"Mrs. Chantry," he acknowledged, and made the monumental mistake of enclosing her hand in his.

When he finally managed to release Amy, the color in her face, already an interesting shade of pink, burned hotter. She continued to meet his gaze, but defiance was fighting a rearguard action.

She looked guilty—as guilty as original sin.

She also looked as tempting.

Marc continued to study the blush suffusing Mrs. Amaris Chantry's cheeks while he fought temptation. There was no doubt about it. His grandmother's latest companion was going to be trouble.

Julia Byrne lives in Australia with her husband, daughter and two overgrown cats. She started her working career as a secretary, taught ballroom dancing after several successful years as a competitor and worked in the history department of a Melbourne university. She and her husband now own a small shop. Although spare time is rare, between manuscripts she enjoys cross-stitch, mah-jongg and studying geneology.

AN INDEPENDENT LADY
JULIA BYRNE

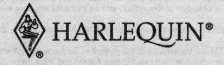

HARLEQUIN®

TORONTO • NEW YORK • LONDON
AMSTERDAM • PARIS • SYDNEY • HAMBURG
STOCKHOLM • ATHENS • TOKYO • MILAN • MADRID
PRAGUE • WARSAW • BUDAPEST • AUCKLAND

If you purchased this book without a cover you should be aware that this book is stolen property. It was reported as "unsold and destroyed" to the publisher, and neither the author nor the publisher has received any payment for this "stripped book."

ISBN 0-373-51153-1

AN INDEPENDENT LADY

First North American Publication 2001.

Copyright © 1999 by Julia Byrne.

All rights reserved. Except for use in any review, the reproduction or utilization of this work in whole or in part in any form by any electronic, mechanical or other means, now known or hereafter invented, including xerography, photocopying and recording, or in any information storage or retrieval system, is forbidden without the written permission of the publisher, Harlequin Enterprises Limited, 225 Duncan Mill Road, Don Mills, Ontario, Canada M3B 3K9.

All characters in this book have no existence outside the imagination of the author and have no relation whatsoever to anyone bearing the same name or names. They are not even distantly inspired by any individual known or unknown to the author, and all incidents are pure invention.

This edition published by arrangement with Harlequin Books S.A.

® and TM are trademarks of the publisher. Trademarks indicated with ® are registered in the United States Patent and Trademark Office, the Canadian Trade Marks Office and in other countries.

Visit us at www.eHarlequin.com

Printed in U.S.A.

Chapter One

'*Good God!* What next?'

The exclamation, though uttered with barely suppressed impatience, was not explosive enough to disturb the mid-morning quiet pertaining in the reading room at White's Club.

One did not, in fact, give vent to explosive exclamations while one was within the dignified portals of a gentlemen's club. Especially when one was the possessor of an old, distinguished title, who took pains to shield from the unwary the fact that he'd inherited every one of the fierce predatory traits that had enabled his ancestors to seize and hold the title in the first place.

The outburst did, however, reach the ears of the fair-haired gentleman lounging in a comfortable leather armchair set at an angle convenient for private conversation.

'Something amiss, Marc, old fellow?' Viscount Eversleigh enquired idly from behind the *Morning Post*. He turned a page. 'Good Lord, a third robbery at Bristol. Situation's getting right out of hand.'

Marcus Benedict Rothwell, Seventh Earl of Hawkridge, clenched his fingers around the letter in his hand and fixed what he could see of the Viscount with a look of narrow-eyed purpose.

'My sister, Augusta,' he began in ominous tones, 'writes to inform me that her butler has taken to falling down drunk every evening while serving dinner; Lucinda has run off to Gretna Green with a half-pay officer; and young Crispin has broken his neck by overfacing one of his father's prize hunters.'

'Dashed inconsiderate,' mumbled Eversleigh. 'I suppose you'll have to post down there and sort everything out, as usual.'

Marc straightened the letter with a snap of his wrist. 'She concludes with the news that your grandfather has finally been gathered to his ancestors after making a new will leaving his fortune to the cook and her husband.'

'*What?*'

The *Morning Post* flew through the air and landed in a small avalanche of paper. Eversleigh sat up with a jerk.

'Ah.' Marc smiled with fiendish satisfaction. 'I trust I now have your full attention, Pel?'

'You do, but that was a damned nasty way of going about it.'

'Inaccurate, too, if I recall your grandfather's cook.'

Eversleigh shuddered. 'I should say so. Wouldn't surprise me if the old boy did turn up his toes after one of her dinners. Can't see him leaving her more than a pension, though. Tight-fisted old bastard.'

'Oh, surely not.'

'Of course he is. Why the devil d'you think I'm hanging out for a rich—?' He caught the gleam in Marc's usually cool grey eyes and grinned. 'You'll have the ancestors spinning in their sepulchres, casting aspersions like that. Stiff-necked lot, the Eversleighs. Not a bastard among 'em. But never mind that. I take it you don't really need to dash off to Gretna, or attend Crispin's funeral?'

The gleam vanished. 'The only funeral I'm likely to attend in the near future is that of my grandmother's latest protégée.'

'Ahh.' Eversleigh nodded as one upon whom light has dawned. Then he frowned. 'Hold on. Thought her ladyship'd sworn off impecunious poets. It was a poet, wasn't it? Wanted her to perch on that rock off the beach at Hawkridge so he could write an ode to a mermaid. Dashed idiotic notion. The tide comes in at that spot before you can blink. Remember the time we were caught—'

'I remember,' Marc informed him, ruthlessly interrupting this excursion into their shared boyhood. 'In the case of the impecunious poet, you're a year out of date. After I sent him packing, we had the artist who was starving in a garret. He needed a profession until he made his name painting portraits; my grandmother decided she needed a secretary to take care of all those plaguey details such as letters of credit and bank drafts.'

'Aha.'

'Indeed. Fortunately, her banker noticed the artistically embellished figures on several transactions and contacted me. He'd never approved of a dowager countess managing her own affairs and was convinced that Grandmama had dropped a rein or two.'

The Viscount looked dubious. 'Very independent old lady, your grandmother. Wouldn't like to be the one to tell her she can't tool her own carriage anymore.'

'You'll be happy to know I don't have to perform that particular task.' Marc glared at the sheets of paper in his hand. 'My dear grandmama is now wide awake to the wiles of struggling artists. Her new companion possesses no skills in that direction at all.'

'There you are, then.'

'Augusta, however, imparts no such assurance that Mrs Chantry—Mrs Amaris Chantry, if you please—won't offer to restore the paintings in the long gallery, while appropriating more portable articles of infinitely greater value.'

'Oh.' A short pause ensued. Eversleigh raised a delicately enquiring eyebrow as he bent to gather up the *Morning Post*. 'Someone offered...'

'Six months ago. A most charming gentleman rented the old Smitton place and promptly joined the Society for the Beautification of Our Village. That, according to Grandmama, immediately put him beyond reproach.'

'Bloody hell!' Eversleigh jerked upright again, leaving the paper to its fate. Sheer horror was stamped on his pleasant features. 'Is that crowd of gossiping old biddies still running amok? One of 'em tanned my hide with her walking cane when I hit a cricket ball through the vestry window twenty years ago. Thought they'd be safely underground by now.'

'Apparently they're still tottering about on walking canes. Grandmother, who's the Society's patron, met Mr Bartle at one of the meetings and was much impressed by his knowledge of history. He purported to be a scholar of art who specialised in the restoration of old paintings.'

'Was he?'

'We never found out. The first painting was taken down, laid on a table and surrounded by an impressive number of bottles and brushes. After two days of working in the strictest seclusion to minimise the danger of ruining the painting, Mr Bartle departed with several silver candlesticks, a handful of snuff boxes, and the first countess's pearls, which for some insane reason were draped over the statue of her husband on horseback.'

Eversleigh laughed. 'Nice to know nothing's changed at Hawkridge since I've been in France.'

'Unfortunately that's not quite true. Mrs Chantry is now in residence. She's a widow.'

'Not exactly a criminal offence, old fellow.'

Marc stared grimly at the letter in his hand. 'There's no mention of Mr Chantry, his style or profession, or how he met his end. The only facts to be gleaned from the crumbs of information scattered between page after page on Lucinda's wilful behaviour and the delicate state of Crispin's health are that Grandmama met Mrs Chantry when she visited Bath a few weeks ago.'

'Dare say she might. Place is full of widows.'

'Mrs Chantry is a *young* widow. "Tragically young",' Marc added, quoting directly from his sister's letter. '"Such a sad situation. Left almost destitute. Forced to earn her own living. And you know what sort of living might be forced upon a penniless girl as lovely as Mrs Chantry." He scowled at the missive again. 'How the hell does Augusta know about things like that?'

Eversleigh grinned. 'I hate to tell you this, Marc, but your sister has been a married woman for quite some time. Not that I can imagine Nettlebed drumming up the energy to carouse with widows—young or otherwise.'

Marc ignored this judicious pronouncement on his cheerfully indolent brother-in-law. 'Unfortunately Augusta's worldly knowledge doesn't extend to Mrs Chantry's parents. They appear to be shrouded in mystery.'

'Probably dead too.'

'Oh, that's a great comfort to me, Pel. I hope you're not going to offer the same explanation when I inform you of the lack of former employers in our widow's history.'

'Perhaps she's been widowed only a short time. You know,

Marc, before you go racing off to Devon to tear the destitute Mrs
Chantry from beneath your grandmother's wing, you might consider that she really is a young widow left tragically bereft.'

'Have you ever heard of a widow named Amaris?'

This demand gave Eversleigh pause. He pursed his lips and bent
his mind to grave consideration of the matter.

'No,' he finally pronounced. And grinned. 'At least, not the type
of widow who hires herself out as a companion to elderly ladies.'

Marc did not feel inclined to share his friend's amusement. 'Exactly. The veracity of this particular widow's tragic past also
comes into question when I tell you that she and my grandmother
met when Mrs Chantry almost fell under the wheels of Grandmama's coach.'

'Good God, how did she manage that?'

'She was faint with hunger. More likely it was the performance
of her life. She could've saved herself the trouble. Grandmama
wouldn't care if she was treading the boards. We've had poets,
artists, restorers. Why quibble at an actress?'

Eversleigh nodded in gloomy agreement. 'Knowing your grandmother, she's probably fascinated. Like to tread the boards, herself.'

'Not at her time of life,' Marc vowed, rising to his feet. 'Pel,
you'll have to convey my apologies to the Scatterthwaites. I was
supposed to attend their ball tonight, but I'll be otherwise engaged.'

'Ask Goring over there to convey both our apologies,' Eversleigh suggested, rising with alacrity. 'I'll be otherwise engaged,
too.'

Marc lifted a brow. 'You're coming with me?'

'Of course I'm coming with you. Urgent family business.'

A look of amusement crossed Marc's face. 'Scatterthwaite's
daughters are worth twenty thousand a year. Each.'

'I'm not that desperate. Besides, you might need help removing
the widow. All very well to toss poets through the library window.
You can hardly do the same to a female.'

Marc muttered something that sounded distinctly like 'Why
not?' Tossing Mrs Amaris Chantry through the library window

would, he decided, go a long way towards relieving his exacerbated feelings.

The situation was getting out of hand. There were far too many people in the world who were prepared to take advantage of his grandmother's affectionate, generous nature. And since no one else seemed capable of doing anything about it, he would have to step into the breach.

A rather nasty sense of inevitability threatened to hover over him. Rather like a sword about to fall. If he didn't want to spend the majority of his time evicting confidence tricksters from his ancestral home he would have to think very seriously about supplying the dowager with a companion of impeccable lineage and proper notions of conduct.

Said companion would also need to be kind enough to tolerate Lady Hawkridge's frequently maddening ways, intelligent enough not to bore him witless within a week, and attractive enough to make facing her across the breakfast table every morning a not impossible task.

In other words, it was about time he made another attempt to supply himself with a wife.

The prospect didn't fill him with delight. The last two attempts, while not exactly disasters, had been crowned by a conspicuous lack of success. Fortunately, only one had been a public lack of success. The other he'd always regarded as more of a lucky escape.

The thought of either situation recurring made him scowl so ferociously that Lord Goring, when cornered, didn't voice even a mild protest at having to face Lady Scatterthwaite and her daughters and inform them that two of the *ton*'s most eligible bachelors would be missing from a ball put on especially to lure them into their coils.

'If only I could decide where to put the Society. Really, Amy, I am quite at my wits' end.'

Mrs Amaris Chantry looked up from the pile of letters she'd been sorting as the Dowager Lady Hawkridge burst into the library like a small, plump, mauve-clad whirlwind.

Her ladyship was armed with a feather duster.

Amy had no idea why her employer felt obliged to dust since

there was a maid assigned for the mundane task, but she'd been living at Hawkridge Manor for a full month now and was quite inured to her ladyship's habit of starting conversations while still *en route* to her auditor.

She also had no trouble following Lady Hawkridge's rambling discourse.

'The winter parlour would be charming now that we have some sunshine after all that rain, but if Mrs Tredgett should attend, she'd be sure to take offence. On the other hand, the drawing-room is far too large, and so *dauntingly* formal that persons such as Miss Pucklenett will be quite overcome.'

Lady Hawkridge took an agitated turn about the library and fetched up in front of the lectern upon which reposed the family Bible, an imposing tome of ponderous proportions in which were recorded the arrivals and departures of several generations of Rothwells.

Her ladyship looked at the duster in her hand and waved it in a vague sort of way over the vellum-bound volume.

'I don't know why the Society's meeting couldn't be held at the Vicarage as usual,' she went on, her cherubic face marred by a frown. 'I know the younger girls aren't well, but they won't be running in and out of the parlour, will they?'

'Ahh.' Amy nodded in complete understanding. 'Mrs ffollifoot has begged that you'll hold the Society's meeting here. I suppose no one else has volunteered. In that case, ma'am, have the drawing-room made ready. Miss Pucklenett positively *delights* in being overcome. Think what a treat it will be for her.'

'Good heavens, you're quite right.' The dowager looked much struck by the notion. 'Poor thing. I suppose she doesn't have a great deal to look forward to. Not that the Mayhews ever treat their staff with anything but the greatest consideration.'

'As do you, dearest ma'am.' Amy rose from her seat, a warm smile curving her mouth as she crossed the room to her employer. 'However, I doubt that Mary will view with anything but the greatest *dismay* the fact that you're doing the dusting.'

'Well, I thought of the drawing-room earlier, but I couldn't remember when we'd last used it. And there always seem to be so many rooms to dust.' Her ladyship looked at the duster again and aimed a swipe in the general direction of a shelf of books. A small cloud of dust motes danced in the air.

Amy stifled a sneeze. 'Even so, ma'am—'

'Now, don't scold, Amy dear. I've a perfectly good explanation.' The dowager paused, then added in accents of doom, 'Chicken-pox.'

'Ohh.'

'It's all the fault of the Vicar's wretched offspring. I hope I'm sympathetic towards children in their sick-beds, Amy, but not when they infect my maids.'

'Perfectly understandable, ma'am. Poor Mary. Would you like me to ask Mrs Cubitt if we should send for the doctor?'

'I don't think housekeepers believe in pampering the maids, but if anyone could persuade her, it would be you. And, after all, I did send for dear Dr Twinhoe when the boys caught the chicken-pox. Not that it did any good. I was hoping he'd give them a draught that would keep them in their beds, but he said the most we could hope for was that they wouldn't run about infecting everyone else.'

'A daunting thought, ma'am.'

Her ladyship shuddered. 'I suppose we should've been grateful that Pelham was visiting here when they both came down with it, but they were the most dreadful patients. Marc and Lord Eversleigh, you know. At least, he's Eversleigh at the moment. When that bad-tempered, gout-ridden old fool is finally pushed into the family vault, he'll be the Earl of Colborough.'

'Er, bad-tempered, gout-ridden...'

'Old fool,' confirmed her ladyship, brandishing her duster with vigour. 'I said old fool and I meant it. Have *you* had the chicken-pox, Amy?'

Amy blinked. 'Yes, ma'am.' And every other childhood ailment known to mankind.

Fascinated by the unaccustomed ire emanating from her employer, she dismissed childhood ailments and probed delicately. 'I collect you're speaking of the elderly gentleman who lives in that house on the other side of the cove.'

'There is no *gentleman* on the other side of the cove.' Lady Hawkridge glared at the duster in her hand, hefted it and charged at a nearby armchair like a knight going into battle. 'Only an old fool who said our Society was a bevy of cackling hens who— Oh, heavens! The Society!' The duster was suspended in mid-air. 'What am I thinking of? Why must Mrs ffollifoot leave it to the last minute to change her plans? We'll have to write notes and— Amy, do you think...?'

'Of course, ma'am. It will take only a few minutes to dash off a quick note to everyone and there's plenty of time before the meeting for the notes to be delivered. Please don't fret about it.'

Lady Hawkridge beamed. 'Dear Amy. So dependable.' She abandoned the assault on the armchair and began to circle the room, flicking the duster over bookshelves and occasional-tables as she passed. Several small ornaments rocked wildly. Amy rushed to avert disaster.

'So kind,' Lady Hawkridge continued, oblivious to the guardian angel of ornaments following in her wake. 'And with all those letters to answer, too. I don't know where I'd be without you, Amy dear. My eyes aren't as good as they once were, you know, and I receive such a volume of mail that I fear they would be quite worn out if I had to deal with it myself.'

Since Lady Hawkridge had, that very morning, espied a rare wildflower blooming on the cliffs several hundred yards away from Hawkridge Manor, Amy had no trouble identifying this remark for the kindness it was.

Gratitude filled her heart, causing tears to well behind her eyes.

She would never cease to thank the benevolent providence that had prompted the Dowager Countess of Hawkridge to call for her carriage that day four weeks ago instead of summoning a chair to negotiate the hilly streets of Bath.

Amy didn't like to think about what might have befallen her if she herself hadn't been on that particular street at the same moment. The thought only had to creep to the edge of her mind to have her flesh turn cold and shivery.

She'd been down to her last shilling. The future had loomed like a crouching malevolent beast, waiting to drag her back into a pit of black despair from which she could never escape.

'Sometimes,' the dowager confided, pausing in her progress to peer at the pile of letters on Amy's desk, 'I wonder if Marc was right when he accused me of indiscriminate patronage of the arts. Oh, dear, that looks like his writing.'

Amy shook off her memories and returned to the desk to pick up the unopened letter she'd laid aside. An arrogant black signature was slashed across one corner of the envelope.

'I thought it might be, ma'am, since the letter is franked by Hawkridge.' She handed it over. 'The only other letter concerning artistic matters this morning is a request for a donation to establish a retreat where a group of sculptors can fashion statues of humans in their, ah, natural forms.'

'Oh, dear, I don't think Marc would approve of that.'

Amy was sure of it. Not that she objected to his disapproval in this particular instance, but she also possessed the uncomfortable suspicion that he wouldn't approve of her either.

She could hardly blame Hawkridge. After hearing the sorry tale of the dowager's previous experiences with people whom she'd taken under her kindly wing, Amy had decided that Hawkridge would immediately assume her to be the latest in a long line of hucksters out to fleece his grandmama of as much as possible in the shortest possible time.

Rehearsing speeches of explanation in the event that she ever met the Earl had not resulted in a feeling of confidence that such a meeting would be pleasant. Hawkridge did not appear to be filled with tolerance and understanding for his fellow human beings.

While the dowager broke the sealed envelope with a distinct lack of enthusiasm, Amy glanced up at the portrait of the Earl that hung over the mantelpiece.

Eyes the colour of sleeting rain stared back at her from beneath level black brows. There was something about those eyes—something the artist had tried to capture, only to have it remain elusively out of reach. Something...

Amy shook her head. The more she tried to pin down the expression, the more it slipped away.

She turned her attention to his other features. Even at the age of twenty they were forbidding; the straight blade of his nose, the high razor-sharp cheekbones and chiselled jaw putting Amy forcibly in mind of the savage Indian warriors fortunately residing in the American colonies. The air of fierce pride and masculine arrogance was echoed in the way he stood, leaning with careless grace against the shoulder of a huge black horse. He held the reins loosely in one large, elegantly-shaped hand, even though the horse looked as if it was about to take a chunk out of anyone foolish enough to approach.

Amy felt a familiar shiver slide down her spine. The same shiver she experienced every time she gazed at the painted image of the Earl of Hawkridge. The portrait had been done fourteen years ago, so Lady Hawkridge had informed her, upon the Earl's succession to his grandfather's title, but Amy had no reason to believe that those years had mellowed the arrogant, handsome face or softened the hard, unsmiling line of his mouth.

The thought wasn't comforting. Even more disturbing was the fact that the painting had the unsettling effect of distracting her from her work at odd moments during the day. Too often she found herself searching those stern features for signs of the boy who'd been catapulted swiftly and tragically into manhood.

The transition seemed to have been complete.

She could, of course, have used any of the other rooms that comprised the sprawling maze that was Hawkridge Manor. Lady Hawkridge had kindly instructed her to avail herself of whatever room took her fancy.

Amy had chosen the library.

And she was honest enough to admit that she'd chosen the room because the portrait fascinated her. She wished it didn't—fascination, unwilling or otherwise, did not augur well if she ever met the original—but that didn't alter the fact.

She was utterly enthralled by the image of the Earl of Hawkridge.

Her only consolation was that she was unlikely to be confronted by the real thing any time soon. The Manor might have been the Earl's boyhood home and principal seat, but it was a long way from London where he apparently preferred to spend his time.

Amy could only be grateful.

She was still busily counting her blessings when the sound of carriage wheels on gravel wafted through the open windows of the library.

'Oh, heavens!' The dowager looked up from her letter. 'You

don't think Mrs ffollifoot has sent notes to everyone and they're arriving already, do you?'

'I doubt it, ma'am. Perhaps Mrs Cubitt has sent for the doctor, after all. Would you like me to find out?'

'If you would, Amy. Oh, dear, if it isn't one thing, it's another. Even dear Mr Tweedy would be rather in the way when I'm so distracted. And this afternoon everyone will want tea and there's Mary with the chicken-pox—'

With the dowager twittering behind her, Amy crossed the room with determined strides. Whoever was arriving would have to be informed that this was not a convenient time to visit. Even if it was 'dear Mr Tweedy' who, in her opinion, was going to prove rather too dear for the dowager's purse.

She reached the door, yanked it open, and gave a squeak of shock as a dark figure loomed over her.

The Earl of Hawkridge stood on the threshold.

The real one.

Amy stumbled back several paces and blinked. It wasn't an illusion. Hawkridge was standing there in the flesh. The impact on her senses was all that she'd feared. After one gasp of dismay, she stopped breathing.

Chapter Two

'Good heavens! Marc!'

The startled exclamation came from his grandmother, not the lady he'd almost bowled over in the doorway.

Marc spared the youthful unknown a quick glance. Fortunately, she'd retreated in a hurry—before he could indulge an utterly insane impulse to catch her about the waist and hold her against him instead of letting her bounce off.

It was not an auspicious beginning. If she was his quarry, several alternatives to ejecting her were already springing to mind. All rendered him distinctly uncomfortable.

Reining in his suddenly wayward thoughts, he manufactured a smile for his grandparent and bent to kiss her cheek. 'Good morning, Grandmama.'

'Marc, what a lovely surprise. I've been wanting you to meet dear Amy for weeks, and here you are.'

'Yes.' He straightened, erasing the smile when he turned to dear Amy. The first thing he noted was the bare fingers of her left hand. He dropped his voice to a tone well below freezing. To his extreme annoyance, it was the only thing about him enjoying that chilly temperature. 'Here I am.'

Mrs Chantry shivered slightly. His satisfaction at the betraying motion was small consolation for the effect she was having on him. It was also brief.

Her chin went up. She thrust out her other hand with equal defiance. 'How do you do, my lord?'

'Mrs Chantry,' he acknowledged, and made the monumental mistake of enclosing her hand in his.

Two wildly opposing impulses assaulted his brain with startling speed. Her hand felt so small in his, so soft, he wanted to cradle it as if he held the finest crystal, while at the same time he was rocked by an equally strong urge to rap his fist against the pointed little chin aimed so pugnaciously at his chest.

Damn it, his plans didn't include letting his victim know she'd thoroughly distracted him from his mission.

Triumph didn't appear to be Mrs Chantry's first reaction to the hard grip of his fingers, however. When he finally managed to release her, the colour in her face, already an interesting shade of pink, burned hotter. She continued to meet his gaze, but defiance was fighting a rearguard action. She looked guilty—as guilty as original sin.

She also looked as tempting.

Marc continued to study the blush suffusing Mrs Amaris Chantry's cheeks while he fought temptation. The faintest hint of lavender water, overlaying warm female flesh, that wafted to his nostrils didn't help the endeavour.

There was no doubt about it. His grandmother's latest companion was going to be trouble.

More than trouble, he concluded grimly, subjecting the total picture to a comprehensive appraisal. She was potential disaster clad in a cream muslin gown the exact tint of skin that threatened to make his mouth water. An elegant primrose spencer, puffed of sleeve and ruffled at the throat, clung like a lover to small, round breasts that *did* make his mouth water.

Resisting the urge to swallow, he jerked his gaze upward.

Hints of the same golden hue as her spencer showed in the rich tawny hair coiled in a neat twist atop her head. He clenched his fingers around the whip still in his hand to stop himself reaching out and tugging at that too-neat coil.

It would have been easy; she barely topped his shoulder.

Eyes narrowed against a vision of silken hair flowing over delicate curves, he lowered his gaze again, and decided that instant lust had overturned his brain. He, who had never waxed lyrical about a woman, found himself in danger of drowning in sable-fringed pools of the clearest, purest crystalline green he'd ever encountered.

And he'd encountered a few. He'd certainly encountered enough to suspect that subtle artifice had been employed to enhance lashes that were much darker than her hair. He would have been happy to prove the theory, but he was too busy being drawn into the beguiling depths of those eyes.

Fathomless eyes that told him their owner had seen too much and hadn't liked much of what she'd seen. Eyes turbulent with defensiveness and defiance, set beneath gently arched brows, and dominating a face too piquant to belong to a diamond of the first water, but so finely drawn his fingers itched to touch the petal-soft skin, to trace the fragile bones beneath.

There was an air of innocence about that face; she looked... untouched. Which was ridiculous. She'd been married, so she was hardly untouched. And if her title was a courtesy one, she'd look even less innocent. And yet, those eyes held an expression that, despite the wariness, despite the shadows that spoke of knowledge hard won, lacked that indefinable something that said 'favours for sale'.

For the first time Marc found himself wondering if she really was what she purported to be. A young widow forced to earn her own living.

The possibility was unexpectedly annoying. Annoying, he admitted wryly, because in that first instant of seeing Mrs Amaris Chantry, he'd pictured her in another position altogether.

Such as under him. In a bed.

He suddenly realised his grandmother had been twittering the whole time he'd been standing as if he'd been bowled over by the Royal Mail, and he hadn't listened to a word she'd said. He vaguely recalled such hopeful phrases as 'delightful company', 'so kind', 'so ready to help...'

'And you'll be happy to know she doesn't approve of me setting up a retreat for naked sculptors.'

That got through. Marc's gaze snapped briefly to his grandmother's impossibly innocent face. She beamed at him. He decided to take charge of a rapidly unravelling situation.

'I'm relieved to hear, Mrs Chantry, that you don't approve of people sculpting while naked.'

'Oh! That isn't...I mean...'

From the corner of her eye Amy saw Lady Hawkridge's lips twitch, and cursed both her employer and the new wave of colour rising to her cheeks. She'd meant to behave with the sort of dignified maturity that would convince the Earl she was fully suited to her position here, and instead was blushing and stammering like a schoolgirl.

It was all Hawkridge's fault, of course. The way he'd pounced on her in the doorway before she'd had any warning was enough to overset the staunchest nerves.

Not that he was exactly like his portrait. In fact, as far as she was concerned, the portrait had a great deal to answer for.

The reality was very much taller for one thing. She had to tilt her chin up in what was sure to appear a challenging angle to look him in the eyes. And there didn't appear to be much daylight between him and the doorway. In any direction.

She tried to tell herself that his elegant greatcoat, adorned with several capes, added to the impression of overwhelming size, but it was clear that Hawkridge's tailor did not need to use an inordinate amount of capes to fill out those broad shoulders, or emphasise the width of chest that met her gaze when she lowered her eyes.

She lowered them further, hoping for something to lessen the impact.

Hope died a swift and ignominious death. Hawkridge's buckskins clung to the long powerful muscles of his thighs in a way that caused her own legs to go unaccountably weak. As for his topboots, she could have climbed into one and disappeared.

A slight movement had her gaze climbing upward in time to see his left hand clench about his whip, as though he was contemplating using it on her. She wasn't surprised; in a mind-numbing burst of knowledge she'd realised precisely what that long-ago artist had so lamentably failed to capture.

Hawkridge might appear civilised; he might dress with the kind of fashionable elegance that drew the eye; he might even behave with civility in polite company. But his instincts were those of the warrior he resembled.

She should know, Amy thought, bracing herself to confront the fierce glitter in those piercing grey eyes. She'd fought enough battles of her own not to recognise another iron-clad will when she met one head-on.

'I see you noticed the absence of a wedding ring, my lord,' she stated, recklessly taking the offensive into enemy territory. 'I had to sell it.'

She didn't appear overly distressed by the circumstance, Marc decided. In fact, her air of youthful innocence was in direct contrast to the cool self-possession that dropped over her like a cloak after she'd looked him up and down. That wide-eyed examination had had its inevitable effect. He was glad he'd left his greatcoat on. The garment hung open, but if he turned slightly away from his grandmother she wouldn't see his unruly body ignoring the commands of his brain for the first time since his youth.

He didn't intend to hide his reaction from Mrs Chantry; he wanted her shaken out of that surface calm. But she appeared not to notice.

Given that his buckskins moulded his form like a second skin, even a mild male response would have been obvious. Mrs Chantry was either so innocent her marriage was a tale of fiction, which might account for the guilty secrets in her eyes—her mysterious husband had been a eunuch, a possibility he dismissed out of hand—or she had turned her back on a positively brilliant career on the stage.

'Now, Amy, I'm sure there's no need to go into all that,' soothed Lady Hawkridge, jabbing him in the ribs with an unsubtle elbow when he opened his mouth to find out.

His glare was met with a guileless smile. 'I'm so glad you're here, Marc, dearest. Augusta is having such a difficult time with Crispin. You know what young boys are like. Not that you ever listened to anyone, but Crispin thinks you're an out-and-outer, so he may listen to you, and heaven knows poor Nettlebed can't—'

'If Nettlebed took a good look at his son instead of taking Augusta's word for it that the brat is delicate, he might do better,' Marc grated, annoyed at the digression.

He saw a flash of approval in Mrs Chantry's eyes, and raised a brow. 'It seems you agree, Mrs Chantry.'

She looked a little self-conscious. 'I wouldn't presume to pass judgement, my lord, when I have no experience with youths.'

'You've never been employed as a governess in your, er, career?'

'No, sir. My place here with Lady Hawkridge is my first position. Um...that is...'

'As a companion,' he murmured.

Her lashes flickered, telling him the shot had hit home.

Not so innocent, then. That untouched, barely-out-of-the-schoolroom appearance must be invaluable to her. He wondered what the hell she was doing as a companion to an elderly lady when she could be earning a fortune in another, more horizontal, position.

No, better keep his mind off the horizontal plane.

'Then I trust the duties of a companion are more to your taste, Mrs Chantry,' he added smoothly.

She tilted that defiant little chin at him again.

'Indeed they are, my lord. And speaking of duties—' Taking a deep breath, she stepped forward, rather in the manner of one about to herd sheep. 'I'm sure you and Lady Hawkridge wish to enjoy a tête-à-tête, so if you'd be so kind as to escort her to the drawing-room, I'll continue with the morning's tasks. Notes,' she added when he raised a brow. 'We're holding a meeting here this afternoon of the Society for the Beautification of Our Village. Chicken-pox at the vicarage, you know. I'm sure the ladies will be agog at your presence, if you mean to join us, that is, but first I have to let them know and...'

She finally ran down through lack of air.

'Yes, indeed,' seconded his grandmother valiantly, taking his arm and tugging.

Before he could argue, Marc found himself back in the hall. The lady he'd come to evict sent him a sweet smile and gently shut the library door in his face.

He glared at the wooden panels an inch from his nose. 'Correct me if I'm wrong, Grandmama,' he began in arctic tones, 'but was I just ordered out of my own library?'

'Of course you were, dearest. You can't expect poor little Amy to write notes to everyone with you looming over her shoulder. You tend to do that a lot, dear. Looming, I mean. You should put a stop to it.'

He gritted his teeth. 'Grandmama, you and I need to have a long talk.'

'How lovely.' Completely undaunted by the prospect, Lady Hawkridge began to steer him towards the drawing-room, waving a feather duster over a vase of flowers as they passed. Several petals floated to the floor.

He decided not to ask.

'I want to hear all the London gossip. You know, Marc, you should convey those interesting little tidbits that we all wish to hear in your letters, instead of warning me against unlikely disasters as if I'm in my dotage.'

'I know you're not in your dotage, Grandmama, but—'

'Now sit down, dearest, while I see what needs to be done. Oh, dear, I do hope Amy is right. Poor Miss Pucklenett. She likes to be daunted by drawing-rooms, you know. It's very sad.'

Marc divested himself of his greatcoat while he counted to ten.

'If Miss Pucklenett is another of your lame ducks—'

'Really, Marc, if you ever paid attention to anything other than my affairs, you'd know that Miss Pucklenett has been the Mayhews' governess forever. And I do not collect lame ducks.'

He couldn't help smiling. 'Of course you do, love. Look at the way you let Pel and me run wild all over the place when we were boys.'

'That,' declared the dowager with dignity, 'was a different matter. You were our grandson—well, you still are, of course—and after that terrible... Well, Pelham had lost his parents, as you had.' She wielded the duster with considerable violence. 'What else could one do when that silly old fool at Colborough Court took no interest in his only grandchild?'

Marc's expression turned wry. 'Colborough lost a son and daughter-in-law, too, Grandmama.'

'Yes,' admitted her ladyship. 'Indeed, he was never quite so irascible until that dreadful day, but to criticise anyone who tries to go about their lives as best they may, although he never goes out himself, is perfectly intolerable.'

'Ah.' Marc grinned. 'Old Colborough still refers to your Society as a bevy of cackling hens.'

His grandmother muttered something unintelligible as she continued to attack various articles of furniture with the duster. There appeared to be no logic to her progression. He wondered if he should point out that several priceless antique urns imported from China by his grandfather were in imminent danger of shattering.

'Grandmama, forgive my ignorance on such matters, but why are you dusting?'

The dusting was suspended, saving the urns from their inevitable fate. 'Marc, are you feeling quite the thing, dearest? Surely you heard Amy say that chicken-pox is everywhere. Mary caught it. So unfortunate, but I'm sure she didn't do it deliberately.'

'Mary being one of your maids.'

'Yes, so you see why Amy and I are in such a pucker.'

The thought of Mrs Chantry in a pucker held a certain appeal. Especially the sort of pucker that sprang in vivid detail to his suddenly fertile brain. His body approved of the fantasy, too.

Annoyed, Marc shoved his hands into his breeches pockets and began to pace. 'Mrs Chantry did not strike me as the sort of person who gets into puckers. On the other hand, for a minute or two there, she did look decidedly guilty.'

'Guilty!' His grandparent glared at him as if he'd accused *her* of nefarious activities. 'What a dreadful thing to say. Poor little Amy. Guilty of what, pray?'

'I don't know, although after the antics of your former secretaries, nothing would surprise me. I merely meant that Mrs Chantry looked at me as if she expected to be evicted in the same manner as that idiot poet and was prepared to fight me every inch of the way.'

'Well, I should think so,' declared the dowager in indignant accents. 'The very idea! Tossing poor little Amy through the library window.'

'Poor little Amy appears to be an enigma,' Marc stated, pausing in his perambulations and fixing his grandmother with a stern eye. 'What precisely do you know about her?'

'Lots of things,' claimed the dowager somewhat defiantly. 'But I don't intend to talk about Amy while you pace about like a tiger ready to pounce on everything I say.'

'All right.' Raising his hands in a gesture of compliance, Marc strode over to a sofa and flung himself on to an over-stuffed cushion. 'There. I won't even loom.'

His grandmother beamed. 'That's much better. Now let me see. Well, Amy reads beautifully. Such verve. Such passion. Such—'

'Yes, it doesn't surprise me to learn that her acting skills are superior.'

Her ladyship's approving smile vanished. 'Marcus, you are becoming extremely cynical, which I take leave to inform you is not an attractive trait. Just because we had that *tiny* bit of trouble with Mr Bartle...'

'Not to mention Ambrose the Artist and that fool poet.'

The dowager had the grace to blush. 'Poor dear Florian. At least he didn't try to rob me.'

'No, he pestered you with attentions, as if you'd marry a man younger than your own grandson. I suppose I should be grateful I only had to toss him through the window instead of chasing after him as I did Bartle to retrieve those damned pearls.'

Lady Hawkridge hung her head, reminding Marc of a chastened schoolgirl standing before a hatchet-faced governess. Even the duster drooped. He felt like a brute.

'Grandmama, I'm sorry.' Rising, he curved his hands around his grandmother's shoulders and squeezed gently. 'I wouldn't distress you for the world, but there's no blinking at the fact that your very nature makes you a target for spongers. If you want a companion I'll find you one. In fact—'

'But, Marc, dearest, I've already found my own companion.' Restored to animation by that indisputable fact, the dowager whisked herself out of his hold and continued her whirlwind circuit of the room. 'I can't imagine why I didn't employ a lady before. Dear Amy is so obliging, so willing, so sweet-natured, so—'

'Who was her husband?' he demanded bluntly, hoping to extract one solid fact from what threatened to become a panegyric on Mrs Chantry's sterling qualities.

The result was a stare of the liveliest astonishment. 'Why, dearest, whoever do you think? Mr Chantry, of course.'

Marc sat down again and put his head in his hands.

'There, there, dear.' The dowager flitted up to him and patted him consolingly with the duster. 'You must be tired. Such a long journey from Town. You should go straight to your room and lie down.'

'Grandmama, I don't need to lie down.' He stared in resignation at the smear of dust on the shoulder of his coat. 'Although I might soon become a candidate for Bedlam. I meant, *what* was Mr Chantry? For all you know, he could have been anything from a respectable businessman to a thief from the stews.'

'Oh, my goodness, how that does take me back. My old nurse, you know. Whenever we had cherries for tea we'd play a game by counting the pips. Rich man, poor man, beggarman, thief. Whatever came last was the man one would marry. Oh, my.' The dowager sighed.

'I'm trying to elicit some facts here, Grandmama, which are not likely to be found in the nursery. So far you don't know who Mr Chantry was, what he did, or when he died. I've never even encountered the name. How old is Mrs Chantry, by the way?'

'Good heavens, I've never asked. And neither will you. Really, Marc! The thought of asking a lady her age.'

'Stow the righteous indignation, Grandmama. Mrs Chantry, for all her elegance and poise, appears extremely young. I'd be surprised to learn she's much above twenty.'

The dowager appeared much struck. She blinked in surprise and gave the matter considerable thought. 'Do you know, Marc, I think you're right. Not that I've wondered, you understand, but now that you mention it, Amy does seem young. When you take a *close* look, that is. And yet, her manner is quite poised, isn't it? One would naturally assume she is older.'

'Probably what she wants you to think,' Marc muttered. 'What about her financial situation? Augusta claimed she was destitute, and she certainly looks as if a puff of wind will blow her over, but she's dressed in the first style of elegance.'

'Well, of course she is. Do you think I'd let my companion go about in rags? Naturally, I gave Amy a little money on account so she could replenish a sadly depleted wardrobe.'

'A little money on account.' Marc nodded grimly. 'Now we're getting to the hub of the matter. How much money?'

'Very little,' declared the dowager triumphantly. 'I tried to persuade Amy to take more, but she wouldn't hear of it. She said she was more than capable of fashioning her own gowns from materials bought from the village draper. And I must say she was right. She has so many useful accomplishments. Why, she can even cook. Such a comfort when Mrs Pickles might be struck down with chicken-pox at any moment.'

'A comfort, indeed. I note that the gown she cleverly fashioned isn't in funereal black. Quite the contrary.'

'Primrose,' stated her ladyship, 'is a very *pale* shade of yellow, and when partnered with cream, is perfectly proper for a young widow out of mourning. Besides, Amy wears her dark green pelisse when she goes out. She made that, too.'

'Hmm. What about more conventional accomplishments?'

His grandmother fixed him with an innocently inquiring eye. 'Do you mean things like torturing the pianoforte or the harp, throwing paint at a canvas, singing that reminds you of cats howling?'

Marc grinned before he could stop himself. 'My remarks after the last crowd of debutantes Augusta paraded before me.' Rising, he seized his grandparent in a fond embrace that lifted her clean off the floor. '*Touché*, love. If I promise not to interrogate you any further about Mrs Chantry, will you let me stay?'

'As if you need to ask to stay in your own home,' protested Lady Hawkridge in somewhat muffled accents. 'You know I'm always delighted to see you, but only if you promise not to intimidate poor little Amy.'

'I promise I won't intimidate Mrs Chantry,' he repeated obediently, setting the dowager on her feet. He decided he could safely make such a promise. If Mrs Chantry had nothing to hide, a few questions shouldn't bother her.

Besides, she didn't appear to be easily intimidated.

Amy leaned against the library door for a good five minutes, both hands clamped over her heart to stop it from leaping clean out of her chest. She seemed to be having a great deal of trouble breathing. No doubt both conditions were caused by relief that she hadn't been hurled forth before she could state her case.

She'd never met anyone more intimidating. She could hardly believe she'd actually faced down the Earl of Hawkridge—the real one—and won a reprieve.

Aided and abetted by the dowager.

The admission had her frowning. She stopped pressing her shoulders to the door as though Hawkridge might burst through it again at any moment, and pondered the point.

For one who had opened her grandson's letter with considerable reluctance, her ladyship had looked inordinately delighted to see the author. Hawkridge, himself, seemed as fond of the dowager. The brief smile he'd given his grandmother had almost startled Amy into peering from him to the portrait to see if she'd mistaken his identity. The fact that she was still standing here, instead of sailing through the library window, was added proof that Hawkridge cared enough about his grandmother not to dismiss her latest companion out of hand.

On the other hand, he could be biding his time.

Amy set her lips in a determined line. It was one thing for her to know how woefully unsuited she was to be residing in a gentleman's house; Hawkridge had no right to look at her as though she'd had a fistful of purloined trinkets in her possession.

Although now she came to think about it, he hadn't looked at her in *quite* that way. His eyes had certainly been hard, and unnervingly intent, but...

Amy shook her head. She suspected it would be a great deal less wearing on her nerves if she *didn't* try to remember the precise expression in Hawkridge's eyes when he'd looked her up and down. Or anything else about him.

Fascination with a portrait was safer.

She glanced up at the painting as though to confirm that comforting conclusion, and waited for the familiar shiver to slide down her spine.

Nothing happened.

Amy frowned and stared harder at the painted image.

Her spine stayed perfectly free of shivers.

Then realisation struck her with the force of a thunder clap.

She was looking at the portrait of a boy. The boy she'd sought all along; matured, even hardened by recent bereavement, but defined by his very youth, the promise of his full strength and manhood still ahead of him.

The man who'd towered over her in the doorway had fulfilled that promise and more. But greater physical strength alone didn't set the man apart from the boy. The difference was in the harnessing of that strength, and the fierce will that drove it. He'd learned to conceal the warrior within. Probably enough to escape detection by most of Polite Society. And it was that—the sheer impact of intense masculinity under ruthless restraint—that was utterly overwhelming.

No wonder he'd taken her breath away.

Amy shivered, unable to stop her errant mind from wondering if Hawkridge's control ever snapped to reveal the man behind the polished façade. And if it did, what would happen if she was in the immediate vicinity when an explosion occurred?

The questions had an unfortunate effect on her senses. She thought of the way Hawkridge had loomed over her in the doorway and her legs trembled. She remembered the piercing glitter in his eyes when he'd looked her up and down and her wits threatened to scatter to the four corners of the room. She remembered the sheer size of him and every nerve in her body quivered, shivered, and generally behaved in a manner that was alarmingly unfamiliar.

Alarm was not something with which she wished to become reacquainted. She had to put a stop to this right now. If she wanted to keep the safe, peaceful existence she was beginning to carve out for herself she was going to need every wit she possessed. Legs would be useful if she had to flee. And her nerves would just have to return to fascination with a portrait, because peace and safety were of more importance to her than fascination with an Earl.

Or any other peer of the realm.

For that matter, they were of more importance to her than fascination with a male of any description.

Amy straightened her shoulders. With that fact resounding in her head she should soon recover her own façade. Heaven knew she'd worked hard enough to perfect it. She would simply stay out of Hawkridge's way until she was sure it was solidly back in place.

Or, she thought, fixing the painting with a narrow-eyed glare of accusation, until she'd better prepared herself to face the subject of a disastrously incompetent portraitist, who had been lamentably lacking in foresight.

Chapter Three

With the praiseworthy goal of avoiding Hawkridge in her sights, Amy set out for the village of Ottersmead as soon as her notes were written.

She anticipated a pleasant outing. Ottersmead was a peaceful place, perfectly suited, she'd decided on her first visit, to the restoration of jangled nerves.

Situated on a spectacular part of the Devon coast, it was sufficiently removed from the post road so that constant traffic did not disturb its sylvan setting, but was still within easy reach of the summer resort town of Teignmouth.

As villages went, Ottersmead was larger than most. A dozen or so genteel shops and houses fronted on its main street, at one end of which stood the Vicarage, a half-timbered edifice surrounded by a very pretty rose garden that dated from Tudor times. The Green Man, a respectable hostelry capable of accommodating the occasional visitor in comfort, presided at the other end of the street; a well-attended market was held on the first Thursday of every month; and the whole was encircled by several fine estates, all of which had been owned by the same aristocratic families for generations.

The residents of Ottersmead were justly proud of their village, none more so than the Society for the Beautification of our Village, and Amy was perfectly happy to assist their efforts at beautification by delivering her notes in person. Especially when the task coincided with her desire to escape from the house.

After despatching a footman to deliver notes to those members of the Society who resided outside the village proper, Amy stepped out at a brisk pace. The sky was a bowl of deep cerulean blue, the sun shone, and the blustery wind she encountered on the road overlooking the rolling swells of the Atlantic was invigorating enough, she hoped, to blow a disturbingly persistent image of Hawkridge out of her mind.

Even a temporary lull would be beneficial. She might be able to convince herself that she'd blown the Earl's impact on her out of all proportion.

The wind had other ideas. Hawkridge materialised at her side as if deposited there by insidious forces of nature, and long before the village, nestled in its crescent-shaped bay between the arms of the surrounding cliffs, had so much as come into sight.

'Mrs Chantry,' he acknowledged in a polite voice that bore no resemblance whatever to his chilling tones of earlier. 'I hope you don't object to my accompanying you.'

'Of course not, my lord.' Amy ordered her heart out of her throat, whence it had jumped at his sudden appearance, and wished she'd had the courage to tackle the path down to the beach. Once on the sand, she would have been invisible to anyone on the cliff top.

Not that it mattered. The tide was in. Though the beach was accessible further along, at this particular point during high tide the waves lapped against the cliff. It was a shame she'd never learnt to swim.

'Thank God you're not one of those females who objects to walking at a smart pace,' he observed, matching her speed without effort. 'I need to stretch my legs after the drive from London.'

Amy stared at him suspiciously. Why was he being civil? He didn't look civil. In fact, he looked distinctly dangerous with his black hair ruffled in the breeze, his coat open and his hands stuffed into his breeches' pockets. Even his cravat appeared to have been released somewhat from its precise folds.

She blinked at him. It was difficult to be sure without actually peering, but the top button of his shirt appeared to be unfastened. The elegant gentleman had been replaced by a brigand. All he needed was a cutlass and earring.

Amy frowned. She didn't approve of pirates.

Unfortunately, disapproval was having little effect on her heart-beat and breathing. Both usually steady functions had accelerated to a disturbing rate.

'You must have left town before dawn, my lord,' she managed to say, surprised she could speak at all, let alone string coherent words together. Her mind scurried to and fro, marshalling arguments, readying her defences—wishing she didn't have an almost compelling urge to study him. Just to make sure she hadn't exaggerated his dangerous qualities, of course.

'Actually, we left yesterday evening and spent the night on the road.'

'Oh. We?' she added when something more seemed called for.

'I drove down with Lord Eversleigh. Colborough's heir.' He jerked his head at the pile of stone perched above the sea on the opposite side of the cove.

'Ah, yes. Lady Hawkridge mentioned Lord Colborough only this morning.'

A swift, unexpectedly wicked grin crossed his face. 'Not by name, I wager.'

'Er...no.' Amy swallowed in an attempt to ease the sudden constriction in her throat. By what bird-witted piece of logic had she considered Hawkridge dangerous when unsmiling? That grin was lethal. Some misguided woman should have married him years ago to save her sisters from galloping heartbeats and irregular breathing.

'I thought not. Grandmama and Colborough enjoy open warfare so much I've often wondered why they never made a match of it.'

Still grappling with the image of that wicked, slashing grin, not to mention the unnerving thought of Hawkridge in the role of husband, Amy struggled to uphold her end of the conversation. 'Lord Colborough and Lady Hawkridge have long been acquainted?'

'Since childhood. When my grandfather died I thought mutual loss might eventually draw them together, but Colborough become a virtual recluse.' He sent her a swift glance. 'Grandmama was widowed six months after my parents and Lord Eversleigh's drowned in a boating accident. The shock was too much for my grandfather.'

'I don't wonder at it,' she murmured, compassion momentarily diverting her. 'When Lady Hawkridge told me...' She shook her head; the task of conveying sympathy for such a tragedy was utterly beyond her. 'There's really nothing one can say, is there?'

Hawkridge's mouth took on a cynical curve. 'The perfect answer. All right, Mrs Chantry. How much?'

If he'd snatched her up and dangled her over the edge of the cliff, Amy couldn't have been more stunned. The change was so sudden, so incisive, that for a moment she couldn't think. Then a surge of heat shot through her.

Oh, he was good. Lull the victim into a false sense of security, then strike. But though her very fingertips tingled with shock, this was something she could fight.

'I have no intention of leaving Lady Hawkridge's employ, my lord, unless she dismisses me.' She schooled her features to cool composure. 'No matter what incentive you offer.'

'You didn't even pretend to misunderstand me.' A brow lifted. 'Unexpectedly refreshing. But what made you think I was offering to buy you off, Mrs Chantry?'

She looked up at him. 'What else would you mean by "how much"?'

He raised his brow again; the sardonic gleam in his eyes all the answer she needed.

This time the surge of heat was so intense she wondered she didn't levitate straight off the ground. She looked away quickly, cursing her fair complexion that showed every change of colour, and reminded herself that Hawkridge could well be trying to provoke her into giving notice.

'I doubt a man would offer to buy a woman he dislikes. But the answer is still no.'

'I admire your restraint,' he murmured, watching her. 'Those offers were blatant insults, but though you refused both, you weren't shocked into retaliation.'

'Women in my position become accustomed to insults, sir.'

'Women in your position. Do you mean widows?'

'Not necessarily.' She met his gaze head-on. 'Single women,

also, may be subject to offers of an insulting nature, even…even hounded…' She broke off, tilting her chin but looking away again. 'It's the way of the world when a woman has no male protector. However, the reason I didn't react as you may have expected is that I know your offer sprang from concern for Lady Hawkridge.'

'Indeed? To which offer do you refer?'

Amy set her teeth. 'The one to buy me off.'

'And when I implied otherwise?'

'I don't believe your implication was meant to do anything more than goad me into impulsive behaviour.'

'An interesting thought,' he murmured.

She clenched her hand around her reticule.

'Careful,' Hawkridge advised, glancing down when a sharp crunch sounded. 'Mrs Tredgett, for one, won't appreciate receiving a crumpled note.'

Amy concentrated on not throwing her reticule at him. A lady did not cast missiles at a gentleman. Even when the gentleman was not behaving like one, didn't look like one, and managed to make her feel very unladylike indeed.

'Perhaps I should make it quite clear from the outset, my lord, that I have no intention of robbing Lady Hawkridge, or of sponging off her. That should render unnecessary any more offers you may have in mind.'

'You come straight to the point, don't you, Mrs Chantry?' He smiled. 'I like that.'

'I'm merely following your example, sir. Besides, under the circumstances, I see no virtue in prevarication.'

'Good. Then I can be equally blunt.' His smile vanished. Eyes the colour of arctic ice bored straight through her. His voice went as cold as fog rolling in across a very dark sea. 'My grandmother tends to see only good in people. She's also kind-hearted and generous to a fault. While those qualities endear her to her family and friends, they also lay her open to disillusionment and hurt. I will do anything, Mrs Chantry—*anything*—to see that she is *not* hurt.'

Amy swallowed. The knowledge that she wouldn't hurt her benefactress for the world didn't prevent chills sprinting up and down her spine at the menace in Hawkridge's tone. A less determined companion would probably flee in total disorder.

A less determined companion wouldn't, for instance, dream of teaching him a lesson in determination.

She wiped the scowl from her face and replaced it with a sweetly approving smile. 'What can I say, my lord, except that your sentiments do you credit.'

His eyes narrowed to glittering slits. Amy decided that teaching Hawkridge a lesson in determination was probably not a good idea while they were negotiating the steep road down to the village. She wanted to arrive in one piece.

She infused her voice with the tone of gentle reason, and tried again. 'Only time will prove that I would never betray Lady Hawkridge's trust, sir. Indeed, I'm more grateful to her than I can ever explain.'

'Try,' he bit out, obviously unmoved by gentle reason.

She sent him a fulminating glare. 'I doubt you would understand what it's like to be down to your last shilling, having spent everything else on appearing presentable so as to gain *respectable* employment.'

This blunt statement seemed to give her opponent food for thought. After a hard-eyed appraisal, he strode along beside her for some distance in silence.

Amy tried to calm the turbulent gyrations of her stomach. There was no reason to be nervous. Hawkridge hadn't dismissed her; she could withstand the odd insult or two. What else could he do to her?

The question had an unfortunate effect on her senses. They scurried about as though seeking refuge from a threat. Such frantic exercise was not conducive to rational thought. She had to keep her wits about her, because she was quite certain that the next salvo wouldn't be long in coming.

'You were not left in fortuitous circumstances, I take it, Mrs Chantry.'

Amy smiled grimly to herself and decided that brevity of reply was her only recourse. 'No.'

'You have no other family?'

'No.'

'I find that difficult to believe. You're little more than a girl. Where are your parents?'

'Dead.'

'Grandparents?'

'I... Dead.' It seemed a safe guess.

'Hmm. Stonewalled. I'm almost afraid to ask. Er...former employers?'

She looked up, startled by the hint of dry humour. Then looked quickly away when the gleam in his eyes sent a sizzle of heat through her veins. 'N-none.'

There was a slight pause. She could feel those light grey eyes aimed at her like twin rapier points. 'You know,' he said at last in a conversational tone she didn't trust for a minute, 'you intrigue me, Mrs Chantry. Every one of my instincts tells me you aren't what you seem. And yet I can't make up my mind about what it is you do seem, or what it is you are. Or even if it's the other way about.'

Since he'd rendered her almost cross-eyed trying to work that out, Amy judged it prudent to remain silent.

'However,' he continued, still in that pleasant tone that caused her to snap back to instant attention, 'it's patently obvious that you dislike lying.'

Heat stung her cheeks; it was useless hoping he'd think it was the natural colour caused by a walk in the brisk wind. 'I'm not lying, my lord. I've never been a companion; therefore I cannot produce any previous employers to speak for me.'

'Perhaps I should warn you, Mrs Chantry, that I have little patience with people who even fiddle with the truth to suit their purposes.'

Her eyes flashed. She lifted her chin, but pressed her lips resolutely together.

'Well done,' he acknowledged softly. 'Whatever else you are, you're familiar with battle tactics. Was your husband a military man, Mrs Chantry?'

Amy's breath caught. Her mind went blank.

'Uh...no.'

'A professional man, perhaps?'

'No.'

He sighed. 'It would really be a great deal less wearing on both our nerves if you'd simply tell me.'

She doubted Hawkridge even had nerves. 'Does it matter?' she demanded, goaded into more than monosyllables.

'I don't know,' he shot back. 'Does it?'

He'd cornered her. Why on earth hadn't she foreseen questions about her husband? Probably because most people hesitated to ask such questions of a young widow, she answered herself. Hawkridge clearly had no such scruples.

Not that any amount of warning would have improved the situation. He was right. She hated lying. Even fiddling with the truth made her feel wretchedly uncomfortable. But she had no choice.

'My husband...invested in certain enterprises,' she finally conceded. And almost collapsed in relief when she saw salvation, in the person of a lady, emerge from the gates of a small estate on the outskirts of the village.

She barely managed to keep her gasp of thankfulness silent. Her acquaintanceship with the estate's chatelaine, Lady Ingham, was of the slightest, but that didn't prevent her from transforming her rigid features into a bright smile of greeting.

'Damn and blast,' muttered Hawkridge, clearly not sharing her feelings on the matter. He scowled. 'Kitty always did have the habit of interrupting at the wrong moment.'

At the sound of his voice, the lady in question looked around. Amy was just hoping her smile didn't appear too desperate, when her rescuer let out a most unladylike shriek of delight and launched herself at Hawkridge.

Amy ground to an astonished halt as Hawkridge not only withstood the assault, but swooped Lady Ingham into his arms and, laughing, his scowl quite banished, twirled her around.

Her ladyship didn't appear to find anything strange in his behaviour. She hung on for dear life and laughed back at him. 'Marc, you wretch, where did you spring from? Oh, heavens, put me down. We're shocking Mrs Chantry.'

Eyes gleaming, Hawkridge set his assailant on her feet and glanced in Amy's direction. 'Mrs Chantry's been at Hawkridge for several weeks, Kitty. She must know you're a hoyden by now.'

'Alas, it's true,' acknowledged Lady Ingham with a rueful smile for Amy. 'But I'm sure you know how it is between old friends, Mrs Chantry. Poor, dear Ingham, though,' she burbled before Amy could answer. 'Such goings on at the gates. He *would* be shocked.'

'How is Ingham?' enquired Hawkridge, a distinctly indulgent smile in his eyes.

Amy could only stare at him in amazement. Was this the same man she'd started out with? She hadn't suspected he was capable of laughter, let alone playful gestures such as twirling a lady around.

Something fluttered inside her as she wondered what it felt like to be locked in those strong arms. Though not necessarily be twirled. If Hawkridge wrapped her in his arms, she strongly suspected her head would spin without any assistance.

The thought paralysed her. Instead of seizing the opportunity to escape, she stood there like a stuffed owl, wondering why she was tingling all over as if she really was enveloped in his embrace.

When Lady Ingham started down the steps built into the cliff opposite her gates with a gay word of farewell and a promise to visit, she was quite incapable of doing more than respond with a weak smile. Fortunately, her ladyship noticed nothing amiss; she was engaged in waving to a little boy who was already industriously at work on the pebbled beach below, assisted by his nurse.

Amy could only be thankful.

'You look as if you'd like to follow Lady Ingham, Mrs Chantry. The beach here is wide enough to walk on without the discomfort of wet sandals. Would you prefer to stroll along the shore?'

And risk looking like a helpless female by clutching the railing all the way down that precipitous descent?

'No!' she uttered with such force that his brows shot up. When colour flooded her cheeks his expression went unnervingly intent.

'A...another acquaintance since childhood, my lord?' she managed to ask in a voice that showed a lamentable tendency to squeak. Forcing her legs into motion, she started walking.

'Yes, as a matter of fact.'

He sounded intrigued. Which was even more nerve-racking.

Then he glanced up and his mouth took on a sardonic curve. 'And aren't you fortunate, Mrs Chantry? Here comes a second saviour in the person of my brother-in-law.'

Relief was plainly writ large on her face. Amy didn't care. Lord
Nettlebed's appearance outside the Vicarage was clearly a gift
from On High. Quickening her pace to something perilously close
to a run, she greeted him with outstretched hand and every sign
of pleasure.

Quite forward behaviour in a mere companion.

'How do you do, Mrs Chantry?' Nettlebed asked, cordially
shaking hands. A smile lit his hazel eyes. 'Just the day for a pleasant stroll, isn't it? After all the rain we've had, you must be glad
to get out of the house.'

She now had serious doubts about that.

'Mrs Chantry prefers to stride,' Hawkridge put in, gripping his
brother-in-law's hand. 'Good to see you, Bevan. How is everyone?'

'I thought Augusta gave you that information in expensive detail,' Nettlebed returned drolly. 'You don't appear to have lost any
sleep over it, however. You're looking disgustingly fit, Marc.' He
let his gaze rest on Hawkridge's less-than-sartorially-arranged cravat. 'If a little informal.'

Hawkridge shrugged. 'I was interrupted in the middle of changing.'

An image of Hawkridge ripping off his cravat promptly flashed
into Amy's mind. It was immediately followed by a picture of him
shrugging those powerful shoulders out of his coat...hooking a
finger in the neck of his shirt...ripping...

The pictures stopped right there—mainly because her brain had
frozen in shock.

Beside him, Marc felt her stiffen and decided his reply had
given the game away. His quarry had finally realised he'd followed
her, regardless of what he'd been doing at the time.

She ought to count herself lucky he hadn't got further along in
the task of changing into more comfortable attire, he thought
grimly, because when he'd caught sight of her heading for the cliff
road at a pace strongly reminiscent of escaping prey, sheer predatory instinct had taken over.

He'd shot out of his room and bounded down the stairs without
a thought for what he was wearing.

For all the good it had done him. Far from obtaining answers, he had several more questions resounding in his brain.

Not least of which was why he experienced a damned painful surge of arousal every time Mrs Chantry aimed that pointed little chin in the air.

'Well, be prepared for a lecture on the proper country attire for gentlemen,' Nettlebed continued, in blissful ignorance of his companions' emotions. 'If, as I presume, you're on your way to call on your sister.'

'I'll drive over later this afternoon,' Marc growled. Then mentally kicked himself when Nettlebed's brows rose lazily at his brusque tone. 'I don't anticipate a lecture, however. As soon as Augusta is informed that I intend to stay at Hawkridge for a week or so, she'll start planning a ball or some such nuisance.'

His brother-in-law was successfully diverted. 'We're already in an uproar over the party we're holding tomorrow night,' he said dryly. 'For God's sake, don't put the idea of a ball into Augusta's mind. She thinks a social whirl will distract Lucinda from the young man we've had haunting the place since she returned from that damned—please excuse me, Mrs Chantry—that exclusive Bath seminary.'

Beside him, Mrs Chantry stiffened again. Marc sent her a swift glance, wondering what had set her off this time. There was a tiny line between her brows, but she didn't appear shocked at Nettlebed's language or the fact that he was discussing family business in her presence.

Then she seemed to shake off whatever had arrested her attention and smiled at his brother-in-law.

'Please think nothing of it, sir. Lady Nettlebed has been kind enough to confide some of her worry to me. Although... I didn't know Miss Nettlebed had met Mr Chatsworth while she'd been at school.'

Nettlebed nodded gloomily. 'You'd think a Young Ladies Academy would take better care, wouldn't you? God knows, they charge enough.'

Her answering nod was so full of sympathy anyone would have thought she had teenaged children herself.

Marc found himself grinding his back teeth, a reaction that gave him a severe jolt. He knew Nettlebed doted on Augusta; even if that hadn't been the case, he suspected Amy was smart enough not to cast out lures to anyone in his presence. But for some odd reason he wanted to tell Nettlebed to keep his problems with Lucinda to himself.

'I can perfectly comprehend your feelings on the matter,' Amy said, startling him until he realised she and Nettlebed still had their heads together like a couple of anxious matrons. 'But speaking of family concerns, you must have a great deal to discuss with Lord Hawkridge. I'll be on my way.'

'Can't be late delivering those notes,' Marc muttered, not knowing if he was more incensed with Amy or himself. He fixed his brother-in-law with a look of heavy meaning. 'You on your way back to the Park, Bevan?'

His lordship remained annoyingly uncooperative. 'No, not really,' he said vaguely. He waved a hand at the residence behind him. 'Had to drop in at the Vicarage. Place is full of chicken-pox. Augusta hasn't had it, nor has Lucinda for that matter, so the task fell to me to do the civil. Didn't realise it was so demanding. Feel like I've had the wretched illness myself, all over again, after listening to Mrs ffollifoot.'

Marc resigned himself to the inevitable. 'A pint at the Green Man should disperse the mists. Come on—' he sent Amy a faintly menacing glance '—Mrs Chantry is in a hurry to be gone.'

She tipped her chin up. 'Only as far as the other end of the village, my lord.'

As a challenge it was without equal. Annoyance exploded into outright male wrath. When she'd exchanged polite farewells with Nettlebed, he deliberately stepped between them, speared her gaze with his, and taking advantage of a passing barouche, issued his own challenge. 'Don't cross swords with me, Mrs Chantry, unless you're willing to take the consequences.'

She flushed; her eyes widened. Then she drew back and lifted her chin at him again.

'So now you're resorting to threats, my lord. I can only wonder, given your opinion of me, why you didn't simply dismiss me out of hand this morning. It would have saved us both from an unpleasant walk, not to mention—'

'I can't dismiss you out of hand,' he interrupted through his teeth. 'Grandmama would be extremely upset. And you know damn well I won't distress her.'

She affixed a smile to her face that made his fingers itch. 'Now why would I presume that, sir? I try to reserve judgement about a person until I'm somewhat better acquainted with him.'

Marc inclined his head in grim acknowledgement, and decided to leave his opponent in possession of the field before he did something he'd regret. Such as throwing her over his shoulder in full view of the village and carting her back to Hawkridge where he could kiss that cat-with-the-cream smile right off her face.

'Your point, Mrs Chantry.' He lifted his hand and, against every sane instinct, touched her cheek briefly in a parody of a fencer's salute. His blood surged in his veins. She was as soft as mist. And as elusive.

'However,' he continued, 'there is another reason why I won't dismiss you out of hand. I intend to know you better, also. To that end we'll continue this conversation on our way back to Hawkridge. You have twenty minutes to deliver your missives before meeting me back here.'

She had delivered her missives in considerably less time.

Amy was still thanking Providence for her narrow escape as the members of the Society began filing into the drawing-room later that afternoon. She was also quaking in her little kid sandals. Defiance had taken on a rather dangerous aspect.

Not that she'd actually agreed to the time limit arbitrarily set by Hawkridge. She'd simply turned on her heel and stalked off; the prospect of another conversation with him, in twenty minutes, not to mention the suddenly unbridled workings of her mind, enough to spur her to unprecedented speed. Never had notes been delivered so fast. She'd been on her way back to the Manor practically before the recipient of the first missive had taken it from the tray presented by her housemaid.

Amy was sure she was still unbecomingly flushed from her uphill dash when Miss Pucklenett paused beside her in the drawing-room doorway, hands clasped to her bony breast.

'The *drawing-room*,' she uttered, justifying Amy's assertion that she would be quite overcome. She seemed oblivious to the elegant, burgundy-draped windows, the magnificent marble fireplace or the exquisitely rendered ceiling murals for which the Manor was famous. 'How *kind* of Lady Hawkridge. How *gracious*. Just as though I was a real person. And she is even staying to attend the meeting.'

Amy suppressed a smile. 'She is the Society's patron, ma'am.'

'Yes, yes, my dear, but patrons aren't required to attend all the meetings, you know. How shall we ever be able to convey our gratitude, our awareness of the very great honour, our—?'

'For heaven's sake, Clara, sit down and keep your tongue between your teeth until your wits catch up with it,' Mrs Tredgett commanded, living up to her reputation as the village dragon. Prodding her friend onwards with her walking cane, she sailed into the room. 'Real person, indeed! What do you think you are? A ghost?'

Miss Pucklenett was too busy being overcome by her surroundings to take offence. Amy doubted she would have resented Mrs Tredgett's stringent comments in any case. The Society's ladies had all known each other for years and, while not members of the upper echelons of local gentry, being made up of the Vicar's wife, various minor squires' relics, one or two governesses and the doctor's sister, were perfectly content with their place in the scheme of things.

Amy was more than happy to be included in their number. It was several steps up from the last social strata she'd occupied, no one frayed her nerves with awkward questions, and there was no reason for her imagination to run riot—unlike its behaviour in the company of certain other persons.

Half an hour into the meeting, however, she was forced to concede that Lord Colborough's opinion of the Society for the Beautification of Our Village had some justification. All of five minutes had been spent on the tricky question of how many ornamental ducks would be ordered from the stonemason to adorn the village wall separating the beach from the gravelled walk optimistically known as the Promenade. Everyone was happy to agree with Lady Hawkridge's suggestion of six, each smaller than the preceding one. The motion thus carried unanimously, the ladies settled down to the main business of the day—gossip.

When Lady Hawkridge was summoned from the room by her butler a few minutes after the tea-tray had been brought in, the gossip promptly swerved to include her grandson.

'I saw it with my own eyes, my dears.' Mrs ffollifoot, as befitting her position as the Vicar's wife and the Society's usual hostess, picked up the teapot and, ignoring Amy's claims as the dowager's deputy, poured tea for the guests. 'There was Hawkridge in the middle of the road, in full view of anyone who happened along, *cuddling* Lady Ingham.'

'*Shameless!*' Miss Twinhoe, a spinster of indeterminate age who kept house for her brother, leaned forward, nose twitching like an eager foxhound.

'*Shocking!*' Miss Pucklenett's skinny form, clad in drab grey wool, quivered with excitement.

'*Scandalous!*' Mrs Tredgett snorted. 'But just like him,' she added, in the tone of one who is an expert on the subject.

'And he then continued on his way with his cravat positively *mussed.*'

'Oh, heavens! Mussing a gentleman's cravat! Whatever was Lady Ingham thinking of?' quavered Miss Pucklenett. 'Why, if dear Mrs Mayhew were to *think* that one of her daughters would behave in such a forward fashion, I would expect to be turned off without a character and end my days in destitution and poverty.'

'There is no need to indulge in exaggeration, Clara,' Mrs ffollifoot admonished, returning the teapot to its stand. Everyone ignored their cups of tea. 'Especially as you are still with us despite Miss Mayhew's attempts to attract Lord Hawkridge last winter.'

Miss Pucklenett had not spent all her adult years as a governess without learning to think fast on her feet. 'Miss Mayhew was no longer under my authority at that time, Eliza,' she declared with dignity. 'And in any case, it was Lady Ingham who encouraged dear Amabel to, er, pursue the Earl.'

'Should've known it was useless,' stated Mrs Tredgett. 'But Kitty Ingham never did have much sense. Not surprised she was cuddling Hawkridge. After all, they were—'

'They weren't cuddling,' Amy burst out, unable to stay silent another minute. She was intervening for Lady Ingham's sake, she told herself. Hawkridge was perfectly capable of looking after himself. 'I was there, since Lord Hawkridge kindly offered me his escort into Ottersmead. Lady Ingham's greeting might have been, er, enthusiastic, but it was perfectly innocent.'

'Yes, yes, my dear Mrs Chantry, we all know that.' Mrs ffollifoot clucked her tongue in affront at having her story stripped of scandalous connotations. 'But it's the *look* of the thing. Dear Mr ffollifoot was grievously shocked, and I could only be thankful Lizzie and Jane were safely in their beds and unable to witness such a hoydenish display, although one could wish that Lizzie hadn't contracted chicken-pox at this particular time.'

'Afraid young Mayhew might sheer off,' muttered Mrs Tredgett in an aside to Amy. 'Shouldn't think so. Dull as dishwater, poor boy. Give me a red-blooded male like Hawkridge any day.'

Amy swallowed. The thought of Hawkridge demonstrating red-blooded maleness was not something she wished to dwell upon.

'I'm sure Lady Ingham meant no harm,' she managed to say weakly, resisting the urge to press a hand to the fluttering in her stomach. 'And Lord Hawkridge's cravat was already mussed because he came chasing after...uh...I mean...'

Everyone sat forward, eyes fastened on her with avid expectation. Amy gazed back at them, her mind unnervingly blank. 'The wind blew it,' she finally got out in a desperate rush.

The ladies sank back in their seats with a collective sigh of disappointment.

Miss Twinhoe recovered first. 'A kind-hearted person such as yourself would naturally say so, Mrs Chantry,' she said, nodding approval at Amy. 'Oh, no need to colour up, my dear. *Your* demeanour is exactly as it should be. I was saying so only yesterday to Miss Pucklenett, wasn't I, Clara? There are several young ladies who would do well to follow your example, but while Hawkridge is in residence you may be sure we'll have all manner of forwardness. Encouraged, I might add, by his own sister, Lady Nettlebed.'

'Not to mention Lady Ingham,' put in Mrs ffollifoot, whose disapproval of that damsel seemed to be increasing in leaps and bounds. 'One would think Hawkridge could have his pick of the

London debutantes, without her throwing every eligible lady in the county at his head.'

'I daresay she wishes his lordship to be as happily settled as herself,' suggested Miss Twinhoe. 'They were engaged, you know,' she added, for Amy's benefit. 'But Miss Ashcroft, as she was then, broke it off, practically on the day of the wedding. Such a scandal.'

'Never understood why,' grumbled Mrs Tredgett, obviously annoyed by her lack of comprehension. 'Hawkridge has wealth, an old, distinguished title and is indecently good-looking into the bargain. What more did the girl want?'

What, indeed?

Amy thought of the affection and easy camaraderie between Hawkridge and Lady Ingham and wondered the same thing. Why *had* Kitty Ingham broken her engagement? And, more to the point, why had a man of Hawkridge's predatory nature accepted the blow?

'His lordship doesn't strike me as the type of man to accept being jilted,' she murmured, unable to resist her curiosity on that particular point.

'Well, he is, after all, a gentleman, my dear,' Mrs ffollifoot informed her, getting her revenge by assuming Amy was ignorant of gentlemanly behaviour. 'What else could he do?'

The question continued to exercise Amy's mind for several minutes. Graceful resignation didn't appear to be Hawkridge's style; perhaps he'd cared so much for Lady Ingham, he'd wanted her happiness despite the cost to himself.

The thought caused a strange pang in her heart. It was immediately followed by a sensation closely akin to fear. Why should she care about his feelings? Hawkridge meant nothing to her; except as a dangerous opponent who had a dismaying habit of invading her mind at inconvenient moments. She would put a stop to it. After all, it was the portrait that had fascinated her; she would simply renew her efforts to avoid its subject.

Unfortunately for this sensible plan, she returned her attention to the conversation to find that Hawkridge was still its main topic.

'Yes, indeed,' Miss Pucklenett was saying. 'I've always found him to be the perfect epitome of gentlemanly behaviour. So gracious. Such manners. So very charming.'

Mrs Tredgett apparently felt compelled to throw in a dash of realism. 'A holy terror when he was a boy.'

'Poor orphaned lad. Quite helpless to do anything,' murmured Miss Twinhoe, shaking her head.

Amy very nearly shook hers as well. A holy terror she could believe, but charming? The perfect epitome of gentlemanly behaviour? *A poor helpless orphan?* Were these ladies *blind*?

'Of course, you don't know anything about that, Mrs Chantry, since you've only just met his lordship.' Mrs ffollifoot sent her an acid smile. 'He always comes down especially to investigate her ladyship's companions.'

'I'm sure it's very touching that he cares enough about dear Lady Hawkridge to assure himself of Mrs Chantry's suitability,' declared Miss Twinhoe hurriedly. 'Not that there can be any doubt about that, my dear.'

'Very protective,' stated Mrs Tredgett. 'Runs in the family.'

'And one must remember that the previous companions were *men*.' Miss Twinhoe made the pronouncement with all the air of one discussing wild and dangerous beasts, whose behaviour could be counted upon to be vastly different from that of more civilised beings.

'Very true,' agreed Miss Pucklenett in hushed accents. She glanced around and lowered her voice still further as though about to divulge a hideous secret. 'And we all know of the Unfortunate Habits that effect certain persons of the Male Persuasion.'

Since the entire Society had several times been regaled with the sorry tale of their friend's long-ago *tendre* for her father's curate, and the scoundrel's subsequent elopement with the daughter of a wealthy tradesman, everyone nodded sagely. A few seconds of silence ensued while respect was paid to the demise of Miss Pucklenett's youthful aspirations to the wedded state.

By the time it was judged proper to continue, Lady Hawkridge returned to the drawing-room and conversation became general.

Amy sat back and contemplated her cup of tea. She completely forgot about her resolution to keep Hawkridge out of her mind; several vastly contradictory images of him were whirling therein in dizzying array. She didn't know which was predominant. The gentleman gracefully accepting his *congé*—her imagination still balked at that one. The boy on the verge of manhood, struggling with bereavement. The rakishly dishevelled, wickedly grinning pirate on the cliff top. Or the relentless interrogator who seemed determined to uncover everything she'd prefer to forget.

And beneath it all, waiting, was the warrior she sensed as surely as she recognised the less-than-civilised side of herself.

A warrior, she suspected, who was going to be more than a little annoyed that she'd eluded him that afternoon.

Chapter Four

Amy attached a tiny lace cap to her upswept hair, checked her appearance one last time in her mirror, and reminded herself that she'd survived worse fates than confronting an irate male across the dinner table. Even one who loomed in doorways, arrived on cliff tops without warning, and asked a lot of questions.

She was prepared. Hawkridge wouldn't take her by surprise again.

Buoyed by that thought, she cracked open her bedchamber door and peered cautiously through the aperture. No one appeared to be looming. Her spirits brightened considerably. Since there were no cliff tops in the house, and she'd rehearsed several pithy answers to a variety of possible questions, the evening might not be so bad after all.

Releasing her pent-up breath, she stepped into the passageway, her head half-turned to close the door.

'Good evening, Mrs Chantry.'

'*Aaagh!*' Amy whirled and cannoned into her door. Unfortunately, in the shock of the moment, she hadn't had time to latch it. The door flew open under the impact. She felt herself reeling backwards and squeaked in dismay.

An arm taut with sinew and muscle caught her about the waist and hauled her to safety against a powerful male body. Except that safety was not the first word that sprang to mind.

Amy squeezed her eyes shut as her head spun like a fairground maypole gone mad. Thank heavens they weren't on twirling terms, she thought wildly. She was having enough trouble coping with the masculine heat and power enveloping her.

She was released before she could melt completely. Senses still whirling, she leaned against the wall, a hand to her heart, and summoned a thread of a voice. 'Thank you, my lord.'

When he didn't answer, she forced her eyelids open. Grey eyes blazed into hers, glittering with enough heat to scorch her pale rose silk evening dress right off her trembling form. 'I mean...' She jerked herself upright. 'So now you've added creeping up on people to the list!'

The muscles in his jaw locked; the flames abated. He shoved his fists into his pockets and glared back at her. 'List?'

'Never mind,' said Amy crossly. She peeled herself away from the wall and started toward the stairway. With luck, her legs would feel steadier than limp muslin by the time they got her there.

It was going to be rather more difficult to erase the fierce intensity in Hawkridge's eyes from her mind. Just for an instant the civilised mask had been ripped aside. He'd looked at her as if he'd been a brigand in truth. A brigand about to throw her to the floor and ravish her.

The shocking part had been the primitive thrill that had coursed through her at the thought.

'I'm sorry if I startled you,' he bit out, not sounding sorry in the least. 'I was on my way to enquire if you'd been unexpectedly struck down by illness since you didn't keep our appointment in the village.' He slanted a mocking glance down at her. 'Chicken-pox, perhaps.'

Amy had no attention to spare for sarcasm. 'Appointment? Oh, yes, appointment.' She tried for a tone of airy unconcern—and resisted the temptation to clutch the balustrade with both hands as they started down the wide sweeping staircase that led to the hall.

'Yes.' He fixed her with a pointed stare. 'The appointment we made before you delivered your notes, Mrs Chantry.'

'Oh, dear, perhaps I misheard you, sir. As I recall, Mrs Mayhew's carriage rattled by at that precise moment. Your words must have been drowned out.' Feeling a little steadier when he didn't challenge this flimsy excuse, she summoned up a polite smile. 'I hope you didn't wait long.'

His smile was equally polite, and a great deal more dangerous. 'Not at all,' he purred. 'I was right behind you all the way back to Hawkridge.'

She gulped, her entire back tingling as if he was stalking behind her at that very moment. The gleam in his eyes had her straightening her spine with an almost audible snap. 'Indeed? In that case, I'm surprised you didn't catch up with me so you could continue your interrogation.'

His smile became even more polite. 'Actually, it was my intention to continue our conversation, but I became distracted by the view.'

She tripped over the bottom step. 'The view?'

Hawkridge steadied her with a large hand beneath her elbow. 'Yes. It was quite fascinating.'

Amy's brows snapped together. 'One would have thought you're quite accustomed to the view, my lord. You've lived here most of your life.'

'Indeed, but there's always something new to be seen, don't you find?'

At this moment, she would be happy to see Lady Hawkridge and a dinner table surrounded by servants.

'But there's no harm done. If you're determined to remain here, Mrs Chantry, we'll have plenty of opportunity for convivial walks to the village.'

'Convivial—' Amy set her teeth. 'Very true, sir. I do trust, however, that you'll refrain from interrogation, at least while we're toiling uphill.'

'Next time we'll take the horses,' he assured her, and bowed before ushering her into the withdrawing-room where the family traditionally congregated before dinner.

Lady Hawkridge was seated before a cosy fire, reading the *Morning Post*. She looked up as they entered. 'Horses?' she queried, putting her paper to one side. 'No, no. Much too large. But, you know, Amy, I'm beginning to have my doubts about those ducks. Perhaps we should have more fully considered Miss Twinhoe's suggestion of dolphins.'

Marc eyed his grandparent with caution. 'Dolphins?' He glanced at Amy as she seated herself at the other end of the dowager's sofa. The faintest of smiles was playing about her mouth. His eyes narrowed. The little wretch knew what his grandmother was twittering about and wasn't above letting him flounder.

'I think you might find the waters around here a little short of dolphins, Grandmama,' he essayed.

Lady Hawkridge stared at him in bewilderment. 'Good heavens, Marc, what has that to say to anything? Were you expecting Mr Brinwell to catch a real one?'

'Er, if you want a dolphin, yes.'

Amy stopped resisting the smile fighting to break free and decided—with great magnanimity, she thought—to come to his rescue.

'Lady Hawkridge refers to the ornamental ducks the Society is commissioning from the stonemason, sir. To adorn the seawall in the village.'

He stared at her, thunderstruck. 'Good God! *Ducks?*'

His grandmother took umbrage at his tone. 'Well, you must admit, Marc, that ducks would be more appropriate than horses!'

'I was talking about riding, love,' he returned, feeling quite incapable of further explanation.

'Oh. Well, in that case I suppose it will have to be the ducks. Although a nice dolphin, in the act of frolicking, would have served as a back-rest if anyone wished to sit upon the wall and drink in the view.'

'How odd,' Marc murmured. He propped his shoulders against the mantelpiece, folded his arms and smiled down at his grandmother. 'Mrs Chantry and I were discussing views only a moment ago.'

Amy glared at him. She had heard enough about views.

Her tormentor hadn't, apparently. 'Perhaps, in the pursuit of searching out interesting views, Mrs Chantry, you'd like to ride tomorrow morning? It promises to be a fine day.'

Amy took up the tablecloth she'd been hemming the evening before and stabbed her needle grimly into the linen. 'I'm here to work, my lord, not jaunter about—'

She stopped as if someone had struck her across the throat, her gaze riveted to the newspaper beside her. Between one heartbeat and the next the withdrawing-room at Hawkridge Manor vanished, and she was catapulted into the past.

'Oh, Amy, dear, you've pricked your finger.'

The dowager's voice came to her from a great distance. Amy shook her head and wrenched herself back to the present.

'It's nothing, ma'am.' She stared at her finger, forcing herself to study the tiny wound so she wouldn't have to look at Hawkridge. She didn't dare look at him. She knew he was watching her. She could feel the sudden tension in him, the coiled waiting stillness of the hunter. 'See. The merest trifle.'

'Only one drop of blood,' her ladyship agreed comfortably. 'But it always gives one such a start. Now, where were we? Ah, yes, jauntering about—'

She was interrupted when the butler entered to announce dinner. Amy breathed a sigh of relief. With luck, Hawkridge might put her abrupt silence down to the sting of her needle.

It seemed he must have; the tension emanating from him abated, and he stepped forward to take his grandmother in to dinner.

Amy followed, hoping that by the time they sat down, her employer's notoriously flighty memory would have forgotten about jauntering.

'You know, Amy, jauntering about the countryside puts me in mind of something,' Lady Hawkridge continued, slaying this hope in one fell swoop. She smiled fondly at her grandson as he held her chair for her. 'While Marc is here to escort us, we should go out and about a little more. You've scarcely met anyone since you've been at Hawkridge, and there's no reason for you to be so retiring because you're my companion. Quite the contrary.'

Amy contemplated, without enthusiasm, the bowl of chicken soup presented to her by Pickles. She had just lost her appetite. 'I'm a widow, ma'am.'

'Yes,' murmured Hawkridge, seated at her right. 'Remember, we don't know the precise date of Mrs Chantry's bereavement, Grandmama.'

He was sent a quelling look. 'Oh, dear, I'm so sorry, Amy. I assumed, since you're out of mourning, that your loss was over a year ago.'

'Well, as to that, you are right, ma'am, but—'

'Then there's no reason why we can't indulge ourselves with a little jollification,' declared Lady Hawkridge, a pleased smile replacing her frown. 'Augusta's party will do nicely for a start. Nothing formal, you understand; merely a gathering of friends to amuse Lucinda until she makes her come-out.'

'But—'

'Now, Amy, you know Augusta will be happy to see you. Why, she was saying only the other day how she values your judgement, how impressed she was by your good sense, how—'

'That's very kind of Lady Nettlebed, I'm sure, but—'

'And no more nonsense about being a companion. That is merely a circumstance; *you* are perfectly presentable.'

'Thanks to your generosity, ma'am. And please don't think me ungrateful—indeed, I'll never be able to repay your kindness—but I'm perfectly happy in the company of Miss Pucklenett and Miss Twinhoe and—'

Her ladyship clucked her tongue. 'Goodness me, no, that won't do. Worthy ladies though they are, you can't wish to end up keeping house for a doctor, even if he is your brother, or losing your wits every time you see a drawing-room.'

'A depressing fate,' concurred Hawkridge, finishing his soup and sitting back in a casual sprawl that managed to look extremely dangerous. He contemplated Amy from beneath half-lowered lids. 'But we've yet to ascertain, Grandmama, if Mrs Chantry has a brother. And if so, is he a doctor?'

Amy met the challenging glitter in those grey eyes with uptilted chin. 'The answer to the first of those questions, my lord, is no. Which leaves the second redundant.' So pleased was she with that reply that her appetite promptly returned. She applied herself with gusto to the second course of lamb cutlets braised in a mint sauce.

'There you are, then,' declared the dowager. She waved a cutlet in the air in triumph. 'If Amy doesn't have a brother, we don't need to worry about him.'

'You relieve my mind, Grandmama.'

Her ladyship was too busy making plans to suspect sarcasm. 'And it isn't as if you're going to be waltzing with every gentleman who crosses your path, Amy. That *would* be too forward in your present circumstances. However, a lady always knows precisely how to behave, and since you're very much a lady, I have no qualms on that account. There can be no objection to your attending Augusta's party. Don't you agree, Marc?'

'No objection,' he muttered.

Mrs Chantry aimed that pointed little chin at him again. She appeared torn between reluctance to embark on a social whirl and indignation at his tone. Her feelings on the subject were the least of his problems, however. He was glad he was sitting down, a napkin over his lap. Apart from his usual reaction to that distinctly feminine challenge—a response that was becoming disturbingly familiar—her mutinous expression re-animated a vivid mental picture of the view he'd found so fascinating that afternoon.

The sight of her pert, rounded little derriere swaying agitatedly back and forth as she'd sped up the hill in front of him had aroused several rather heated fantasies. He'd wanted to curl his hands around those tantalising globes, to stroke, to caress, to savour that uniquely feminine softness.

And that was only the start.

Once the seed was sown, his mind had proved disastrously fertile. The delicately curved ankles revealed every few seconds by the violent upward flipping of her skirts hadn't rendered the trip any less painful. Something had to be done before Mrs Chantry caused permanent damage.

The first step was to get her away from the house again.

'And since you now have Grandmama's approval in the matter of jollification, Mrs Chantry, there can also be no objection to us riding together tomorrow morning. Shall we say ten o'clock? You'll notice there are no carriages rattling by, so I'll expect you to the minute.'

Amy blinked at him, her wits momentarily suspended. It wasn't Hawkridge's somewhat menacingly uttered rider that bothered her; she had just discovered a rather significant gap in her education.

She must have looked as blank as she felt, because Hawkridge raised a brow. 'You do ride, Mrs Chantry?'

'Er, no.'

The dowager looked vaguely surprised. 'You don't ride, dear? Well, not every lady cares for horses, you know.'

Amy thought quickly. An instant's silent debate had her aban-

doning the idea of following her ladyship's lead. If Hawkridge
thought she didn't care for horses, he was perfectly capable of
marching her down to the stables and introducing her to the animals, regardless of her feelings on the matter. Her reply had to be
prosaic.

It also had the advantage of being the truth.

'It isn't that. My mother and I did live in the country for a time,
but I was so young I scarcely remember it. Then we moved to
town.'

'Ah, so you did have a mother, Mrs Chantry.'

'Marcus!' His grandmother bent a severe frown upon him. 'That
was very rude. Pay no heed to him, Amy.'

'I don't intend to, ma'am.' Amy took her time over the last
mouthful on her plate, placed her knife and fork neatly side by
side and set her lips in a prim line. 'I've already learned that your
grandson does not always behave like a gentleman.'

'Yes, I know. And nothing can be done about it. Though if the
gossip one hears is the truth, several ladies have attempted the
task.'

'I would be obliged to you both if you'd stop discussing me as
if I'm not here,' Hawkridge stated. He raised an ironic brow at
Amy. 'My apologies if I seemed rude, Mrs Chantry. Such was not
my intention.'

She sent him a sidelong look, gently mocking. 'I believe you,
my lord. You seem to manage the feat without any prior intent at
all.'

Lady Hawkridge choked and lifted her napkin hastily to her lips.
'Oh, dear.' She coughed discreetly. 'That last mouthful must have
gone down the wrong way.' Ignoring her grandson's abruptly narrowed gaze, she beamed at Amy. 'Have you finished, Amy, dear?
Perhaps we should leave Marc to his port. It might improve his
mood.'

Amy rose from her chair as though propelled by springs. 'An
excellent idea, ma'am.'

Hawkridge sighed and stood also. 'Given the female conspiracy
to which I find myself falling victim, I feel I should accompany
you. Merely to defend my character, of course.'

'If you say so, dearest.' Lady Hawkridge patted his arm as she passed him. 'I'm sure Amy will be glad of your company. I don't know how it is, but every time I attend one of the Society's meetings I feel…quite…exhausted…afterwards. Oh, dear…'

To Amy's dismay the dowager began to wilt. To her horror, her ladyship didn't stop at wilting. Before her very eyes, Lady Hawkridge transformed herself from a still-spritely elderly lady to one whose air of enfeeblement was positively ghastly.

A tiny, claw-like hand reached, shaking pitifully, for Amy's arm; she leaned heavily, her weight quite disproportionate to her suddenly shrunken size. Her voice quavered with the weak tones of one croaking out last wishes. 'Perhaps you wouldn't mind ringing for Giddings, Amy? To assist me up the stairs.'

'I'll certainly ring for Giddings, ma'am, but first allow me to escort you to your room.' She would have hauled the dowager towards the door in her haste, except that Lady Hawkridge drooped even more. Amy had to grab hold of her ladyship with her other hand to prevent her from slithering all the way to the floor.

'No, no, Amy, dear. I know you won't take it amiss, but I'd like to have Giddings. When one is overtaken by the wretched weakness engendered by advancing years, one needs long-familiar faces about one.'

'I'm sure that's quite understandable, ma'am, but—'

'And it would take such a load off my mind to know you'll keep Marc company on his first night at home.' Blue eyes lifted pleadingly. 'He likes a cup of tea, you know, and who will pour it when Pickles brings in the tea-tray if you're upstairs with me?'

'Well, as to that—'

The bird-like claw patted her arm. 'I knew I could depend on you, Amy, dear. So kind. Thank you.'

Amy sent a frantic glance at Hawkridge. He had taken up his post against the mantelpiece again, arms folded across his chest, and was watching the performance with a smile of unholy amusement in his eyes.

Which was all very well for him, she thought frantically. What if the dowager really was overcome by exhaustion, unlikely though it seemed? It was part of her job to see to her ladyship's comfort, to accede to her wishes.

'Would you please ring the bell, my lord,' she directed, glaring at him when he grinned.

'I already have. Giddings should be here at any second.'

The door opened on his words. Giddings bustled in, apparently not at all surprised to see her mistress in an advanced state of decrepitude.

'There, I knew how it would be after all that dusting,' she scolded. 'Now just leave her ladyship to me, Mrs Chantry. I'll have her put to bed and resting in a trice.'

'So kind,' croaked the dowager, waving feebly. With a smile for Hawkridge and Amy that appeared to take the last of her rapidly dwindling stores of strength, she tottered from the room, supported by Giddings.

Amy could only gaze after her employer in awed admiration—until a chuckle from the vicinity of the fireplace reminded her of the remaining company.

'What convinced you that Grandmama wasn't about to expire in your arms, Mrs Chantry?' Hawkridge pushed himself away from the mantelpiece and crossed the room to a table that held a decanter and several crystal glasses. He poured himself a small measure of brandy and turned to face her.

Her gaze rested thoughtfully on the glass in his hand. 'For some odd reason, my lord, I can't imagine you drinking tea.'

He raised a brow.

'It would be far too civilised.'

'You consider me uncivilised?'

'I'm sure you can be perfectly civil, my lord.'

A smile touched his mouth. 'That wasn't quite what I asked.'

When she didn't answer, the smile turned wicked. 'Your unspoken accusation is positively reverberating in the ether, Mrs Chantry.'

She wasn't going to rise to that bait either.

He laughed softly. 'We'll reserve the discussion of my uncivilised tendencies for a later date. You still haven't answered my original question. Quite an innocuous one, I thought.'

She narrowed her eyes at him. 'After my first shock, sir, I realised you weren't at all worried about your grandmother's health.

Nor was Giddings, come to that. The conclusion was obvious. However, a companion doesn't argue with her employer.'

'And you are a very proper companion, aren't you, Mrs Chantry?'

'I hope so. However, I have no obligation to be a companion to you, my lord. I'm sure you're quite capable of amusing yourself until you retire, so I'll wish you good—'

'But my grandmother expressly asked you to keep me company, Mrs Chantry.'

Amy paused, one foot half-suspended from the floor. 'That was part of her act, as I'm sure you're aware.'

'Yes. I did wonder if your lack of concern sprang from instant recognition of a superlative performance. Merely a fleeting thought, you understand.'

She stifled a sigh, returned her heel to the floor and looked back over her shoulder. 'Since I've never had the opportunity to attend a playhouse, my lord, I'm glad the thought was merely fleeting. My answer to your query as to my lack of concern was the simple truth, no more, no less.'

'Excellent. Why don't you sit down so we can explore some more simple truths together?'

The notion of exploring anything with Hawkridge caused a tremor to ripple through her. Amy turned very slowly. He stood watching her, one brow raised, the half-smile playing about his lips holding amusement, a hint of appeal—and an unnerving amount of charm.

Fascination stirred; tantalising, teasing. Curiosity tip-toed in its wake.

Miss Pucklenett had been right. He could be charming. How many guises did he use to mask the fierce intensity that was evident only in the stillness with which he waited and the intent glitter in his eyes?

It was probably foolish to ask the question, let alone stay in the expectation of an answer, but hadn't she prepared herself for this very situation? Her earlier evasiveness had only aroused Hawkridge's predatory instincts. If she gave him nothing to sink his teeth into—another tremor rippled through her—he might cease his questioning.

Perhaps Lady Hawkridge, knowing her grandson, had reached a similar conclusion and created the opportunity.

Amy swallowed, walked over to a chair and sat down. 'Very well, my lord. I can see you won't be content until you've completed your interrogation.'

'Not at all, Mrs Chantry. I'm merely endeavouring to make polite conversation. It's what one does after dinner, you know.'

'You appear to need practice at it, sir.'

He laughed aloud at that, the sound causing a *frisson* of sensation to feather over her skin. For some odd reason she found herself holding her breath until he'd strolled over to the sofa opposite her armchair and sat down.

'Then let us practice, Mrs Chantry, by all means. I see yesterday's news is at hand to assist us.' He retrieved his grandmother's discarded newspaper and, sending her a swift glance, began to read. '"Another shocking robbery at Bristol. Last night thieves broke into a gentleman's residence, tied the terrified occupants hand and foot, including the unfortunate servants, and proceeded to ransack the house. This newspaper considers transportation too lenient for such scurrilous rogues." What do you think, Mrs Chantry? Should the wretches be hanged when they're laid by the heels?'

He glanced up as he spoke—and immediately narrowed his eyes on her face.

Thank God she'd had that warning earlier. Even so it was a struggle to force her frozen features into an expression of mild interest. Only sheer determination to hold on to her place here had her managing the task.

'A very frightening experience,' she remarked, neatly dodging a debate on transportation or hanging. If Hawkridge suspected such a discussion had the power to disturb her, he wouldn't rest until he knew why. 'But there's no need to delve into the newspaper for a topic of conversation, my lord. I'm quite happy to answer your questions.'

'Hmm.' Hawkridge tossed aside the *Morning Post* and crossed one booted foot over his knee. He still watched her narrowly, but the expression in his eyes turned ironic. 'Why do I get the feeling I'm not going to learn much?'

'Why should you wish to, sir?'

'A good question,' he muttered. 'When I do learn more, I might have an answer.'

'Well, unless you're still labouring under the misapprehension that I'm here to fleece Lady Hawkridge and so must possess a shady past—'

'No,' he interrupted. 'Actually, having had the opportunity to observe you further, Mrs Chantry, I believe you're genuinely fond of my grandmother. Under those circumstances, I can't imagine you cheating her.'

'Oh.' Amy flushed. The very small, very scared part of herself that was always wary, relaxed some of her defences. 'Thank you, sir. In that case—' She made to rise.

'However, I am interested to learn how it comes about that a lady of your tender years finds herself completely alone in the world.'

Amy dug her fingers into the arms of her chair, resisted an urge to grind her teeth, and sat back.

Hawkridge smiled faintly. 'You say you have no family living. What of your husband's relatives?'

'I don't know, my lord.'

His brows shot up. 'You don't know?'

'My husband never mentioned his family.' She shifted slightly. 'Perhaps I should make it plain that my marriage was very brief.'

'I see. I'm sorry to hear that, Mrs Chantry.'

'Yes. And since my own mother died only a few weeks before I le—er, lost my husband, I was forced to find some means of support.'

He studied her somewhat thoughtfully, making her nerves jump as she wondered if he'd noticed her slip.

'It must have been very frightening to be left alone like that. Were there no friends you could turn to? You mentioned living in town. Surely somewhere in London...'

'My mother and I lived in Branscombe, sir.'

When he lifted a brow, she added, 'It's near Cheltenham.'

'Ah.' Another smile touched his mouth. 'Too small to possess a livery stable, no doubt.'

Amy frowned. 'Really, my lord, are you still wondering why I don't ride? Why on earth would you belabour such an insignificant point?'

'A grave fault, I know, but insignificant points sometimes have a way of turning out to be crucial.' His smile turned apologetic. 'Your family, for instance. Are you quite sure there's no one?'

'No one.'

A quizzical gleam came into his eyes. 'No one *at all*? No aunts, uncles, third cousins in the fourth degree, crusty old great-uncles living in seclusion?'

Amy had to smile. 'None that I know of, sir.'

'Who was your father, Mrs Chantry?'

'No one with any connections who might have come to my aid, if that's where this is leading,' she said somewhat drily. 'He was merely the son of a vicar, destined to follow his father into the church.'

'Destined? I take it from that, he didn't do as expected?'

'No.' She shifted again and tried to relax muscles that were drawing tighter with each question. She had nothing to hide about her parents. Not compared to the rest. 'Unless one has private means, the remuneration for newly ordained curates is not enough to support a wife and family. However, my father had fallen in love with my mother and wished to marry her immediately, so he left home to find other work. My grandfather disowned him.'

Hawkridge frowned. 'A rather extreme method of bringing your father to heel.'

'But quite common, my lord. Even in your own circle.'

He inclined his head. 'Indeed. Although the laws of inheritance protect elder sons. And some of us...' He hesitated; his gaze shifting to the fire. 'Some of us are fortunate enough to have parents who care about their offspring.'

His brows drew together. He sent her a swift glance before getting to his feet and bending to place another log on the fire. 'So, what happened to your parents in the end, Mrs Chantry?'

Amy barely heard the question; her attention was suddenly riveted to him. He straightened, but stayed where he was, staring down into the flames. She wished she could see more of his face than a half-profile. That fleeting moment had left her strangely shaken. He'd spoken quite matter-of-factly about his parents' deaths that afternoon. But just now...had the mask slipped again? This time to reveal vulnerability? Was he aware of it—or was he using it to lure her into confiding in him?

'Mrs Chantry?'

Amy started and glanced up. She hadn't even been aware that her gaze had fallen to her hands, gripped tightly in her lap, but now her senses were painfully alert, and almost...waiting. The quietness was so intense she felt Hawkridge's presence as if they were touching, although he wasn't particularly close. The fire flickered lazily, sending wisps of smoke drifting up the chimney. The clock on the mantel ticked, sonorously, as though time had slowed in the silence of the room.

The entire house seemed to wait for her answer.

'They eloped,' she murmured, throwing off the odd notion that, in that moment, her life had stilled, before moving on in another, unknown, direction. 'Mama told me they travelled about for some time, seeking work, and then my father died of a fever a month before I was born.'

Hawkridge frowned. 'And your mother returned home?'

'No, my lord. Apparently my maternal grandfather was also lacking in sympathy.' Her chin went up. 'Possibly because my parents didn't manage to get themselves married during their travels.'

'I see.' He was silent for a moment, then added, 'Inconvenient of them.'

The gentle humour eased some of her tension. Amy smiled wryly. 'They were both under age. Without their parents' consent, any marriage would have been illegal.'

'Unlike your own, Mrs Chantry.'

'Yes.' She made a sound that wasn't quite a laugh. 'I made sure of it.' And had regretted it ever since.

The abrupt silence that followed had her entire body tingling. She hadn't said those last words aloud, had she? No, that wasn't why she was suddenly frozen where she sat.

He'd done it again. Distracted her, slipped under her guard and—

She came to her feet with a rush that almost sent her chair toppling backwards. Her hands fisted at her sides. 'Oh, you are an excellent interrogator, my lord. I noticed it this afternoon, but apparently the lesson didn't last long enough. How dare you imply that I'm masquerading under false pretenses, that I wasn't married at all?'

He stepped forward a pace, brows drawing together. 'Before you whip yourself into a fit of the vapours, Mrs Chantry, I implied no such—'

'Yes you did! Your statement was deliberately designed to trip me up. To...to...trick me into confessing—'

She stopped short, clamping her lips shut on the rest.

His voice went very soft, very gentle. 'Confess what, Mrs Chantry?'

Amy shuddered and made a desperate grab for her composure. What was she doing? If she wasn't careful, she *would* be confessing everything.

She pushed away a sudden insane desire to do just that. Pushed it away violently.

'I was speaking metaphorically, my lord.' She took a breath; let it out. 'If you have any doubts about that, I'd be perfectly happy to go upstairs and fetch my marriage lines for your perusal. Perhaps *that* will put an end to your questioning.'

She wheeled about on the words, but Hawkridge was beside her before she'd taken a step. He caught her above the elbow, his long fingers completely encircling her arm. Amy gasped once, then went very still. Even her breathing stopped. His hand felt hard and warm, his fingers terrifyingly strong against the softness of her inner arm.

She shivered, threw off the sensation of having been captured, and turned, brows raised in haughty enquiry. The expression apparently needed practice; Hawkridge gentled his grip, but he didn't release her.

And his eyes were glittering, intent on her face.

'That won't be necessary, Mrs Chantry. I was merely remarking that your parents' experience no doubt influenced your own. I didn't mean to discompose you.'

Her chin lifted. 'You didn't, sir. I was objecting to your methods. Now, if you don't mind...'

He ignored the tug she gave her arm. His voice went even softer.

'You, on the other hand, are definitely discomposing me.'

'That, my lord, is not my concern. I'm sure a man of your intelligence will be able to think of a solution. Good evening, sir.'

Amy jerked her arm out of his grasp as she spoke, and swung about with a flip of her skirts. Somewhere in the back of her mind she was aware of Hawkridge's narrow-eyed gaze on her as she stalked towards the door. No doubt he was contemplating the view again. She hoped the defiant twitch of her hips accurately conveyed her mood.

Unfortunately, she had not accurately assessed his reaction. Instead of eyeing the view from a distance as he'd done that afternoon, Hawkridge crossed the room with the speed of lightning, slammed his hand flat on the door, and banged it shut before she'd opened it more than an inch.

Amy whirled, and promptly plastered her spine to the panels behind her. In front of her Hawkridge loomed, one arm extended past her shoulder, his hand still holding the door shut, so close she could feel the brush of his clothing against hers, could feel him breathe. His face was taut with annoyance, and something else that sent heat rushing through her veins.

She swallowed. Breathing was well nigh impossible. Masculine purpose and power swirled about her in crashing waves.

And yet she wasn't afraid. Furious, fascinated, befuddled. But not afraid.

Which was enough to spur her to a woefully belated protest.

'Really, my lord, I believe I've answered quite enough—'

'Not even half of them,' he grated. His free hand came up to capture her face. He leaned closer until Amy was sure she was going to merge either with him or the door. Both were hard, utterly unyielding; of the two the door was safer.

But Hawkridge was far more potent. His rain-coloured eyes glittered into hers, sending rational thought to the four winds. His long fingers moved, tilting her face up to his and sending a fresh wave of heat swirling through her.

He lowered his head until his breath washed over her lips. 'You haven't answered the most important question of all, Mrs Chantry.'

'But...' Her voice was a breathless squeak. 'Aren't you satisfied *yet*?'

'Far from it,' he growled softly. 'I intend to alter that unhappy situation.'

Before she could make any suggestions, his mouth came down on hers.

Chapter Five

Hunger surged through him, insatiable, ravenous. He forgot Amy was smaller than he, forgot she was weaker. Holding her captive with the weight of his body, Marc parted her lips and plundered.

She gave a muffled squeak of protest, but the roaring of his blood was louder. She tensed with resistance; he felt only the first instant of startled surrender.

Soft. Sweet. Slender. Almost fragile against him, but quivering and intensely alive.

The sensations tore through him in such rapid succession that for the space of several pounding heartbeats he was oblivious to the fact that Amy was fighting him. No longer resisting; really fighting. Her hands were fisted against his chest and she was shoving, struggling, straining to free her mouth.

The jolt cleared the mists from Marc's mind. He jerked back, stunned by his own behaviour. He, who had always taken care to control his more primitive instincts when dealing with women, had assaulted his grandmother's companion like a marauding barbarian.

He stared at her, wondering why she wasn't screaming the house down. Her eyes were huge in her flushed face, her breasts heaved. Her lips were parted and trembling; moist and reddened from the force of his, they were a temptation he didn't dare linger over.

He wrenched his gaze from the luscious sight, released his hold on her, and stepped back.

And was promptly snapped back another pace by a teeth-jarring right to the jaw. The blow was hard enough to blur his vision. Marc blinked—and decided not to shake his head. It wouldn't be wise while his brain was rattling.

'You *bastard*!'

Amy was calling him a bastard? She had obviously been rendered completely irrational with shock.

He blinked again and revised his opinion. His grandmother's proper companion had vanished. In her place was a quivering bundle of sheer feminine fury. Her eyes flashed green fire, the sparks threatening to ignite another explosion of wrath at any moment. Her entire body shook. He could almost feel her blood pulsing, hot and fast, beneath her skin.

His body, shocked momentarily under control by her blow, hardened again with a rush that nearly doubled him over.

He cursed, and slammed the cage shut on instincts that had always been savagely reined.

'Mrs Chantry,' he began. And couldn't think of another thing to say.

His victim didn't have the same problem.

'I may be illegitimate, my lord,' she raged. 'And beneath the other women of your acquaintance because of it, but that does not give you the right to use me for your amusement the minute you learn the fact!'

Whirling, she pulled the door open, whisked herself through the aperture and slammed the door shut with the full force of her arm.

Marc winced as the reverberations shook the room. A small painting hanging beside the door fell to the floor with a crash. The windows rattled in sympathy. The din didn't help the ringing still going on in his ears.

God, what had he done? The kiss itself wasn't such a crime. After all, he'd been driven mad all day by the paradox presented by Amy's innocent appearance and the wary knowledge in her eyes...he'd been so aware of her he'd practically felt her every move...the last provocative flip of her skirts had been the final straw... Was it any wonder he'd kissed her?

But his timing had been absolutely appalling.

'*Bloody hell!*'

Marc turned abruptly and began to pace. He strode the length of the room, wheeled and started back. He wished there was something in his path so he could kick it aside. He was painfully aroused, frustrated, and furious with himself.

Mrs Amaris Chantry was a tantalising mixture of knowledge and innocence, but she *was* innocent.

At least, innocent of the type of career he'd suspected. No enterprising widow with an eye to the main chance would have reacted with such fury to a mere kiss.

Marc groaned aloud. 'A mere kiss' didn't begin to describe the sensations aroused by the feel of her mouth beneath his. Damn it, she'd even tasted innocent. Innocent and sweet; almost virginal. He was too experienced not to recognise the genuine article.

Especially when it hit him in the face.

He stopped pacing and cautiously felt his jaw. Where the devil had Amy learned to throw a punch like that? She might be young, and heart-breakingly vulnerable, but she wasn't defenceless. She'd fought back. She'd treated him to the cutting edge of her tongue.

She'd yielded. For one tiny infinitesimal second, her mouth had trembled and softened beneath his.

Was that why she'd reacted so violently, when his earlier insults had elicited no reaction at all?

Something deep within him was suddenly alert; a sleeping predator abruptly wakened.

He started pacing again, fast. He was still aroused, still frustrated, still furious with himself. But beneath it all, a fierce elation was beginning to burn.

He hadn't frightened her. For three or four mind-spinning seconds he'd given his instincts full rein, and Amy had neither swooned, shrieked nor thrown a fit of the vapours. Every eligible lady his sister had dangled in his way over the years would have indulged in one of those options.

His last fiancée had treated him to all three.

His grandmother's mysterious companion had matched him. He'd have preferred a passionate response to his kiss rather than a blow to the jaw, but she'd matched him.

He stopped pacing, and stared, eyes narrowed in thought, at the door. Somehow he had to find a way out of the disastrous pit he'd dug for himself. Because it was suddenly, vitally, imperative, that he discover everything he could about Mrs Amaris Chantry.

Amy had packed and unpacked her single bandbox three times in an agony of indecision before she realised the futility of the exercise. Not only did she have nowhere to go, she had no way of getting there.

And how could she repay her kind employer by creeping out of the house like a thief in the night?

The answer was simple. She couldn't.

Frustrated, and inexplicably on the verge of tears, she kicked her bandbox under the bed and paced to the window. Her agitated reflection stared back at her.

What was she going to do?

The night-shrouded woods glimpsed beyond the south lawn didn't provide an answer.

Amy stalked back across the room and sat down on the bed.

An instant later she was up and pacing again. She couldn't sit still; she felt as if all her nerves were dancing on the surface of her skin. None of the practised, calculated embraces from her husband before their marriage, nor the perfunctory pecks that had come later, had prepared her for such an onslaught of sensation.

The mere memory of the fierce pressure of Hawkridge's mouth on hers caused lightning to streak through her all over again. He hadn't asked, he hadn't persuaded, he hadn't even seduced. He'd taken as if he'd had the right.

How had she so badly miscalculated as to credit him with *any* civilised propensities? The man wasn't a warrior. He belonged in a cave.

Amy shivered and wrapped her arms about herself. Outrage aside, it wasn't Hawkridge's primitive tendencies that worried her—one could get very primitive when food was handed out where she'd been.

What caused her entire being to quake with alarm was a persistent, nerve-tingling vision of herself sharing the cave with him.

Amy sank down on her bed and put her face in her hands. This was the result of fascination with a portrait. Present her with the real thing and she promptly lost her wits, and reverted to some rather uncivilised behaviour herself.

Heat flooded her cheeks as she remembered her actions, her *words*. No lady would have behaved like that. She had sunk herself utterly beneath reproach—and she'd been doing so well. Her only consolation was that no one else had witnessed her lapse. She doubted Hawkridge would inform his grandmother of the encounter. The dowager had obviously retired to her bedchamber in the sadly mistaken belief that Hawkridge wouldn't attack her companion the minute her back was turned. He wouldn't be likely to disillusion her.

Especially when the entire episode was all his fault.

That thought provided an effective antidote to self-castigation. Amy sat up straighter and frowned at the opposite wall.

It was no use sitting here wallowing in mortification. The situation could have been worse. She might have succumbed to the wild torrent of excitement that had swept through her the instant Hawkridge's mouth touched hers; she might have let him sweep *her* away to realms as yet unexplored.

But she hadn't been swept away. She'd escaped. And now she wouldn't think about it again. She wouldn't think about the heat and power of his body, the hard, thrilling demand of his mouth. She'd do what she had always done. Put it out of her mind and go forward.

But...forward to where? Why should she be driven from the only safe haven she'd known—although safe was a moot point at the moment? Still, Hawkridge wouldn't be staying forever. Surely she could cope with his presence for a few days.

Planning how to do so provided a welcome distraction. Amy bent her mind to the task. Avoiding Hawkridge was proving unexpectedly difficult; given his conqueror's response to any challenge, she doubted the situation would improve. But she could ensure she was never alone with him. Even if it meant joining the dowager in her quest for jollification.

Embarking on a social whirl was, after all, more ladylike than another bout of fisticuffs.

Amy glanced down at her hand and flexed her fingers. Her

knuckles felt somewhat bruised. So, for some strange reason, did her heart.

She pushed the notion aside. Naturally she felt shaken. It was a perfectly normal reaction, but nothing to do with her heart. Now that she was calmer, she'd get undressed, climb into bed, and contemplate ways and means of sticking to the dowager like a shadow. And then she would go to sleep.

Dreamlessly.

Doing so shouldn't present a problem. What with one thing and another, it had been a rather exhausting day.

Her careful planning came undone the minute she knocked on Lady Hawkridge's door the next morning, only to be informed by Giddings that her ladyship had left the house to pay morning calls on several tenants.

Amy stared at Giddings in surprise. It was Lady Hawkridge's custom to take breakfast in her bedchamber before summoning her companion to discuss the day's activities. Amy then left the dowager to the ministrations of her dresser while she, herself, attended to any secretarial duties that fell to her lot. What on earth had possessed her employer to deviate from her usual course?

When she put this question to Giddings, that worthy individual launched into a monologue on the miraculous recovery enjoyed by the dowager after a good night's sleep.

Amy wished she could make the same claim. Thanks to a restless, dream-filled slumber, she had woken considerably later than her usual time. To find herself abandoned.

There was only one thing to do. Cutting short Giddings's earnest speech on the restorative properties of sleep, she descended the stairs in search of Pickles. The way the morning was shaping up, Hawkridge was probably lying in wait in the breakfast parlour. She would have a tray sent in to the library.

It took some time to put this plan into action. When she finally located Pickles, who was putting away billiard balls that looked as if they'd been rather violently cannoned all over the billiard table, he reproachfully informed her that no one had touched the tea-tray he'd borne into the withdrawing-room on the previous evening. And Mrs Pickles had especially baked Amy's favourite macaroons.

Amy adjourned to the kitchen to soothe Mrs Pickles's wounded feelings. She accomplished the task by letting Mrs Pickles ply her with bread and butter dripping with honey, followed by a cup of coffee, while Mrs Cubitt provided a homily on missing meals when she needed to build up her strength.

Consequently, the imposing clock in the hall was solemnly striking eleven by the time Amy carried a second cup of coffee into the library—after first ascertaining that Hawkridge wasn't lying in wait for her there.

He wasn't. Amy breathed a sigh of relief and locked the door. She wasn't precisely sure about the propriety of locking an Earl out of his own library, but that didn't prevent her from defiantly turning the key.

She made sure the windows were latched for good measure.

Then, refusing to so much as glance at the portrait above the fireplace, she marched over to a shelf of books and commenced work.

Since her normal duties took up very little time, she had asked Lady Hawkridge to let her sort and catalogue the vast collection of tomes acquired by various Rothwells over the decades. It was a task she relished. For years the only book she and her mother had possessed was a tattered Bible; access to all the books she could read was a feast to one starved of formal learning.

Amy settled down to the search she'd been conducting for over a week. So far, she was forced to the conclusion that no Rothwells had felt it expedient to purchase treatises or papers on the laws pertaining to marriage. Perhaps Parliamentary Acts would help—if she could find them.

She was so intent on her quest that when a section of shelving beside the fireplace began to swing inwards with a particularly blood-curdling groan of ancient hinges, she merely glanced around in mild surprise.

Every drop of blood stilled in her veins as mild surprise turned to shock.

Hawkridge strolled out of the dark cavern beyond the opening, contemplated the locked door for precisely two seconds, then looked at her, brows raised. 'Good morning, Mrs Chantry.'

Amy stared back at him, both hands clutching a heavy book to her breast. It was no use asking how he'd got in; the answer was perfectly obvious. She searched wildly for something else to say.

'You deserved to be locked out, my lord.'

As an opening remark it was rather undiplomatic, if true.

He retaliated with a faintly menacing smile. 'Well, now we're both locked in.'

Her eyes blinked wide.

Before she could think of a solution to her dilemma, Hawkridge glanced down, frowned, and flicked a large spider off his sleeve. It landed on the floor with a plop and scuttled under the desk.

Amy gazed after it in consternation. She was locked in with Hawkridge and a spider. A large spider. Things were getting worse.

'And the only way out,' he purred, as though reading her mind, 'is the spider-infested way I came in.'

She shuddered.

'But don't worry, Mrs Chantry. Fortunately for you, I do occasionally succumb to the odd chivalrous impulse.' He pushed the bookshelves closed and walked across to the door.

Amy shuddered again as the hinges protested with another nerve-shattering screech. Then watched in astonishment as Hawkridge unlocked the door.

'That takes care of the proprieties,' he remarked and turned to face her.

She gazed owlishly back at him over the top of her book. It seemed to be getting heavier, but its bulk gave an illusion of protection. Hawkridge might have succumbed to a chivalrous impulse, but he was between her and escape. She clutched her burden tighter.

'However, we'll leave the door closed for the moment. I wish to speak to you alone, Mrs Chantry—'

She took a step back.

'—to apologise.'

Amy's jaw dropped.

He gave a short laugh. 'I thought that might be your reaction.

You know, Mrs Chantry, I believe you've been guilty of the same crime as myself.'

'*What?*' Oh, thank goodness. She'd finally relocated her voice. 'Prejudgement.'

'Oh.' She considered the charge. 'Well, perhaps, my lord, but—'

'And,' he continued inexorably, 'as if that isn't bad enough, your method of retaliation last night was rather unexpected. For a lady.'

Amy blushed to the roots of her hair. 'I am fully aware of that, sir, but I take leave to tell you that you did not behave like a gentleman.'

A rueful smile curved his mouth. Coming forward, he touched his fingertips to her cheek. 'I know,' he admitted gently. 'In fact, my behaviour was atrocious, and I do beg your pardon for it.'

Amy froze at the brief touch; her mind reeled. Hawkridge's evident sincerity startled her as much as his unexpected appearance. Despite all her resolutions, she felt a softening inside. There was something rather disarming about a man who admitted he was wrong, without making excuses for it.

She groped for some sort of response. 'Well... Thank you, my lord. I mean...I accept your apology. That is...so long as you promise—'

'I never make promises I might not be able to keep,' he murmured, still in such a soft tone that his meaning took a moment to register. When she levelled a suspicious glare at him, he smiled wickedly. 'Perhaps I should make it clear that I'm not apologising for kissing you, but for my appalling lack of finesse during the process.'

'What! But... That... You...'

She stopped before she spluttered herself to a complete standstill, and tried again. 'Really, sir, if you think that sort of apology is sufficient, you're fair and far out. I told you last night that I won't be used for your amusement and—'

'I was not,' he stated with great precision, 'using you for my amusement.'

'Indeed?' She tilted her chin at him. 'Was last night the way you treat all the ladies of your acquaintance?'

'No,' he admitted ruefully. 'But not for the reason you're probably thinking.'

'Hmph!' Her chin went higher. 'Clearly, you have more respect for them. What else am I to think?'

Every trace of amusement vanished from his eyes. He lifted his hand and taking her chin between thumb and forefinger, gave it a little shake. 'Let me make one thing very clear, Mrs Chantry. I *do* consider you to be the equal of the other ladies of my acquaintance, regardless of your birth. Furthermore, I had no thought last night of repaying your confidences by insulting you.'

She blinked at him.

His gaze dropped briefly to her lips before he released her. 'I kissed you for another reason entirely, which we won't go into at the moment.'

'We won't? No.' She shook her head. 'Of course we won't.' Her mind seethed with possibilities. Only one made sense. He was going to offer her a *carte blanche* without the insult of 'how much' attached to it.

The thought should have horrified her. She should have felt affronted at the very least—although logic told her she could hardly expect a more respectable offer. Instead, a shiver that felt very like anticipation brushed her skin.

'However,' he went on, the amused gleam returning, 'I did derive some benefit from last night's salutory lesson.'

Still grappling with her horrifying lack of horror, Amy could only stare at him.

He grinned. 'I've finally discovered what your husband did.'

She went utterly still; shock blanked out everything. For a minute she couldn't even think. Then, very slowly, she turned and carefully returned her book to its place.

'Oh?'

The sudden intensity of his gaze was palpable. 'Do you know, Mrs Chantry, you've gone quite pale. Why should that be?'

Amy took a deep breath and forced her features into an expression of unconcern. 'It…must be my shock at your powers of deduction, sir.'

When he didn't answer, she risked a glance at him. She couldn't do much about her lack of colour; every drop of blood in her veins had plummeted southwards along with her heart. 'Well? What did my husband do?'

After another long, nerve-racking moment of contemplation, Hawkridge started to grin. 'He was a prize-fighter.'

Amy's colour returned in a rush. She wished she could sink through the floor in mortification. Failing that, she would have been happy to sink into insensibility, but even as she wondered how to achieve that helpful state, the devilish gleam in Hawkridge's eyes saved her. To her utter astonishment, she giggled.

Then clapped both hands over her mouth and stared at him over the tops of her fingers, her eyes as round as saucers.

And in that moment he knew.

This was the one. This was the woman he'd been waiting for.

A wave of sheer primitive possessiveness hit him with all the force of a raging torrent. He wanted to reach out, snatch Amy into his arms and carry her off to a cave somewhere. The sheer violence of the need startled him. And he *knew* how ruthless he could be.

Fortunately, common sense reasserted itself. The nearest cave was some distance away. He suspected that long before they reached it, Amy would have reacted to his primitive tactics with another blow to the jaw. It wasn't the response he wanted.

He pushed ruthlessness back into its cage, took a deep breath, and smiled.

Amy lowered her hands very slowly. For a minute there, she'd wondered if she really was going to swoon away for the first time in her life. Something had flashed into Hawkridge's eyes. Something so fierce, so utterly implacable, she'd frozen like a rabbit staring into the eyes of a hawk. Unable to see anything else. Unable to hear. Unable to feel anything but the frantic beating of her heart.

Then the expression was gone. He smiled, and a completely inexplicable feeling of happiness welled up inside her. Before she could contemplate the wisdom of such a response, she found herself twinkling back at him.

'That statement, sir, was extremely ungallant. And quite incorrect. I told you yesterday that my husband invested in, uh...'

He raised a brow when she faltered.

'Never mind,' she muttered, flushing. 'It isn't important.'

Another smile curved his mouth. 'You don't like to talk about him, do you?'

Amy hesitated, then shook her head. 'He wasn't a very nice person.'

'Good. We needn't scruple to speak ill of the dear departed.'

She giggled again, a delightful gurgle of sound that had Marc feeling ridiculously pleased with himself.

Captivated by a playfulness he suspected was new and very fragile, he was about to continue along the same lines when the library door slammed open.

He glanced up, frowned at the exquisitely fashionable damsel storming across the threshold, and with some difficulty recognised his niece.

'Good God, Lucinda. Is that you?'

The visitor didn't waste time on this unflattering greeting. She caught up the full skirts of a powder-blue riding habit that was braided and frogged wherever braiding and frogging could be placed, marched straight up to her uncle and fixed him with a steely gaze. The effect was ruined somewhat by the sweeping black plume adorning her cap *à la hussar* that fell over her eyes, practically obscuring her vision.

'Hawkridge, you have to help me get married.'

Amy felt her face go blank again with shock. Hawkridge remained singularly unimpressed.

'Hawkridge?' he repeated, eyeing his niece up and down. 'What the devil happened to Uncle Marc?'

Lucinda dropped her skirts, elevated her small nose and swept the plume aside. It promptly bounced back into place. 'You may have noticed that I'm quite grown up now.' She extended a powder-blue gloved hand. 'How do you do, Hawkridge? It seems an age since I've seen you.'

Hawkridge contemplated the hand poised under his nose, studied the bobbing plume and burst out laughing. 'No wonder Bevan cursed that Bath academy,' he observed. 'Come down off your high horse, brat.'

His niece narrowed her striking blue eyes to glittering slits. 'The name,' she said through set teeth, 'is Lucinda.' Snatching her hand back, she yanked the feather aside with enough force to snap its delicate quill. The plume subsided sadly on to her shoulder. 'No wonder Mama despairs of you ever finding a wife. No woman in her right mind would have you.'

'Very likely not,' he agreed. 'But before we delve further into such a fascinating subject, I expect your newfound manners to extend to Mrs Chantry.'

Lucinda flushed, but tossed her ebony curls. 'Amy and I are friends. We don't need to stand upon ceremony. Besides, she's only—'

Hawkridge took a threatening step forward. Lucinda stopped in mid-protest and swallowed visibly.

'I was only going to say she's not much older than me,' she muttered after a moment. 'Hello, Amy.'

'Miss Nettlebed,' Amy acknowledged and, responding to the visitor's imperious air, instinctively dropped a curtsy. Or started to.

Hawkridge wheeled and strode over to the desk, bending close as he passed her. 'Curtsy to that little minx, Mrs Chantry, and you won't sit down for a week.'

Amy halted in mid-curtsy. When her knees threatened to wobble, she straightened and glared at him over her shoulder.

He returned her scowl with a bland smile and propped himself against the desk.

'Now, *Lucinda*, what's all this idiocy about getting married at the age of sixteen?'

'I've turned seventeen, which you'd know if you ever stayed in Devon for longer than a minute. And it isn't idiocy, Uncle Marc, it's—' She stopped, and thrust out her lower lip. 'Oh, now look what you've done! You've spoilt it.'

'You mean your nonsensical pose of maturity slipped,' he corrected drily. 'I didn't think it'd last long.'

'Ohh!' Lucinda stamped her foot. 'You're as bad as Mama and Papa. Not to mention that horrid little toad, Crispin.'

'Dear me,' Amy murmured, finally gathering enough wit to remove herself from the battlefield. She began edging towards the door. 'Where has the morning gone? I'd better go and enquire after—'

'No, Amy, don't go.' Lucinda halted her progress by grabbing her arm. Short of tearing the sleeve out of her peach cambric gown, and being obliged to sew it in again, Amy was caught.

'You know all about Jeremy. Besides, it's thanks to you that he's attending our party tonight.'

'Indeed?' enquired Hawkridge, his tone suddenly so glacial that Lucinda released her captive in surprise.

Amy returned to the desk, ostensibly to pick up her coffee cup. 'Would you rather Lucinda met Mr Chatsworth clandestinely, sir?' she enquired in the same undertone he'd used to her.

'I'll reserve judgement until I meet him myself,' he replied, scowling. Then replaced the expression with a pleased smile. 'Why, I do believe your good influence is working on me already, Mrs Chantry.'

'If you have something to say about my affairs, Hawkridge, you may address yourself to me,' Lucinda interposed, advancing on her uncle before Amy could reply to this patently untrue statement.

'I wouldn't come too close to this desk, if I were you, Lucinda,' Hawkridge countered. 'There's a spider in the vicinity. A very large, black, hairy spider.'

Amy had forgotten the spider. Snatching up her skirts, she scanned the floor around her feet—mercifully spiderless—and backed off in a hurry. So did Lucinda.

'A spider?' she squeaked. 'How on earth did a spider get inside your library?'

'I was showing Mrs Chantry the secret passage.' He glanced at Amy, a devil in his eyes. 'She was struck speechless with amazement.'

'I should think so,' Lucinda declared indignantly. 'Really, Uncle Marc, aren't you a little *old* to be scaring people with spiders? I'd expect that sort of thing from that horrid toad, Crispin.'

Hawkridge raised his eyes heavenwards.

'But never mind that,' Lucinda continued, returning to the subject at hand with the tenacity of the young and self-absorbed. 'What are you going to do to help me?'

'Nothing.'

Her eyes narrowed again.

'For one thing, you're too young to be married, and for another, if Jeremy is the bounder Augusta mentioned in her letter, he hasn't even asked your father's permission to address you.'

'N...o...o,' Lucinda admitted reluctantly. 'But how can he when Papa won't grant him an interview?' Apparently feeling she'd stonewalled Hawkridge with this rhetorical question, she turned to Amy in appeal. 'You know how it is, Amy? After all, you must have been about my age when you were married.'

'A little older,' Amy demurred, conscious of Hawkridge's suddenly intent gaze. She waved a hand in studied carelessness. 'But, you know, I always wondered what a London Season would have been like. The balls, the parties, driving in the Park, all those young gentlemen vying for one's attention. Such fun. You must be looking forward to it.'

Lucinda looked a little startled. 'Well, yes, but...I'll still be able to have a Season. Dearest Jeremy and I will settle in Town. We'll be the most fashionable couple you've—'

'Dearest Jeremy is flush with funds, I take it?' Hawkridge put in silkily. 'He'll need to be to pay the dressmaker's bills, if that ridiculous get-up you're wearing is any example.'

'*Ridiculous?*' Lucinda's voice and colour rose alarmingly.

Amy hurried into the breach. 'I'm sure it's a very pretty habit, Miss Nettlebed. I'd like to wear that shade, myself, but it wouldn't appear to advantage on me.'

Lucinda subsided. 'Thank you, Amy.' She sent a disdainful glance in her uncle's direction. 'For your information, Hawkridge, Jeremy thinks I'd look delightful in sackcloth.'

'Sounds as if he's preparing you for a lifetime in the stuff.'

His niece ground her teeth audibly. 'Just because Jeremy doesn't have a title or a vault of money like you do is no reason to be sarcastic. I'll have plenty for the two of us from that estate old Aunt Cordelia left in trust for me.'

'And no doubt Jeremy is aware of that interesting fact.'

'No, he isn't,' Lucinda informed him, nose in the air. 'He told me he wouldn't have had the courage to approach me, if he thought I was wealthy.' A besotted smile spread over her face. 'Isn't that noble? Isn't that gallant? He's so charming, so—'

Hawkridge cast another long-suffering glance at the ceiling. 'Of course he is, you goose. It's his stock-in-trade.'

Lucinda stopped rhapsodising and glared at him. 'You don't know anything about it,' she cried. 'And, what's more, you don't know anything about gallantry or charm either. In fact, you're *worse* than that horrid little toad, Crispin.'

This was obviously an insult of the highest order. Hiding a smile, Amy glanced at Hawkridge to see how he was taking his niece's reversion to childhood. He wasn't bothering to hide his amusement.

'It seems to be the fate of younger brothers to always be referred to as horrid little toads,' he observed thoughtfully.

Lucinda stuck out her lower lip. 'What would you know about it?'

'I am a younger brother. And that reminds me. According to your mother, Crispin is about to totter straight into the grave. What's wrong with him? Apart from his toad-like qualities, that is.'

'Nothing.' Lucinda continued to pout. 'Just because he used to have those wheezing fits for days on end when he was a little boy, Mama fusses and worries until there's no bearing it. She wouldn't let Papa send Crispin to school—which would at least have stopped him tormenting me. I mean, what is the use of having a brother in the house if he won't help me?'

Amy gaped at this evidence of self-interest, but Hawkridge nodded approval.

'Crispin must have more sense than anyone's giving him credit for.'

'Ohh!' The floor received another stamp.

'Never mind the tantrum, Lucinda. I take it your brother isn't at death's door.'

'Of course he isn't. He only reclines on couches and looks pale so Mama will fetch and carry for him. No one cares about *my* suffering.'

'Now, that's not quite true. Your Papa mentioned yesterday that you haven't had the chicken-pox, and I've just remembered that the house is rife with it. You'd better be off. Maids are dropping right and left.'

'*What!* You're talking about *chicken-pox* when my whole life might be *blighted*? Ohh!' Lucinda stamped one foot then the other, clenched her fists and began to pace. 'This is the most heartless family I've ever encountered,' she wailed. She kicked a foot-rest out of her path, causing Amy to step hastily aside. 'I came here to ask for your help, and what do I get?'

'A spanking if you're not careful,' Hawkridge threatened, amusement vanishing as he came upright in one swift movement. 'Behave yourself or leave.'

Lucinda blinked at him in shock, then tossed her head and retrieved her pose of offended dignity. Unfortunately, all the pacing, stamping and tossing had her plume abandoning dignity. It slid lower.

'I will certainly take my leave,' Lucinda replied with great hauteur. 'And don't bother looking for me any time in the near future. I don't intend to cross this threshold again until you learn some manners.'

Hawkridge grinned and promptly swept her an elegant bow. 'Miss Nettlebed, thank you so much for deigning to grace us with your presence this morning. Our delight at the brevity of your visit is exceeded only by our relief.'

'*Aaagh!*' After one shriek of frustration, Lucinda stormed towards the door. It was all too much for the plume. It slipped its moorings and floated to the floor, barely escaping decapitation by the violently slammed door.

'One can only hope,' Hawkridge murmured as a second muffled slam indicated that the front door had been subjected to the same treatment, 'that the doors in this house will withstand the recent violence visited upon them.'

Amy heard herself giggle for the third time that morning with a kind of stunned amazement. She'd never giggled before in her entire life. Now she seemed to be doing it every five minutes. The pained look Hawkridge gave her nearly set her off again.

'Oh, dear,' she managed, trying for a suitably sympathetic expression. 'I'm so sorry, my lord. Are you quite deafened?'

'Not quite,' he said, scowling. 'What the devil happened to Lucinda? She was always a brat, but a likeable one. A year or two ago she'd have been in that secret passage regardless of what might be lurking there, and probably dragging Crispin along with her. In fact, I'm sure the little wretches hid there one day in the hope of scaring the wits out of Pickles.'

'I'm afraid certain Young Ladies Academies pride themselves on turning out very *proper* young ladies, sir. But don't worry. I believe the effect is only temporary.'

He cocked a brow. 'How do you know?'

'I had a position in a school before my marriage,' she replied composedly. 'For a very brief time. Now, I really should go and make sure the maids are *not* dropping right and left, so if you'll excuse me—'

'No, don't go,' Hawkridge said quickly, putting out a detaining hand as she turned away.

Amy jerked back, more in surprise than real alarm, and he withdrew his hand at once. 'I mean,' he said, resuming his seat against the edge of the desk, 'you don't have to run away because we're alone. I have no intention of attacking you.'

She eyed his hands, clenched hard around the solid mahogany of the desk. 'That's very reassuring, my lord, but—'

'Tell me about this Chatsworth character. What's he like?'

Amy hesitated, conscious of a need for caution, but strangely reluctant to leave. 'I don't know. I haven't met him.'

He studied her wary expression, his smile wry. 'I'm not going to criticise your advice to Augusta, Mrs Chantry. I know it's preferable for Lucinda to meet Chatsworth under her parents' roof rather than clandestinely.'

'Oh. Well...I'm glad you approve, sir. Now, I really do have things...' She faltered again, flustered by a faintly amused regard that yet held something deeper, and utterly steady.

Then Hawkridge turned aside, indicating the nearest shelves and releasing her from the intensity in his grey eyes. 'Cataloguing the library,' he murmured. 'Grandmama told me you volunteered for the task. Since we seem to have exhausted the current topic of conversation, it is I, therefore, who should leave you in peace to continue.'

But he made no move to go.

Amy glanced towards the door, not quite sure whether she ought to agree or demur. After all, it *was* his library. Then as he looked back at her, a thought occurred that had her smiling.

'On the contrary, my lord. A task awaits you here that takes precedence over anything I may need to do.'

She crossed the room, opened the door, and glanced back. And this time her smile was alight with mischief. 'You have a very large, very black, very hairy spider to dispatch.'

Chapter Six

How was he supposed to concentrate on catching a spider after that smile?

Marc gave up the task after a fruitless five minutes, during which time he concluded that the spider had gone to ground. He couldn't keep his mind on the job anyway. Thoughts of Amy kept distracting him.

Little details. Like the fine arch of her brows; the delicacy of her hands. The shy mischief in her eyes and the tiny dimples that had appeared at the corners of her mouth when she'd smiled at him from the doorway.

She'd been lucky the entire length of the library had separated them, he thought, wryly amused at himself, because he'd been on the verge of doing something that wouldn't have helped his cause in the least. This hunt needed skill and patience. He'd mended a few fences this morning, but Amy was still wary, still controlled. Even to letting herself laugh.

His eyes narrowed as he thought about that. She wasn't intimidated, he decided after a moment, just…conscious of her behaviour. He could hardly blame her after their initial encounter.

Damn it, he'd never been so wrong about anyone—and the clues had been there, if he'd stopped being annoyed at his own response long enough to see them. The innocence in her clear gaze, the courage inherent in the tilt of that determined little chin. Even her scent was all wrong. The widow he'd imagined would have worn something cloying, far too sweet. The sweetness was there, but, like Amy herself, it was fragile, elusive, reminding him of lavender buds, tiny petals defensively closed until kissed by the warmth of the sun.

He had the feeling there'd been little sunshine in Amy's life.

Marc frowned again. If he hadn't been blinded by prejudice yesterday he would have seen immediately beneath Amy's guilty defiance without having to resort to force to get his answers.

On the other hand, he couldn't regret kissing her. Not when the conflict between suspicion and his instinctive male response to her had, for a few fleeting seconds, flushed from hiding the real woman behind her ladylike façade.

He intended to do it again. And in the process find out whatever it was she was hiding. That it was something to do with her husband he had no doubt, but he also didn't doubt for a minute that he'd be able to coax, persuade or otherwise prise the information out of her.

The sound of a carriage bowling up the drive interrupted his thoughts and drew him to the window. He grinned at the sight of his grandmother sitting in solitary splendour as her barouche swept up to the front door. He must remember to thank her for making herself scarce this morning—a decision he suspected had been deliberate. His beloved grandparent might be maddening on occasion, but she was no fool.

Somehow she'd known before he had. And approved.

With such an ally in his camp, Amy's fate was sealed.

The light-hearted mood that swept Amy out of the library that morning had vanished by mid-afternoon. She couldn't have said precisely when the clouds began to gather on her horizon but, as she walked back to the Manor after a trip to the village draper, they began to assume ominous proportions.

For some reason Lucinda's visit kept turning over and over in her mind. Several facts that she'd either been unaware of before, or unworried by—such as Jeremy Chatsworth sharing the same initials as her husband—suddenly assumed a significance that had apprehension sprinting around her stomach.

Instead of immediately sitting down to fashion a three-quarter overdress of silvery-grey gauze for her rose silk evening gown, she hunted up the *Morning Post* for a closer perusal of the report on the robberies at Bristol.

Nothing she read allayed her uneasiness in the slightest. The clouds slunk over the horizon and crept closer.

By the time she studied her reflection in her dressing-table mirror that evening, preparatory to setting out for Nettlebed Place, impending doom hovered about her like a persistent fog. She was not in the mood for a party.

Unfortunately, she had no choice but to attend. It was better to confront her suspicions immediately; to see Mr Chatsworth for herself—preferably before he clapped eyes on her—and to hope he had nothing to do with her past.

If he did, she could always feign illness and return home. It wouldn't take a great deal of effort.

Her plan was not destined to run smoothly.

Half an hour after the family dinner that preceded the Nettlebeds' party, Amy had discovered a very peculiar thing about such gatherings. It was impossible to search for one particular person while making sure she wasn't first seen by that person herself.

Of course, if Hawkridge would only behave himself, she'd be able to take cover behind one of the potted ferns with which Lady Nettlebed had adorned her drawing-room, and search to her heart's content. But every time she showed signs of retreating thereto, Hawkridge loomed at her side, cutting off retreat and introducing her to yet another guest.

Amy didn't know whether to feel guilty for being where she was, or annoyed at his high-handed tactics. What was worse, every time she gathered her wits, intending to deliver a protest, the sight of him, tall and darkly handsome in elegant black evening clothes, sent her thoughts off on several highly unsuitable tangents.

It was extremely unfair of him.

'I say, Mrs Chantry, you look bang up to the nines, but why are you wearing a cap?'

The demand had her turning to see Crispin, a dark-haired, willowy youth still some weeks short of his sixteenth birthday, come bounding up to her. He skidded to a halt, a pleased smile on his face, rather in the manner of an over-eager puppy waiting for a pat.

Amy's heart sank. She was torn between relief at the interruption, which enabled her to take a discreet step away from the immediate circle of guests, and dismay at the expression of canine devotion on Crispin's face.

'I'm a widow, Mr Nettlebed,' she explained, trying for a repressive tone that wouldn't entirely crush her youthful admirer.

'Yes, I know, but you don't look like one. In fact—'

Amy ceased to listen. Out of the corner of her eye she saw Hawkridge disengage from his conversation with one of his neighbours and turn a narrow-eyed stare of speculation on his nephew.

'—didn't have a chance to tell you at dinner,' Crispin concluded.

She had no idea what he'd been talking about. 'Yes, well, dinner was rather, er...'

'Rendered hideous by Lucinda's sulks,' Hawkridge finished for her.

'Told her Chatsworth wouldn't be there,' Crispin confided, his attention diverted from Amy. His eager expression didn't falter, lending credence to the dowager's assertion that Crispin considered Hawkridge an out-and-outer. Narrow-eyed stares were clearly to be expected.

'Why should Papa invite him to a family dinner?' he continued. 'Fellow isn't a member of the family. I say, Uncle Marc, were you serious about teaching me to sail?'

'Yes. But there are conditions.'

The caveat didn't appear to bother Crispin. He launched into an enthusiastic description of an old sail-boat he'd discovered in an unused barn.

Amy glanced quickly at Hawkridge. The dinner table had been rendered hideous by Lucinda's displeasure that her darling Jeremy had been excluded from the intimate gathering; a distinct pall had also been cast over the meal when Hawkridge had demanded that his nephew render an account of the sports and pastimes he enjoyed.

The list had been disastrously short. Reclining on a couch while listening to his mama play soothing music had been at the top, followed closely by having her bathe his brow with lavender water. Only the sarcastic tone in which this information had been delivered had saved Crispin from instant annihilation. That had been reserved for Lord and Lady Nettlebed.

As the ensuing battle had raged about her ears, Amy would have been happy to call an end to the evening then and there. Her presence when she was almost as much a stranger to the family as Mr Chatsworth was bad enough. The fact that everyone—except Lady Hawkridge, who blithely provided a Greek chorus totally unrelated to the prevailing subject—felt free to rage and argue in front of her was singularly unnerving.

As Crispin's conversation began to include such mysterious terms as luffs, gaffs and booms, she cast a longing glance at the row of ferns placed artistically behind the sofa where her employer was holding court. *That* was her proper place. Not here beside Hawkridge, where she was being forced to wonder whether her assumption that morning that he was thinking of offering her a *carte blanche* was somewhat wide of the mark.

After all, a man didn't present his potential mistress to his family and friends when the female concerned didn't move in those circles in the first place.

At least, she didn't think so. But if he hadn't meant to insult her, if he hadn't been amusing himself, why had he kissed her?

Amy started to worry again—which worried her even more, because if her reactions to the possibility of a *carte blanche* were those of a proper lady, there wouldn't be any need to worry in the first place. Especially when she already had Mr Chatsworth to worry about.

Hmm.

She eyed the glass of champagne in her hand and wondered if the single sip she'd taken had gone straight to her head. Her thoughts seemed to be spinning in circles.

When she caught a glimpse of Lucinda, the centre of an animated group of young people, nervousness danced an accompanying reel in her stomach. Without conscious thought, Amy started edging towards the ferns again.

Propriety wasn't the only reason propelling her thence. If she could just catch a glimpse of Mr Chatsworth, just convince herself

that he had nothing to do with her, that Lucinda's situation was
sadly commonplace, that she *knew* he couldn't be—

'Hah! So you're the new companion, are you? Well, you're a
demmed sight prettier than the last one.'

Amy froze several steps short of the ferns. She turned her head
to find herself being examined by two pairs of critical blue eyes,
one belonging to an elderly, silver-haired gentleman who was leaning heavily on a cane, the other to a younger man enough like his
companion for her to make a reasonably accurate guess as to their
identities.

It was all of a piece, she decided, turning fully. Nothing was
going as planned tonight.

Before she could reply to the older gentleman's somewhat un-
conventional greeting, Lady Hawkridge rose from her sofa and
flitted up to them, an innocently enquiring smile on her face.

'Good heavens, Bartholomew! Are you finally having Colborough Court redecorated? It's the only reason I can think of that
would account for your separation from that armchair in front of
the fire.'

'Very amusing, Clarissa.' Colborough's bushy grey brows drew
together over a decidedly hawk-like nose. 'You can blame Eversleigh, here, for my presence. Young idiot's got no sense. See how
many parties he'll feel like attending when he's over seventy and
plagued by a gouty foot.'

'Your foot is no more gouty than mine is,' retorted her ladyship.
'You just use it as an excuse to grumble and grouch.'

'Much you know,' grumbled Colborough. 'Where's that man-
nerless grandson of yours? I've got a thing or two to say to him.'

Her ladyship rolled her eyes. 'Amy, as you've no doubt guessed,
this is Lord Colborough and Viscount Eversleigh.' She patted the
Viscount's arm. 'Marc's friend since boyhood, you know.'

Eversleigh bowed, a twinkle in his eyes. 'How do you do, Mrs
Chantry? I'm glad to see that Marc managed to restrain himself.'

Amy's knees wobbled in the middle of a curtsy. Apparently
Hawkridge's methods of dismissing his grandmother's companions were known far and wide.

Worse was to come.

As she straightened, Colborough subjected her to another close stare. 'Mrs Chantry, is it? Don't know the name. Recognise those eyes, though. So, you're a connection of the Daltons.'

'Uh...'

'A remote one, possibly,' murmured Hawkridge from directly behind her.

Amy jumped. Awareness rippled up and down her spine on a wave of tingling heat. He was so close the merest intake of air would bring her into contact with him.

Before she could do anything so perilous, a very small, still-rational part of her brain ordered her take a careful step to the left.

Hawkridge moved at the same time. In the same direction.

'Going somewhere, Mrs Chantry?' he enquired in a low growl.

She didn't have breath to answer. Bracing herself, she took a careful step to the right. With the same result.

Eversleigh grinned at them. 'You know, if you two wish to dance, they're making up sets in the upper room.'

Hawkridge curved his hands firmly around her shoulders to hold her in place and moved to stand beside her.

'Stow it, Pel,' he advised, and in the most fleeting of caresses, unnoticed by anyone but herself, let his hands slide an inch or two down her arms, pressed gently and released her.

'Colborough,' he acknowledged coolly, as if he hadn't managed to addle her wits all over again by what she could have sworn was reassurance. 'I'm surprised to see you here.'

'Not as surprised as I am,' growled his lordship. 'About time you came down to check on things, Hawkridge. Clarissa's been pestering me to hold a Public Day; she can pester you instead. And there's a man-milliner by the name of Tweedy hanging around her. You may oblige me by getting rid of him.'

'Oh, I never interfere in Grandmama's life,' Hawkridge stated, with a blithe disregard for the truth that had Eversleigh choking on a mouthful of champagne.

Lady Hawkridge, completely unperturbed by this reaction, slipped a hand into the crook of Colborough's arm. 'Why don't we take up Pelham's suggestion, Tolly, and join the country dance they're getting up.'

His lordship gaped at the dowager as if she'd suggested they fly through the window on his walking cane. 'Have you finally lost the few wits you possessed, Clarissa?'

'Of course not. But if you want Marc to hold a Public Day, we'll have to leave him to arrange it with Pel. We'll take a little walk instead.' Smiling sunnily, she whisked the cane out of Colborough's hand and tossed it over her shoulder. 'You won't need that.'

Colborough's face turned an alarming shade of red as his cane crashed into the ferns. 'By God, Clarissa, I ought to—'

'I refuse to promenade about the room with a man hobbling along on a cane.'

'*Promenade*—' The Earl made noises suggestive of an impending seizure. 'Where the devil do you think we are? The Steyne at Brighton?'

'Good heavens! Brighton! I haven't been there in years. Such fun as we used to have. Visiting Prinny's little cottage and...'

Still burbling on about the delights of Brighton, her ladyship led Colborough away.

Eversleigh regarded their departing backs and shook his head. 'You know, Marc, I'm as fond of your grandmother as if she was my own, but one of these days someone's going to wring her neck. She didn't even check her aim.'

'No need,' observed Hawkridge, slanting a sardonic look down at Amy. 'Who'd be lurking behind the ferns?'

'Well, there is that,' agreed Eversleigh. 'I suppose I'd better retrieve the dashed cane. When the old boy remembers to hobble, he'll probably use it on me if I don't get to it first.'

Amy came to life with a start. Taking a leaf from the dowager's book, she smiled brightly up at his lordship. 'Allow me, my lord.' She started to sidle towards the ferns. 'I'm sure Lord Colborough won't use his cane on *me*, and you have a Public Day to plan with Lord Hawkridge.'

'Oh, nothing in that,' Eversleigh assured her, brows lifting as she continued to sidle. 'Hold 'em every summer. Enjoyable day, actually. Marc's people and mine hold a cricket match, and there's a picnic, and games for the children. You know the sort of thing.'

Amy didn't, but that didn't deter her from smiling more sunnily than before. The look that flashed into Hawkridge's eyes had her sidling faster, but the Fates finally decided to do a little smiling themselves. Lady Ingham swept up to them, greeting the gentlemen with her usual enthusiasm.

Amy felt a fern frond brush her shoulder and whisked herself out of sight while Hawkridge's attention was diverted.

Not that she couldn't easily be found, but at least she had a perfectly good excuse for lurking behind the ferns.

And Hawkridge looked as if he was going to be engaged for several minutes. Three or four other ladies had drifted across the room in Lady Ingham's wake, seemingly drawn to him like filings to a magnet. As Amy watched, he bowed to the latest arrival, a faint smile curving his mouth.

He'd been right about one thing, she reflected somewhat darkly. He could be perfectly civil. So civil that every lady in the room seemed completely unaware of the warrior concealed beneath his polite façade. Perhaps because the dangerous glitter in his grey eyes had been cloaked by a cool amusement that dared rather than daunted.

Another mask. Fascinating to watch.

Amy shook her head and wrenched her gaze away. She was not here to be fascinated by Hawkridge. She had someone else to study. Someone, she realised abruptly, pushing a fern frond aside, whose appearance was unknown to her. An instant later she told herself it didn't matter. The whole point of the exercise was *not* to see anyone she recognised.

She located Lucinda almost immediately. Several young couples were engaged in an impromptu dance in the upper half of the drawing-room, but Lucinda had dropped out, and appeared to be arguing with someone who was moving swiftly towards the doorway leading to the hall.

The crowd shifted, re-formed; a kaleidoscope of black and white, interspersed with brilliant colours. She could only see the back of the man's head and shoulders, but when Lucinda placed a hand on his arm, gazing up with pleading eyes and indicating the room as though urging him to stay, Amy was convinced of the gentleman's identity.

Tall. Quite broad across the shoulders. Brown hair.

Her husband had been slim—*oh, thank God!*—and very fair.

She sagged against the nearest window frame as tension leached from her body. She hardly dared believe it. She was safe. Safe! Mr Chatsworth was totally unknown to her.

Her eyelids closed in relief, then, suddenly realising that some-one might notice her propped against the wall as if she was about to collapse, she snapped them open again and straightened.

There was no need to collapse. Everything was all right. She was safe. And now that she wasn't worried sick, she could see that all those small similarities between her husband and Mr Chats-worth were really quite logical. Given the number of wealthy, well-born girls attending Young Ladies Academies, there was sure to be more than one gentleman who made a living by preying on such innocents. And sure to be more than one gentleman with the same initials as her husband.

She'd worried herself into a frenzy over nothing.

Relief rendered her positively euphoric. At that moment the en-tire world looked rosy; she was even prepared to believe that Mr Chatsworth was genuinely in love with Lucinda.

Remembering the glass of champagne in her hand, Amy lifted it to her lips and drained it with several healthy swallows. Then had to fan her suddenly warm face with her other hand.

'Mrs Chantry, will you stop doing that?'

Amy's hand paused in mid-flutter. Some of her rosy glow faded. Danger of an entirely different sort had arrived. She looked up at Hawkridge's exasperated countenance and promptly plastered a look of innocent enquiry on her face. 'Fanning myself, sir?'

'And don't give me that fluff-brained stare. You know very well what I'm talking about.'

She exchanged the fluff-brained stare for a disapproving frown. 'Well, if you would refrain from introducing me to all and sundry as though I was a friend of the family, I wouldn't need to hide behind ferns. Which, I might add, is my proper place.' She paused, and thought about that. 'No, not ferns precisely, but not in the middle of the dinner table. I mean, the middle of a party.'

Hawkridge eyed her empty glass and thoughtfully removed it from her hand.

Warming to her lecture, Amy swept on. 'And see what has come of it. Lord Colborough thinks I'm a member of the Dalton family, whoever they may be.'

'You probably are,' he murmured. 'Your father might have been destined for a humble curacy, Mrs Chantry, but I wouldn't be surprised to learn that your mother sprang from a minor branch of a noble family. In this case, the Daltons.'

She stared at him. 'Good heavens. What makes you say so?'

'Because you have more than surface elegance and manners. You have breeding.'

Her eyes went round.

'In fact, it didn't occur to me until Colborough mentioned it, probably because your hair is much lighter, but your eyes and lashes are exactly like Nick's.'

'Nick?'

'The Earl of Ravensdene. A friend of mine.'

'Oh. Another earl. There seem to be a lot of you. Earls, that is. Although there's a lot of you, as well.' She looked him up and down, and frowned. 'I don't think I meant to say that.'

Hawkridge's lips twitched. 'Tell me something, Mrs Chantry. Have you ever had champagne before tonight?'

'No,' Amy confessed. Drawing closer, she added confidingly, 'It wasn't on the menu at the poorhouse.'

His brows went up.

Amy didn't notice. She was too busy wondering why she'd said that, too. She caught sight of the glass in Hawkridge's hand and a dismaying explanation occurred to her. 'Oh, my goodness! I'm inebriated!'

This time the smile reached his eyes. 'Not at all, Mrs Chantry. Merely a little hazy. Probably because you hardly ate a morsel at dinner. Some fresh air should do the trick.' Depositing her glass on the edge of a fern-pot, he offered his arm. 'We'll go outside.'

'We certainly will not,' Amy contradicted, deciding to ignore his strictures on her eating habits. Owing to the faint spinning sensation in her head, she could only concentrate on one of his iniquities at a time. 'It would be most improper.'

Hawkridge fixed her with a look of heavy meaning. 'Trust me, it isn't as improper as the two of us continuing to lurk behind the ferns in this furtive fashion.'

An Independent Lady

'But *I* have a reason to lurk.' She frowned.

'Don't bother trying to recall it,' he said, correctly divining the cause of her expression. 'Besides, you may have noticed that the schoolroom brigade have adjourned to the terrace. Augusta ordered me to make sure their antics don't get out of hand since, according to her, I'm overly concerned about the well-being of her offspring. I came in search of you to request your assistance.'

'Ah. Now, that,' she pronounced, nodding incautiously, 'is exactly what a companion should do.' She placed her hand on his arm—mainly for balance, since nodding had caused the room to tilt in a very strange manner—and smiled sunnily up at him. 'Where is the terrace, my lord?'

Marc took a deep breath, resisted the temptation to take advantage of his quarry's delightfully hazy state, not to mention the cover afforded by his sister's over-enthusiasm for ferns, and began to steer Amy towards the nearest french windows. He felt extremely noble. The last thing he wanted was the company of the noisy crowd on the terrace. On the other hand, there wasn't a lot he could do at a party.

Although an interrogation on the subject of poorhouses wouldn't be a bad idea.

This piece of inspiration vanished as soon as they crossed the threshold. So did his feelings of nobility.

The softest of early-summer breezes enfolded them, carrying a heady combination of scents from the garden. It mingled with Amy's unique feminine essence, and, drifting upward on the warmth of her skin, rose to tease and tantalise.

Marc tensed as desire roared to life within him. The crowd on the terrace vanished. Every precept of civilised behaviour threatened to do the same. He wanted to sweep Amy into his arms and carry her into the dark recesses of the garden, to lie her down, cover her with his body; to sink into the warmth and scent of her until he was sated. Every instinct he possessed strained towards her, wanting...wanting...

Aching, he jolted to a stop a mere foot beyond the window, anchored only by the touch of her hand on his arm. A touch so light he barely felt it, and yet that alone held him back, even while his entire body hardened.

Shaken, Marc clenched his free hand and thanked Providence that the light spilling from the drawing-room was behind them.

And that the object of his fantasy had problems of her own.

She tripped when he halted so abruptly, and frowned down at the flagstones beneath her feet. 'I think the paving needs attention, my lord.'

'Take a deep breath,' he grated. And did the same. It didn't help. He focused on the crowd at the other end of the terrace and tried to remember why they were there.

'Is that a lot of people over there, or do I need to take some more deep breaths?'

A smile tugged at his lips despite himself. 'It's a lot of people,' he confirmed. 'Noisy people. We can supervise them from here. Would you like to sit down, Mrs Chantry?'

'I don't think so,' she said, subjecting the question to lengthy consideration.

'Then let us take a short stroll to those steps while we discuss—'

'Earls!'

The interruption was as abrupt as the sudden tension in the little hand resting on his arm. Marc looked down, brows raised. He got the distinct impression that Amy was avoiding his gaze.

'I don't have anything to do with them,' she said, flushing.

His eyes narrowed. She was recovering fast if she could come up with an apt red herring at short notice. On the other hand, red herrings could sometimes be just as informative as the truth. He decided to follow the bait.

'I hesitate to contradict you, Mrs Chantry, but you're talking to an earl right this minute.'

Amy waved that aside. 'I mean, I'm not a close connection of any earls.' She shook her head, apparently quite worried by the possibility. 'My mother would have told me.'

'I didn't say you were a close connection of the Daltons,' he corrected gently. 'However, we'll know for certain when I discover the name of your maternal grandfather.'

'What! But...' She stared up at him in dismay. 'I don't want you to discover any such thing. Why should you wish to do so? He's probably dead and—'

'Probably? I thought you said he was dead.'

Her colour deepened. 'It seemed a logical assumption, sir. You must know that I can't be sure, however. Besides—' she lifted her chin '—he's dead as far as I'm concerned.'

'An understandable sentiment, Mrs Chantry, especially if you did indeed spend time in a—'

'So there you are, Hawkridge.' Lucinda stormed up to them, a vision in white sarcenet decorated with pink and white rosebuds. The same flowers were placed artfully among her curls. Unfortunately, the sweetly feminine costume did not match her expression. 'Now that you've forced poor Jeremy to leave, I hope you're satisfied.'

Marc resigned himself to postponing questions about Amy's acquaintanceship with the poorhouse. 'Spare us the histrionics, Lucinda. How did I cause Chatsworth to leave?'

'He said he was intimidated.'

Marc snorted. 'Since I exchanged no more than half a dozen words with him, I suggest he was intimidated by his surroundings. You should be grateful to be spared future embarrassment. If he feels out of place here, how's he going to cope in London?'

A good question, Amy mused. She found herself harbouring a sneaky fellow feeling for Mr Chatsworth. Since he wasn't her husband come inconveniently to life, she could afford it—even if it was highly unlikely that anyone was going to fall in love with her and carry her off to the terrors of the metropolis.

The thought had a surprisingly lowering effect.

She pushed it aside in time to hear Hawkridge advise his niece to take herself off.

'I shall be happy to oblige you,' Lucinda retorted. 'Fortunately, there are others who show more sympathy for the agony endured by—'

'Lucinda, please.' Lady Nettlebed, an attractive dark-haired matron, fashionably attired in midnight-blue silk, stepped on to the terrace. She had a shawl draped over one arm. 'You can be heard in the drawing-room. And you shouldn't have come straight from a warm room without a shawl.'

'Wrap it around Uncle Marc,' Lucinda recommended, stomping back to her friends. 'Preferably around his neck.'

Lady Nettlebed gazed after her daughter with acute dismay before turning a look of displeasure on Hawkridge. Since she was several years older than her brother, and was blessed with the same cool grey eyes and patrician features, the look might have been effective had it been turned on anyone else.

'As if encouraging Crispin to defy me isn't bad enough, you're now upsetting Lucinda. I hope you're satisfied, Marc.'

'I wish people would stop hoping that,' he muttered. 'It's not an imminent possibility.'

At the growled comment Amy felt a craven desire to melt into the shadows. Unfortunately, her hand was still resting on Hawkridge's arm; though the flagstones had ceased their sudden tendency to move, she wasn't as confident about the steadiness of her head. She made a mental note never to touch champagne again. It obviously had a very detrimental effect on her senses.

Rather like Hawkridge, actually.

As if to prove the point, the muscles beneath her hand tensed. The thrill that rippled through her at the awareness of leashed power was quite shocking. It was also totally unwarranted, because Hawkridge was clearly taking a grip on nothing more than his patience.

'If you'd calm down, Gussie, you'd see the wisdom of—'

'Calm down?' Lady Nettlebed's voice rose. 'When you wilfully intend to lead my only son into *danger*? No wonder Lucinda is so stubborn. I know who she gets it from.'

Amy cleared her throat discreetly. Since she couldn't melt into the shadows, her second impulse was to help.

'Ah...if Lucinda is stubborn, ma'am, perhaps it's no bad thing. She's unlikely to be led astray, or—or cozened into a hurried marriage.'

Lady Nettlebed glanced at her as though surprised to see her there, then shook her head. 'Oh, dear, how very rude of me. I'm so sorry, Amy. What with Lucinda giving me no peace, and Crispin not speaking to me at all, I scarcely know if I'm on my head or my heels. And all Grandmama can say is that Marc knows what he's doing.' She whisked a scrap of lace out of the dainty reticule hanging from her wrist and dabbed at her suddenly brimming eyes. 'Nobody understands.'

Hawkridge's mouth curved wryly. 'Gus, you know I won't let

anything happen to your precious cub. I'll come over tomorrow and we'll talk about it. In the meantime, I can see Colborough getting redder in the face, so you'd better go back inside before Grandmama succeeds in driving him insane.'

'She's probably telling him about that awful Mr Tweedy inviting her to the Assembly Rooms at Teignmouth.' Lady Nettlebed sniffed and dabbed harder. 'You see what happens when you're in London, Marc? But *I* don't interfere. *I* don't tell you what you should do, or that you should visit more often, because I know why you stay away.'

With a final muffled sob, her ladyship whisked about and fled into the drawing-room.

'Well, well,' Hawkridge murmured, brows raised. He glanced down at Amy and smiled faintly. 'I'd apologise, Mrs Chantry, but you might as well know the worst.'

'Worst?' Amy eyed him suspiciously. 'What worst?'

'Families,' he said cryptically. 'I suspect you've never experienced the dubious delights of domesticity at its most basic. Brace yourself. The next few weeks should prove enlightening. Now, I think we've spent enough time as chaperons. We shall adjourn to the supper table, where you will eat more than you did at dinner, if I have to feed you myself.'

This rather high-handed decree sailed right over Amy's head. She was far too busy contemplating the dubious delight welling up inside her at the knowledge that Hawkridge wasn't planning an early departure.

She wasn't sure which emotion was uppermost, dubiety or delight; both shimmered through her in equal proportions. The unsettling mix threatened to make her head spin all over again.

She tried to tell herself that she had no business feeling delight. After all, it was Hawkridge's portrait that had enthralled her, not the man. She told herself that dubiety wasn't necessary, because he would be kept too busy with a Public Day, teaching his nephew to sail, preventing his niece from eloping, and getting rid of Mr Tweedy, to enthrall her any further.

The result was not what she'd hoped for. Anticipation continued to swirl inside her until she felt as though she stood poised on the brink of a precipice. The sensation was somewhat alarming. Especially for one who had never coped very well with heights.

Under the circumstances, teetering on the brink of a precipice was not a good idea.

It was not a good idea at all.

Chapter Seven

It would have been too much to state that squirrels wearing very heavy boots had taken up residence inside Amy's head the following morning, but she felt a trifle frayed when she descended the stairs at an hour considerably later than her usual time of arising.

She couldn't entirely attribute her fragile state to the glass of champagne she'd imbibed the night before. Not when she'd spent several sleepless hours worrying about her indiscreet utterances at Lady Nettlebed's party. Not after the inordinate amount of time she'd spent remembering the gentle understanding in Hawkridge's voice when he'd tried to reassure his sister about Crispin.

Not when she'd passed the long hours before dawn contemplating the lowering suspicion that, like Lady Nettlebed, she knew why Hawkridge didn't spend a great deal of time in Devon. After all, constant encounters with the lady he'd wished to make his wife, only to see her married to another, could be nothing but painful.

Brooding over that explanation had caused another hour or two of unrest. All in all she had definitely lost the euphoric glow occasioned by her glimpse of Mr Chatsworth.

The sight that greeted her when she reached the hall did not augur well for its return any time in the near future. Mr Tweedy was standing in the library doorway, contemplating the hall as though assessing the value of its contents.

Amy regarded his portly form with displeasure. A scarlet waistcoat was stretched over his girth, making him look like a particularly well-fed robin. When he turned his head in her direction, beady eyes, a short beaky nose and ruddy cheeks adorned with side whiskers added to the illusion. His pursed lips curled upwards in a smile that set her teeth on edge.

'Ah, Mrs Chantry.' Tweedy minced forward, beaming and rubbing his hands together. 'And how are we this morning, after our little party last night? Not too overcome by the honour?'

Amy raised her brows. '*I* enjoyed a most convivial evening, sir.'

Tweedy's smile lost some of its brilliance. 'How fortunate. I believe one of the other guests—a Certain Young Gentleman, shall we say—left rather early. I thought you may have felt the same, er, discomfort. On the other hand, one must grasp one's opportunities to study the ways of polite company, mustn't one?'

The stony stare she sent him in response to this question bounced off Tweedy's armour of determined geniality without so much as inflicting a dent. Amy set her lips.

'Were you expecting to see Lady Hawkridge, sir? She has not yet come downstairs.'

'Oh, no, dear lady, I wouldn't dream of disturbing her ladyship. I merely stopped by to pay my respects on my way back from the village. Hawkridge's groom—Mawson, I believe—offered me a lift up the hill. I was happy to accept. The climb sometimes proves rather too much for one of my, er, mature years.'

Amy inclined her head. Since Tweedy's rented house was half a mile beyond the Manor and he usually made the trip to Ottersmead in his gig, she suspected he'd deliberately set out on foot, hoping for an 'accidental' meeting with Lady Hawkridge.

'Not that you young people will enter into my feelings on the matter,' he continued. 'I was saying so only a little while ago as I was chatting to Mr Chatsworth.' Tweedy tittered at his mild play on words. 'He was standing outside the Receiving Office, you know, when Mawson and I were both collecting mail.'

'Indeed, sir.'

'Always delightful to receive communications from one's friends, isn't it? However, the walk back to my cottage is rather long. When Hawkridge's groom gave me a lift, I offered to deposit your mail here in the library by way of thanks. I have seen your butler do so, and knew precisely where to put it.'

'I see.' Amy glanced quickly past Mr Tweedy into the library. The pile of letters on her desk—or rather, Hawkridge's desk— proved the veracity of Tweedy's excuse. She resigned herself to being polite. 'Thank you, sir.'

'Don't mention it, my dear. I'm always happy to be of service. Every little attention must be observed, mustn't it. I'm sure you understand. After all, your own position depends upon such careful observances, does it not?'

'I try to make myself useful to Lady Hawkridge,' Amy replied with as much patience as growing irritation allowed. She'd sensed Tweedy's dislike of her at their previous encounters, but the dowager's presence had prevented him from firing such openly barbed darts.

His smile slipped a little further. 'Indeed, Mrs Chantry, indeed. However, your usefulness has its limits. Ladies of a Certain Age need a man about the place to take care of those little matters of business that tend to puzzle the female mind.'

'This female mind is a little less easily puzzled than you might suppose,' Amy said drily. 'Besides, you may have noticed that Lord Hawkridge is in residence?' An ironic smile curved her mouth. 'He is quite enough man about the place.'

Tweedy permitted himself another titter. 'No doubt you find him rather intimidating,' he agreed archly. 'But he won't be here forever. I've heard he never stays longer than a week at the outside. Perhaps you, too, should start planning your departure, Mrs Chantry.'

Amy's brows rose. 'At your suggestion, sir? I hardly think so.'

'I merely suggest that you consider the future, my dear. Circumstances are forever changing, are they not? One should never dismiss advice out of hand. You could return to Bath and consider, er, employment with a gentleman. One with reasonable means, of course.'

'That advice, sir, is as unnecessary as it is unwarranted,' Amy informed him roundly. 'I have no intention of leaving Lady Hawkridge's employment. Nor do I anticipate any change in her ladyship's circumstances that would cause my employment to be terminated. Now, if you will excuse me...'

Tweedy's pursed lips puffed out in a small pout. 'Of course, Mrs Chantry, of course. Far be it from me to keep you from your duties. Perform them well, my dear, but keep in mind that informing Lady Hawkridge of this conversation is not one of them.'

'I wouldn't dream of repeating a conversation of such little significance, sir.'

'Yes, you are very confident, Mrs Chantry.' The pout became a spiteful sneer. 'No doubt you have become quite the favourite. I suspected as much. However—' with another glance about the hall '—there appears to be enough for two.' Tweedy stepped away from the library doorway to retrieve the beaver hat he'd placed on the hall table, and sent her a malicious smile. 'Perhaps Mr Chatsworth will be more amenable to advice from one who is older and wiser. Ottersmead is quite a large place, but I doubt it can accommodate all three of us.'

Already halfway to the front door to see off her unwelcome guest, Amy wheeled about and stared at him. 'What on earth do you mean by that, sir?'

'Think about it, my dear.' Tweedy minced past her to the door, opened it and started down the front steps. His parting words fell into the sunny morning like cold little pellets of rain. 'When one person in our walk of life is unmasked, people tend to ask questions about other newcomers to the district.'

Amy stared after him, frowning. Unease stirred faintly at the back of her mind. Though Tweedy clearly considered her a rival for the dowager's patronage, he'd always been perfectly civil to her, if not downright unctuous. He'd never given her any indication that he considered her anything other than a lady forced to find employment due to straitened circumstances.

What had made him suspect she was something else?

She closed the front door and walked slowly towards the library, pausing in front of the enormous gilt-framed mirror hanging above the hall table to examine her reflection. This morning, in deference to the faint ache behind her eyes, she'd tied her hair back with a simple band of Wellington green silk, leaving it free at the back to fall in artless ringlets to her shoulders. One or two tendrils had defied the ribbon to curl at her brow and temples, rendering the style rather informal for a companion. But not, she decided, studying her cream muslin gown adorned, today, with a green sash to match the ribbon, unsuitable for a morning at home.

What had Tweedy seen that apparently put her on a par with him and Mr Chatsworth?

What, for that matter, did Tweedy know of Mr Chatsworth? Did he suspect him of dishonesty merely because he himself lived by his wits, or did he have some definite knowledge that would discredit Lucinda's suitor? If he did, should she warn someone? Hawkridge? Lord Nettlebed? What could she say?

More uneasy than ever, Amy wandered into the library, her gaze going straight to the pile of mail. Her frown deepened as she remembered that Pickles hadn't been in the hall. No doubt Tweedy had entered the house without ringing the bell; she had no trouble imagining him doing so. But most people on an errand of courtesy would have left the handful of letters in the hall, not made themselves further at home by strolling into the library as if they owned the place.

Simple presumption?

Or, she thought, focusing abruptly on the top of the pile where a folded and sealed square of paper bore her name and direction, had Tweedy originally intended to express his sentiments in writing?

Amy contemplated the missive for a moment, then picked it up and broke the seal. The sheet was devoid of message or signature, but as she smoothed out the folds another smaller piece of paper fluttered out. It appeared to be a cutting from a newspaper. She opened it.

And felt the blood drain from her face with a speed that had her grabbing for the edge of the desk for support. Shock coated her entire body in a sheet of ice. She couldn't move, couldn't think. Could only hold the report of the robbery at Bristol clenched in a hand that wanted to fling the paper aside and could not.

Dear God. Who would send her such a thing?

A violent tremor shuddered through her, breaking her frozen paralysis. Shaking with reaction, hardly able to look at the cutting without feeling sick, she hurried over to the fireplace. Paper and kindling were always laid, although since the advent of warmer weather a fire hadn't been necessary. She crouched, reaching for the tinder-box, then halted abruptly as rational thought reasserted itself.

How could she explain why she'd lit a fire on such a warm, sunny morning?

Amy eased her grip around the paper, took a deep breath, and forced herself to think.

No ghost had sent her that cutting; she'd established that Mr Chatsworth wasn't her husband—the only other person to whom the article would mean something. It had to be Tweedy; trying to frighten her away, but unable to resist baiting her verbally when he'd seen her.

No wonder he'd deposited the mail in the library where she would probably be the first to see it.

But why the cutting? Why would he assume it meant anything to her? She'd never encountered him before she'd come to live at Hawkridge Manor. Had he known her husband? Seen her with James from a distance? It was possible. Those who lived by their wits on the fringes of Society must sometimes encounter others of their ilk.

The more intelligent denizens of the criminal world were even more tightly knit.

But if Tweedy knew about her past, why hadn't he threatened her with outright exposure just now, instead of merely rendering advice?

Amy shook her head. There were too many unanswerable questions for the puzzle to be easily solved, but one thing seemed clear. Tweedy couldn't know everything or he would have used his knowledge to discredit her.

Amy set her lips in a determined line and stuffed the cutting into the pocket of her gown. If Tweedy thought he could intimidate her into leaving, he was in for a sad disappointment. Without proof, he could do nothing.

Feeling more defiant than brave, despite the logic of her reasoning, she put her hand on the woodbox to push herself upright. One of the logs shifted slightly. Before she could blink, something large, black and hairy scuttled into her line of vision. It stopped less than an inch from her fingers and stared at her with tiny malevolent eyes.

Amy forgot all about Mr Tweedy.

Marc strode into the hall, and was halfway up the stairs when an ear-splitting scream, reverberating with feminine fear and outrage, threatened to bring the house down.

Wheeling, he put his hand on the bannister, vaulted it and landed in the hall running.

When he burst through the library doorway a pounding heart-beat later, the sight that met his eyes pulled him up short.

Amy was standing on top of his desk, one hand clutching her throat, the other holding her skirts at a level that was not quite shocking and more than a little tantalising.

He allowed himself one quick glance at elegantly turned ankles and slender calves clad in white cotton stockings that for some odd reason sent a jolt of pure lust through him before lifting his gaze to her face.

'*You didn't get rid of that spider!*' she shrieked, still at the top of her lungs.

Marc closed the door, leaned back against it and decided it wouldn't improve matters to inform Amy that she'd just scared the wits out of him. 'I did try,' he said, with great self-restraint. The remark didn't appear to soothe her in the least.

'Well, you'll have to try again, my lord! And this time you'd better succeed!'

He took a deep breath, determinedly kept his gaze on her face— mainly for his own sanity—and relaxed the battle-ready tension in his muscles. 'Certainly, Mrs Chantry. If you'd give me the spider's precise location, I shall be happy to oblige you.'

'There.' Amy pointed a shaking hand at the woodbox. 'It climbed on to that log and...and stared at me.'

Marc quirked a brow. 'Stared at you.'

'Yes! As if I was its next meal!'

A muscle quivered in his cheek.

'Don't you dare laugh at me, sir.'

'I wouldn't dream of it, Mrs Chantry. Over here, you say?' He strode over to the fireplace and hunkered down to examine the log. A long thin leg protruded from beneath it. No doubt about it. The spider had taken refuge, its nerves shattered by the scream at close quarters. It would be an act of mercy to put the creature out of its misery.

Marc picked up the log and smacked it smartly down on the one beneath it, spider undermost.

Amy let out another shriek and clapped her hands over her ears.

Sternly suppressing a grin, Marc shook the corpse into the fire-place and straightened, brushing his hands. 'There. Nothing like rescuing a fair maiden from a spider to start the day.'

The fair maiden uncovered her ears and glared at him. 'Well, I'm very grateful for the rescue, my lord, but did you have to kill the poor creature?'

'Poor creature? A minute ago it was a carnivorous monster.'

Amy blushed and bit her lip.

Releasing the grin tugging at his lips, Marc strolled towards her. 'To tell you the truth, Mrs Chantry, I considered a speedy dispatch to be more merciful than chasing the spider all over the room, prior to showing it the door.'

'Oh.' She shuddered at the very thought. 'I see what you mean, sir. I dare say even a spider would be terrified by such an ordeal.'

'I meant it was more merciful for you,' he corrected drily. He stopped beside the desk and held out his hand. 'As it is, you may descend from your perch in perfect safety.'

Amy glanced briefly at his hand. He was apparently under the impression that descending from the desk was going to be easy.

When she didn't immediately avail herself of his assistance, he raised a brow. 'I assure you, Mrs Chantry, your assailant is quite dead.'

'Yes, I know that, sir. Thank you.'

'Well?'

Amy felt herself blushing again. 'Um—perhaps if you were to leave the room...'

Both brows went up. 'I beg your pardon?'

'I mean, what if the servants heard me scream? It would be very worrying for them, and—'

'This house is very old, Mrs Chantry. Its walls are thick. I doubt if anyone heard you from the servants' quarters. However, in case

I'm mistaken, you'd better come down from there before someone feels moved to investigate.'

Amy sighed and gave up the task of trying to get rid of her rescuer so she could sit down on the desk and slither off. 'This is no doubt going to sound absurd, my lord, but...I have a small problem with heights.'

'*Heights?*' The quizzical gleam in his eyes turned incredulous. She watched in resignation as he measured the distance to the floor.

'Mrs Chantry,' he began in a reasonable tone that made her seriously consider screaming again, 'the road to the village is situated at a "height". You didn't appear to have any trouble with that. What is the problem here?'

'The problem, sir, is that this desk is not the road to the village. The road to the village, you might have noticed, is set at some distance from the edge of the cliff, causing one to look out over the sea. In fact, in several places there are trees blocking one's view of the descent. However, if I was to stand at the edge of the cliff and look straight down, I would probably *fall* down. That is not a desirable outcome, my lord.'

There was a suspicious hint of movement about his mouth. 'A most *un*desirable outcome, Mrs Chantry. However, take a look at your feet in relation to the floor. You are not standing on the edge of a cliff. The top of that desk is about three feet high. That is hardly what one would call a great height.'

Amy began to feel slightly desperate. 'From your point of view that may be true, sir, but my eyes are not in my feet. They're in my head—which is more than another five feet higher. That is over eight feet, my lord. Eight feet! And when I look directly down it seems a lot worse.'

'Then don't look down,' he suggested, the curve of his mouth suddenly, inexplicably, tender. 'Just step over the edge.'

When she stared at him, aghast at this reckless suggestion, he added softly, 'I'll catch you.'

Amy's breath caught instead. She had the strangest feeling he was talking about something far removed from stepping off a desk. Before she could decide precisely what, however, Hawkridge lowered his hand and tilted his head consideringly.

'Of course if you consider that too risky an option, I can always lift you down.'

It was the gently musing tone that did it. Amy straightened her spine and glared at him. 'Kindly give me your hand, sir.' She took a determined step forward. 'And if you say one word about this to—'

The door crashed open as Lady Hawkridge burst into the library in her usual whirlwind fashion.

Already teetering on the brink, Amy jerked her head up, wobbled for several unnerving seconds, then pitched forward.

'Good morning, Grandmama,' Hawkridge said calmly as she tumbled into his arms.

'Good morning, Marc dearest. How kind of you to help Amy off the desk.'

Amy made a strangled sound of shock and virtually leapt from Hawkridge's arms. The thought flashed through her mind that he'd let her go only because of his grandmother's presence, but there was no time to contemplate the hard tension in his body. The crumpled piece of paper in her pocket, shoved too hurriedly out of sight while she'd been in a crouched position, chose that moment to fall out.

Everyone watched its progress to the floor. When Hawkridge moved to retrieve it, Amy pounced. Snatching it out from under his fingers, she stuffed the paper back in her pocket.

'A...a recipe for Denmark Lotion,' she stammered wildly, straightening like a marionette whose strings had been violently tugged.

Hawkridge studied her flushed face, his eyes so intent she wondered they didn't bore straight through to her scrambling wits. She turned to the dowager, knowing she should leave well alone but unable to stop babbling.

'I hope you don't mind me cutting it out of the paper, ma'am. It's very good for freckles, you know.'

'No, of course not, dear. But—' Lady Hawkridge tilted her head '—you don't have any freckles.'

'Well, no, but one never knows when a freckle may appear, does one? And since I take quite frequent walks to the village, I thought...'

She caught a glimpse of Hawkridge's politely raised brows and knew he didn't believe a word she was saying.

'Oh, dear, and I was about to ask if you'd take a basket of clothes to Lavender Cottage,' the dowager murmured, earning Amy's undying gratitude. 'But you may go in the barouche if you don't wish to walk, Amy.'

'Not at all, ma'am.' Her voice still sounded as if someone was shaking her back and forth. Amy took a steadying breath, and carefully avoided Hawkridge's gaze. 'I enjoy my walks to the village, especially when the objective is a visit at the Cottage.'

Her ladyship beamed. 'I know you take a great interest in our little project, dear. And the children love to see you.'

'Yes, well...' She started towards the door with what she hoped was a firm step. 'Let me fetch my bonnet and pelisse and—'

'Be back here in five minutes, Mrs Chantry. I'll drive you to the village.'

Amy's firm step faltered rather badly. There wasn't a single hint of suggestion in Hawkridge's tone. It was an order. She looked back over her shoulder.

He smiled—like a cat who had just put out a very large paw and pinned down a mouse intent on escape. 'After all, we wouldn't want to expose your complexion to the elements any longer than is necessary, would we? And my greys are overdue for some exercise.'

She was in a great deal of trouble. Hawkridge seemed to have developed the habit of setting neat little traps for her without any warning. She could have refused a favour on her own account, but there was no gracious way to do so if he was going out anyway.

'Thank you, my lord,' she managed to say with creditable calm. 'I won't keep you above a moment.'

The curve of his mouth still held far too much satisfaction for her peace of mind. Amy tilted her chin. She might have been outwitted, but she was far from pinned down. She left the room as if driving into Ottersmead with Hawkridge was all her own idea.

'Are you quite comfortable, Mrs Chantry?'

As comfortable as one could be when expecting an interrogation to start at any moment.

'Yes, thank you, my lord. Your phaeton is exceptionally well sprung.'

Hawkridge cast an amused glance down at her as they bowled through the gates and turned on to the main road to Ottersmead. 'So that's why you have a death grip on the hood. You're afraid you'll bounce off at the first bump.'

Amy flushed and removed her hand, folding it over its clenched twin in her lap. 'I trust the road is not that perilous,' she returned somewhat drily.

'I trust so, too,' Hawkridge murmured. 'Especially as I thought this route might be less harrowing for you than the cliff road.'

She blinked at him, wondering if she'd heard correctly. The road they were on wound inland past woods and fields for a mile or two before dividing into two branches; the right leading to the main post road, the left curving back towards Ottersmead. The route lacked spectacular views and was longer. She'd thought Hawkridge had chosen it so he'd have plenty of time for interrogation.

Instead, he was taking her foolish fear of heights seriously.

No, she thought immediately. Impossible. He must be teasing her. After all, anyone who had trouble descending from a desk had to expect a little raillery on the subject.

'Thank you, my lord. But as long as I see *terra firma* around my feet in every direction, or I have something to hold on to, I do not have a problem.'

His smile was wry. 'Does that mean I put the hood up to no purpose? I thought you might feel more secure in a high carriage if you couldn't look down.'

This time she gaped at him. Her brain seemed to be having a great deal of trouble catching up with the conversation. Such a small thing: raising the hood because she was perched several feet above the ground. She wouldn't have thought of it herself until it was too late.

She shook her head in bemusement. 'I don't know what to say, my lord. Thank you.'

He cast her a searching glance. 'You sound positively astonished, Mrs Chantry. Do you think me so incapable of care or consideration?'

'No...no...of course not. I...' She floundered; caught in a morass of surprise and conjecture. 'I mean, I know you care about your family, but—'

When he raised a brow she sank deeper. 'Well, you only have to look at the way you tell them how to run their—'

'Yes, Mrs Chantry?'

Amy took a firm grip on her wits. 'What I mean, sir, is that you show great consideration for the welfare of your family.'

'To the point of telling them how to run their lives.'

The gleam in his eyes had her winning free of the verbal quagmire tugging at her feet. 'If you must know, sir, it seemed that way at last night's dinner. However, I quite understand that you don't wish to see your young relatives fall into trouble because of over-protection by one parent and a disinclination to bestir—'

She finally managed to put a halt on her runaway tongue.

'A disinclination to bestir himself on the part of the other,' Hawkridge finished for her. 'A telling summation, Mrs Chantry.'

He sounded more thoughtful than annoyed, but Amy flushed. 'And one I had no right to make,' she said immediately. 'Please forgive me, sir, I—'

'Stop that,' he said very quietly.

She stopped. So did her breathing.

'You may say anything you wish to me, Mrs Chantry.' His gaze was very direct. 'Anything. On any subject.'

Anything? On any subject?

'Uh, my lord...the road? It is starting to curve towards Ottersmead, and unless your horses know the way...'

He returned his gaze to the road, but not before she caught the quick flash of laughter in his eyes. 'That wasn't the subject I had in mind,' he murmured. His mouth curved in a faintly crooked smile. 'I want you to trust me, Amy.'

'I...I do trust you, sir.'

'One wouldn't have thought so the other night when, after I'd assured you I no longer suspected you of ulterior motives, I was attempting to discover something of your background.'

When silence greeted that remark, he continued as if they were discussing nothing more innocuous than the weather.

'But tell me where you received such an accurate insight into my family. Was your own mother over-protective or weak? Either would account for a marriage entered into when you were scarcely past childhood.'

'I was seventeen!' Amy exclaimed indignantly. And obviously no more sensible now. He had just managed to slip under her guard again by saying her name in that spine-tingling, velvety dark tone. It was a tone he'd never used before.

She didn't want to think about why he was using it now. Or why he'd used her name. Or why he wanted her to trust him. He was going somewhere with this, but she was too bemused by the entire conversation to pay much attention to its point.

'And my mother was neither over-protective nor weak. In fact, she had very little to do with my marriage.'

'You managed the business yourself?'

'I had no choice, sir. Mama was ill for a long time before her death. I had to manage for both of us.'

'You're used to that, aren't you?' he said, glancing down. 'It's not a matter of trust, although you don't trust easily. It's a matter of independence.'

'You should be able to understand that, my lord. You, too, had to take charge at a young age. I dare say that's why everyone has become accustomed to leaning on you.'

'Never mind my family for the moment, Mrs Chantry. It's your reticence on the subject of your past that interests me. Although a predilection for fighting your own battles goes a long way towards explaining it.'

'I'm glad something's been made clear,' she muttered.

'The point I'm trying to make,' he said, sounding as if his patience was beginning to wear thin, 'is that you no longer need to be so independent.'

'Why not?'

'Because you're living under my protection, damn it. That means if you're in any kind of—'

'I don't see why I should stop fighting my own battles just because I'm living in your house. You don't lean on anyone.'

'That's different,' he bit out. 'I'm a man.'

'All the more reason to keep my independence,' Amy retorted, starting to feel rather annoyed herself. 'When a man is in charge, disaster usually results.'

'Is that why you lied about that scrap of paper this morning? To avoid disaster?'

She slammed back in her seat as if he'd whipped the horses into a headlong gallop.

Although why she should be so stunned was a mystery. He was merely running true to form.

'Perhaps I should have explained in greater detail, Mrs Chantry, the consequences of your continuing to fiddle with the truth.'

The very faintest thread of warning wound through the velvet of his tone. Outrage rescued Amy from her stunned paralysis. She actually felt her breasts swell as she drew in enough air to rend him limb from limb.

Metaphorically speaking.

'Let me tell you, sir, that a request for my trust is not of much use when it's immediately followed by threats! Yes, I did lie about that wretched piece of paper, and you would have done exactly the same in my place. In fact, you do do it. All the time!'

That switched his attention away from her iniquities.

He hauled on the reins so abruptly Amy had to grab for the hood to prevent herself being catapulted into the air. The horses plunged to a stop, snorting and squealing their indignation at their unaccustomed treatment.

Their owner added a few muttered curses to the din before they settled down. Tying the reins around the brake, he turned to her with a distinctly menacing glitter in his eyes. 'Would you care to explain that statement, Mrs Chantry?'

Amy swallowed, and decided she didn't particularly care to explain that statement in the least. She could hardly tell a prominent member of polite society that, despite his façade of civility, she had no trouble picturing him prowling through tracts of icy wilderness, hunting woolly mammoths and other such prehistoric creatures.

'You take me up much too fast, sir,' she muttered. 'All I meant was that you use the same social...*lies*, if you will, that we all use to spare people's feelings.'

To her relief, the hard line of Hawkridge's mouth softened. An instant later he started to grin. 'Several members of polite society might argue with you on that score, Mrs Chantry.' Then, more soberly, 'Very well, I agree with you to a point. Most of us try to behave with some semblance of civility, but—'

'Indeed, we do, my lord. Just think what a shambles we'd be in without polite platitudes and—'

'I said I agree *to a point*. What I wish to know is whose feelings were you trying to spare this morning? And why?'

She clamped her lips together and lifted her chin.

'You don't want to look at me like that, Mrs Chantry. The result might be more than you'd expect.'

'More threats, sir?'

'Damn it, Amy, you were worried about something—and I'm not talking about that blasted spider. I understand you sparing my grandmother's feelings; mine are a damn sight less easily overset. Kindly forget your distrust of the male sex for a moment and tell me what the devil was on that paper?'

Amy sighed. Hawkridge was quite capable of sitting here in the middle of the road until he got an answer. She might as well give him one. If he asked to see the paper, she could always say she'd destroyed it.

Uncomfortably aware that lies seemed to be piling up on top of each other, she resolved to stick as closely to the truth as possible.

'If you must know, sir, I received a message from Mr Tweedy, warning me not to interfere in his pursuit of Lady Hawkridge.'

'What!' Hawkridge's eyes narrowed. 'You deduced all that from a newspaper cutting?'

'It was particularly applicable to my situation, sir.' *That* was certainly the truth. 'I thought such a thing would only upset her ladyship. Now, may we continue to Ottersmead before—'

'Particularly applicable— In what way?'

'It referred to the behaviour of servants. You know, if another carriage were to come around that bend—'

'Good God! Do you think that's going to be the end of the matter? For one thing, Mrs Chantry, you are not a servant. And for another, you will hand over any more warning letters to me. Is that clear?'

'It was *my* warning letter,' she retorted, wincing at the idiocy of the statement.

Hawkridge made a snarling sound in his throat and reached for the reins. Amy received the distinct impression he wanted to reach for her throat.

'This is no time for your stubborn independence,' he grated. 'Especially when your reasoning seems to lack any semblance of logic. Did you stop to consider for one moment that a modicum of distress on Grandmama's part *now*, might be preferable to the greater distress caused the longer Tweedy is allowed to run his course?'

'Lady Hawkridge would be no more distressed to see the back of Mr Tweedy than you would, sir. She is, however, kind-hearted enough to be upset on *my* account. *That* is what I wished to avoid.'

He whipped his head around to study her for a moment, then shortened the reins and gave his horses the office to start. 'Did Tweedy threaten you?'

'Not in so many words. He seemed to be labouring under a similar misapprehension about my past as your own.' Still smarting under the lash of his words, she elevated her nose. 'I would like to know what it is about me that immediately causes *some* people to assume the worst.'

Hawkridge winced. Amy was incensed enough to derive considerable pleasure from his reaction. It was small consolation for that remark about her lack of logic.

'In Tweedy's case, Mrs Chantry, he would probably assume the worst about anyone in your position. It isn't personal.'

'Hmph.'

'As for myself, I did admit I was wrong about you.'

'Hmmph!'

'And in all fairness, you must admit that Grandmama's previous lack of judgement, not to mention the lack of information about your background, greatly influenced my opinion.'

'*Hmmph!*'

'However, I'm happy to inform you that, even if I wasn't already convinced of your innocence in respect to your past, your present behaviour would do the trick.'

'I *beg* your pardon, sir?'

'That mutinous little chin is just begging to be captured so its owner can be thoroughly kissed.'

'Wha—?'

'Fortunately for you, the village is upon us.'

They swept into the main street of Ottersmead before Amy could get her mouth closed again.

Chapter Eight

'By the way,' Hawkridge said, as if he hadn't just sent her thoughts whirling off on several shockingly unsuitable tangents. 'Who are the clothes for?' He cast a glance at the basket reposing at her feet. 'Obviously not naked sculptors.'

Amy choked and regained her powers of speech. 'Really, my lord!'

He grinned. 'Yes, Mrs Chantry?'

Despite grappling with a nerve-tingling memory of the last time he'd kissed her, Amy giggled. It was useless trying to think of a quelling response in the face of that wicked grin. Besides, wickedness was rather reassuring. His remark about kissing her could be put down to the same diabolical tendency.

She sternly quelled a niggling feeling of disappointment.

'The clothes are intended for the children at Lavender Cottage,' she informed him with as much dignity as she could muster.

'Yes, I deduced that there were children at Lavender Cottage. Where is the place? I don't recall a house of that name in Ottersmead.'

'I believe it used to be known as the old Smitton residence. Lady Hawkridge rented it last month on behalf of the orphaned children and...and unmarried mothers of the parish.'

She felt the sharp glance he sent her like a flash of heat against her cheek and resolutely kept her eyes to the front. 'I'm surprised Lady Hawkridge hasn't mentioned the project to you.'

'I'm not,' he returned somewhat drily. 'The last tenant tried to rob her. Although how she could equate Bartle with orphans is beyond me. However, the Smitton place is on a steepish street. We'll leave my phaeton at the Green Man and walk.'

Amy took a moment or two to digest this information. She'd been rigidly braced for criticism or comment, even an implication, about the influence she must have asserted on behalf of the local orphans and unwed mothers; by the time she realised nothing of the sort was forthcoming, Hawkridge was turning his horses into the cobbled space in front of the inn.

She was instantly diverted by a noise from the Esplanade opposite that sounded like the squawking of several seagulls.

'I was under the impression the Society for the Beautification of our Village had already met this week,' Hawkridge remarked, frowning at the small crowd of ladies responsible for the racket. He drew his horses to a halt.

'They have, sir.'

'Then why is a good proportion of the membership waving to us from across the road?'

'I have no idea, my lord.' She waved back to the crowd of chattering ladies, hoping the excitement on every face wasn't caused by the fact that she was out driving with Hawkridge. 'Perhaps Lord Nettlebed can enlighten you. I believe the horse tethered a few yards away to your left is the chestnut he usually rides.'

Hawkridge followed her gaze as he tied off the reins. 'Hmm. And a bay gelding keeping it company.' He descended from the phaeton and strode around to her side. 'I wonder if it's too much to hope that Bevan is partaking of some exercise in company with his son.'

Before she could venture an opinion on the subject, another phaeton, driven by Viscount Eversleigh, clattered into the yard and pulled up next to them. Lord Colborough's gruff tones smote her ears.

'Morning, Mrs Chantry. Hawkridge. Where the devil is Jennings? Hey! Jennings! Jennings, I say!'

'No need to yell, sir,' Eversleigh said, wincing. 'Good morning, Mrs Chantry. You're looking in tune with the season. That shade of green becomes you.'

Amy smiled at him. 'Thank you, my lord.'

Hawkridge scowled, seized her about the waist and whisked her out of the carriage before she could blink.

'Mrs Chantry is a widow,' he informed Eversleigh, setting her on her feet with a distinct thump. 'Widows wear dark colours.'

Amy snatched her hands away from his shoulders—where they'd shown a distressing tendency to linger—and glared at him, torn between umbrage at his lack of gallantry and relief that her exit from the phaeton had been accomplished so easily.

When she saw Eversleigh grinning, she all but dived back into the carriage in search of her basket.

'Going on a picnic?' he enquired innocently when she emerged with her property.

'We're dancing attendance on my grandmother's latest project,' said Hawkridge, sounding as if he was speaking through clenched teeth.

'Where is Clarissa?' growled Colborough in much the same tone. 'Off somewhere with that Tweedy fellow, I suppose.'

Hawkridge turned, an evil smile curling his lips. 'I have no idea,' he purred. 'But since Grandmama decreed this morning that our Public Day will be held in three days' time, you may be sure he'll take every opportunity on that occasion to push his suit.'

'Might as well hold it here and now,' Eversleigh remarked, forestalling the explosion gathering on his grandparent's countenance. 'Half the village seems to have gathered across the way, and here comes Nettlebed with Lucinda and the Inghams.'

'Hah!' barked Colborough, momentarily distracted. He watched the others stroll towards them for a moment before turning back to Hawkridge. 'You had a lucky escape there, Hawkridge, even though you might not have thought so at the time. Know Ashcroft had his doubts about letting his daughter marry you, and he was right. Sweet gal, Kitty Ingham, but not up to your weight. Would have bolted in fright at the first fence.' He chuckled.

Amy suddenly decided that she really ought to be on her way to Lavender Cottage. 'Uh...my lord—'

'I say, sir,' Eversleigh expostulated at the same moment. 'There's a lady present.'

'What's that got to do with anything?' demanded his grandparent. 'Mrs Chantry was married, wasn't she? She isn't going to swoon at a few blunt words. Stands to reason,' he added, as one throwing in a clincher. 'Hardy lot, the Daltons.'

'Good morning, everyone,' Lady Ingham called, before anyone could comment on this pronouncement. 'Isn't it a lovely day?' She caught sight of Amy as she rounded Eversleigh's phaeton, and promptly cut off her retreat. 'Oh, Mrs Chantry, did I hear Lord Colborough say you're a connection of the Daltons? Sarah is one of my dearest friends, you know. I saw her in London during the Season, but she and Ravensdene had to cut their stay short since she was expecting to be confined. Have you heard how she goes on? And the dear little baby?'

'Nick wrote to me a few weeks ago,' Hawkridge answered while Amy was still frantically sorting through a variety of responses. 'From the tone of his letter, I deduced that Sarah was in the pink of health and they're both besotted with the heir. And by the way, Kitty—' he sent Lady Ingham a very straight look '—Mrs Chantry's connection with the Daltons, if any, is very distant. She's never met them.'

'I understand,' Lady Ingham said immediately. She turned a warm smile on Amy. 'Don't worry, Mrs Chantry. I won't say anything. There's nothing more awkward than people assuming something about one that may not be true. But I'm sure Marc will find out the facts for you if you wish it. He's very good at that sort of thing.'

The remark was obviously meant as reassurance. Amy returned her ladyship's smile with a weak one of her own and wondered what that exchange of looks between Hawkridge and Kitty Ingham was all about. She already knew Hawkridge was a stickler for the truth on matters of importance. But she wasn't sure if Lady Ingham meant that the proper connections were also important to him.

Either alternative was disturbing as far as she was concerned.

She shook off the thought and took a firmer grip on her basket. 'My lord, if you don't mind, I'll...'

'Amy! There you are!' Lucinda appeared at her other side, clad in a scarlet riding-habit adorned with gold braid and epaulettes. The sight was so startling, it took Amy a moment to hear what Lucinda was saying. 'I'm so sorry you didn't meet Jeremy last night,' she rattled on. 'He particularly wished to speak to you because I told him you wanted to help us.'

'I beg your—'

'After all, you know what it's like to be in love.'

'Well—'

'But Jeremy is looking forward to meeting you at the Public Day.'

'Excellent,' said Hawkridge, drawing his niece's attention. 'Perhaps you'll remind me, Mrs Chantry, to recruit Chatsworth for the cricket team.' He raised a brow at Lucinda. 'I presume he did learn the game at school.'

Lucinda scowled and stuck out her lower lip.

'He did go to school, didn't he?'

'I think you'd better leave it right there,' Nettlebed advised as his daughter's countenance took on a dangerously angry hue. 'Are you ready to go, Lucinda? Your mama will be wondering what's become of us.'

'Yes, indeed, and so will little Anthony,' put in Lady Ingham. She tucked her hand in the crook of her husband's arm, neatly distracting him from his conversation with Colborough and Eversleigh.

Amy watched as he smiled down at his wife. He was some years older than Hawkridge, unremarkable in countenance, unassuming in manner, clearly happy to indulge his much younger wife.

'Ready to go, my dear?' He patted her hand, the glance he swept over the assembled company, resting for a moment on Amy. 'Mrs Chantry, I do hope you'll come and visit one day soon. Anthony is always talking about the pretty lady who helped him pick flowers a couple of weeks ago. Of course, he and his nurse were trespassing,' he added drolly to Hawkridge. 'The little scamp caught sight of your grandmother's roses when he was out for a walk, and was bound and determined to bring some home to his mama.'

'As if we don't have enough of our own,' Lady Ingham said, laughing. 'But do come, Mrs Chantry. Please don't feel you must wait on Lady Hawkridge. We're much of an age, you know, and I would so like us to be friends.'

Amy promptly sank beneath a tidal wave of guilt. The deluge came out of nowhere, swamping the faint ripples she'd felt before, and sending her hurtling into a maelstrom of regret, worry and recrimination.

By the time she surfaced the Inghams had departed and Nettlebed was assisting his daughter into the saddle.

As he reached for his own reins, he caught her eye and gave her a wry smile. 'I think you'd better come and visit us, too, Mrs Chantry. We could do with some sensible advice.'

Another wave of guilt threatened to roll over her. Amy braced herself, determined not to lose her footing. When had the trickle she'd been living with become a flood? she wondered. Even last night hadn't been this bad. Until then, the only person she'd deceived was Lady Hawkridge, and she'd tried to make up for it by anticipating her ladyship's every whim; had even told herself that she might eventually confide in her benefactress.

Since Hawkridge had arrived, the list of people she was deceiving was growing to nightmarish proportions. She'd thought she would be living retired with an elderly widow, not becoming the recipient of all this kindly attention.

She didn't like it. She didn't want any attention. Unless it was Hawkridge paying—

No! She didn't mean that. She was becoming overwrought. Was it any wonder?

'What's Crispin doing this morning?' Hawkridge demanded, jolting her back to her surroundings.

'Who cares about him?' Lucinda retorted. 'Papa asked him to come riding with us, but he preferred to go off to some mouldy old barn.'

'Painting that yacht in the old boathouse,' Nettlebed explained. 'You'd better talk to Augusta, Marc. She's not happy. Not happy at all.'

'Later,' Hawkridge said briefly.

Amy suddenly realised he was watching her closely. She instantly plastered a smile to her face and looked up at Eversleigh, who had just emerged from the inn.

'God knows where Jennings is,' he remarked. 'Can't find him anywhere.'

'Does the fellow expect us to sit here all day?' barked Colborough. 'Although I can't say I blame him for making himself scarce with that screeching going on across the road. *Stop that infernal din!*' he roared suddenly, raising his voice to a pitch that could have been heard over cannon-shot. 'A man can't hear himself think!'

The ladies stopped chattering as if hands had been clapped over their mouths. They stared across the road, shock and horror on every countenance. Then, as Colborough half rose from his seat, they turned as one and fled down the street like a flock of panicked grey partridges.

Eversleigh groaned. 'Oh, very nicely done, sir. That should add to your reputation as a gentleman.'

Colborough glared at his grandson. 'It worked, didn't it?'

Hawkridge started to grin.

The Viscount raised his eyes heavenward. 'I don't see Jennings reappearing,' he pointed out. Then, with a swift glance at Hawkridge, he looked at Amy and winked. 'Do you want to try flushing him from cover, Mrs Chantry? Old Jennings always has an eye for a fetching female. You might have more success.'

The grin was wiped from Hawkridge's face in a flash. 'That,' he stated in nothing less than a snarl, 'was not amusing, Pel. Find him yourself. And you can tell him that if he wants to continue running the Green—'

He stopped dead as he caught sight of the sign hanging over the door.

Everyone except Nettlebed followed his gaze.

'*Frog?*' they chorused, in accents ranging from outrage to disbelief.

The painted image of a very fat, self-important green frog smirked back at them.

'Meant to warn you,' Nettlebed said gloomily. 'That's why the Society are so dashed excited. They thought a Green Frog made more sense than a Green Man. Poor old Jennings didn't stand a chance. Found him putting up the new sign not half an hour ago. Probably drowning his sorrows in the cellar.'

'Good God!' muttered Hawkridge. He seized Amy by the wrist. 'Pel, we have an errand to run. Track down Jennings and make him take down that ridiculous sign. I don't care what the Society thinks. This time they've gone too far.'

'I'm not telling them that,' Eversleigh began. 'They've probably gone to bring up Mrs ffollifoot and that Tredgett woman as reinforcements.'

'Then tell them Jennings will lose business if he changes the name of the inn. Tell them the damn sign fell down. Tell them anything you please. Just do it!'

He yanked the basket out of Amy's hand. 'As for you, Mrs Chantry, if you've quite finished receiving compliments and invitations from every male in the place, we'll depart before the Society has stone ducks waddling about the yard.'

'Stone doesn't waddle,' Amy informed him in stony accents. 'And I was not—'

She was hauled out of the yard with startling velocity.

'For heaven's sake, my lord!'

It was a testament to her outrage that she still had breath to protest. But Amy eyed the steep hill in front of her and decided to postpone the rest of her lecture until they arrived at Lavender Cottage. It wouldn't take long. She was being towed upwards with relentless despatch.

'You do realise, I suppose, that Lords Colborough and Nettlebed are staring after us with their mouths hanging open, and that Lord Eversleigh is doubled over with laughter,' she began when they halted at their destination.

Marc looked back over his shoulder. Since the cottage was situated less than a minute's walk from the inn and commanded an excellent view of its yard, the most cursory glance was all he needed to see that Amy was right.

He scowled, shoved the wicket gate open, and towed Amy up the path. 'I'm glad Pel finds the situation so amusing,' he growled, thumping a peremptory fist against the front door. 'He might not laugh so hard when I inform him that he has an odd notion of compliments.'

'He was only being kind, my lord. There was no need for you to stand there wielding a club.'

'Wielding a *club*?'

'Um...' She wasn't going to explain *that*.

'Never mind,' he said grimly. 'I've grasped the general picture.'

He glared at the door. 'Doesn't Grandmama have a superintendent or someone running this place?'

'The matron is probably busy, sir. Charitable institutions are not like private residences where people are forever visiting.'

'And that reminds me. What the devil was Ingham about, issuing invitations for you to call? You only met him last night.'

'Lord Ingham is a gentleman, sir.' Her pointed stare told him he could have taken lessons in gentlemanly behaviour. 'He, too, was merely being kind.'

'Well, he can keep his gentlemanly kindness for Kitty. It's why she married him.'

The door opened just as he raised his fist again. The stout, motherly-looking woman in the doorway fell back a pace or two with a startled squawk.

Marc lowered his hand and turned his scowl into a smile. He noticed that Amy manufactured a similar expression. It rivalled the yellow front door for brilliance.

Obviously she felt even less like smiling than he did, but he didn't have time to contemplate the matter. The lady in the doorway was looking at him with bright-eyed expectation. He cast his mind back a couple of decades and came up with a name.

'Good morning, Mrs Fidler. How are you?'

'Well, if it isn't your lordship! Fancy you remembering me. I swear you weren't no more than a schoolboy when I left my place with Lady Hawkridge to marry Mr Fidler. I'm very well, sir, and enjoying my position here. It keeps me busy, Mr Fidler having been gathered to his reward two years ago.' She smiled and nodded, apparently not heart-broken by Mr Fidler's departure. 'And Mrs Chantry's brought you to see her ladyship's good work, which is only right and proper, I'm sure. Good morning, ma'am.'

'Good morning, Mrs Fidler. May we come in?'

'Lawks! Whatever is the matter with me, chattering here on the step? Of course, ma'am, of course. No doubt you'll want to see the children. Cora's taken them into the garden for their lessons.'

'What a lovely idea. Yes, I would like to see them. Perhaps you could show Lord Hawkridge about while I step outside.'

'Aye, that I will, ma'am. Are those the clothes Lady Hawkridge promised to send? Just pop them down right there, m'lord, and come this way.'

The fervent light of the charitably inclined gleamed in Mrs Fidler's eyes. As Amy took advantage of the situation to vanish down a short passage leading to another door, Marc resigned himself to a thorough tour of the premises. Fortunately the house was small. He saw and heard everything he needed to see and hear in twenty minutes. It was enough to inform him that, thanks to Amy's influence, Lavender Cottage was unlike every other almshouse in the entire country.

Escaping at last with the excuse that his horses would be growing restless, he made his way to the garden.

It, too, was small, but charmingly laid out with a winding path that followed the slope of the hillside in a series of descending steps as it meandered through a maze of flower beds. Wild roses ran amok among more formal arrangements, jasmine draped itself over the surrounding hedge, and everywhere he looked lavender nodded gently in the breeze, adding its perfume to the mix and making his head spin.

It must have been something like that, he thought, because the minute he saw Amy he felt as if he'd been kicked in the chest. All the air vanished from his lungs, the bright colours at the edges of his vision dimmed, as if the garden had disappeared in a mist, leaving only Amy framed in an incandescent circle of light.

He stopped, eyes narrowed against the brightness; the circle widened, and he saw that she was sitting on a child-sized chair in front of a group of half a dozen very small children, reading from a book open on her lap. Every little face upturned to her wore the same expression. Rapt attention.

He knew exactly how they felt, Marc thought suddenly. He could have sat there himself, endlessly, absorbing the play of expressions chasing each other across her face, listening to the soft lilt of her voice, filling himself with her essence every time he drew in a breath.

It wasn't desire, the strange longing that shook him then, although desire raked across his flesh with increasingly fiery claws whenever he saw her.

This was something else; something deeper, something so much a part of him that, if it was ever torn away, the loss would threaten his very soul.

He loved her.

The knowledge hit him with such finality he didn't even question it. As if he'd known the instant he'd learned she could match him, but had called it desire, protectiveness, anything, to prevent himself from again becoming a hostage to fate.

His entire body shuddered as a sense of unbearable vulnerability swept over him. For an infinitesimal second he was twenty again, waiting, helpless, for the news that two of the people he'd loved most in the world had been taken from him.

Then his hands fisted at his sides and he reminded himself that this time he wasn't helpless, this time he *could* protect. And this time, by God, if the same malevolent twist of fate stopped him protecting Amy, then he'd go with her into whatever lay beyond.

He clenched his teeth as a primal roar of human defiance rose in his throat, and as if Amy felt the storm of emotion raging within him, she looked up, her clear green eyes wide, her lips slightly parted.

He fought down instincts that were as violent as they were primitive, steeled himself against agonising need, and strolled forward.

'My lord! Are you ready to go?' She leapt to her feet, causing the children to blink and transfer their attention to him. Their expressions went from rapt to severely disapproving.

Marc couldn't help smiling, albeit wryly. 'Something tells me I'm not going to be very popular if I take you away before you finish your story, Mrs Chantry, but I don't want to keep my horses standing any longer than is necessary.'

'It's all right, my lord. I'd just started another rhyme. Cora will be happy to finish it when she returns from putting her baby down for his nap.' She glanced down at the circle of faces. 'Stand up and say good morning to his lordship, children.'

There was a general scramble as the group got to their feet. 'Good morning, his lordship.'

Marc grinned. 'I'm afraid I must take Mrs Chantry home now,' he told them. 'But she will visit you again very soon, and you may see her at our Public Day if you wish.'

One urchin removed his thumb from his mouth. 'Will we see your horses, too?' he demanded.

'Yes, as long as you do precisely what my grooms instruct you to do while you're in the stables.'

Everyone nodded solemnly.

'Well, then,' said Amy, bestowing a smile on her charges that had his eyes narrowing thoughtfully. 'You may go and watch the kittens until Cora comes back, but no touching them, mind. Not until they're bigger.'

'I 'member,' lisped one little girl. ''Cos the mama cat will smell us on them and leave, and then they'll be orphans like us.'

'Yes, but you have Mrs Fidler to look after you now, Emmy. She isn't going to leave you.'

The child gave a shy smile, nodded and ran off. The rest streamed after her without wasting time on social niceties.

'You have a way with children, Mrs Chantry,' Marc observed, taking her arm to lead her out of the garden.

She eluded him the instant his fingers made contact, her smile winking out like a snuffed candle. 'Thank you, my lord. You would appear to possess a similar way, if you truly meant they may visit your stables.'

'I meant it. Mawson will see that neither they nor my horses come to any harm.'

'That's very kind of you. Now, if you don't mind waiting a second or two, I'll take my leave of Mrs Fidler and—'

'I've already taken the liberty of doing so on your behalf. If we go along this path, it will take us back to the street without having to go through the house. Mrs Fidler is an excellent woman, but she does tend to chatter.'

'Oh. Well...'

'Of course, chatter can sometimes be useful. I believe there are two other girls living here.'

'Uh...yes. Jane and Ellen.' Amy tried to pull herself together with the stern reminder that engaging Hawkridge's interest in the dowager's project was of more importance than the confused state of her emotions.

Unfortunately, it was difficult to ignore the fact that since they'd arrived at the cottage, she felt as if she'd been caught in a whirl-pool.

First there'd been the strange cloud of depression that had descended on her when Hawkridge had made that comment about the reason for Kitty Ingham's choice of husband. If anything had been needed to confirm her assumption about his reasons for staying away from Devon, it had been those words.

Her reaction had given her quite a jolt. Her throat had felt tight; there'd been an odd ache in her chest. The last thing she'd felt like doing was smiling and chatting to Mrs Fidler as if there was nothing wrong.

She'd managed to throw off the sensation—after all, there *was* nothing wrong—but it had taken a surprising amount of effort. And then Hawkridge had managed to overturn her senses again when she'd glanced up to find him watching her with that piercing intensity in his grey eyes. It was the look she'd glimpsed in the library, only more so.

Utterly implacable. Fiercely determined. Almost...brutally relentless.

No, she thought at once, Hawkridge would never be brutal, but that look had been enough to cause her heart to leap quite violently into her throat and lodge there for several seconds.

And now he was being so polite, she was beginning to wonder if her disordered mind had been playing tricks on her.

'Jane and Ellen?' he prompted.

Amy jumped. 'Oh, yes.' Really! This wouldn't do. She'd presented a happy face to the children, she could manage a composed visage for Hawkridge. 'They've found positions as housemaids, sir. However, most such positions require people without dependents, which is why the children are housed at Lavender Cottage until they're older. The girls contribute a little towards their food and Cora is teaching them their letters.'

There, that was better. All she had to do was keep her mind on what was important, and forget what was not.

'And Cora's story?' he asked, holding the gate open for her.

'An all-too-common one, I'm afraid. She was seduced, abandoned by the man who had promised to marry her, and then lost her place when her mistress discovered her situation. Parish relief was her only recourse—respectable recourse, that is—but I can assure you, such relief is grudging and insufficient at best.'

He sent her a swift glance as they started down the hill. 'A sadly commonplace tale, indeed. Very similar to your mother's, except that her destitution was caused by your father's death.'

Amy felt her breath catch, even though she'd been expecting something of the sort since Hawkridge had discovered the purpose of Lavender Cottage.

'In case you're wondering, sir, Lady Hawkridge knows nothing of my mother, or of my own circumstances except that I'm— except that I was married. I admit I interceded when poor Cora was caught trying to milk one of your cows, but—'

'I wasn't criticising you, Mrs Chantry.' He smiled down at her, a smile so gently reassuring she felt her heart hesitate and flutter before it resumed its usual rhythm. 'I would expect nothing less of you than that you'd help a girl in Cora's situation. As for Grandmama, I'm only too happy for her to be involved in such a project. Her patronage of poets and artists and the like only seems to land her in trouble,' he finished drily.

Fortunately for her beleaguered mind, they reached the inn at that moment, saving her from the necessity of a reply. As Jennings bustled out, full of thanks and excuses, Amy leaned against a handy carriage wheel and tried to gather her wits.

She hoped the task wouldn't take long. She still had the conversational shoals of the drive home to negotiate.

Chapter Nine

They took the cliff road. Amy didn't know whether Hawkridge chose the route by force of habit or because he'd accepted her earlier assurances, and didn't have time to enquire. They had barely passed the vicarage when he returned to the subject of her past.

'Tell me about your mother, Mrs Chantry.' He glanced down at her. 'If I was correct in assuming her situation to be similar to Cora's, she must have been an exceptionally courageous young woman to rear you as she did.'

Amy debated for a moment, then decided that after visiting Lavender Cottage, his interest sprang from genuine concern.

'My mother's situation was somewhat worse, sir. At least Cora hasn't had to go into the poorhouse. You see, parish officials are loathe to support able-bodied adults. One must work. Which is all very well, but work isn't easy to find when one has a babe in arms, or even a young child clinging to one's skirts. Whenever Mama found a position, no matter how lowly, there were always... compromises to be made.'

'Involving the men in the situation?'

She made a small, assenting gesture. 'I was too young to know anything about it, of course, but I remember how she would sink into despair sometimes, that she often looked afraid. Eventually the poorhouse, or workhouse as they're coming to be known, must have seemed safer for both of us.'

'And harder to get out of than the Fleet, I imagine.'

'No one wants to lose free labour,' she said drily. 'You can't leave unless you can prove you won't be a charge on the parish, but how can one search for employment when one is forever kept busy and confined? It's a circle of hopelessness, especially for the simple, the old and sick, or children who, like myself, lack formal education.'

'You have more than formal education, Mrs Chantry. Thanks to your mother, I presume.'

Amy nodded. 'Most workhouses have classes for the younger children, but I was considered too old by the time we entered one. So, at night, Mama taught me everything she could remember from her own schooling.'

'Even how a lady should behave,' he murmured.

'She was a lady, sir! Not only by birth, but in all the ways that matter.'

He smiled faintly. 'Having met you, Mrs Chantry, I have no doubt on that score.'

Slightly mollified, Amy subsided. 'Eventually I was taken into the superintendent's house to be trained as a maid...'

'But?' he prompted.

'I grew older, sir. Old enough to draw the attention of the son of the house and...his friends.'

'Hmm. I think I hear ''doltish'' friends in there somewhere.'

The comment drew a smile from her. 'I began to look for another position,' she continued, more at ease. 'Whenever I was sent out on some errand or another. Eventually I found a place at the Misses Appleton's Academy for Young Gentlewomen. I...'

She glanced down, then lifted her chin. In this instance, at least, she would give him the truth. And hope it would pacify her conscience for a while.

'I lied, sir, to gain a position as a junior schoolmistress. I even had Mama write a reference purporting to be from a school in Yorkshire. It wasn't difficult to play the role. A junior mistress is more of a maid than anything else. She's expected to wait at table, supervise the laundering, serve tea to the senior teachers, that sort of thing. Any teaching is done by rote from *Miss Mangnell's Historical and Miscellaneous Questions,* and is restricted to the very youngest girls. And the Misses Appleton ran only a modest establishment. They didn't cater to the Upper Ten Thousand, as Mama put it.' Her confident façade wavered a little. 'I know I'm sadly lacking in the sort of accomplishments that might be expected of a companion, indeed of a lady, but—'

'Amy.'

The gentle tone, his steady gaze, had the rest of her speech vanishing into the ether.

'You are a lady,' he said quietly. 'A lady waiting for the right setting.'

He held her gaze an instant longer, then returned his attention to the road.

'Yorkshire?' he queried after a moment.

Amy tried to answer and discovered she'd just lost the thread of the conversation. 'Um... It was the first remote place I could think of, sir.'

He smiled at that. 'I expect the superintendent at the workhouse wasn't too pleased about your advancement in the world.'

'I told him only that I'd found another maid's position,' she confessed, still feeling strangely disoriented. 'Even that enraged him, although heaven knows he had plenty of other girls to choose from. He called me every name he could think of and threatened to throw Mama into the street.'

Marc's eyes narrowed. 'What stopped him?'

'She was ill by then, mainly because of the conditions in the place, and he was answerable to higher authorities. Not that I knew that at the time, but I told him I'd go to the local magistrate unless he allowed Mama to stay until I could find another place for her. Fortunately, it didn't take long. I paid for a small room off the kitchen of an inn, and Mama helped out with the work whenever she could in return for her food. We were lucky; they were good people.'

He nodded. 'She was there when you met your husband?'

'Yes.' Amy fixed her gaze on her hands. 'Actually, she met him first. He was staying there, and she became quite attached to him. He was...kind to her.'

Marc watched the myriad expressions cross her piquant little face and wondered at the last. Sadness and regret he understood, but there'd been...hesitation. Uncertainty. As if she might have said more, but had retreated into the safety of silence.

He stamped down on a surge of impatience to know the entire story. He *needed* to know. She'd been desperate to get her mother out of the poorhouse. Her dying mother. Desperate to get herself away from its superintendent—probably sensing, with the instincts of the small and vulnerable, that the man had another purpose in taking her into his house. But how desperate? She'd lied—he was glad of it; his blood ran cold when he thought of how close she'd come to having her innocence brutally stripped from her—but to what other straits had she gone?

He needed to know to protect her from any consequences.

'You were very close to your mother, weren't you?' he said, making his voice as soft and unthreatening as possible. 'You took care of each other.'

Her gaze flicked upwards, then away. She nodded. 'There were only the two of us, you see. All my life. When she died...'

There was silence for a moment, filled only with the sounds of birdsong, and the steady clip-clop of the horses' hooves. They topped the rise overlooking the sea, and he reined in, transferring the ribbons to one hand.

'I know,' he said, very low. He reached out and took one tightly clenched little fist in his free hand. 'I know.' And raising her hand to his mouth, he turned it and pressed his lips to the delicate tracery of veins at her wrist.

The pulse beneath her skin leapt and quivered. Probably because he'd startled her rather than in response to the caress, but even as he felt an answering tension invade his own muscles, she was drawing her hand away.

Faint colour tinted her cheeks. 'You...always manage to surprise me, my lord. I don't know why.'

His mouth curved in a somewhat crooked smile. 'Don't you?' he asked wryly. 'Given your opinion of my, er, tendency to wield a club, I find that hard to believe.'

Amy felt herself blushing again. The heat seemed to emanate directly from the faintly throbbing place where his lips had touched. It even threatened to cloud her mind, because, despite knowing that Hawkridge would find the rest of her story even harder to believe, she was rocked by an unexpected urge to tell it.

As if she hadn't already said enough! No wonder she was feeling rattled; as though someone had picked her up and shaken her to see what fell out.

The trouble was, she'd never trusted anyone enough to confide in them; the sense of vulnerability was nerve-racking. Although Hawkridge had prompted her with nothing more than the briefest of questions, spoken in the gentlest of tones.

And just now, his quiet acknowledgement of her loss—a loss he'd known himself—had aroused a sense...almost of kinship with him. A closeness she'd never expected to share with a man.

For some reason, that made her feel more vulnerable than ever, as if she'd just skated out on to very thin ice.

She resisted the urge to rub the still-tingling spot on her wrist, and scrambled back to safer ground.

'Goodness me, my lord! The view from here *is* quite spectacular, isn't it? I can see why Lady Hawkridge was so eager to show the spot to Mr Tweed—'

She stopped dead as another patch of thin ice threatened to crack beneath her feet. The heart-shaking smile on Hawkridge's face was abruptly replaced by narrow-eyed purpose.

'I think I'll have a word with this Tweedy fellow,' he growled. 'He's been a little too busy for my liking.'

'I can assure you, sir, that Lady Hawkridge is in no danger of being taken in.'

He scowled at her. 'Then what the devil does she think she's doing, running about the countryside, looking at views with Tweedy?'

Amy had a sudden vision of Lord Colborough's irascible countenance when discussing the same subject. 'You could always wait and see,' she suggested, wondering if her startling suspicion was correct.

The expression in Hawkridge's eyes seemed rather to imply that she'd taken leave of her senses. 'Wait around for the situation to deteriorate?' he demanded. He took up the reins and flicked them against the horses' rumps. 'No, thank you, Mrs Chantry. I know better.'

Somewhat incensed at having her suggestion summarily dismissed, she sat back and folded her arms. 'I'm sure you do, sir.'

'What does that mean? That you think you know more about the situation than I do?'

'Not at all, my lord.'

'Oh, yes, it does.' His scowl darkened. 'I know what's going on in that independent little mind. You think Grandmama should enjoy limitless freedom to get herself into trouble.'

'She might get herself out of it, too.'

'The way you were going to get yourself off that desk?' he asked silkily.

Amy stuck her nose in the air. 'I was going to sit down upon the desk and slide off it,' she informed him.

Marc had a sudden vision of her dress sliding upwards as she did so. The image nearly caused him to rip a layer of paint off his phaeton as he turned in at the gates.

The narrow escape didn't improve his mood. Not only was Amy sitting there beside him with a distinctly disapproving look on her face, he had just been struck by the several disagreeable facts.

He grimaced inwardly as he remembered his half-amused, supremely confident assertion that she belonged to him. As if possessing her physically was all; as if making her his wife, while needing skill and patience, was inevitable.

After what he'd learned this morning, marrying Amy might not be as easy as he'd supposed.

And his own position was to blame. The social gulf between them was wide. Though the circumstances of her birth were unknown, everyone was aware, at the very least, that she was a penniless widow without connections.

Not that he gave a damn about that, but Amy would. If he showed his hand too plainly in public, it would give rise to the sort of gossip that would shred her vulnerable little soul to pieces. Some well-meaning, but misguided, fool might even try to warn her against responding to him.

On the other hand, given her mother's situation and her general distrust of the male sex—rather justified, he had to admit—he suspected too overt a pursuit in private would send her fleeing again.

And then there was her damnable independence.

Marc scowled again. The entire business threatened to be a long, painstaking process. He didn't want painstaking. He wanted *her*. Now! Immediately! If not sooner.

He wanted the right to protect her, to ravish, to love. He wanted to make her laugh again. He wanted—

'Excuse me, my lord, but are you still exercising your horses? Or have you forgotten the way to the stables?'

Marc jerked his attention back to his driving to discover he'd just overshot the turn to the stableyard. His horses, being the polite, well-bred animals they were, hadn't argued his apparent decision to circle the house.

He thought fast.

'It just occurred to me, Mrs Chantry, that if you don't ride, you probably don't drive.'

'Well, no, but—'

'Then this would be an excellent opportunity for me to teach you.'

'Oh.' For a second or two, she looked adorably confused. 'Thank you, my lord, but...I do have a considerable pile of mail waiting on my...I mean, waiting on your desk.'

They turned a corner. The gravel strip between terrace and lawn narrowed considerably. He didn't want to think about the damage his off-side wheels were doing to the grass.

'Some other time, perhaps,' he said smoothly. 'Tyrant though I am, I do believe that ladies should be able to drive themselves if the need arises.'

She frowned. 'I didn't say you were a tyrant, sir. Merely...extremely conscious of your responsibilities.' Her frown vanished. She looked inordinately pleased with the pronouncement.

Marc winced. 'It's a good thing I'm not inclined to be puffed up with my own importance,' he said drily. 'You would soon burst that particular bubble, Mrs Chantry.'

'Oh, dear.' She looked up at him in apparent concern, but he didn't miss the quick flash of mischief in her gaze. 'I'm sorry if I offended you, my lord. You did grant me leave to say anything I pleased to you. On any subject.'

'Something tells me I may have been a bit too liberal with that permission,' he muttered. 'Since you're exercising the license, however, tell me what I should have done on the previous occasions when Grandmama got herself into strife? Allowed her to be pestered by unwanted attentions or robbed blind? Waved Bartle off with the pearls, perhaps, or— Damn it! Now look what's happened!'

The horses trotted dutifully past the stable turn-off again. Amy glanced around as they swept by, and had to resist an insane urge to pat Hawkridge soothingly on the hand.

'I can certainly understand why you chased after Mr Bartle,' she said placatingly. 'But before that, have you ever waited for an outcome other than a continuance of trouble?'

To her surprise, every trace of wry humour vanished from his face. He flicked the reins against the horses' rumps with a white-knuckled restraint that sent her an abrupt reminder of the warrior beneath the gentleman. If he hadn't been confined in a carriage, Amy knew he'd be pacing.

'Once,' he said flatly. 'Once I waited for my parents to return from an afternoon's sailing. I waited too long to save them.'

Her lips formed a silent 'oh' of comprehension. Compassion welled inside her, wrenching at her heart. This time it was imperative she touch him, if not physically, as he'd touched her, then emotionally; that she let him know he wasn't alone in feeling loss and grief. Or guilt.

'Was it a storm?' she asked softly.

He was silent for the few seconds it took them to round the corner of the house and bowl along the carriageway to the front door. There he stopped the horses and tied off the reins, but he made no move to descend from the phaeton. Merely leaned forward slightly, resting his forearms on his thighs, his hands clasped loosely between them as he stared straight ahead.

Her heart ached when she thought of what he must be seeing in his mind's eye. 'I'm sorry,' she murmured. 'You don't have to—'

'No,' he said, and half-turned his head towards her, briefly. 'Time heals, Amy. I want you to know.' He paused for a second, as though remembering. 'There was a calm that afternoon, and fog. Not bad when the wind came up again, but still dangerous in patches. And though Pelham's father and mine had probably been rowing during the calm, they'd been too far out to sea to reach the cove and safety before dark. They were run down by a revenue cutter in pursuit of another craft. Smugglers, using the fog as cover.'

'I'm so sorry,' she whispered. 'That sort of waiting must have been terrible.'

He glanced down at his hands. 'It didn't get bad until nightfall. There was no reason to worry, we thought. Both my father and Pel's were experienced sailors, had often run under lights, in all weathers. But eventually my grandfather and I, with Pel and Colborough, went out looking for them. We found the cutter. They'd gone back, searching for survivors, but their speed had been such at the moment of impact that, by the time they came about, patched up the damage to their own boat, and tacked back to the spot, there was nothing.'

Nothing but wreckage, floating on the surface of the sea.

'Their bodies eventually washed ashore along the coast. Dr Twinhoe said it was very likely they'd all been killed on impact. Or injured so badly that even a minute's delay in rescue would have been too long once they were in the water. But I'll never be certain. If we'd gone out earlier...sailed back with them...the cutter might have seen two boats.'

'You weren't to know that such a thing would happen,' Amy said gently.

'No.' He turned his head at that, smiled faintly. 'Hindsight is a wonderful thing, isn't it? The revenue officer in charge probably regretted his decision to run without lights, in hindsight. He was hauled over the coals for it, of course, but he'd been chasing smugglers. No one was going to reprimand him too strongly for that. It was put down as an accident. Unfortunate, but unforeseen.'

'I'm glad you told me,' she murmured. 'Now I can better understand Lady Nettlebed's distress at the thought of Crispin sailing.'

'She'll soon become reconciled. It's in his blood. We all learnt to sail practically before we could walk. Even Augusta. In fact, I think poor old Bevan paid his addresses to her out on the water more often than not.'

Amy tilted her head, instinctively finding the way to lead him back to the present. 'You allowed your sister to sail, my lord?' She widened her eyes at him. 'How very liberal of you.'

He grinned. 'Minx. I had nothing to do with it. At the time, I was still at the horrid little toad stage.' Then, more soberly, 'I hope you also better understand my own, er—'

She smiled at him. 'The word you're searching for is protectiveness, sir. It does you credit.'

His brows went up. 'A rather surprising remark, considering our earlier conversation.'

'Not at all,' she replied composedly. 'A woman appreciates a man who can be relied upon, no matter how independent she may be. So long as he respects her own abilities.'

'Oh, I respect your abilities, Amy. Believe me.'

The softly voiced assurance had her composure threatening to beat a hasty retreat into caution. 'Yes, well, according to Mrs Tredgett, protectiveness runs in your family, so—'

The rest was swallowed on a startled gulp as she realised what she'd said. It was useless hoping that Hawkridge hadn't been similarly struck.

'Aha!' He pinned her to her seat with a fiendishly anticipatory gleam. 'Gossiping with the Society, I see.'

Amy blushed as if she'd been found out in a heinous crime. 'Um...'

'Denial is useless, Mrs Chantry. You may as well tell me what else was said. I don't want you going about with any erroneous impressions.'

The words 'poor helpless orphan' jangled loudly in her head. 'Helpless' now made more sense, but she didn't think Hawkridge would appreciate hearing it.

'Good heavens, my lord! Just look where the sun is. I really must be—'

She sprang up, remembered where she was, and sat down again.

Hawkridge smiled his cat-with-the-captured-mouse smile. 'Let me save you the trouble of sparing my sensibilities, Mrs Chantry. Knowing Mrs Tredgett and company, you were probably treated to an inaccurate description of my broken engagement to Kitty Ingham. God knows, they've all been speculating about it for the past five years.'

Amy's embarrassment vanished. She stopped worrying about how she was going to escape when she couldn't even manage the simple task of descending from a phaeton. She was suddenly, intensely interested in broken engagements. 'Inaccurate, sir? I mean, Miss Twinhoe did happen to mention...'

'Yes, I'm sure she did. She mentions it to everyone. To hear Miss Twinhoe tell it, I was jilted at the altar. The simple truth was that I'd proposed to Kitty in the mistaken belief that, because we'd known each other since childhood, she'd make me an excellent wife.'

'That seems a most, ah, logical decision, my lord.'

'A little too logical. The only reason I made it was that everyone was in a frenzy about the succession because I'd been held up on the road to Newmarket a few weeks earlier. And at that point I hadn't met anyone else who— Well, never mind.'

'Oh, dear. I'm so sorry, sir. I didn't mean to cause you to recall more painful memories.'

'The only painful part was getting myself winged by a high-wayman before I managed to disarm him,' he said, grinning. 'There's no need to picture me as a heartbroken suitor. For one thing, my heart wasn't involved in the first place, and, for another, I began to suspect that Kitty, too, had a few misgivings. When I asked her about it, she was very grateful to be given the opportunity to cry off. Unfortunately, she felt so guilty about accepting in the first place, she's been trying to find a replacement ever since.'

'Good heavens. That was five *years* ago?'

'Yes.'

'And in all that time she hasn't found a lady to put up wi— I...I mean—'

He grinned again. 'Kitty hasn't. A couple of years ago, I thought I had, but I discovered—fortunately before any formal notices were sent out—that the lady concerned was acting under instructions from her very ambitious parents. When she was given a taste of one of her, er, duties, her acting skills proved unequal to the task.'

Amy was quite certain her eyes were going to pop right out of her head with astonishment. 'Oh, my,' she uttered, and was only prevented from adding 'how foolish of her' by the opening of the front door.

She almost slid off her seat in relief when she saw Lady Hawkridge.

'Yoo hoo! Amy. Marc.' The dowager waved from the top step. 'I think you'd better come in now. Amy will be getting freckles. And Marc, dearest, there seem to be some very peculiar ruts in the south lawn. Perhaps you'd have a word with Thorpe about them.'

Her ladyship disappeared.

'Pel was right,' Hawkridge muttered as the front door shut again. 'One of these days someone is going to wring Grandmama's neck.'

Amy didn't hear him. She was too busy trying to suppress a blush that wouldn't have left room for the smallest freckle. As Hawkridge sprang down from the phaeton and strode around to her side, she jumped to her feet, this time determined to leap to the ground and flee.

She had grievously underestimated the size of the carriage step and the distance of the leap.

Before she could make a fool of herself, Hawkridge was there. 'It's all right,' he said. 'I'll lift you down.'

Amy forgot about blushing and glared at him. 'This,' she declared, 'is ridiculous. I am not going through life being lifted down from desks and carriages.' She grabbed hold of the hood. 'Kindly stand aside, sir. I'm going to do this even if my head spins so fast it whirls right off my shoulders.'

He started to smile. 'Amy, *every* lady needs assistance descending from a high-perch phaeton. That's why they invented the things. We'll compromise. I'll hold your other hand while you step down.'

That sounded reasonable. Amy put out her hand and had it enveloped in a hold that felt rock steady. She could have been clinging to the iron railing adorning the Inghams' access to the beach.

Two steps and she was on the ground.

A delighted smile spread across her face. 'I did it!'

'No,' he contradicted very softly. '*We* did it. Think about that, Mrs Chantry.'

'Ah...yes. Well...' All she could think about was the hard grip of his fingers and the compelling purpose in his eyes. 'Thank you, my lord.'

His fingers tightened for an instant before he released her.

Amy stepped back. She had the distinct impression that she should keep stepping back, that she shouldn't stop stepping back until she was safely in the house. But something else, something quite alien to her naturally wary nature, was driving her.

She put out her hand, touched his arm—the merest butterfly touch, but the awareness of leashed power beneath her fingers was even stronger than it had been last night. She hoped her voice wouldn't betray that for some strange reason she was trembling inside. 'I do understand why you dislike waiting,' she said softly. 'But, this time...there can be no harm in it. Please.'

His eyes went light, and brilliantly intense.

Amy didn't wait to see with what expression. Wondering what on earth had possessed her, she snatched her hand away, turned, and fled into the house.

Marc wheeled and clamped both hands hard around the nearest object. The rim of the front off-side wheel dug into his palms. He didn't dare let it go, didn't dare watch Amy race into the house.

God, one little touch and his entire body was hard and throbbing. One little plea and he was shaking with the need to go after her, toss her over his shoulder and carry her upstairs to his bed, where he could demand the rest of the story—and a whole lot more.

He wondered if she'd understand *that*. Or the fact that the soft, sweetly serious expression in her eyes had threatened to tear apart the bars keeping his instincts caged.

Wait? He'd never felt less like waiting. Only one thing reconciled him to that course of non-action.

The promise he made to himself in that moment that, once he

knew the whole story, he really was going to toss Amy over his shoulder and carry her off to his bed. And there she would stay until she agreed to marry him, even if he had to keep her tied up and helpless.

The thought had a certain appeal. But there was a catch.

He wanted Amy to love him in return, and that couldn't be forced.

Chapter Ten

The next few days were not spent in the peace and quiet that Amy had anticipated when she'd come to live at Hawkridge Manor.

Nor did she have a lot of time to wonder if she'd done the right thing in asking Hawkridge to wait, instead of interfering in any schemes hatched by his grandmother. When she'd dashed into the house after their excursion to Lavender Cottage, Pickles had been waiting to inform her that since a Public Day was to be held in three days' time, Things Would Have To Be Done.

Amy had gone in search of her employer, only to find that the dowager had departed to enjoy a picnic with Mr Tweedy on the beach below Colborough Court. Even though there was a perfectly good beach at Hawkridge.

This provocative behaviour confirmed Amy's opinion of her ladyship's intentions—in fact, she wondered with some amusement how long Lady Hawkridge had been trying to bring Colborough to heel, only to have her grandson put unwitting spokes in her wheel.

Less amusing was the realisation that her plan to join the dowager in her quest for jollification, and thus avoid danger, was rapidly coming to nought. In fact, she'd forgotten all about it.

Her lapse in memory had been bad enough although, in view of Hawkridge's apology after he'd kissed her the other night, quite understandable. What threatened to suspend her wits over a precipice was the added realisation that the scheme had lost its appeal.

Amy seized gratefully on the distraction of a Public Day. The Manor became a veritable hive of activity. Dust covers were removed from the state rooms; a section of the south lawn was rolled for a cricket pitch, causing several footmen to go about practising their bowling action; and, to the accompaniment of Mrs Pickles's instructions and exhortations, a seemingly endless army of macaroons marched out of the ovens.

At first, Hawkridge prudently removed himself from the fray by spending several hours at Nettlebed Place, helping Crispin prepare his boat to a state of seaworthiness that would satisfy that young man's mother.

Amy was glad of his absence. Truly she was. She decided it was a great deal easier to keep him out of her mind when he wasn't always underfoot. Unfortunately for this happy exercise in logic, there appeared to be no predictable pattern to his comings and goings. Instead of departing for Nettlebed Place in the morning and staying there until evening, he developed the knack of appearing just when she was returning a pile of books to a shelf an inch or two above her head, or lifting large vases of flowers.

There was nothing in his manner to give cause for alarm, but Amy began to feel...small. Delicate. Even fragile. Which was rather alarming in itself.

She began peering around corners whenever she had to carry anything heavy.

Then there were the disturbingly persistent thoughts that wafted through her head at odd moments during the day—whether Hawkridge was there or not. The warmth that enfolded her when she remembered the touch of his mouth against her inner wrist; the tingling little arrows of heat that darted about inside her when she recalled the sudden intensity in his eyes before she'd fled into the house.

She made valiant efforts to put the tantalising memories out of her mind. Truly she did. She studied the portrait diligently, for instance, willing fascination with an inanimate object to return.

Hawkridge overturned the scheme by striding into the library in search of a boat-hook he'd mysteriously left there. And when she glared accusingly from him to the painting, he had the temerity to explain that it *had* been done fourteen years ago. The grin he wore when he left the room nearly caused her to heave the nearest available object at his head.

She brooded on his narrow escape for some time.

Finally, on the general principle that doubling her duties would leave her no time to think at all, Amy offered her assistance to the housekeeper.

It worked. Until Hawkridge managed to outwit her by cantering past the drawing-room windows at the precise moment she was dusting an extremely expensive jade statue. She managed not to drop the statue, but it was a near thing.

There were no two ways about it. The man appeared to great advantage on horseback.

Amy found herself entertaining a rather wistful longing to ride with him. Until her uncharacteristic lapse into the realms of fantasy was interrupted by a very junior housemaid, who had been instructed to inform her that his lordship refused to allow his grandmother to turn the state drawing-room, which housed innumerable priceless *objets d'art*, into a skittles alley in case the weather turned inclement.

At that point she decided that Hawkridge had formed a fiendish plot to overturn her wits, for diabolical reasons of his own, and sallied forth to try her own skills at distraction on the dowager.

Fortunately for the *objets d'art*, the weather was inclined to clemency. Everyone awoke on the appointed day to a soft misty haze that transformed itself into cloudless blue skies and brilliant sunshine by the time the gates were opened at nine o'clock.

Marc descended the stairs shortly beforehand, anticipating the pleasures of pursuit while he had an excellent excuse to spend an entire day with his quarry. Not that the past few days had been fruitless. Amy had started blushing, then frowning disapprovingly, whenever she saw him. It was a very encouraging sign.

A considerable setback, however, awaited him at the breakfast table. Crispin was sitting in Amy's place, under the doting eye of his great-grandmother, devouring food as if he hadn't seen any in a week.

'Thought I'd come over early to fetch that jib you have stored in your boathouse, Uncle Marc,' he said by way of greeting. 'Why are you dressed like that? You are going to help me clean it up, aren't you?'

'Good God, Crispin, you're as single-minded as your sister. Did you happen to notice the booths and tents set up on either side of the carriageway? We're holding a Public Day today. Good morning, Grandmama.' He bent to kiss her ladyship's cheek. 'You're looking delightful as usual. That's a very frivolous cap.'

'Thank you, dear.' The dowager twinkled up at him. 'I believe Pelham is bringing Bartholomew over. One must look one's best for such a momentous occasion.'

Marc eyed his grandparent's guileless countenance with suspicion. 'And since everyone for miles around attends these things, Mr Tweedy is sure to make an appearance. What are you up to, Grandmama?'

'Oh, just tying up a few loose ends, dearest. Have you seen Amy this morning? I wish she wouldn't work so hard, but the dear girl insisted on writing replies to those letters I gave her yesterday.'

'Don't worry. I'll see that she has the rest of the day free.'

Her ladyship beamed. 'Thank you, Marc. I thought you would.'

'What about my boat?' Crispin objected, as Marc walked over to the sideboard to help himself to a liberal portion of ham.

He turned to appraise his nephew's willowy build. 'Today you can play cricket. We need an extra man.'

Crispin looked taken aback for a moment. Then a broad smile spread across his face. 'Thank you, Uncle Marc. I haven't played cricket all that often, you know—dare say I'll be bowled out at the first ball—but it's capital sport.'

'Almost as much fun as sailing,' Marc murmured with an answering grin. 'You'd better go home, Crispin, and change out of those disreputable clothes. Put on something comfortable, it's going to be hot.'

'Right. See you later, Grandmama.' With a violent shove of his chair, Crispin was off. Pounding footsteps sounded in the hall; a second later the front door slammed.

'That boy is crying out for some male pursuits,' Marc observed as he carried his plate back to the table. 'Can't you have a word with Augusta, Grandmama?'

'I think you've already given her enough food for thought, dearest. She doesn't really wish to see Crispin become spoilt, you know, but old habits are hard to break. And he was very sickly as a small boy. To watch him struggle for air was quite terrifying.'

'Yes, I know. But Bevan should have taken a stand when Crispin grew older and got him out on the water. God knows, he used to sail as much as any of us, and it probably would've done the boy the world of good.'

'Of course, dear. I've always thought so, but you must remember that, in this particular matter, Nettlebed's feelings for your sister constrain him. It isn't only Crispin's health that concerns her. Her fear of sailing is very real. Indeed, you, too, still feel the effects of your parents' deaths.' Lady Hawkridge rose and patted his cheek on her way to the door. 'I'm so glad you've found a reason to stay at Hawkridge, Marc.'

Marc watched the door close gently behind his grandmother and gave a wry smile. His sister wasn't the only member of his family gifted with perception on that particular subject. Not that sailing held any fears for him, although he'd severely curtailed the activity out of consideration for the dowager. His reaction had gone much deeper.

He'd spent as little time as possible at Hawkridge.

He pushed his plate aside and rose to stroll over to the windows overlooking the small ornamental lake.

Mine, he thought, with a rush of possessiveness he hadn't allowed himself to feel for a very long time. Every field, every tree, every simple cotter's dwelling: his. He loved the place, had always loved riding over the land, keeping a watchful eye on the crops, discussing the latest methods of cattle-breeding with knowledgeable farmers. But those days had lost their magic when his father and grandfather had no longer been there to ride with him.

With the links to his immediate familial past abruptly severed, his future yet to unfold, emotionless duty had taken the place of the soul-deep sense of belonging that was his birthright.

But it hadn't entirely left him, he realised now. He'd been waiting; without knowing. Waiting for a reason to return home to stay. To live, to love, to reclaim his future.

With Amy.

Seized by a sudden sense of urgency, Marc wheeled, strode over to the door and flung it open. He crossed the hall in several long strides, subjected the library door to the same cavalier treatment, and opened his mouth to issue a comprehensive edict on the writing of letters when the sun was shining.

The effort was wasted. No widow possessed of a tantalising mixture of maddening reserve and mischievous charm was there to receive it.

His quarry had flown.

Amy was busily congratulating herself on finishing the dowager's letters before the crowd gathering on the lawn outside the library became too noisy. After sealing the last missive, she had exited through the french windows just as the occupants of Lavender Cottage, accompanied by Mrs Fidler and Cora, rounded the corner from the carriageway.

Shrill cries of delight greeted her appearance. Beneath the din she thought she heard a door slam somewhere, but she found herself being swept away on a tide of small children before she could glance back.

Eventually, leaving Mrs Fidler chatting with several acquaintances, the tide veered towards the stables, where her escort was rendered speechless with excitement at the offer of a ride on one of the farm horses.

'They'll talk about nothing else for a week,' Cora remarked, as the children lined up for the treat. She bounced the rosy-cheeked baby on her hip, and clucked at him.

Amy smiled and nodded, struck, not for the first time, by Cora's quiet manner of speech. She was a tall girl, too thin for her inches, but with her guinea-gold hair and blue eyes, already regaining her looks after a fortnight at Lavender Cottage. She was also a talented seamstress.

Amy was determined to see Cora set up her own dressmaker's establishment, where she'd be able to keep her child with her and earn enough to do more than survive.

'How is the little man?' she cooed, as the baby grinned at her with toothless charm. 'May I hold him a moment, Cora? He's so adorable.'

'He's likely to dribble on your pretty gown, ma'am.'

'As if that matters,' Amy said, taking the baby. 'Are you cutting a tooth, then, little fellow?' She planted a kiss on one flushed cheek and nuzzled his neck, breathing in the sweet baby scent. He gurgled happily in response and batted her with a playful fist. Taking the hint, Amy lifted him into the air.

That was how Marc found her as he strode into the stableyard. The sun shone on the tawny curls peeping from beneath the most ridiculous little cap he'd ever seen, her muslin gown shifted lovingly over her curves, and she was laughing, swooping a baby into the air and making the child laugh, too.

The kick of desire caught him so hard it almost knocked him backwards. He stopped short, braced against a raging torrent of lust, until he thought he had himself under control. At this point it wouldn't help his cause to throw Amy into the nearest stall and take her on a pile of straw until she was helpless and clinging to him.

But that was precisely what he wanted to do. And seeing her with the baby made it worse. He wanted it to be *his* baby she was holding. He wanted her to belong to him in the most primitive way possible. To plant his seed in her body and watch her grow big with his child. He wanted it with a fierce longing that startled even him.

He had a sudden premonition that it was going to be like this for the rest of his life. Every time he came upon Amy unexpectedly. Baby or no baby.

The thought didn't bother him particularly—given his nature he could expect nothing less—but if he didn't put them both into a position where he could do something about it in the immediate future, he simply wouldn't be answerable for the consequences.

To hell with discretion in public, he decided in that moment. He'd just have to see that no one got near enough to Amy to meddle before he'd declared himself in private.

Setting his jaw, he strode forward.

The baby took one look at his face and burst into tears.

Chaos and mayhem erupted.

Dogs started barking wildly, leaping about, overturning pails and sending what had been an orderly line of children shrieking in all directions. His horses, unaccustomed to ear-splitting wails and loud clanging disturbing the peace of their existence, set up an accompanying chorus of protest and threatened to kick their stalls to pieces.

Amy and a girl he assumed was the baby's mother both started cooing like agitated pigeons in an attempt to stem the flood.

Everyone else turned to see what had caused the commotion. His grooms, who had all been standing around with vacuous smiles on their faces as they watched Amy play with the infant, indulged in one second of shock at his presence, then leapt into action. One scurried around gathering up children, another tried to quiet the dogs, the rest vanished into the stables to calm their precious charges.

Marc smiled grimly after them, then tried to soften the expression when he reached Amy.

The baby cried harder.

'Oh, dear, I can't imagine what is the matter with him,' Amy was saying, frantically trying to soothe her burden. 'Perhaps his tooth came through.'

'Here, give him to me, ma'am. He might have a bit of wind.'

'If I could make a suggestion,' Marc began.

Amy squeaked and jumped. 'Good heavens, my lord! Must you creep up on me like that? I almost dropped the baby.'

Marc eyed the bundle sobbing pitifully on its mother's shoulder and winced. 'I think I might have startled him,' he confessed.

'Well, if you insist on sneaking up on people like that, I'm not surprised. Go away at once.'

'For heaven's sake, ma'am...'

'It's all right...Cora, isn't it?' He smiled at the girl. 'Mrs Chantry is correct, as usual. We shall depart forthwith.'

'We?' Amy blinked at him. 'I didn't say—'

He cut her off by the simple expedient of taking her hand and tucking it into the crook of his arm. Then covered it with his other hand to prevent any escape. 'I really must insist that you accompany me, Mrs Chantry. Who knows how many susceptible infants may be scattered about the place? I'll need you to steer me clear of them.'

'But—' She glanced distractedly about the yard. The dogs were sulking at having their fun cut short, pails had been righted, the children were back in their places. 'The children haven't finished their rides.'

'All the more reason for us to leave while they're occupied.'

'But—'

With a conspiratory smile for Cora, which left her open-mouthed, he led Amy away. 'Amy, my love, I applaud your motives in starting Lavender Cottage. I will be more than happy for you to expand on the project if you wish, but I don't intend to be accompanied by a tribe of small children for the rest of the day.'

Amy's head threatened to spin as she tried to sort all that out. Several things rang ominous warning bells. The trouble was, she didn't know which bell was ringing loudest. The warm weight of Hawkridge's hand over hers didn't help in the decision.

'Um...I don't think it's proper for you to address me so informally, sir.' She might as well start at the top of the list.

'Why not?' he asked, refusing to co-operate.

She frowned. 'It supposes a closer relationship than, er...'

'Don't tell me you're a servant, Amy, because you're not.'

'Well, not precisely, but—'

'You can call me Marc, if it will make you feel better.'

She almost tasted his name on the tip of her tongue. Fortunately she stopped herself in time. 'That would be most improper, my lord. A companion does not put herself forward.'

'Just as well,' he murmured with a startling about-face. He came to a halt where the path from the stables met the carriageway. On their left lay the shrubbery. To the right the windows of the Manor gleamed benignly down on the crowds scattered over the lawn. 'I won't have to worry about you throwing yourself into the front line before hostilities commence.'

'What!' Her brain reeled anew. 'What *are* you talking about now, sir?'

'Colborough has arrived, armed with cane. And if I'm not mistaken, the smugly smiling butterball mincing along with Grandmama on his arm is Tweedy. Remind me to have a word with him when Colborough's finished. If there's anything left.'

'Oh, my goodness!' She stared in dismay from one party to the other. Colborough had clearly sighted prey and, brows beetling, head thrust forward, was bent on a collision course. 'Do something, my lord! We can't have bloodshed on the south lawn!'

'Why not? Tweedy deserves to lose a pint or two. For threatening you, if nothing else.'

'But...' She made a grab for her wits as they whirled past on the carousel that was her mind. 'He didn't threaten me. At least, not precisely. And I told you the other day he means nothing to Lady—'

'You told me not to interfere,' he interrupted ruthlessly. 'You also implied that Grandmama knows what she's doing.' He studied Colborough's rapidly reddening countenance. 'I hope you're right.'

'Oh, heavens!' Amy would have wrung her hands, but she was too busy trying to push Hawkridge towards the rapidly closing space between the combatants. It was like trying to push a wall. He didn't resist; he simply didn't move.

'This is no time for levity, my lord. Speak to Lord Colborough! Fetch Lord Eversleigh! *Do something!*'

He grinned. 'You may cease panicking, Mrs Chantry. Grandmama is veering off into the shrubbery in a manoeuvre that would turn Wellington green with envy. What are the odds that by the time Colborough reaches the spot, she and Tweedy will have vanished?'

'I am not interested in betting, my lord. Oh, my goodness, what am I saying? This won't be the end of it. You'll still have to—'

'Good God, you're right.' Turning on his heel in a move as rapidly executed as the dowager's, Hawkridge started towards the other side of the house. Amy had the choice of being whisked off her feet, or accompanying him. She chose the more dignified option.

'What are you doing, sir? It is no use leaving. Lord Colborough will only confront Mr Tweedy another time.'

'Grandmama can fight her own battles.' He slanted a challenging glance down at her. 'Isn't that what you prefer to do, Mrs Chantry? Which, I might add, is an attitude directly opposed to your attempt just now to shove me into the breach.'

She flushed. 'I didn't think you'd noticed.'

'I notice everything.'

'Indeed?' She glared at him. 'Then why didn't you go where I was trying to put you?'

'Because I didn't feel like being mowed down by Colborough. Nothing short of knocking him down would have prevented that unhappy outcome. Of course, if you have any other suggestions as to the disposal of my person, I'd be happy to hear them.'

'Don't tempt me, sir.'

He started to grin. 'You must admit the day promises to be interesting.' They turned the far corner of the house as he spoke and he paused to cast a comprehensive glance over the colourful throng on the lawn. 'In fact,' he added rather thoughtfully, 'very interesting.'

Amy followed his gaze. Several people seemed to be eyeing their sudden appearance with smiles of approval and satisfaction. She realised her hand was still tucked snugly in Hawkridge's arm and snatched it free.

'You appear to be very popular, my lord. No doubt everyone is happy to see you in residence.'

'If it comforts you to think so, Mrs Chantry.' He met her suspicious stare with a bland smile. 'Since we've arrived at the area set aside for civilised pastimes, would you like to try something? Archery, perhaps?'

Amy was not in the mood for civilised pastimes. 'Only if you're the target,' she retorted. Then closed her eyes in horror. 'Oh, no. Tell me I didn't say that.'

His shout of laughter had her cautiously slitting one eyelid open.

'You said it.' Wicked grey eyes glinted down at her. 'But on second thoughts, we'll try something else. Your aim, Mrs Chantry, is already far too accurate.'

Amy decided not to ask for clarification on anything Hawkridge might say that day. It was all too nerve-racking.

Deliciously nerve-racking.

She promptly read herself a lecture on the dangers of deliciously tingling nerves.

Despite the lecture, her nerves continued to tingle at odd moments during the morning. Hawkridge was entirely to blame for the phenomenon. Whenever he was stopped by a visitor, or drawn into conversation with one of his tenants, Amy very properly continued on her way, only to find him back at her side when she walked around a booth or paused to watch a game of horse-shoes.

She was wondering whether she should issue a protest in the interests of propriety—and whether he'd take any notice of it—when she caught a glimpse of the dowager through a gap in the crowd and was promptly distracted.

'Look there, sir! Lady Hawkridge has exchanged Mr Tweedy for Lord Colborough.'

Hawkridge turned his head, his height giving him a considerable advantage in locating his grandparent. 'So she has. I wonder how she managed the task, or if she had some assistance from Colborough?'

'Oh, dear. How can you say that with such unconcern? What do you think has become of Mr Tweedy?'

'I neither know nor care.' He cast a curious glance down at her. 'I wouldn't have thought you cared a fig for Tweedy's fate, either.'

'I don't wish to see the man come to any harm. After all, he didn't actually threaten me in person.'

'Good God,' he muttered. 'A babe in the woods. You should be locked up for your own good.'

Amy glared at him. 'I'm not quite the fragile little flower you seem to think me, sir. What's more, Mr Tweedy doesn't frighten me. And I must say it would serve you right if his lifeless body was to be discovered by some innocent visitor.'

His frown vanished in a burst of laughter. 'God, you're a delight. You know, Amy, when you cease being a companion, you might try your hand at writing Gothic tales.'

Amy's eyes widened. She stopped walking so abruptly her hand slipped from his arm. A quite hideous tremor of uncertainty caused the bright morning to dim suddenly, as if a cloud had passed over the sun. 'Why should I cease being a companion, sir?'

'For no reason that should alarm you,' he said immediately, sounding contrite. When she didn't respond, he touched a finger to her chin, tilting her face up to his. 'Don't worry,' he said softly. 'I phrased that rather badly. I certainly don't wish to see you depart.'

Just try it and see what happens, he added silently.

'Oh, well...' Amy lowered her lashes and looked away, flustered by the sudden fierceness in his grey eyes. Fortunately, Lady Hawkridge hove into view again, flitting from group to group like an animated butterfly towing a large cocoon in its wake. She noticed that Colborough had abandoned his cane in the interests of keeping up with the dowager's erratic progress.

It suddenly occurred to her that though her ladyship's progress appeared erratic, she was forging a similar path through the crowd to the one she and Hawkridge were taking, rather in the manner of an advance guard.

The notion struck her forcibly enough to have her digging in her heels when Hawkridge started off again.

'What's the matter?' he demanded. 'We can't stand here. Mrs Tredgett's seen us.'

'What? Oh...'

'Good morning, Mrs Chantry. My lord.' Mrs Tredgett's voice boomed out over the crowd, rendering escape impossible.

'Good morning, ma'am,' they chorused like a pair of obedient children. Amy met his eyes and had to smother a giggle.

Mrs Tredgett marched up to them. 'Perfect day,' she barked. 'See your roses are well advanced.' Having disposed of the niceties, she looked at Amy and waved her stick in the direction of her head. 'What's that you've got on your head, child?'

Amy blinked. 'A cap, ma'am.'

'Ridiculous piece of nonsense. No, don't start blathering on about being a widow. I've been a widow for forty years, but no one ever saw me wearing such fripperies. Might as well put a brand on a girl when she's still got her life ahead of her. Take it off. You're young enough to get away with it.'

Amy managed to close her mouth on yet another repetition that she was a widow. Thank goodness she hadn't needed to utter it; for a minute there she'd thought Mrs Tredgett had wanted to save her the trouble because she wouldn't have believed the statement.

She realised her fingers were gripping Hawkridge's arm, and relaxed her hold.

'I couldn't agree more, ma'am,' he said, watching her narrowly under the guise of examining her offending headwear. 'But such fripperies have their uses, you know.'

Mrs Tredgett chortled wheezily. 'And I'd wager you know 'em all,' she said, punching him playfully on the arm.

Hawkridge stood up manfully under the blow. 'A gentleman never contradicts a lady,' he murmured.

Amy nearly choked as Mrs Tredgett rocked about with laughter. Fortunately a seizure was prevented by Miss Pucklenett's breathless arrival.

'Good heavens, Maude, are you all right? You've gone quite purple in the face. How do you do, my lord? How do you do, Mrs Chantry? I've just been on a tour of the state rooms. Such elegance. Such exquisitely rendered ceiling murals. We were even permitted a tiny peep into the muniment room and the winter parlour, although they weren't strictly included in the tour.'

Mrs Tredgett recovered her voice and snorted. 'Anyone would think you'd never seen it all before, Clara. Pack of busybodies, if you ask me. Surprised you didn't march right through his lordship's bedchamber.'

'Heavens, Maude!' Miss Pucklenett's face turned bright red. 'What a thing to say. I assure you, sir...'

'It's all right, Miss Pucklenett. I gave strict instructions that my bedchamber was to be locked.'

Miss Pucklenett eyed him as one would an incendiary firecracker.

'And how are the Society's ducks coming along?' he asked with a fiendish smile. 'They *are* still ducks, I presume, and haven't been transformed into frogs?'

Miss Pucklenett promptly fell into a morass of half-sentences, flustered explanations and stammered excuses. She was eventually stopped by Mrs Tredgett who took her arm in a firm hold. 'Told you so, Clara. Silliest idea I ever heard, changing the name of the inn. Don't wonder his lordship put his foot down. But come along. We've taken up enough of everyone's time. Plenty more people waiting to meet Mrs Chantry, you know.'

She led Miss Pucklenett, whose mouth was still mutely opening and closing, towards the refreshment stall.

Amy gazed after them in consternation.

'No wonder Mrs Tredgett's been a widow for forty years,'

Hawkridge observed. 'Mr Tredgett obviously departed for safer surroundings.'

'Um...'

'Her presence also explains why we haven't seen Pel all morning.'

'Yes, I dare say. My lord, what did Mrs Tredgett mean about people wanting to meet me?'

'Nothing in particular,' he said, resisting the urge to bend down and kiss the frown from her brow. 'Merely the natural interest everyone has in the happenings on the estates roundabout.'

'Oh.' That was a reasonable explanation, Amy supposed.

They started off again and she caught another glimpse of the dowager, still moving ahead of them. Perhaps there was a set pattern to these things. After all, what did she know about Public Days?

She proceeded to learn. She learned that she'd been right in saying that Hawkridge was popular and that everyone was happy to see him—but the level of happiness seemed beyond what was usual, as if he'd never attended a Public Day before.

She learned that everyone wanted a chance to greet the lord of the manor—but that their greetings were so enthusiastic they struck her as more in the manner of a welcome; as if he'd returned after an absence of years, instead of paying regular, if brief, visits to his home.

She learned that nobody thought it odd that her hand remained tucked snugly into the crook of Hawkridge's arm, and decided, tentatively, that anyone who lived under his aegis was automatically accepted.

But it was all very odd. And there was something else about the beaming smiles on everyone's face that puzzled her. A kind of pleased satisfaction.

She would have been happy to join in the general air of approval, but she had the distinct feeling that she formed an unenlightened minority of one.

After a while, however, she forgot to worry about it. Once she and Hawkridge had traversed the lawn a couple of times, he declared his duty to be done and that it was time to enjoy themselves.

And Amy learned something else, something utterly irresistible. That, with Hawkridge, she could have fun.

Suddenly it was incredibly easy to converse with him, to laugh at the antics of a pair of puppets; to scold when they encountered Miss Twinhoe and he promptly threw that lady into confusion by expressing the hope that her heart-rending tale had lost nothing in the telling; to tease and coax him into letting her try her skill with a bow and arrow after all.

She learned how very safe she felt half-encircled in his arms as he showed her how to aim and release the bowstring; and how ridiculously thrilled she could be when she actually hit the target.

She learned that magic existed.

Somewhere, far, far back in her mind, a little voice warned that the sunny hours would disappear, taking the magic with them, but as morning flowed into afternoon it was easy to ignore the voice of caution. By the time a crowd gathered to watch the traditional cricket match, and she found herself ensconced on a rug beneath an ancient oak in company with the dowager and Lady Nettlebed, it had been silenced completely.

She settled back happily while Eversleigh's team accumulated an impressive number of runs, laughing with the rest whenever Nettlebed, who was the referee, had his decisions hotly debated.

'I don't know why Bevan puts himself through this year after year,' observed Augusta, idly waving a fan to move the warm, still air beneath the trees.

'Yes you do, dear.' The dowager patted her hand. 'Nettlebed would far rather argue than run up and down a cricket pitch.'

'Well, at least he can keep an eye on Crispin while he's out there. You don't think he's looking a little over-heated, do you, Grandmama?'

'Nettlebed, definitely. Crispin looks perfectly stout.'

Lady Nettlebed sighed. 'Oh, dear. I am *trying* not to be a fuss-budget.'

'Yes, I know, dear.'

'Do the boy good to run about a little,' Colborough put in gruffly.

He was ensconced in a rather magisterial fashion on a chair next to Lady Hawkridge, keeping up a running commentary on the players' skill, or lack of it. Amy cast a glance from him to the dowager, and was suddenly struck by something in their expressions. There was nothing blatantly obvious in their manner, but her ladyship's usual bright smile seemed to have a touch of smugness about it, while Colborough wore a resigned, but definitely proprietary air whenever he glanced at her.

She found herself wondering, not for the first time, about Tweedy's fate.

'Good God!' Colborough exploded, making her jump and switch her attention to the match. 'Told Pelham he should've given the lads a few pointers, but no. Said they'd played before. Where, might I ask? Look at that fool up at bat. Doesn't know a thing about the game. There! What did I tell you? Caught out!'

'Never mind, Tolly. That was the last of your batsmen. We can have tea.'

They had tea under the oaks; Pickles leading a procession of servants, bearing drinks and delicacies, out from the house. Everyone else who had stayed to watch the match converged on the stalls set up to dispense lemonade and ices.

And Amy forgot all about Colborough, Tweedy and the dowager. She took the teacup a maid handed her without taking her eyes off Hawkridge as he strode across the lawn towards her.

He'd stripped off his coat and cravat at the start of the match, but now his sleeves were rolled up to the elbows and he'd loosened the neck of his shirt. With his muscled forearms exposed, his face and throat sheened with sweat, and his black hair hanging over his brow, he looked more like one of his own grooms than a peer of the realm. Until one saw the authority stamped on his face.

He also looked thoroughly disreputable, heart-stoppingly handsome and more than a little dangerous.

Amy found herself fanning her face with a leafy twig, although she couldn't have said why she suddenly felt so flushed. It didn't help her soaring temperature that he came directly to her side and hunkered down on his heels, his eyes glittering, appearing lighter than ever in his tanned face.

'Enjoying yourself?' he asked, smiling at her with that warm light she'd noticed several times that day.

Quite ridiculously thrown by the question, she nodded and took cover behind her tea.

'Here you are, Marc.' Lady Nettlebed handed her brother a tall glass of chilled tea. 'I thought you might prefer this to a cup.'

'You thought correctly,' he said, and standing, tipped his head back and drained the glass with several long swallows.

Amy's gaze widened as she watched the process. One stray drop of tea escaped, trickled over his chin, and travelled downwards, slowly. Down over tanned, gleaming flesh, down over the rippling muscles of his throat, down into the opening of his shirt. Down.

She followed it. In her imagination. Down through the thicket of hair glimpsed through the fine lawn of his shirt, all the way down to his waist.

That's where she stopped, because suddenly she was looking at his face again where his waist had been a second ago.

She blinked, and went absolutely still, staring straight into eyes that had gone from warm to scorching in seconds.

He wanted her. There was no mistaking it. She'd never seen such savage, searing desire in a man's eyes, but every feminine instinct she possessed recognised it—and responded. She felt a shuddering urge to lie down, a need to *surrender*. The sense of acceptance, of awareness, that struck her in that moment was absolute, and utterly terrifying.

To her everlasting relief, Lady Nettlebed returned with another drink, and broke the spell.

'I hope you noticed that I haven't run, clucking, to Crispin's side,' she said archly as Hawkridge stood up. 'Although I'd rather he played cricket than sail.'

Hawkridge took the glass, demolished its contents—Amy didn't dare watch this time—and thrust it back into his sister's hand. 'I noticed.'

Lady Nettlebed's brows rose.

'Listen, Gus,' he said, in the same curt tone. 'If Crispin is boat-mad, the best thing I can do is teach him the proper way of going about things. And you might have a word to Bevan to that effect. God knows, the damn boat used to be his.'

'I already have,' Lady Nettlebed admitted. Then gave a rather resigned sigh. 'If nothing else, the situation has brought Crispin closer to his father. Thank you for that, Marc.'

A faint smile touched his mouth. 'I'll repeat what I've already told you, Gussie. We won't sail out of the cove until Crispin knows what he's doing, he's promised he won't sail alone, and he'll wear a life-belt whenever we're out on the water. All right?'

His sister returned his smile with a wry one of her own, gave him a swift hug and returned to her husband's side.

Hawkridge watched her for a second, half-turned as though he would speak to Amy, then wheeled and strode back out to the pitch, his hands fisted at his sides.

Amy discovered she'd been holding her breath throughout the entire exchange. She gasped in some badly needed air. Good heavens, the heat must have melted her brain. She must have lost her senses. Surely Hawkridge hadn't looked at her as if...as if...

But he had.

And that wasn't all. She had the dreadful feeling that if he'd made one move towards her, just one, she would have lain back on the grass and let him...

Oh, heavens. She didn't know what, didn't dare think about it.

No wonder Kitty Ingham had broken her engagement, she thought suddenly as her restless, darting gaze halted on that lady.

Lord Colborough's remarks flashed through her mind; comprehension exploded with blinding clarity. No wonder Lord Ashcroft had entertained doubts about the entire business. Hawkridge might be able to conceal his true nature from society in general, but not from men who'd known him all his life. What father would want his innocent, gently bred daughter to face that blistering intensity on her wedding night?

The knowledge that she'd not only faced it when Hawkridge had kissed her, but thrilled to it, sent streamers of heat flowing through her.

But he'd done nothing since.

Amy clutched her tea-cup as if the delicate china could somehow anchor her while she sorted out her wildly spinning thoughts. Hawkridge hadn't made any advances. At least, not the sort of advances a woman in her position could expect.

Of course, until she'd stared at him in that very improper manner, she hadn't given him any reason to suppose she would be amenable to improper advances. The thought that he might do something about it, *now*, made her tremble.

The realisation that immediately followed, that he would not, had her lips parting on a silent gasp of discovery.

Her gaze flew to where he was standing, tall and powerful, as he waited for Pelham to send down the first ball; the hard line of his mouth and the determined set of his jaw indicative of the fierce will that drove him. He possessed all the natural arrogance of a man used to commanding what he wanted, but it was also the dominance of a man whose first instinct was to protect, whose strength of will was built on a foundation of unshakeable honour.

He would no more dishonour her than he would himself.

Amy put her tea-cup carefully on the grass and contemplated the discovery that somehow, at some point in the past few days, she'd come to trust him. It made her feel incredibly safe. At the same time, the faintest whisper of sadness stirred at the back of her mind.

No, not sadness precisely. Wistfulness, perhaps.

She pushed the notion aside. She should be grateful for the sense of security that wrapped her around. She *was* grateful. No one knew the dangers to a woman of clandestine relationships better than she.

But as the match resumed, the dangers of improper liaisons faded slowly into oblivion. The vision of Hawkridge wielding a devastatingly effective bat drove every thought out of her head— except a deliciously improper, purely feminine appreciation of sheer masculine power.

The sight was riveting.

The return to earth, when it came, was shattering.

There was no warning. Nothing. She heard Lucinda call her name, looked up—

And looked straight into the face of disaster; into the face of the one man she had hoped never to see again.

Into the face of her husband.

Chapter Eleven

Amy froze. There was nothing else she could do. She went absolutely still while ice-cold fear trickled down her spine and her hands dampened. Lucinda's lips were moving, but she couldn't hear what the girl was saying. The world she'd created was shattering at her feet in vicious, razor-edged shards, waiting for her to take the first mis-step that would tear her to pieces.

Then, as a sharp crack from the direction of the lawn heralded another six, the world snapped back into place. A different world, perhaps, but one worth fighting for. Her mind went as cold and clear as the sheen of ice on her skin. As cold and clear as the mocking smile in the eyes of the man Lucinda was introducing as Jeremy Chatsworth.

He bowed. 'How do you do, Mrs Chantry?'

Oh, yes, she remembered those smooth tones, the polished bow. He held out his hand, quite confident she would respond.

And she did. She had no choice. Not here. Not now. She extended her hand; her fingers were enveloped, and pressed around the folded square of paper he slid into her palm.

'Mr Chatsworth,' she acknowledged coolly, and knew she hadn't betrayed herself. And *he* wouldn't expose her; to do so would be to expose his own lies. He would want a meeting before he did anything. He'd been very good at arranging meetings.

She laid her hand on her lap and waited. She was even able to summon a faint smile for Lucinda as the girl sat beside her.

'Is he not charming?' she whispered to Amy, as Chatsworth

began talking to the dowager under the cold gaze of Lady ̶
bed. 'Is he not the most elegant gentleman you've ever seen?'

'Actually,' Amy returned coolly, 'I consider your uncle to be more elegant.'

'What! Uncle Marc!' Lucinda gaped across the lawn. 'Well, all I can say, Amy, is that you have a very odd notion of elegance. And, what's more, Jeremy is a great deal more amusing than Hawkridge.'

'I'm sure you think so.'

Lucinda's brows met for an instant. 'You sound rather strange. Are you feeling quite the thing?'

'No, as a matter of fact. I think it's the heat.' An avenue of escape opened.

'But you're quite pale.' Lucinda peered closer. 'Very pale, actually. You're not going to faint, are you? Jeremy particularly wishes to become acquainted with you.'

'I'm afraid our acquaintance will have to wait,' Amy said, rising to her feet. She managed the task of staying upright by the simple expedient of imagining the furore that would ensue if she didn't. Fortunately, her movement caught Lady Hawkridge's attention, making it unnecessary for her to intrude on the conversation.

'If you don't mind, ma'am,' she began before anyone else could comment on her lack of colour. 'I'll return to the house for a while. I have a slight headache.'

'Oh, dear. Are you sure, Amy? You'll miss the rest of the match.'

'Yes, I know. I'm sorry. I think it's the heat.' She wondered how often she'd be required to repeat the excuse before she could get away.

But the dowager nodded. 'I don't wonder at it. Lie down with a cool cloth over your brow, and you'll be better in a trice. Lucinda, go with her.'

'*No!* Please,' Amy added in a milder tone as several heads turned. 'I just need to be somewhere cooler for a while.'

'Of course, dear. Off you go.'

'Perhaps I could escort you, Mrs Chantry.' Jeremy Chatsworth leapt to his feet with what he no doubt considered to be the epitome of masculine grace.

She'd once thought so, too, Amy remembered.

She swept him an uninterested gaze, determined to have a moment alone before she had to confront him. 'No, thank you, sir.'

Turning, she walked away towards the house, conscious of a vague sense of astonishment that she could move at all when every joint and muscle felt frozen. Even when she emerged from the trees into full sunlight, there was no difference. The heat bounced off her as if she was encased in stone.

But her mind moved swiftly; thinking, thinking.

She wondered if Hawkridge had seen her leave.

That caused her to falter. She stopped, looked back. Everyone appeared very small and far away, she thought vaguely. Almost... faded. As if she'd stepped out of a misty painting.

But she could see Hawkridge clearly.

Something tore at her heart. A swift burning slash.

Perhaps it was the last tiny thread of magic being ripped away. It was silly, really, but she couldn't stop the sudden pang of wistful longing for what might have been. If the magic of the day had been real.

If it had been Hawkridge she'd met two years ago.

If he'd been of her station.

If.

Amy shook her head, set wistfulness firmly to one side, and, realising in that second that she was completely unobserved, took the few sideways steps necessary to take her into the shrubbery and out of sight.

The note had told her to meet him on the beach in ten minutes.

Well, he would just have to wait, Amy thought as she trod resolutely down the steps outside the Inghams' gates. She wasn't tackling the stony path leading to the beach below Hawkridge Manor for anyone. The stairs at least had a railing to hold on to. And the time spent walking back towards the Manor was necessary to prepare herself.

She stepped on to the pebbled beach, keeping her eyes on the uneven surface as she made her way around outcroppings of rock and small sunlit pools, until the pebbles became more scattered and she was walking on the strip of sand that formed a narrow crescent-shaped beach at the foot of the cliffs at Hawkridge. The sea whispered a few yards away, its secrets hidden beneath the sparkling blue surface.

She'd been here once before, with the dowager, and had been enchanted by the wild solitude of the place, the rugged cliffs, the crenellated formations of rocks that gave the beach the appearance of another world.

Now the almost-empty landscape looked strangely forbidding, even in the mellow golden light of late afternoon. A few people were still about, but they were some distance away and strolling in the same direction as herself, making their way back to the path and the Manor.

Not that she wanted anyone to witness her meeting with Chatsworth. So far she'd been lucky. Most of the people whom she'd met that morning were at the cricket match, and other visitors had been leaving in large enough quantities for her exit through the side gate to go unremarked.

Chatsworth had chosen his time well.

She wondered if Lucinda knew of the meeting. If the girl had been told a clandestine meeting with Amy was necessary if she was to help them. She wished she'd thought to mention it to Lucinda, herself. She might not want witnesses, but the thought that no one knew where she was, or who she was with, was suddenly very disquieting.

But it was too late. She glanced up to find the man she'd known as James Chantry leaning against a large rock a few paces away and staring out to sea.

The cynical thought that the pose allowed her to admire his profile had a surprisingly calming effect on her nerves.

Amy took a deep breath and walked forward.

He turned his head as she approached. 'You took your time,' he said without preamble.

She gave a short inward laugh. A good thing she hadn't expected a concerned query about how she'd survived the past year. 'I didn't think you'd leave Lucinda so soon, James,' she answered mildly. 'Especially when you appear to have just arrived.'

He shrugged that off. 'Have to keep her eager for my company.'

His lips twisted contemptuously. 'And the rest were only too happy to see me go.'

'Yes, well, you can hardly blame them for that.' She studied him, seeing few changes since their last meeting, when the scales had well and truly fallen from her eyes. 'Is that your real name?' she asked abruptly. 'James Chantry? Or is it Jeremy Chatsworth?'

'The first,' he said. And studied her thoughtfully. 'Don't worry, Amy. We're definitely married. I've been standing here wondering if that's an advantage or not.'

'Feel free to procure a divorce at any time,' she retorted.

He gave a short laugh. 'Still an innocent. Divorce requires several expensive steps, dear wife, resulting in an Act of Parliament. People of our station don't trot into the House of Lords every day and demand one. And an annulment,' he added smoothly, 'would prove most embarrassing for you. After all, I was perfectly capable of performing my husbandly duties. It was you who always found an excuse to avoid your obligations.'

Her chin lifted. 'I deserved more than a hurried tumble on your mistress's bed, James.'

'You didn't know Nan was my mistress at the time.'

'Maybe I sensed she was more than a friend when I discovered you were living with her! But that doesn't matter. We've had this argument before. You found me employment where the maids had to live in and were supposed to be unmarried. Did you expect me to open the back door and smuggle you into the house at night?'

'Why not?' he asked carelessly. 'You made sure I knew about the broken latch on the dining-room window so I could rob the place.'

She gasped and flinched back as if he'd struck her. 'That was unintentional. You *questioned* me, before I knew—'

She broke off as accusations and explanations tumbled through her mind with a speed that left her utterly sure of the conclusions. But she still had to ask. She still had to *hear* it.

Perhaps it was a perverse sense of her own guilt that had her wanting the final confirmation. Like probing a continually aching wound.

'Are you responsible for those robberies at Bristol? Did you set your friend up as a maid in one of those houses, like you did me, so she could let you in and pretend to be tied up with the rest?'

His smile mocked the memories evident in her shaking voice. 'You weren't as co-operative, if you recall, Amy. Bloody ungrateful, in fact, considering all the trouble I went to for you. Yes, the Bristol robberies were my work. I needed money after I met Lucinda.'

'But the last robbery was less than a week ago.'

'God, Amy, you ought to know that money doesn't stretch far when you're living in this sort of style.' He ran his gaze over her. 'You must have spent a bit yourself.'

She ignored that. 'So...it was you who sent me that cutting. It wasn't Tweedy.'

'Tweedy? What made you think it was him?'

'He brought the mail into the house that morning. The paper with my name on it was on top. Do you mean he had nothing to do with it? You don't know him?'

'Never met the man until a fortnight ago. He was merely a distraction for Hawkridge's groom. It was easy to slip the note into the pile of mail on the seat of Mawson's gig while Tweedy was begging a lift. I didn't expect him to actually deliver it, but I'm not surprised he couldn't resist nosing through the stack.'

So Tweedy was of no importance to her. His words that day had been pure spite, motivated by his ambitions towards the dowager. And, she thought suddenly, she wouldn't be surprised if they never saw him again. Colborough appeared to have routed him completely.

She realised Chatsworth was still speaking. Somehow it was easier to call him that in her mind. To give herself some badly needed distance from the threat he posed.

'I thought the cutting would give you a little warning before I turned up out of the blue,' he was saying. 'Which is more than the bloody nasty start you gave me when I saw you at Nettlebed Place the other night.'

He rapped it out as if she should have had more consideration. Amy inwardly shook her head. 'I saw you, too, but I thought...' She gestured slightly. 'The dyed hair is obvious, but...'

He shrugged. 'A little padding in the shoulders of my coat, a higher heel on the shoes. It's amazing how one's appearance can be changed with a little ingenuity and effort.'

'Costly effort, I imagine. You look finer than when I met you.'

'All in a worthy cause. But you can relax, Amy. The third robbery was the last. Nan's gone back to London. You can't have the same maid hiring on and disappearing too many times in the one town, and she was starting to nag me to tell her what else I'm getting up to. Still, it netted me enough to last until—'

'Until what? Until you seduce Lucinda? You won't find her so easy, James. She's headstrong, but she knows her own worth.'

'Then she won't refuse marriage. And headstrong suits my purposes very well.'

Amy stared at him, horrified. 'But you *can't* marry her! It would be bigamy!'

He laughed aloud at that, but a second later his eyes narrowed, almost with hatred. 'You know, you're a dangerous woman, Amy. That innocent, fragile look pulls a man in, makes him want to look after you. Until he discovers the truth.'

'And that is?'

'You're strong-minded. Too bloody strong-minded. It's not a trait men want in a woman. Especially when added to stubbornness, independence, and a damned inconvenient set of morals. If you want to get on in this world, let our situation be a lesson to you. You quickly lose your appeal and become a nuisance.'

'Thank you,' she said drily. 'I'm glad you explained that to me. For several weeks I actually blamed myself for driving you into another woman's arms, because I wouldn't join you in London until Mama...'

'You *were* to blame,' he interjected nastily when she faltered. 'But never mind that. Just make sure your morals don't get in my way this time.'

'I don't know why you expect me to put a spoke in your wheel, James. Lord Nettlebed is no fool. If you offer for his daughter, he'll immediately make enquiries into your background and that will be the end of it.'

'Not quite. When Nettlebed discovers that Jeremy Chatsworth has no background, he'll pay handsomely through the nose to be rid of me. Especially when he knows his darling, headstrong daughter is capable of eloping.'

'And if Lucinda refuses to elope?'

'I've already thought of that,' he said, in such a dismissive tone that she hoped, fervently, that Lucinda's heart wasn't truly engaged. 'Seeing you with the old lady the other night gave me the idea. If nothing else works out, you're perfectly placed to help me toss the Manor. Some of the stuff in there must be worth a bloody fortune.'

'Are you *mad*?' She stared at him in amazement. 'If I wouldn't help you before, what makes you think I'll help you now?'

'Because if you don't,' he said very softly, 'if you even breathe a word to anyone about anything I've told you, I'll be forced to reveal the details of the Tinsley job to the proper authorities. Anonymously.'

Fear clamped an ice-cold vise around her heart. Her stomach churned. 'I didn't know what you intended! I—'

A snap of his fingers cut her off. 'Do you think they'll care a fig for that? Oh, no, Amy. Not when you took your share of the proceeds and ran.'

He was right. Dear God, he was right, and the knowledge haunted her every waking moment. And most of her sleeping ones as well.

'It was that or sell myself. Or go back...'

'To the poorhouse,' he finished for her. 'Well, whenever you feel like refusing to co-operate, remember that life in the Hulks or on a convict ship is worse than the poorhouse.'

She didn't answer. Let him think her frightened, cowed by the threat of transportation or worse. He was looking so satisfied, so smugly confident that his threat would keep her under control.

And why not? She'd never defied him before. Never flatly refused to fall in with his plans. She'd been horrified, disillusioned, frightened by the glimpse of violent temper he'd shown her. She'd argued. She'd pleaded. But she hadn't defied him.

She'd fled.

'We'd better go back,' she said quietly, and turned away to retrace her steps. 'It's getting late.'

He gave a satisfied grunt and straightened away from the rock. 'Where the hell are you going? The path's over here.'

'I prefer to use the stairs beyond that outcrop of rocks.'

'Don't be an idiot, Amy. The tide's coming in.'

She stared in dismay as she realised Chatsworth was right. They hadn't been on the beach all that long, but apparently time made no difference to the tide. Water was sweeping up to the rocks, cascading into the pools she'd picked her way around earlier, rushing into crevices and exploding in fountains of spray when it could go no further. Even from where she stood, the power of the waves was awesome. Apart from the inconvenience of getting wet to the knees—or higher by the time she reached the spot—if she lost her footing on that treacherous section of beach she'd be swept under before she knew it.

But the path didn't look any more inviting.

Amy glanced up at it and called herself every kind of fool for being where she was in the first place. The cliff at this point wasn't precisely vertical, but it was steep enough to make the ascent look like a daunting task. The thought that everyone at the Manor no doubt spent most of the summer months scampering up and down it made her shudder.

'What's the matter?' Chatsworth demanded, giving her an impatient scowl. Then his frown cleared and he grasped her arm with ungentle fingers.

'God, don't tell me you're still indulging that stupid fear of heights. Get moving, Amy, before there's no beach left for us to stand on.'

He jerked her towards the path as he spoke. Amy let the momentum carry her up the first few feet before she shook her arm free.

'It's all right, James. Your gallant assistance is no longer needed.' She grabbed hold of a protruding chunk of rock and used it for balance while she gathered her skirts in her other hand. They were going *up*, she told herself. She wouldn't have to look down.

'Then hurry,' he snapped behind her. 'There might be awkward questions asked if people see us together. We don't want any suspicions about you until your usefulness is finished.'

'So considerate,' she muttered.

'Yes, that's all very well, but we could have finished our business and walked back a few minutes apart if you hadn't felt obliged to question everything I said. But that's you all over, Amy. Nothing but trouble.'

Amy raised her eyes heavenward and started climbing. In truth, the path wasn't as daunting as it had appeared from the beach, in some places there was even a natural step or two, but with only one hand free and several loose stones underfoot, progress was slow.

Despite that, however, she was doing rather well. She was even beginning to congratulate herself on conquering her fear—as long as she didn't look down—until the path made a slight turn that took it on a parallel course across the cliffside for several feet, and from the corner of her eye she saw nothing but space.

'Oh, God.'

She ground to a halt, closing her eyes before her head started swimming.

But that only made it worse. Without sight, her other senses sharpened. The wind, which until then had been nothing more than a mild breeze, suddenly seemed to buffet her with the express intention of knocking her off her feet.

She opened her eyes again, keeping her gaze to the right. A stunted bush grew out of the cliff almost level with her face. She stared at it until her eyes watered, trying to pretend that bushes were all around her, but her limbs were so rigid, she couldn't even put out a hand to grab a branch in case the movement caused her to lose her balance.

'For God's sake, Amy. What's the matter now? We're nearly there.'

The sound of Chatsworth's impatient voice snapped open some of her mental shackles. She could breathe again.

'James, I'm sorry, but do you think you could go ahead and let me hold on to your hand? I don't think I can trust my balance.'

'Hold my *hand*? Are you out of your mind? How's that going to look when we get to the top? This path doesn't take us back to the road, you know; we're going to end up on the other side of Hawkridge's home wood. What if people are still wandering about?'

'I'm sure they'll only think—'

'God, anyone would think you hadn't been living here for a month. Get out of my way, Amy. I'm not your bloody nursemaid.'

He pushed roughly past her as he spoke, but not to her left as Amy half-expected. Stung by his scorn, she had just managed a tentative lean towards the cliff when he stormed by on the inside of the path, shoving her sideways and sending her stumbling into the top branches of another shrub that was growing up only a few inches below the path.

Amy gave a short gasping scream as she felt the shrub tear loose beneath her weight. As if at a signal, the entire edge of the path crumbled, seeming to gather momentum as the first stones she'd dislodged in her stumble began bouncing down the cliff. She didn't have time to turn, to grab hold of anything, to dig in her heels.

In the single sickening instant before she lost her footing and the world turned over, she caught a glimpse of Chatsworth's startled face. Then the ground dropped from beneath her feet.

Marc was not in a good mood. He didn't know how one small female could manage to disappear between one second and the next, and stay missing, but he was going to find out. And then he was going to put a stop to it.

Amy was supposed to be in the house. More specifically, in her bedchamber. Recovering from a headache.

She wasn't anywhere in the house. He knew because he'd just spent a fruitless thirty minutes searching the place. He also knew she wasn't in her bedchamber because he'd damned propriety and looked in there, too.

She had obviously taken herself and her headache elsewhere.

Perhaps she'd walked back to Lavender Cottage with its inhabitants.

He paced up and down the terrace while he considered the notion. It would have made sense, except that she wouldn't have gone for a long walk in the heat if she'd had a headache.

But if her head wasn't aching, why had she left? She'd seemed perfectly happy sitting under the trees watching him play cricket. The fact that her gaze had been on him whenever he'd glanced across the lawn had been very encouraging. Unfortunately, it had also been frustrating, because she'd looked so deliciously flushed and soft, he'd wanted to drag her behind the nearest tree and see how much more flushed and soft he could get her.

His frustration wasn't eased when he'd walked off the field at tea to find Amy looking up at him in a way that had caused him to resort to the recitation of complicated mathematical equations in order to stand up with some degree of comfort.

He'd managed to keep his mind on the task, but only because they'd had an audience.

Things had improved a fraction when play had resumed. There he'd been, systematically demolishing every ball Pelham sent down to him, with a single-minded ruthlessness that at least gave him an outlet for his physical frustration, and the next instant he'd looked across to the trees to discover that Amy had disappeared.

So had his concentration. The next ball had thudded into the stumps, sending bailes flying to the accompaniment of relieved cheers from the opposition.

Marc scowled at the memory. He'd been well on his way to a century, damn it. Mrs Amaris Chantry had a lot to answer for.

'Marc? What are you doing out here? Your grandmama wants to know if you wish to eat dinner, or have supper later.'

He wheeled about to see Kitty Ingham step through the French windows from the library.

'I don't know about you,' she continued, 'but I've been eating all day. Dinner is the last thing on my mind.'

'Hello, Kitty. I didn't know you and Ingham were still here.'

'Anthony's nurse took him home a couple of hours ago,' she said, reaching him and slipping a hand through his arm. 'But Lady Hawkridge invited us to stay if we wished. I was looking forward to a chat with Mrs Chantry, but I believe she's indisposed.'

'So she said, but she's not in her room.' He frowned, sweeping the outskirts of the home wood with an all-seeing gaze. Nothing moved in the shadows that had formed now that the sun had slipped below the horizon.

'Are you worried about her, Marc? She might have gone for a walk now that it's cooler.'

'I'm not particularly worried; there's still plenty of light and she wouldn't go near the cliff, but I didn't realise the dinner-hour had arrived. If she has gone for a walk, she should be back by now.' He glanced down and gave Kitty a quick smile. 'Tell Grandmama supper will be fine. I think I'll go for a walk, myself.'

'But your sister is here, too, and Pelham and Lord Colborough.'

'They'll survive without my presence.'

Her lips curved upward. 'I'm sure they will. Would you like some company on your walk?'

He grinned. 'No, I wouldn't.'

Kitty laughed. 'I didn't think so. Is Mrs Chantry the one, Marc? I do hope so. Augusta and I are running out of eligible cousins, friends and acquaintances. Not that any of the girls we've cast in your way for the past five years would have done anything except make you thoroughly miserable.'

'Thank you very much,' he said sardonically. 'Why did you keep trotting them out in that case?'

'I meant that none of them were capable of feeling as you do,' she said gently. 'I wasn't, myself.'

His ironic smile disappeared. 'Did I frighten you, Kitty? Is that the true reason you broke our engagement? I know you married Ingham because he's the gentle, unassuming sort, but—'

'No!' She shook her head vigorously. 'I wasn't afraid of *you*, only of disappointing you. I know I tried to explain it at the time, and couldn't. But I hadn't been married myself, then, so I didn't know about intimate relationships.'

'For God's sake, Kitty, what did you think I was going to do to you? I'm not a brute. I am capable of treating a wife with consideration.'

'Oh, dear, now I've made you cross. Marc, I didn't mean that at all. Of course you're capable of consideration. You're the best person I know. Apart from Ingham, that is,' she added with a smile. 'But some people feel more...*passionately* than others. I know I'm not one of them, and that suits me perfectly well, but you couldn't be happy in a marriage where polite consideration was the order of the day.' She raised herself on tiptoe to kiss his cheek. 'And I do want you to be happy, my best and dearest friend.'

'Apart from Ingham, that is.'

She giggled and gave him a little shove. 'Go and find Mrs Chantry. I think she may cast a few obstacles in your way, but something tells me you won't give her up as easily as you did me.'

'I won't give her up at all,' he said, and grinned.

She was alive. And the world had stopped spinning.

Amy clung to that knowledge and didn't let herself think about anything else until her heart stopped pounding. She wished it would hurry up and settle down, because she wanted to hear if rescue was on the way.

Then she realised she could hear other sounds. The wind; the rushing of the sea; the startled screech of a gull as it swooped past her. She even heard the quick flap of the bird's wings as it veered away.

But she couldn't hear anyone hurrying to the rescue.

'James?'

The name emerged from her throat in a tentative croak. Nothing stirred; no one answered.

She called again, louder.

Silence.

Of course he was gone. He probably hadn't even waited to see if she'd fallen all the way to the beach.

Perhaps she had.

She opened her eyes, cautiously.

And immediately choked on a strangled cry of terror. *Oh, God.* She was lying face down on some sort of ledge, so close to the brink she could see over it. The space she occupied was tiny, barely enough to take her full length. If her legs had been stretched out her feet would have dangled over the edge.

Below her the sea swirled and eddied as the tide continued to rush in. She almost felt the pull of it, dragging her over, dragging her down.

No!

The cry of denial tore from her throat and was whipped away by the wind. Her fingers dug into the stony ground so desperately her nails broke. She squeezed her eyes shut again on the realisation that in front of her and on both sides there was nothing but empty sky.

Something was whimpering. Several seconds passed before Amy realised it was herself making those terrified animal sounds. Had she fainted? Dear God, don't let her faint. She would fall over the edge for sure.

The edge. She had to get away from it. She couldn't stay here all night. Clearly, no one except James had witnessed her fall, and he would think first of himself. As far as he was concerned, she might be dead and he might be blamed if anyone saw him near the scene. He would be long gone. There was no one to raise the alarm; no one would realise she was missing. Why should they indeed? Everyone thought she was lying down in her room, not lying on a stony ledge suspended over nothing.

Don't think of it! Don't think of it!

Her hands were still clutching dirt and stones. Think about that, she ordered herself. She wouldn't fall while she still clung to the earth beneath her. It only felt like she was about to fall when she opened her eyes. So she wouldn't open her eyes and she wouldn't let go.

But if she didn't open her eyes, how was she going to crawl back from the edge? She didn't even know if there was enough room to crawl backwards.

Don't think about that either. There was room. There had to be.

She dug her fingers in harder, and concentrated on breathing. Only on breathing. James had said she was strong-minded. If ever there was a time to demonstrate strong-mindedness, this was it.

In. Out.

Dust tickled her nose. Grit shifted somewhere.

She shut out the distractions and concentrated. After a while breathing became easier. She started to imagine that the ledge was wider. Very carefully, she built up the picture in her mind. She could move. There wasn't a sheer drop right in front of her face. She could ease some of the tension in her fingers. She even imagined that the ledge sloped upward a little, making it safer, that there were bushes on either side, closing her in.

And that Hawkridge was waiting for her, his hand outstretched, ready to steady her if she stumbled, to lead her to safety.

When his image was firm in her mind she moved one leg backwards, very slowly. There was room. At least a yard, maybe more. Taking a deep breath, keeping her eyes tightly shut, Amy shifted, one muscle at a time, until she was lying against the cliff.

The tiny sense of security afforded by the rock digging into her side had her muscles turning to water. Tears of relief welled in her eyes; she started to cry. Heaven knew what the combination of dust and dirt and tears was doing to her face, she thought, and started to laugh instead. The laugh ended in a hiccup, but at least it stopped her crying. She began to wonder if she was injured, and was vaguely astonished that the question hadn't occurred to her before.

Well, it had occurred now. She put the picture of a wide ledge surrounded by bushes to one side of her mind and concentrated on herself, beginning with her head. It was difficult to be sure with her eyes closed, but if she didn't count incipient hysteria, she seemed to be in one piece. She ached and throbbed in several places, her left thigh stung rather badly, but nothing appeared to be broken. Despite a hazy memory of landing with a jarring thud, it was clear she hadn't fallen all that far.

The knowledge didn't provide her with any great comfort. Given her terror of falling any further, it was useless trying to get back to the path. She didn't even know if there still was a path.

After reaching that conclusion, there was really nothing left for her to do except call out every few seconds, and wait to be rescued.

By the time dusk was more than a grey tinge in the sky, Marc had exchanged vague concern for real worry. He'd combed the shrubbery, the orchard, the home wood, and even the stables, without result, and had despatched a groom to Lavender Cottage, only to be informed on the man's return that no one had seen Amy since the middle of the afternoon.

Frowning, he watched the groom retreat to the servants' hall. Then, struck by the sudden notion that Amy might have run away for some obscure reason, he returned to her room and flung open the doors of her wardrobe.

Her clothes were still there, hanging in a neat row; her rose silk evening gown, the peach cambric, a warmer dress of biscuit-coloured wool, and her green pelisse. She'd been wearing her cream muslin.

Something stabbed at his heart at the sight of the tiny collection, but he didn't spare the time to think about that, or his relief that she hadn't run away. Worry congealed into a ball of fear that lay cold and heavy in his gut.

For some reason, his certainty that Amy wouldn't go near the cliff was no longer rock-solid. He didn't think she would go willingly, but when he considered the fact that she was hiding something, and that Tweedy hadn't been seen since the dowager had apparently abandoned him for Colborough, certainty tottered and threatened to crumble.

Wheeling, Marc strode out of Amy's room, took the stairs in several perilous bounds and left the house through the front door. He didn't stop to tell anyone of his suspicions—he'd already entered the drawing-room once, ascertained that Amy wasn't there, and stalked out under the astonished stares of its occupants. No need to give the crowd in there any more reason to speculate on his sanity.

But as he headed back towards the woods, he saw Crispin approaching from the direction of the lake.

'I say, Uncle Marc, that's a capital little row—' His nephew stopped, goggle-eyed, as he strode past him without pause.

An instant later, the boy was on his heels. 'What's up?' he asked breathlessly. 'Where are you going?'

'The beach.'

'The beach? But the tide's in. Probably up to the high-water mark by now.'

He didn't need Crispin to tell him that. Fear spread its ice-cold fingers wider.

The sensation wasn't pleasant. Anger, he decided, was a very good antidote. When he found Amy he was going to throttle her. And then he was going to tell her in no uncertain terms that she was never to go anywhere without him again. In time, if she behaved herself, he might let her go from room to room without an escort, but that was all she could expect.

The absurd thoughts didn't alleviate his fear one bit.

'Amy's missing,' he said curtly to his nephew. 'She might have gone to the beach, and she hasn't a notion of how fast the tide comes in.'

There was one thing to be said for the boy. He didn't need to have things spelled out.

'It's all right, Uncle Marc. If she couldn't get back to the path in time, she'd climb the rock where that dim-witted poet wanted Grandmama to sit for him.'

'Maybe. Heights upset her balance.'

'Better to feel giddy than to drown.'

Marc sent his nephew a quick, wryly amused glance. 'Right on the nail,' he said. 'Thanks, Crispin, I needed that.'

'You like Amy, don't you, Uncle Marc? So does Mama. She thinks bad things have happened to her. She says that sometimes when Amy doesn't know anyone's watching her, she looks frightened.'

'Your mama is a clever lady.'

'Well, sometimes. Look, there's the path. Good thing it's not really dark yet. Can you see anyone down there?'

Marc swore. 'Damn it, I should have taken the time to grab a lantern. Stay behind me, Crispin. Something's not quite—' He broke off before he'd descended more than a dozen steps, and swore again. Comprehensively.

The landscape looked terrifyingly different to the last time he'd seen it.

Crispin peered past his arm. 'Good Lord! Half the path's gone.'

The boy's voice rang out in the still air. A faint echo carried back to them. And then another voice.

'Crispin? Is that you?'

The cry had Marc's head coming up like a hunter scenting prey.

'*Amy!*' He started downwards again, moving as fast as possible with rubble shifting beneath his feet. 'Crispin, stay where you are! The path starts again further down, but this section appears to have fallen straight down the cliff.'

'No, wait, Uncle Marc!' Crispin yelled excitedly. 'I can see her.' He pointed a steady finger. 'Look! Through those bushes over there. There's some sort of ledge, and I can see a scrap of white.'

Marc turned his head in the direction Crispin was pointing, and felt his heart shudder to a stop. From where he stood, balanced on the cliff-side, the view was better than Crispin's. The small huddled form his nephew had glimpsed was lying only feet from the edge of a sheer fifty-foot drop to the sea.

He swept the scene around her with swiftly assessing eyes. 'Christ! She must have gone over with the landslide. And the ledge broke her fall.'

'How are we going to get to her?'

'I'll get to her. Crispin, I want you to go back to the house as fast as you can without running yourself short of breath.'

'I'll be all right, Uncle Marc. What do you want me to do?'

'Fetch Pelham and half a dozen strong men. The strongest; they'll have to take both our weights. We'll need lanterns, plenty of thick rope—' he glanced in Amy's direction again, thinking of injuries '—and blankets. You'd better warn everyone else, but tell them not to panic. Amy's alive. That's all they have to worry about at present.'

Crispin followed his gaze. 'She hasn't called out again. Do you think she's all right?'

Marc refused to contemplate any alternative. 'She'd better bloody well be all right,' he grated, 'because when I get her out of this, I'm going to beat her to within an inch of her life!'

'Good Lord!' Even from where he stood, Marc saw his nephew's eyes widen. 'You're not really, are you, Uncle Marc?'

'Of course I'm not. But the fantasy is extraordinarily satisfying.'

Crispin flashed him a quick grin. 'We'll be back before you know it,' he said, and disappeared.

Chapter Twelve

She hadn't called out again because she was struggling to hold back the torrent of tears dammed up behind her eyelids.

He was here. The relief of it threatened to overwhelm her fragile reserves of strength.

'Amy!'

Marc. His voice came from somewhere above her, but closer than before.

'*Amy!* Answer me, damn it!'

She dragged in a breath. 'Yes.'

'All right.' His voice lowered. She counted two heartbeats before he spoke again.

'Can you cover your head with your arms? There's a slight overhang above you. I'm going to lower myself over it to reach your ledge, and I'll probably dislodge a few stones in the process.'

Her eyes flew open in alarm. She knew immediately that she'd made a ghastly mistake. Without daylight to dazzle her eyes after they'd been closed so long, she could see with hideous clarity. Her carefully constructed vision of a wide ledge shattered and vanished.

'You can't!' She clamped her eyes shut as the sky spun dizzily. Her fingers dug into rock. If she could have crawled inside the ledge beneath her, she would have. 'There isn't room!'

'Yes, there is. It's all right. Just lie very still.'

He didn't have to tell her to do that. She'd been still for so long, she didn't think she could move. Even to obey his instruction to cover her head. What did it matter, anyway? She was already covered in dust and rubble.

A hail of pebbles rained down on her as she contemplated that aspect of the situation. A light thud sounded a mere inch or two away, and she sensed a darker shadow come between herself and the early-night sky.

He must have landed like a cat.

The thought vanished when she felt his hands touch her hair.

'Marc.' It was a whisper of thankfulness.

'Yes,' he murmured. 'I'm here, love. Let me see if you're hurt.'

'No, I'm...' Her voice wobbled and she took another shuddering breath. She wanted to cry again. It was weak and foolish, but she couldn't help it.

'Shh.' His hands moved over her head and face, brushing away dust and dirt. Then, as if he was examining something incredibly fragile, he ran his hands over her arms, gently circled her ribs, carefully felt the length of her spine, stroked downwards.

And flipped her tangled skirts up to her thigh.

'My lord!' The urge to cry vanished.

'Yes?'

'What are you doing?'

'Seeing if anything's broken.'

'But...' She started to shiver inside. Her fingers dug in harder, but only because the warmth of his touch startled her so. She almost forgot her precarious position for a few heady moments. 'There's nothing broken,' she managed to say.

'I'm blocking out what little light there is, but I think you're right.'

'Of course I'm right. They're my bones. I ought to know if they're broken or not.'

'Hmm. If you're well enough for indignation, you can't be too badly hurt. Can you sit up? I'll check your other leg.'

Amy contemplated the question. Momentary forgetfulness was one thing; moving quite another. 'No.'

He was back at her head in a flash, cradling it in one large hand. She felt him bend closer.

'Is there something wrong with your back? Is that why you can't move? Are you in pain?'

His urgency had her feeling stupidly weepy again. She began to feel as if she was on a see-saw. 'It's not that,' she said wretchedly. 'I can't move, or I'll fall.'

He exhaled on a long breath. 'No. You won't fall, Amy. I won't let you.'

'You don't understand. I have to open my eyes to move, and I can't.' Her lower lip trembled. 'I *can't*.'

He touched his fingers to her face, brushed them over her lashes. 'Yes, you can, darling. I'm between you and the edge. Just open your eyes and look at me.'

His voice was so deeply tender, she simply did as he asked. As if she was impelled by something that would have bade her follow him—even over the edge if he'd suggested it.

Her lashes fluttered up. She blinked rapidly a couple of times, ready to retreat into darkness, then her gaze focused on the reassuring bulk that leaned over her in the gloom, and stayed.

'That's better. Now...' He covered her hands with his, gently easing the tension in her fingers. 'Slowly.'

The instant she felt Marc lift her into a sitting position, Amy grabbed hold of his arms and hung on. The muscles beneath her hands were like iron. She wanted to fling herself against him and burrow in.

'I thought of you, you know.' The shaky admission was out before she knew it.

'Did you?' He propped her against the cliff and, without making any attempt to pry her fingers loose from his arms, carefully probed the side she'd been lying on.

'Yes.' She shivered as his hand moved over her ribs. 'Whenever my pretend ledge wavered, I'd think of the way you held my hand when I stepped down from the carriage, and it would steady again.'

She felt the swift glance he sent her, but he continued checking downwards.

'I called out, too. Until my voice got too croaky. I didn't think anyone would come until morning.'

His hand stilled, tightened fractionally, then continued.

'Did Tweedy bring you here?'

'Tweedy?' She took a moment to bring the man's image to mind. 'No.'

'Then what in the world possessed—? No, never mind. We'll get you home first.'

That was good. But for some unaccountable reason she couldn't think why. Everything began to take on a strange, dream-like quality. As if it was happening to someone else. Even the touch of Marc's hand on her thigh evoked nothing more than a rather detached interest in her various wounds.

'Is anything broken?' she asked without any real concern.

'No, but I think this leg's been bleeding.'

'It was stinging,' she said vaguely, and tried to remember what she'd been doing before it all started. 'Did you win the cricket?' she asked suddenly.

'Yes.'

'That's nice.'

'Oh, God, Amy—'

'Yes, my lord?'

'Nothing. I—'

A shout from above interrupted him. He loosened the grip she had on him and shackled her wrists in his hands. But that was all right, she thought. As long as he was holding on to her, she'd be safe. She heard him shout something back. The conversation seemed to go on for a long time; she recognised Eversleigh's voice, heard one or two others, then a rope came snaking down from somewhere and Marc reached out to pull it in.

She kept her gaze where it was. On his face. His eyes were washed of colour in the night, but, glittering faintly, utterly steady, they stayed on hers, commanding her trust.

'Amy, I'm going to tie the rope around myself. You can hold on to me while I do it.'

She nodded, and hung on when he transferred her hands to his shoulders.

'Good girl. Now I'm going to stand up with you. We won't fall because there's at least six men up there holding the rope, and I'll be holding you.'

Her heart lodged in her throat. Some of the dream-like quality faded, but before she could protest against standing on that precariously small ledge in the middle of nowhere, she was on her feet and locked in Marc's arms.

She flung her own arms around his neck, pressed her face to his shoulder. Reality crept terrifyingly closer. 'Don't let me go!'

'Never,' he vowed, his mouth very close to her ear. Then, looking upwards and raising his voice, 'All right, Pel. Keep the rope taut, even when we're back on the path.'

A confirming shout came back.

'What are we going to do?' she asked, trying to keep her voice from shaking.

'I'm going to carry you up to the top of the cliff,' he said as calmly as if they were going for a walk in the gardens.

'But—'

Her voice dried up completely when he swept her skirts upward again and lifted her against him.

'Put your legs around me,' he ordered.

The sharp command didn't give her any choice. Amy obeyed, simply because she sensed the alternative would be a great deal worse. Such as hanging over his shoulder with an excellent view of the drop below them.

To her dismay, the last comforting threads of detachment were whipped away by the cool wind gusting against her bare legs. She was abruptly, *excruciatingly*, aware that she was clinging to Hawkridge in the most intimate way possible, as if she was going to crawl right inside his clothes and cling to his bare flesh.

'Oh, my goodness!'

'Hold on tight,' he said, transferring one hand to the rope. 'You'll feel us drop a little when I step off the ledge, but we're perfectly safe.'

He hoped. Marc prayed his men had a good grip on the rope. This was the moment when they were most at risk—for the few seconds between swinging out from the ledge and making contact with the cliff again—when the sudden jolt on the men's arms as they took his and Amy's combined weights would test their strength, and the strength of their life-line.

The rope around his chest was also going to tighten rather painfully. It was for that reason he hadn't tied Amy to him. If he was safe, she would be, too, because he had no intention of letting her go. And judging by the way she was clinging to him, nothing short of an earthquake was going to wrench her loose.

Deciding not to give either of them any more time to think about it, he stepped over the edge.

Amy gave a short gasping scream and clung tighter. Then gasped again when his feet slammed into the cliff with a force that jolted every bone in his body.

'Are you all right?' he grated. He'd tried to protect her as much as possible, but there wasn't a lot he could do with only one arm to shield her from the impact.

'Yes.' Her voice was a squeak. 'Are we there?'

'Not quite. We're making for the path.' He forebore to tell her that he was virtually walking her across the treacherous face of the landslide, with their safety dependent on the men above them, until they reached the place where the path started again.

But she obviously had a good imagination. And it was running riot.

'Oh, my goodness!' She pressed her face harder into his shoulder. 'Are you sure those men know what they're doing?'

'I'm sure.'

'What if the path falls to pieces again when we get to it?'

'We've still got the rope.'

'What if the rope breaks?'

'It won't.'

'But what if——?'

'Amy, are you always this pessimistic?'

Her legs tightened, pressing her more intimately against him. He took a moment to reflect on the perversity of a body that could harden instantly in response even in the face of mortal danger.

'Only when I'm dangling over a cliff at the end of a rope in the dark,' she quavered.

He didn't feel like smiling at the breathless answer. 'Just keep quiet and hold on.'

Ten seconds later, she was off again.

'Have you done this a lot, my lord?'

He set his teeth. 'All the time when I was a boy.'

'You climbed this cliff with a rope when you were a boy?'

'It seemed like an interesting challenge at the time.'

'But—'

'Amy, I know you're terrified, but could you refrain from conversation until a more convenient time?'

'Terrified. Yes, you could say that.' She waited a breath. 'I was only going to say that one would have to assume you were lighter then.'

'*Amy*—'

His feet hit a patch of flat ground and he knew they'd reached the path. Easing his grip on the rope for a second, he prised Amy's arms from around his neck and hitched her over his shoulder before she had any warning. Her legs fell from around his waist and he used his free hand to return her skirts to a state of modesty before clamping his arm about them.

'I liked it better the other way,' she said in a very small voice. Wonderful. She liked torturing him.

'I don't suppose... No. I dare say it must have been very uncomfortable for you, my lord.'

'Uncomf—' Gritting his teeth, he started upwards. 'Amy, when I get you out of this, I'm going to either kiss you witless or put you over my knee. I haven't decided yet. Unless you wish me to make the decision while your pretty little rear is so close to hand, I suggest you shut up.'

She shut up all the rest of the way to the top of the cliff.

She remained silent when they finally reached safety. But that was probably because several people began talking at once.

Eager hands reached to pull them over the top. He recognised his grandmother's anxious tones. Colborough was barking instructions. His sister and Nettlebed joined in. Crispin was yelling encouragement as he continued to haul in rope with an action that would have earned him line-honours at a regatta.

'What the devil—' Marc began, lowering Amy to the ground and releasing her. He yanked the rope from around his chest before he was hauled in with it, then, warned by the tiniest of sighs, whirled and snatched Amy back into his arms as she sank against him in a dead faint.

'Such a dreadful thing to happen, Dr Twinhoe. Why, we've all been up and down that path hundreds of times, with never a thought that it might collapse.'

The dowager wrung her hands, then scurried over to the bed where Amy was lying, an unwilling prisoner. She began plumping up pillows. 'There, that's better, isn't it, dear?' She didn't wait for an answer, but flitted across to the windows, where she drew the curtains against the bright morning sunlight.

'From what his lordship was telling me last night, dear lady, all the rain we've had recently must have softened the soil.' Dr Twinhoe closed up his bag and patted Amy's hand. 'When Mrs Chantry tripped and stumbled against a shrub on the side of the path, the roots tore loose, together with a great chunk of earth and stones, and started a small landslide.'

'Dreadful!'

'Yes, indeed. But, fortunately, Mrs Chantry's injuries are minor. A nasty bump on the head, a bad gash and various scratches and bruises. I won't remove the bandage on her leg this morning. Just dropped in to see how she was going on. Dare say you have a touch of the headache, my dear.'

Amy opened her mouth.

'Who could wonder at it?' exclaimed the dowager, pattering back to the bedside. 'So very kind of you to call in, Dr Twinhoe. What would we do without you?'

Amy closed her mouth again.

'I expect you would go on perfectly well,' he responded, twinkling. 'A day or two in bed and plenty of quiet is what's needed here. I'll leave a dose of laudanum with you, m'lady, now that we know the head injury isn't serious. Sleep is the best cure for a shock of such magnitude, but I expect Mrs Chantry to be able to drop off without any assistance.'

'Especially after very little sleep last night,' her ladyship agreed. 'Marc kept poking his head in every hour or so and telling us to wake her to see if she was still sensible. Quite absurd of him. Amy is always sensible, aren't you, dear?'

Amy's lips parted.

'Bit of a new-fangled thing that, waking the patient for a bump on the head.'

Her lips closed again.

Dr Twinhoe shook his own head. 'Hawkridge told me he'd seen it done in the Peninsula. Can't do any harm, I suppose. Now, before I go—' he raised his bushy brows at the dowager '—tell me who informed Mr Tweedy that chicken-pox is rife in the village?'

Her ladyship's eyes opened to their widest extent. 'Good heavens, I've no idea. What makes you ask?'

'Merely that Tweedy came knocking on my front door before I'd swallowed my breakfast this morning, and wanted my opinion about a spot on his nose. Man's an idiot. Told him he'd been out in the sun too long yesterday, but he insisted that chicken-pox was all over the place.'

'Well, fancy that. Of course, I did tell Lord Colborough that one of our maids had come down with it, but I can't imagine why he would pass the information on to dear Mr Tweedy. Why do you think, Amy?'

She took a breath.

'Mumbled something about a walking cane and being threatened with the ffollifoot girls.'

Amy exhaled and subsided into the bedclothes.

Dr Twinhoe frowned. 'The man must have been drinking, and at a disgracefully early hour, too.'

'Disgraceful,' agreed the dowager. 'I shall tell him so, if I see him again.'

'Don't think you will,' said Dr Twinhoe, picking up his bag and heading for the door. 'He was driving his gig, and there was a chest and a carpet-bag in the back. I'll call in again tomorrow, Mrs Chantry. In the meantime I don't want you to leave that bed. No reason to.'

'No, indeed, Amy, dear.' Her ladyship scurried around the bed and produced a small silver bell which she placed by Amy's hand. 'I'm sure you must be perfectly exhausted, answering questions every few minutes. Now, you have a nice, long sleep before you worry about receiving all the visitors who are calling in to see how you go on. If you need even the smallest thing, just ring this little bell.' After straightening the already straight quilt and giving the pillows a final pat, Lady Hawkridge tip-toed out of the room after Dr Twinhoe.

Amy contemplated the closed door for several seconds. When she was quite sure that the dowager was being true to her promise to keep visitors away, she sat up. No dire consequences followed.

She could have told Dr Twinhoe, if he or anyone else had allowed her to speak, that such would prove to be the case. Lying about in bed, for whatever reason, had not been encouraged in the poorhouse.

And she had every reason to leave her bed. Her mind had been made up last night when she'd recovered her senses, when all the fuss and commotion had died down, when everyone had come to the conclusion that she'd gone down to the beach for some fresh air and had tripped on the path.

She had a vague recollection that it was Hawkridge who'd put the tale about, but, despite the aches and pains and confusion that had constituted the rest of her night, she hadn't been fooled into thinking he believed the story.

A quick frown creased her brow. There was something else he'd said. When they were on the ledge. Something she felt was important, but that had been lost in the confusion that followed.

After a moment she shook her head. It no longer mattered. She was going to tell him everything. No matter what the risk. It wasn't only for Lucinda's safety. She truly believed her intervention wouldn't be necessary; the girl was too closely guarded. She simply couldn't continue to lie to him.

Not any more. Not to him.

She would have to leave, of course. She didn't think Hawkridge would throw her to the wolves—remembering the way he'd cradled her all the way back to the house, she didn't think he could be so gentle and tender one moment, and behave with such heartlessness the next—but he would hardly want her to stay. She knew he disliked lies and pretence—she could hardly blame him—and she'd lied to him, to his grandmother, to everyone. And they'd all been so kind to her.

The weight of guilt threatened to drag her under the bedclothes again, to hide until she could creep out of the house unobserved. But that was the coward's way, and she wouldn't be able to live with herself if she took it.

Moving gingerly, Amy climbed out of bed and proceeded to

dress herself in her peach cambric gown. The cream muslin was but a memory; even Amy's thrifty soul conceded that no amount of scrubbing and mending could restore its tatters to anything resembling a dress.

Clothed, she examined her reflection in the mirror. It was the first time she'd seen herself since the accident. The sight made her wince. Her arms were decorated with darkening bruises intersected by scratches of varying lengths, and a wide bandage circled her head, holding a cold compress in place over one eyebrow. Thanks to its presence, her hair fell to her shoulders in wildly tousled ringlets, despite Lady Nettlebed's ministrations last night which had removed a collection of leaves and twigs.

There was another bandage around her thigh, but that, at least, was out of sight. The same couldn't be said for the graze along one collarbone. As for her hands...

Amy shuddered and set about rectifying the situation.

Ten minutes later she tip-toed to the door, opened it and peeped out. Given that the bell Lady Hawkridge had left with her wouldn't have been heard more than a few feet away, she half-expected to see a maid on duty outside her room.

The passage was empty.

On a sigh of relief, she slipped silently out of the room and, moving like a wary, slightly battered little ghost, set off in search of Hawkridge.

Pacing up and down the terrace—or anywhere else for that matter—was becoming something of a habit.

Marc brooded grimly on the fact that he was going to wear a path in the flagstones, or in any one of a number of carpets.

On the other hand, the exercise did serve to keep his tightly coiled body occupied, while he planned strategies in his mind.

Unfortunately, only one strategy had any appeal. As soon as Amy awoke from her nap, he was going to lay everything out for her in no uncertain terms.

Politely, of course. He wasn't going to yell. After all, she'd been through a harrowing ordeal. But he would be firm.

He paused at the far end of the terrace and considered the plan.

A slight modification was necessary. He was going to lay *almost* everything out for her in no uncertain terms.

Enough to give him the right to look after her from now on. Enough to protect her. To cherish her. To win her heart.

Enough to make sure she didn't get herself into any more situations that threatened to shred his self-control into tiny, little pieces and toss them to the four winds.

He started pacing again.

She was going to marry him. He wasn't going to brook any defiance. She could forget her independence for five minutes and admit that she needed him. He'd saved her life, damn it. He'd proved that when a male took over, disaster didn't ensue. In fact, if anyone had caused a disaster, it was Amy for going to the beach in the first place.

He ground to another halt, eyes narrowed in thought, as he remembered that he still didn't know why she'd indulged in a pastime guaranteed to terrify her.

Something told him the answer to that little question would prove very enlightening.

'Uh...my lord? May I have a word with you?'

Several words. And then—

He stopped in mid-thought, whipping around when he realised the tentative little voice he'd heard wasn't in his head.

A giant fist slammed into his heart. Every strategy involving politeness, consideration and even a modicum of civilised behaviour fell at his feet and smashed on the flagstones. Amy stood a few feet away, looking as if someone had taken a club to her.

'What the devil are you doing out of bed?' he yelled. 'Damn it, Amy, do I have to climb in there with you to make sure you stay put?'

Amy blinked at the outraged question and resisted an insane urge to nod. She had the feeling that if she did, she'd be back in bed, with Hawkridge, before she could take another breath.

The thought caused such a pang of longing, she forgot why she'd left her bed in the first place.

'This is it!' he snarled, starting to pace with an abruptness that made her jump. 'This is the final straw!'

She blinked again, wondering what she'd missed.

'I waited.' He halted and transfixed her with an accusing glare. 'I did what you asked, and look what happened! You nearly got yourself killed!'

'But—'

'And why? Because I was *waiting*. For you to tell me what was going on. For you to trust me. And have you? No! You'd rather cling to your stubborn independence.'

'But—'

'Well, no more! You've had a free rein long enough. I'm pulling it in.'

She narrowed her eyes at him. 'I beg your pardon, my lord?'

'Look at you!' he demanded, running his gaze over her with glittering thoroughness. 'Just look at yourself.'

Before she could tell him that she already had, and didn't wish to repeat the experience, he closed the distance between them in three long strides. One sharp tug and he'd whisked away the shawl she'd draped about her arms. It went sailing on to the flagstones.

Amy gazed after it in bemusement. Then jumped when Hawkridge touched the scratches on her arms.

A visible tremor shuddered through him. His voice went hoarse. 'God, Amy. Look at you.'

She looked at him instead, her eyes widening at the sudden raw emotion in his face.

He studied her injuries for a moment, then still holding her wrists as if she was made of fragile glass, raised her hands to his mouth and pressed first one abraded little palm to his lips, then the other.

A river of sensation flowed all the way to Amy's toes and back again. She forgot about everything except the heart-shaking tenderness with which he touched her. He was warmth and strength and safety. Everything she needed in that moment.

'My lord...' She gazed up into the darkening grey of his eyes and couldn't remember what she'd been about to say.

'Hush,' he murmured, and releasing her hands, drew her into his arms. 'It's going to be all right, little Amy.'

Bending his head, he took her mouth with his.

It was the sweetest, gentlest, most intensely cherishing kiss Amy could have imagined. No, she thought hazily in the instant before

her mind blanked and she softened against him. She could never
have imagined a kiss like this.

His arms tightened about her with the utmost care, cradling her.
He parted her lips, but so tenderly she yielded without a qualm.
He stroked his tongue into her mouth with a deep, slow, possessive
caress that had every muscle in her body melting to the consistency
of warm honey.

She stopped thinking and let herself feel. Just for this moment.
Just for this one kiss. Surely no one could begrudge her this, before
she had to destroy everything she held—

No!

Awareness, barely acknowledged and almost instantly suppressed, dashed a wave of cold reality over her in the same moment that Hawkridge broke the kiss.

He continued to hold her, but she felt as if a yawning chasm
had opened between them. Heat blazed in his eyes; it couldn't
warm her. His body felt like coiled steel, but her senses had gone
numb.

She didn't dare think what she'd just thought.

She didn't *dare*.

His brows drew together and he touched a hand to her face.
'Amy? What is it, love?'

She stiffened and drew herself out of his arms. 'I...have to talk
to you.'

'Yes, I know. But not here.' His gaze swept over the windows
opening onto the terrace. 'The place is swarming with concerned
neighbours, who will very likely feel obliged to interrupt us if they
catch sight of you. Can you walk as far as the shrubbery?'

She nodded. It was all she could manage. His sudden shift from
outrage to tenderness already had her emotions teetering precariously on the brink. Her voice threatened to fail her completely
when she thought of the kindness of the people she'd come to
know.

The people she'd deceived, she reminded herself ruthlessly. She
had no right to indulge in foolish tears and wistful yearnings. Even
less right to be treated like a fragile lady who was going to shatter
if handled too carelessly.

'We can go further afield, if you wish, my lord.' She deliberately made her voice cool and polite. 'I really am much better this morning. And I assure you, I have as little desire to be interrupted as yourself.'

He sent her a quick, frowning glance. 'Not for the same reason, I suspect. Don't worry, Amy. I've done this the wrong way around, but there's nothing to distress you.'

'I seem to be rather less distressed than yourself, my lord. And...' her pose of remote politeness trembled on its shaky foundations '...I haven't thanked you yet for saving my life. Indeed, at risk to your own.'

'That's all right,' he said with a wicked grin. 'I'll savour my reward when you recover.'

'Well, you've already kissed me wit—'

His eyes flashed silver fire.

Amy swallowed and tried to recover lost ground with a touch of humour. It took an incredible effort. 'I mean...I trust you're not going to carry out your threat to beat me.'

'So you remember what I said last night.'

'Yes.' They turned into the shrubbery as she spoke. 'But since you were under a considerable strain at the time, I didn't place a lot of credence in it.'

Hawkridge jerked to a stop. Without warning, he was looming over her.

'Considering that kiss we shared not two minutes ago,' he grated menacingly, 'that was a big mistake. The only reason I'm not putting you over my knee, Mrs Chantry, is that it would be difficult to find a spot that isn't already black and blue.'

Amy stared into the blazing eyes so close to hers, and decided it would be better to stay silent until she had her thoughts in some sort of order. She seemed to be having a great deal of trouble keeping up with Hawkridge's changes of mood. He was bouncing from outrage to concern to a rather ominous edge of danger with a speed that left her already shaken wits reeling.

'Here,' he growled, straightening. 'Sit down before you fall down.'

She was steered over to one of the benches set at intervals along the enclosed walk, and released. Her legs gave way thankfully.

'Now—'

'Before you start, my lord—' *and before she lost her courage* '—I have something to say.'

'So do I,' he said. 'And I've already waited long enough to say it. In fact, more than long enough to confirm my opinion that waiting for certain people to come to their senses is extremely unrewarding.'

Her spine straightened. She lifted her chin. 'You consider waiting *three days* to be excessive, my lord?'

'More than excessive.'

'Well! All I can say is—' She stopped, suddenly realising she *didn't* know what to say. In fact, she was completely baffled.

'Why are we having this conversation?' she asked, her voice rising. 'Nothing has happened to Lady Hawkridge. What were you waiting for, anyway? Why should you care if I trusted you or not? Why—?'

'Because you're going to marry me, damn it! It would be gratifying if you trusted me, too.' He glared at her astonished face for a second, then turned aside and took several impatient strides along the path. *'Bloody hell!'*

Amy gazed after him, her brain reeling in shock. She couldn't think. She couldn't speak. She couldn't move.

Perhaps she hadn't heard correctly.

When Hawkridge wheeled about and strode back to her, she hadn't moved so much as an eyelash.

He sat down, laid his arm along the back of the bench and covered the small fists clenched in her lap with his other hand. His eyes blazed, demanding her compliance.

'Amy, I know you prefer to fight your own battles, but last night made it patently obvious that you can't fight every battle alone. I want the right to protect you. To…care for you. You're going to marry me.'

'But…' Something shuddered and threatened to break open deep inside her. She trembled.

'There's no need to be afraid,' he said at once. 'I know we've only known each other a week; that doesn't matter.'

The words aroused a faint sense of surprise. She felt as if she'd known him forever. As if she'd recognised him that very first day.

The terrifying awareness inside her shuddered again, harder.

He tightened his hold on her hands. 'Say yes.'

A flicker of indignation sprang to life. She hung on to it, almost as desperately as she'd clung to Hawkridge last night. 'How can I do that, my lord, when you haven't asked me a question?'

He half-smiled at that. 'And give you the chance to say no? Do I look like a fool?'

No, never. He looked like the man she loved.

Oh, God!

She squeezed her eyes shut, as if cutting out the sight of him would take the knowledge away. She couldn't breathe. Because if she took another breath, then time would move on and awareness would become knowledge and—

But sheer physical reflex, far beyond her fragile control, released the breath she was holding, and like the tide sweeping over the rocky beach below them, awareness, knowledge, acceptance, broke free and flooded every part of her being. Heart and mind and soul.

She loved him.

How had it happened? How had she not known it until this moment?

The questions meant nothing; they were gone as soon as she asked them. All she knew was that she'd been offered a piece of heaven—and had to stay in the hell of her own making.

'Amy?'

She opened her eyes, looked at him. At those stern, handsome features. At eyes that could glitter with fierce intensity or gleam with wicked laughter. At the hard mouth that had possessed hers with devastating gentleness. At the face that would haunt her for the rest of her life.

She was vaguely aware that Hawkridge was speaking again. Vaguely aware of his rueful laughter as he said, 'All right, Amy, if it's the question you want, you shall have it. Will you do me the very great honour of becoming my wife?'

'I...can't,' she said almost inaudibly. And almost doubled over with the pain of saying the words. Oh, how could she bear it? If she'd been alone she would have fallen to the ground in a tiny ball of agony and waited there for her heart to finish bleeding.

As it was, she had to draw back, to wrench one hand free, to press her fingers to her stomach. She was dying inside. And it was going to take forever; she could see by his expression that he wasn't going to accept her refusal.

'Why can't you?' he asked with a gentleness that tore at her soul. She wondered if knives could be as sharp, as brutally cutting. The pain stole her breath. She couldn't speak, couldn't answer him.

'You're not still entertaining the idiotic notion that you're a servant, are you, Amy? Because if you are—'

A quick shake of her head cut him off.

He waited for a moment, then his eyes narrowed, his voice went hard. 'Is it because you're illegitimate? I don't care about that; it isn't your fault, anyway.'

'No.' She uttered the word through dry lips. 'It isn't that. I—' She broke off, turned her face away. If she'd been able to, she would have turned away completely, shielding herself from the storm she sensed building within him.

'Then why, damn it? Do you think I'll tell you how to run your life? Is that it? I won't. I respect your independence. Your strength. It's one of the things I—'

'*Please,*' she whispered, almost choking on the lump in her throat. She had to stop this. She had to get away until she'd regained control of herself, until the pain eased. If it ever did. She owed him an explanation, she knew that. But not now.

'Please *what*?' he exploded, getting abruptly to his feet. He took a step or two away from the bench before whirling to face her. There was a white line about his mouth, but she was too distressed to worry about the reason for it.

'God, Amy, you can't leave it like that!'

She wondered vaguely why not. He'd accepted Kitty Ingham's refusal, hadn't he?

'Did Chantry mistreat you?' he demanded. 'Do you think I will? Tell me *why*.'

'All right!' she cried, breaking under his insistence. When he took a step towards her, she sprang to her feet, holding out a hand to ward him off. Her breath kept catching. She had to wait until she had enough air to say it quickly.

'I can't marry you...because my husband isn't dead.'

She saw the shock hit him, turn his face white. Then his eyes narrowed, and she knew he was thinking back, searching for anything that might have given her away.

Pain stabbed through her, relentless, brutal, crippling.

'I know...there's more...but...' Her voice became wholly suspended by tears. 'Later,' she whispered. 'When I can speak. When I can...'

It was impossible to continue. Turning blindly, Amy walked towards the shrubbery entrance. She didn't know how she managed it; even then she had to stop for an instant. She drew in a breath, wondered how she would get to the house; told herself she would crawl there before she gave in to the agony tearing her apart.

She knew Hawkridge was standing where she'd left him. She could feel the violent storm of emotion raging around him. But she couldn't look back, couldn't let him see...

'I'm sorry,' she uttered. 'I'm so sorry. I wish...'

Gathering her last ounce of resolve, she took an experimental step. And another. Then, knowing she was out of the shrubbery, and out of his sight, she broke into a stumbling run, gaining momentum, until she was fleeing towards the house as if every demon inhabiting her personal hell howled after her in savage, triumphant glee.

Chapter Thirteen

She made straight for the library. She didn't know why. Sheer instinct, perhaps. A hunted creature fleeing to the place where she'd found a measure of safety.

Or had she fled here in a last desperate bid to deny the pain, and the cause of it?

But there was no denial. No shield against pain. No hiding from the truth.

Amy stared up at the portrait, her arms held tight across her waist, and knew with an anguish that tore at her heart that, without noticing, without knowing, she'd taken the step from fascination with an image to love of the man.

How could she not? she thought, groping her way to a chair and sinking on to it. The portrait was of a boy, striking, commanding interest, but ultimately meaning little.

The reality was a man, strong, protective, honourable; commanding all, meaning everything.

Amy made a tiny sound of pain and began to rock back and forth. She couldn't think clearly. And yet, somewhere in her mind, she knew she'd have to go upstairs, pack, make sure she hadn't left her room untidy.

She'd have to speak to Lady Hawkridge. Tell her...

She stopped rocking, seizing on the thought. Yes. That she could do. Before anything else, she'd end this deception, tell the dowager the truth, apologise.

As if that would make it better, she thought, getting stiffly to her feet. The cut on her leg ached; she scarcely felt it. What was a cut on the leg compared to the vicious claws embedded in her heart?

She deserved it, she thought suddenly in an agony of self-blame. Not only because she'd deceived people, but because she'd been so heedless, so foolish. What had she been thinking? What...?

But that was it. She'd been thinking only of Hawkridge, focusing so intently on him, on his actions, his words, that she'd ignored the love blossoming secretly in her heart.

Well, no more hiding from the truth, she told herself, moving towards the door. She could never put him out of her mind, she was his into eternity, but one day, maybe, the worst of the pain would ease, and if she set things right with the dowager, she would still have some pride.

The door opened on the thought, causing her to jump. Lady Hawkridge peeped into the room.

'Why, Amy, dear...what are you doing out of bed? I just looked in upstairs to see if you were sleeping and you weren't there.'

Amy took a moment to let her startled nerves settle. For a second there she'd thought...hoped...feared...

'You've been crying,' continued the dowager, coming into the room and closing the door. 'You know, Amy, I don't wish to scold, but you really shouldn't—'

Her ladyship broke off, her suddenly shrewd gaze studying Amy's face. She nodded. 'This isn't because of last night. It's not because you're in pain.'

'No, ma'am.' Amy glanced down at her arms, still clasped tightly across her waist. 'At least, not that sort of pain.'

'Well...' Lady Hawkridge crossed the room and sat down on the sofa set to one side of the fireplace. 'That explains why Marc went charging off on that wicked black stallion of his not five minutes ago. Come and sit down, dear, and tell me all about it.' She patted the seat next to her.

Amy felt her lower lip tremble. She sank her teeth into it until it steadied, then complied, seating herself beside her employer and clasping her hands tightly together.

'I presume Marc made you an offer,' the dowager began, startling Amy into looking at her. 'And since I've never seen anyone looking so miserable after accepting one, I presume you refused.'

'Yes, ma'am. I— How did you know?'

Her ladyship smiled. 'Amy dear, I've known since I met you that you're perfect for Marc. He obviously didn't take much longer to come to the same conclusion.'

'Perfect?' She shook her head. 'Ma'am, even excluding the facts of which you're as yet unaware, I'm penniless. I have no family. At least, none that I know of. I—'

The dowager clucked her tongue. 'Good heavens! Marc must have expressed himself with an extraordinary lack of address if you think that sort of thing is important to him.'

'It isn't only my lack of connections,' she said very low. 'My parents weren't even married. Mama and I spent years in the poorhouse. I...I've lied to you consistently, ma'am. Mostly by omission, but also in pretending to be a widow. There was good reason for it. At least, I thought so at the time, and if you'll allow me to explain—'

'Amy, dearest, explanations will make no difference at all.'

Amy's eyes widened in dismay. Every drop of blood drained from her face. 'They won't?'

'Oh, you poor child.' Her ladyship moved closer and put a comforting arm about her shoulders. 'I seem to be as *maladroite* as Marc is today. It must be the disappointment. I was so sure everything was going along swimmingly. Of course, you may explain, Amy. But it won't make any difference to the way I feel about you.' Perhaps sensing from her companion's rigid posture that comfort would only shred her control further, Lady Hawkridge removed her arm from about Amy's shoulders and sat back. 'I still wish to welcome you into the family, and I fully intend to do so.'

'But...' Amy shook her head in bemusement. 'You don't seem to understand, ma'am. I'm illegitimate. My first proper post was as a kitchenmaid to the superintendent of the poorhouse, and after that I wasn't much more than a housemaid. I've been masquerading as a lady's companion. Indeed, as a lady. And—' She took a shaky breath. 'Far from being a widow, I have a husband who is very much alive.'

'Oh, dear,' said the dowager, pursing her lips in grave consideration. 'Yes, indeed. That is a problem. I wonder what we should do about him?'

Amy could only stare at her employer in mute confusion. Her mind, battered already by heartbreak, remorse and unbearable pain, was completely unable to cope with anything else. She simply waited. For judgement. Castigation. She knew not what.

Lady Hawkridge lapsed into silent contemplation for several minutes, then sat up with an air of decision. 'Have you told Marc about your husband, Amy?'

She nodded. 'And I just realised... I'm sorry. I should have thought of it before... But I was so distressed, and... I have to warn Lord Nettlebed.'

The dowager untangled this incoherent speech and seized on the point that was missing. 'Why?'

Amy took a ragged breath. 'Ma'am, my husband is Mr Chatsworth.'

'Good heavens!' Lady Hawkridge fell back against the sofa, a hand to her heart.

'Yes.' Amy braced herself for blame, recrimination, and revulsion.

'God bless my soul, what a dreadful shock to have one's husband return from the grave like that. Not that I wouldn't have wished to see Marc's grandpapa, because I was very much attached to him. But he was a good person, which it seems to me your husband is not.'

'Uh...'

'When did you find out?'

Amy's brain reeled anew. 'Yesterday. Oh, ma'am, you don't have any reason to believe me when I've lied to you, but I truly didn't know. You see, he left the party early the other night, and—'

'Well, of course, you didn't know, Amy. And you haven't actually lied to me, dear, except about being a widow, which I dare say is quite understandable now that I know Mr Chatsworth is your husband. What's more, I wager you've told Marc a great deal more about yourself *without* lying.'

'Yes.' She glanced down at her hands. 'I wanted to tell him everything, but...I didn't know why. *Then.*'

'Hmm.' Lady Hawkridge's mind was clearly on more pressing matters. 'What did Marc say about Mr Chatsworth?'

'I only told him my husband was alive, and Marc...that is, Lord Hawkridge didn't say *anything*. Not that I wondered about that. I could scarcely speak, myself.'

'No, indeed.' The dowager sat up again and patted her hand sympathetically. 'As for Marc's uncharacteristic silence, well, you must have given him quite a shock. You know, Amy, when a man has laid bare his heart, and been rejected, for whatever reason, he will not be thinking with any clarity of intellect.'

'He didn't mention his heart,' Amy pointed out in a very small voice.

Lady Hawkridge shook her head. 'Really, Amy, I can only imagine that your head must have received a harder bump than we first believed. Why else would Marc ask you to marry him if he wasn't in love with you?'

'Because he wants me, ma'am. Oh, dear, that sounds terrible. I mean, I think he does. That is, he looked at me as if he does. I think.'

The dowager frowned. 'It seems to me that you both require assistance in clarifying *what* you think. Let me make one thing clear. Marc would not offer marriage purely to satisfy his physical urges.'

'I know that, ma'am. If I'd expected any sort of offer at all, it would have been a *carte blanche*. But I've come to know him, you see. He's very protective, and honourable, and...'

'Yes, Marc is protective and honourable,' affirmed his fond grandparent, ignoring the sudden sheen of tears in Amy's eyes. 'But he's also an unattached, exceptionally healthy young man. He's taken mistresses before from what one would term the ranks of respectable widows. If that had been his intention in regard to you, the only circumstance that might have stopped him is the fact that you're my companion. And that could easily be overcome. I don't wish to cause you further distress, Amy, but, once you'd responded to his advances, he would simply have made you an offer that would ensure your future financial security and thus satisfy any male notions of honour.'

Amy felt a faint spark of interest. 'He's done that before, ma'am?'

A rather mischievous gleam lit her ladyship's eyes. 'One shouldn't confess to knowing about such things, but yes. When you're married, it will be different, of course. Knowing Marc as I do, I shouldn't think he'd even look at another woman.'

'But we're not going to be married.' Anguish, momentarily stifled in talking about Hawkridge, returned with devastating force. Amy dug her ragged nails into her palms to stop another onrush of tears. The sting of last night's grazes barely registered. 'Whatever his reason for proposing marriage...I've destroyed it. Even if I wasn't already married, I deceived him. Just like that other lady. He won't want to see me again.'

'Of course he will,' declared her ladyship stoutly. 'And when he does, you will have to tell him everything.'

'I intend to, ma'am. If he'll listen.' Imbued by her employer's determination, she stiffened her spine. 'If he won't, I'll write him a letter. Perhaps you'd give it to him when I'm gone.'

'I don't think you should make any plans to go anywhere, Amy. It sounds as if Marc already has enough to overset his temper. Chasing you all over the countryside isn't likely to improve his mood.'

'No, ma'am.'

'What we shall do is go upstairs so you can rest in bed while we decide what to tell Bevan.'

'Yes, ma'am.'

'A brief note to the effect that an acquaintance recognised Mr Chatsworth yesterday and warned us that he's a fortune-hunter of the worst kind should suffice. Until Marc is aware of the facts, the fewer people who know Chatsworth is your husband, the better.'

'Yes, ma'am.'

'And then, Amy, after you've told me the entire story, you are going have a nice, long sleep, even if I have to tip Dr Twinhoe's laudanum down your throat.'

'But, ma'am—'

'You don't wish to show Marc a haggard countenance, do you?'

'No, ma'am.'

'That's better.'

* * *

Surprisingly, she did sleep—for several hours—the vicissitudes of the past two days proving more effective than Dr Twinhoe's laudanum. The long rest enabled Amy to rise from her bed with nerves fluttering in her stomach, but decision firming her spine.

None of the decisions involved leaving Hawkridge Manor. At least, not yet. She couldn't leave before finding out if the dowager was right in thinking that Hawkridge was in love with her.

And if he was...

Oh, if he was...

But Amy suppressed the pang of yearning immediately. She'd sealed pain away in a dark corner of her mind, but there it crouched, waiting to spring out and devour the tiny flicker of hope that burned, valiant but terrifyingly fragile, in the deepest recesses of her heart. She couldn't risk that vulnerable flame by thinking too far ahead. It would be enough if he still wanted her.

Besides, her ladyship hadn't known all the facts when she'd voiced that opinion. Hawkridge did know her background and, knowing it, would never have proposed an improper liaison.

Which meant that she would have to propose it.

Amy reached for her clothes and began dressing. It was a good thing she was accustomed to fighting her own battles, she mused, because she was going to need every ounce of determination she possessed. She couldn't afford to stumble. If she hesitated just once, if Hawkridge suspected for one instant that she was quaking inside, his highly developed protective instincts would strip her of all hope.

So she planned. And she waited. She waited so long that when the front door banged, hours after the dowager had looked in on her way to bed, she leapt out of her chair and almost stumbled from sitting curled up for so long.

Putting a hand to the mantel to steady herself, Amy stood poised, listening, hardly daring to breathe in case she missed the sound of his footsteps passing her door. Until she was sure it was him.

A faint echo of his voice came to her as he spoke to Pickles. He must have reached the top of the stairs. She slumped, only then acknowledging that she'd been worried about him. He'd been gone so long and—

His footsteps, muted by the carpet, stopped outside her door.

Amy froze, her gaze flying to the doorknob. A pulse pounded in her temples; her breath seized.

His footsteps moved on. A door closed further along the hall.

She gasped in air, dashed over to the door and flung it open.

The empty hall, lit by candelabra at regular intervals, stretched before her.

Amy pressed a hand to her breast to slow her breathing. Her heart thudded against her palm, her vision blurred. And in the misty haze that formed before her eyes she saw her mother, Cora and every unmarried woman she'd ever encountered in the poorhouse, their thin hands clasped, warning in their faces, despair stealing their youth.

Except her mother. The misty image smiled with a serenity never attainable in life, and, for the first time, Amy understood why her mother had left home and family, casting aside every semblance of security, for a love that was stronger than any fear of consequence. A love that was worth any risk. A love that needed to give, of everything she was.

Lifting her chin, she walked down the hall and knocked softly on Hawkridge's door.

It was opened before she'd lowered her hand. He loomed over her, big and powerful, just as she'd first seen him, his brows drawing together in a quick frown.

'Amy? What the devil—?'

He broke off, glanced swiftly towards the stairs, then grabbed her hand and yanked her into the room. 'What the devil are you doing here at this time of night?' he demanded in a wrathful undertone. 'Don't you know that Pickles is going about the house snuffing out candles?'

He thumped the door shut, making her start. Amy's eyes widened. She hadn't anticipated a flood of reproaches, but Hawkridge looked neither heartbroken nor filled with revulsion. His fingers were still gripping her hand, but the frown between his brows indicated annoyance more than anything else.

'I have to speak to you,' she said at last, and tried to stop the fingers of her other hand from shredding her skirts.

He studied her frowningly for an instant, then released her hand, raising his own to touch the faint bruise on her forehead. 'You've taken your bandage off,' he murmured.

And he'd removed his coat and cravat. But she registered the small details only because she didn't want to think about the remote calmness in his voice, the lightness of his touch.

Had she destroyed everything? Was it too late?

But even as the pain so carefully locked away threatened to break free, his gaze flashed back to hers and without warning his eyes turned molten, brilliant, searing. The blast of heat hit her like a wall of flame. She gasped, almost staggering back. He wheeled, strode across the room to the windows, and shoved his fists into his breeches pockets.

'All right. I'm listening.'

Amy swallowed. She was shaking all over after that coruscating look, but not with doubt. He still wanted her.

She clutched determination to her like a shield and launched into the speech she'd rehearsed for hours.

'My lord, you did me the very great honour, this morning, of asking me to be your wife, and though I had to refuse, I wasn't…specific enough in my refusal.'

He turned slowly to face her. She couldn't be sure in the shadows where he stood, but she thought his mouth quirked. 'Amy, I think "I can't marry you because my husband isn't dead", is rather specific.'

'As far as marriage goes, yes.' She swallowed again. 'But—I could be your mistress.' Despite her resolve, the last words were whispered.

But he heard them. He came forward, until only a few feet separated them. When she looked into his eyes, her heart started racing like the hooves of a runaway team.

'You're willing to be my mistress? To put yourself in such a vulnerable position?'

'Yes.'

'Why?'

'Because last night…we could have been killed, and I would never have known…' She shook her head sharply. 'I realised that being with you, belonging to you, is more important than safety or logic or all the sensible things that say I shouldn't do this. I know you won't abandon me if there should be a child, or leave me destitute if you tire of me. And—'

'Tire of you?' Marc stared at her, trying to clear the haze that seemed to be impeding his thought processes. He couldn't remember everything Amy had said. An explanation for her offer hammered somewhere in his brain, but all he could think about was the offer itself.

She was willing to give herself to him without any assurances as to her future, without the security of marriage, to take the risks her mother had taken.

She was willing to trust him.

'Why?' he said again.

Amy lifted her chin. She would give him this. She would give him everything. 'Because I love you.'

A shudder racked his powerful body. She could see it from where she stood. He whipped his hands out of his pockets, closed the distance between them in two long strides and caught her up in his arms.

'Oh, God, Amy! Amy! It's going to be all right. I promise. You don't have to worry. I—'

He broke off, pressing his mouth to her hair, her face, her throat. He was shaking, she realised in wonder. The strength in him was overwhelming—he could have crushed her without thinking about it—but he was shaking, shuddering like a blooded stallion straining at the bit.

She couldn't think beyond that. He'd seemed so invulnerable. Not to hurt, but to her. His was the position of power, his the control. She hadn't suspected she could affect him so. Just for an instant, she had a glimmer of understanding, that there was more here, in his fierce embrace, than simple desire, but he was speaking again, his voice so low she couldn't make out the words, and the feeling slipped away. All she knew was that urgent male hunger roughened his voice in a way that sent chills of excitement feathering over her flesh, that the coiled tension in his body made her press against him in a purely feminine instinct to assuage that hunger.

Then he lifted her, strode over to the bed and lowered her on to it, and she ceased thinking at all. He came down over her, pinning her to the bed before she'd taken another breath.

Amy trembled as she felt his weight for the first time, gasped as he pressed a knee between her thighs, parting them, bringing their bodies into such intimate contact that her senses swam. She'd known he was big, but lying beneath him like this, completely at the mercy of his much greater strength, was too much. Too soon. Too fast. Excitement set fire to every nerve-ending, but she hadn't expected him to claim her seconds after her offer to become his mistress.

She gripped his shoulders, not certain if she was going to cling or try to hold him off. 'My lord...'

'Marc,' he said, pressing urgent little kisses over her face. 'Say it.'

'Marc—'

The rest was smothered as his mouth came down on hers. His fingers speared through her hair, holding her head still; his tongue plundered, penetrating, retreating, over and over until she couldn't think beyond the demands he was making. Every muscle in her body trembled and went weak, preparing for surrender.

Every muscle in his shuddered and went rigid, ready to conquer. The arms about her were like iron; his shoulders tensed, seeming to curve over her, around her. He crushed her into the bedding, moving against her with a fierce urgency that rendered their clothing well nigh invisible.

She made a small frantic sound, the hard thrust of his body overwhelming her almost to the point of insensibility, and as abruptly as the storm had broken, it ceased. Marc wrenched his mouth from hers and stared down at her.

'Amy. God, what am I doing? I can't make love to you like this.'

She gazed back at him, shaking. Her eyes felt as if they were eclipsing her entire face. His were blazing. 'You can't?'

'No.' The word was a hoarse groan. His chest heaved as he struggled to control his breathing. 'I've never been so close to losing control. I could hurt you.' He moved again, this time with a slow yearning thrust that sent a wave of piercingly sweet pleasure through her. If his weight hadn't held her down, she would have arched.

He let his head fall forward until his brow rested on hers. His teeth clenched. 'And, apart from that, I can't make love to you here.'

'Why—?'

'Don't move.'

She blinked at him. 'I didn't move.'

'You're breathing, damn it.' He took a breath himself. 'Bloody hell!'

Flattening his hands on either side of her head, he pushed himself away from her with such force she felt as if part of her had gone with him. But even as the wrenching sense of loss took hold, he was scooping her up off the bed and carrying her across the room.

'Not a word,' he growled softly, and set her on her feet to one side of the door.

He opened it, glanced up and down the hall, then, drawing her out of the room, shut the door and led her back to her own chamber.

The instant he closed her door she was in his arms again and his mouth was on hers.

Just as well, Amy thought hazily. Her legs weren't going to hold her up another second. She was trembling like a leaf in a tempest, tossed this way and that, but even as she quivered in anticipation of another storm, she realised his embrace was different. He held her as if he'd never let her go, the rigid male flesh pressed to her was no less intimidating, but she sensed the urgency driving him was under an iron-fisted control.

And knowing it, she yielded, sinking into the warmth and strength enfolding her, lifting her mouth for his kiss, parting her lips for his possession, until a new and pulsing heat began throbbing deep inside her.

'God,' he muttered, lifting his head and staring down into her dazed eyes. 'I don't know what's worse. Not kissing you at all, or kissing you knowing that's all we're going to do for the moment.'

'It is?' she asked hazily. She looked about the room and finally caught up with him. 'Is that why you brought me back here?'

'No.' He bent to nip her lower lip in the gentlest of tiny bites, then put her firmly away from him. 'I brought you back here because we don't want the maids finding you in the wrong bed in the morning, or wondering why you're up and dressed before dawn. My appearance at that hour won't arouse any questions. I often ride early.'

'Oh.' That tiny bite had obviously unhinged her wits. She couldn't seem to think straight. Did that mean he was going to stay all night? But in that case, why was he pacing over to the window as if he wanted to put as much distance between them as possible?

'I thought you meant that because I was hurt, we weren't... But I really am much better now and—'

She forgot the rest when he swung about to face her. The fierce desire in his eyes had the muscles in her lower body dissolving into liquid fire.

'Oh, yes,' he said, very softly, as if she'd asked a question. 'I'm more than capable of making love to you without adding to your bruises. I'm just trying to keep my distance long enough for us to talk.'

'Talk? Oh, heavens!' She made her shaky way to a chair and sank onto it. 'Yes, my lord. I think you *had* better stay over there. I just remembered that I have a great deal to say.'

Despite the barely contained intensity vibrating in the air around him, a wicked smile dawned. 'Say it fast.'

Amy swallowed. 'This will come as something of a shock.'

'After this morning, Amy, I'm immune to shocks.'

'I don't think so, sir. You see, my husband is Mr Chatsworth.'

'*What?*'

'Yes.' She clasped her hands. 'I didn't know until yesterday because I didn't see him at Nettlebed Place, but it's all right because Lady Hawkridge wrote a note to Lord Nettlebed warning him that James is a fortune-hunter who preys on innocent schoolgirls. That's one of the things he does. He knows the parents will pay him off rather than risk a scandal. Not that he actually elopes with them. He used to disappear, and now he's married to me, but nobody knows that except you and Lady Hawkridge.'

This breathless speech was destined to remain unacknowledged for several seconds. Not that Hawkridge appeared to be struck dumb with shock, Amy thought, studying him anxiously. He was watching her, but the frown in his eyes seemed more thoughtful than anything else.

'That isn't all,' she went on, determined to get everything out at once. 'He slipped me a note yesterday, telling me to meet him on the beach so he could blackmail me into helping him with Lucinda, and if she won't elope with him, he thinks I'll help him rob you and Lady Hawkridge. But I won't.' She leaned forward, her eyes pleading. 'I *won't*! I'd rather be transported than betray you so.'

His eyes narrowed with sudden attention. 'Why is transportation a threat?'

'I helped him before.' The memory washed the colour from her cheeks. Her fingers gripped, entwined, tangled. 'But I didn't mean to. I didn't *know*.'

'Amy.' He came forward and hunkered down before her, covering her restless hands with one of his. 'It's all right, sweetheart. I had to ask, to know what you'd done so I can protect you, but there's no need to be afraid. No one's going to hurt you. This is what you almost told me the other day, isn't it?'

'Yes. I wanted to tell you.' She clung to the steady reassurance in his eyes, the strength of his hand. 'You see, a few weeks after I met James, he asked me to marry him. I think...I think it was impulse. Perhaps he wanted me and knew I'd accept nothing less than marriage. He said he wanted to take care of me, although it was I who was employed. That was odd. He had money, but no apparent means of support. When I asked about it, he talked vaguely of investments. I believed him—what did I know of such things?'

He nodded. 'Go on.'

'After we married James wanted us to move to London where he had friends, but Mama was too ill. She couldn't travel and I wouldn't leave her, so he went alone, saying he'd find work and a place for us to live. I had to leave the school to nurse Mama and, at first, James did send money, but his letters became fewer, and angrier, and finally stopped altogether.'

Hawkridge stroked his thumb across her hands. 'And then?'

She glanced down briefly. 'After Mama died I followed James to London. He got quite a shock when I turned up. It was almost as if he'd forgotten my existence. I even had to spend that first night at a coffee-house because there was no room where he was living—or so he said. But the next day he found me a place as housemaid to Lord Tinsley.'

'An exceedingly wealthy Viscount,' Hawkridge put in drily. 'You don't need to tell me the rest, Amy. Several pieces have finally dropped into place. Such as your reaction to that report in the *Morning Post*.'

'You know what that cutting was about?' she asked, her eyes widening.

'I looked through my own copy of the paper. That article was the only one that seemed apt.' A wry smile curved his mouth. 'I know you asked me to wait until you confided in me, but, as *you* know, waiting is not my favourite pastime. I intended to find out what had upset you, one way or another.'

She blinked at him. 'Asked you to wait—? But...I was talking about your grandmother.'

His brows went up. 'Grandmama seems to be doing quite well on her own account, if the conversation I had earlier today with Colborough is any indication. But never mind that. Am I right in assuming that Chatsworth broke into Tinsley's house, tied you up along with the rest of the servants and robbed the place?'

'Yes.' She would have wrung her hands again if Hawkridge hadn't been holding them. 'I didn't mean to help him, but James asked questions about the family and their movements and so forth, and I answered. I felt so guilty about leaving him on his own for weeks and weeks, and then we still couldn't live together. The only way we could meet was when I was sent out to the market or given a half-hour off. I was so anxious to make up for my neglect, for my coldness, as he put it, that I didn't think twice when he questioned me. I thought he was making an effort to be nicer.' She shook her head. 'Stupid! *Stupid!*'

'No,' he said sharply. 'Innocent. Frightened. Alone.' His fingers tightened on each word, until, realising he might be hurting her, he released her and stood up.

'Do you think a judge will take that into account?' she asked shakily, watching him pace over to the window again. She wished she still had his warmth to cling to. 'You see, that isn't all. When I realised what I'd done, what James had done, we had the most dreadful argument. I'd been totally mistaken in him. He told me he'd struck up an acquaintance with Mama and I to find out if there were any wealthy pupils at the Misses Appleton's school, and since he'd given up the scheme for my sake, I had to help him in his other endeavours.

'The Tinsley robbery wasn't the first, nor did he intend it to be the last. I refused, of course. I threatened to inform against him, but he laughed. He pointed out that the money he'd given me previously, indeed, the money he forced on me then, would convict me along with him. After all, who would believe a girl from the poorhouse? So...I took the money and ran.'

He turned. 'To Bath?'

'No. Not then. I went to some little town... I can't even remember its name. I found work at an inn, but, after a while, the innkeeper... Well, I had to wedge a chair against my door every night. One night he started to smash his way in, and I climbed out of the window and ran away again. He hadn't paid me, of course. I'd been there less than the half-year, but I still had some of the money that James had given me. This time I managed to think—running from a drunken innkeeper wasn't as frightening as running from transportation or the gallows—so while I walked to the next town, I planned.

'I'd heard the Tinsleys' housekeeper talk about Bath, that it was full of elderly widows, so I bought a fashionable dress, travelled by various stages to Bath and took a room at a respectable inn. I thought if I posed as a widow, I might have a better chance of being employed by one.'

When no comment on that assumption was forthcoming, she made a little gesture. 'That's all.'

That probably wasn't even half of it, Marc thought savagely, pacing restlessly about the room. He couldn't be still. His entire body was coiled and tense with the need to lash out at something.

If that drunken lout of an innkeeper had appeared before him, he would have smashed his fist into the man's face, and once started, he probably wouldn't be able to stop.

As for Amy's matter-of-fact account of walking about the countryside, alone, in the middle of the night, his blood ran cold at the thought of what might have happened to her.

Not frightened? She must have been terrified. Facing the world with nothing and no one; with the spectre of criminal charges hanging over her. And then to find safety, only to have the past rear its head.

'On the other hand,' he said aloud, wheeling abruptly to face her, 'that makes things easier.'

She looked confused. 'Posing as a widow?'

Yes, he thought grimly. That made things very much easier. But he wasn't going to inform Amy of that.

'The coincidence that caused Chatsworth to choose Lucinda and follow her home,' he said.

She shook her head. 'I should have realised that a place like Bath, with its Young Ladies' Academies and wealthy older people, would be a target for someone like James.'

'You could have stumbled across him at any time, Amy. That sort of criminal life requires regular changes of residence. But it doesn't matter now. The point is, he's here, where we can deal with him.'

Chaining the primitive savage prowling beneath the surface, he crossed the room, took her hands and drew her to her feet. 'But we'll talk about that later.'

'What are you going to do?' she whispered.

'Right now?' he asked very softly, and framed her face in his hands. 'I'm going to make love to you.'

He watched her eyes widen, felt the tremor that rippled through her, and had to clamp a firmer hold around the reins of control. She'd been hurt scarcely more than twenty-four hours ago. Tonight she needed gentleness.

If he kept telling himself that, he might be able to manage it.

He lowered his head to kiss her.

'Um...my lord?'

It was the tone of voice that warned him. He paused, looked into her eyes, and felt a reluctant smile tug at his lips. 'Yes?'

One little hand came up to rest against his chest. 'There's just one more thing.'

'This time I'm not making any predictions as to my immunity to shocks. What is it?'

'At first I wasn't going to tell you, but I promised myself I wouldn't lie to you again, even by omission.'

'You never lied to me about your true nature, Amy. That's all I cared about. Now, tell me.'

'You promise you'll still make love to me?'

'Yes, damn it. What—?'

'I haven't done this before.'

He thought his heart stopped. He knew his brain had. 'I beg your pardon?' he asked very politely.

'I never lived with James. The day we married I had to go right back to the school, and in London he was living with another woman, although I didn't know it at the time. We never—' She blushed, enchanting him. 'Made love.'

He took several deep breaths. It was a good thing he was already prepared to be gentle, he thought, because the knowledge that Amy was innocent, that she was his, *only* his, threatened to banish every instinct except the violently throbbing need to possess her.

'Did you love him?' he asked abruptly, and knew he hadn't asked before because he hadn't wanted to hear the answer.

'No.' She regarded him solemnly. 'I know that now. If I'd loved him, I would have made more of an effort to be a true wife. I liked him. He was very charming at first, but I didn't love him. Maybe I was afraid of being alone after Mama died.'

Her gaze dropped to her hand, still resting against his shirt, then lifted again. 'I'm not afraid of being alone any more. I was prepared to leave, when I thought you wouldn't want me because I'd lied to you. I know I can survive on my own. I've done it. That isn't why I went to your room tonight. I *choose* to be with you, to be your mistress, for as long as you want me.'

'Oh, God, Amy—'

He swooped, taking her mouth before the next words were clear in his mind. Forever, he thought hazily. He wanted her forever. As his mistress, his wife, the mother of his children.

He had to tell her that, had to reassure her that everything would be all right, but coherent thought was impossible with her lips softening and parting beneath his, with the sweet scent of her skin filling his senses, with her body trembling before he'd even touched her.

Later. He was going to need every ounce of control he possessed to take her gently. If the savage inside him had to wait, so could reassurance.

He broke the kiss long enough to pick her up and carry her over to the bed, the soft surrender in her eyes enough to bring his body to full aching arousal in seconds.

But she blinked it away when he stood her beside the bed, and he felt her tense.

'Don't be frightened,' he murmured. 'You took me by surprise before. I won't lose control this time. I won't hurt you.'

'It wasn't exactly frightening,' she said, so earnestly he had to smile. 'Just...faster than I expected.' She blushed, and met his gaze shyly. 'But it was exciting. I liked it.'

The smile reached his eyes. 'Let's see how you like slow,' he murmured and, holding her gaze with his, reached behind her to unfasten the buttons at the back of her dress.

Chapter Fourteen

Slow promised to dazzle her senses.

His arms encircled her; sweet captivity. His hands exerted the gentlest pressure to draw her closer as his fingers slipped buttons free of their fastenings. Her dress loosened, fell away to pool at her ankles.

Amy tipped her head back, wanting Marc to kiss her, to distract her from the nervousness quivering inside her. She wanted him, but she'd never stood before a man and let him undress her. When he loosened the ribbons of her chemise and swept the straps aside, the sudden shyness took her by surprise.

Then he lifted a finger to trace the long scratch across her collarbone, bent and repeated the caress with his mouth, and shyness vanished in the wave of emotion that swept over her.

She swayed and brought her hands up to his chest. The fine lawn of his shirt bunched in her fists, making her blink as she realised that she, too, wanted to touch, to see him without the trappings of civilisation.

'Yes,' he said huskily, straightening as her hands fluttered over his chest. 'Take my shirt off, sweetheart.'

Amy tilted her head, distracted by the practicalities of the task. He'd unfastened the garment earlier, but she'd have to tug it free of his breeches and lift it over his head. And her arms were restricted.

But the goal was too seductive. Without a second's thought, she shimmied free of the confining straps drooping down her arms and reached for his shirt. A quick flick of his fingers had the top button of his breeches undone to facilitate her task. Then she hit a snag.

Her chemise shifted minutely. She glanced down to see its lacy edge clinging precariously to the upper slopes of her breasts. She wasn't built to keep a chemise in place by gravity alone. It was one thing for Marc to remove her garments with gentle care; quite another for her to toss aside years of modesty while flinging shirts about.

She looked up at him. 'You're too tall for me.'

A pulse was beating rapidly in his throat, but he smiled. 'Stand on tip-toe and pull. I'll help.'

Amy took a deep breath, hoped it would improve the situation, and obeyed. The shirt came off, her chemise succumbed to gravity, and she overbalanced into his arms.

They came around her instantly, holding her crushed to his chest. Wild little sunbursts of heat exploded inside her as her nipples rasped against hair-roughened muscle. She forgot about modesty. The sensations winging through her were too enthralling to leave room for anything else. She would have cried out in wonder at the piercing intensity of the pleasure, but Marc's mouth was on hers, swallowing the sound and taking the soft little whimpers that followed.

She flung her arms around his waist, clinging to his strength; her own had deserted her. His mouth was hot, his arms hard, the smooth flesh of his back burning her hands as she pressed them to the long muscles bracketing his spine. She parted her lips, aching for the intimacy of having him inside her mouth, needing to be part of him and knowing only that way.

Marc shuddered heavily as Amy's tongue met his with shy eagerness, as she joined him in a sensuous dance of demand and retreat. Sliding, stroking, tasting, taking. Her wild response went to his head like potent brandy; the softness of her breasts, their firm little peaks pressed to his chest, had his body hardening to the point of agony.

He tore his mouth from hers before he gave in to the urge to take her right there on the floor.

'Amy, sweetheart, we have to slow down.'

She blinked up at him, her eyes dazed with the beginnings of arousal. 'I thought we were going slow.'

'In that case, we'd better try slower.'

'I don't think that's a good idea,' she said weakly. 'I'm finding it very difficult to stand.'

He gritted his teeth against another wave of need, and prayed he'd have the strength to keep his footing against the undertow of aching desire. The sweet openness of her response almost brought him to his knees; it also threatened to shred his control.

'Then we'll lie down,' he said hoarsely, and lifted her on to the bed, turning away immediately before he managed to shock her right out of her dazed state. The single glance he had of soft round breasts, their rosy little crowns begging mutely for attention had the reins of control slipping and sliding through his fingers as though he'd never seen a naked woman before. He didn't dare look at her until he'd retrieved them.

Unfortunately, Amy wasn't co-operating. She slithered down the bed and reached out to touch his thigh. The need to turn, to move so that questing little hand could slide over the front of his breeches, had his teeth clenching so hard his jaw cracked.

'It's very odd, my lord, but when I touch you, it makes me feel quite incredibly weak.'

'And you make me feel incredibly powerful,' he grated, sitting down to yank off his boots. Too damn powerful. For the first time he understood how his primitive ancestors had been capable of dragging the women of their choice into a cave and taking them whether they were willing or not. He, too, could have plundered, ravaged, devoured. And he would, he promised himself as the second boot hit the floor. But not this time.

She was already bruised.

He turned his head on the thought. Amy made a move as though she would cover her breasts, then went still, watching him. The love and trust in her eyes shook him to his soul, clearing the mists of desire long enough for him to see the pale blue mark that curved around her ribs. He already knew her arms looked like she'd been dragged through a row of hedges. God knew what he couldn't see.

Grimly determined to find out, Marc turned fully towards her and pushed her petticoats up to her knees. She'd put on her white stockings but no shoes. He drew her stockings off, taking note of each small wound as it was revealed. None were serious, but he glimpsed the bandage beneath the froth of her petticoats, remembered the sight of her blood on his hands when they'd returned to the house last night, and shook with the need to pull her up into his arms, to feel her against him, warm and safe and alive.

When he got his hands on her husband—

He shut off the thought instantly. Chantry, or Chatsworth or whatever he chose to call himself, had no place here.

Amy stirred and reached out to touch the hand he'd fisted beside her hip. 'See. I'm not really black and blue all over.'

Marc sent her a look that told her precisely what he thought of that assessment, but his touch was gentle as he lifted one little foot and brushed his lips across the scratch on her instep.

Amy felt her toes curl.

Her petticoat slid higher as he touched his mouth to the faint graze on her calf. Heat bloomed. He kissed the bruise on her knee; she sank deeper into the bed. He swirled his tongue gently around another on her thigh; every muscle quivered and went limp.

'Marc?'

'Hmmm.'

'Are you going to kiss every single bruise?'

'Every single one,' he murmured, and turned his attention to her other leg.

Amy thought of the various locations of her wounds. 'Oh, my goodness.'

His mouth curved against her inner thigh. The hot tingle of excitement that resulted distracted her so much she didn't realise her bunched-up petticoat and chemise were being removed until cool air brushed her skin.

She shivered, but not with cold. He curved his hand to her waist, brushed his thumb across the underside of her breast, stroked downward until the heel of his palm rested above the soft triangle shielding her femininity. And everywhere he touched, she burned.

'You're so tiny,' he whispered. 'So soft.'

'You're not,' she breathed, scarcely able to speak. She didn't have to touch him to know the truth of that statement; sudden tension defined his muscles in a way that had her softening inside in a response as primitive as the sheer physical power of his body. She wanted to move, to arch into his touch, but the shuddering stillness in him held her in a vise of almost unbearable anticipation.

'No,' he said, and her eyes widened at the guttural tone of his voice. 'I'm bigger than you. Harder. Stronger.' His gaze flashed to hers, silver fires burning, and she trembled with helpless excitement. 'Does that frighten you?'

Very slowly she moved her head from side to side.

'It should,' he said. And suddenly his hand was shaking against her flesh. 'It should, because it scares the hell out of me. Oh, God, Amy—'

He bent; his arms went around her, clasping her hips as he pressed his face to the softness of her belly. She felt the sharp edge of his teeth, the hot sweep of his tongue. 'I could devour you,' he said hoarsely. 'Take you to places you haven't even dreamed of. Dark places, where all you'll know, all you'll want, all you'll feel, is me, inside you, taking you, until you scream with the pleasure of it. And I'll keep you there forever. Mine! Always!' His arms tightened. 'Now are you scared?'

For a moment she couldn't speak. Her lips parted, but she couldn't answer. Love flooded her entire being, love so powerful, so all-encompassing she wondered her heart didn't simply shatter with the pressure of it. And with it came a swift bright flash of awareness—that in the battle he waged between savage desire and equally fierce protectiveness, it was she who held the balance.

She lifted her hand, touched his head. 'I'll never be afraid with you, Marc. No matter where you take me. No matter how long you keep me there. I know you'll never hurt me.'

'No,' he vowed. 'Never. You never have to be afraid again.' He shuddered as a measure of control returned, wondering how she'd done it, how she'd drawn him back from the brink of savagery. And knew, when he straightened to look at her, that it was her fragility and trusting innocence that had given him the strength to harness his instincts. Not the easy control he'd used with other women.

A fragility that was all too apparent in the delicate body he could have lifted with one hand; an innocence that brought a blush to her cheeks even as she smiled.

'I'm not afraid now,' she said softly, and held out her hand.
'And I won't break.'

'I hope not,' he rasped as his fingers enveloped hers. 'Because
I can't seem to concentrate on bruises when so many other sweet
places are waiting to be kissed.'

She blushed again, but her gaze travelled over him as if she,
too, wanted to savour. The tip of her tongue moistened her lips
and with a hoarse sound of need, Marc lowered himself over her.

Amy cried out softly as his weight came down on her. He was
so big, so strong. The dark pelt on his chest brushed her breasts,
excitingly male to her female. She stroked her hands through it,
slid them upwards. Such hard muscle beneath warm supple skin.
She felt both safe and deliciously wanton lying beneath him like
this, the sense of vulnerability that had overwhelmed her before
lessened with her legs locked between his.

'We're so different,' she murmured, stroking her hands downward again. Her fingers found two hard male nipples nestled in
whorls of hair and she stroked curiously.

His breath hissed between his teeth.

'Oh, I'm sorry.' Her gaze flew to his. 'Did that hurt?'

A smile glittered through the blazing intensity in his eyes. 'You
tell me,' he growled. And cupping one breast in his hand, he
stroked his thumb across its ruched pink tip.

Amy gasped and jerked as a thrilling little *frisson* of pleasure
darted through her.

'Did it hurt?' he murmured.

'N...no.'

'Good,' he said, and did it again, slower, firmer.

Fire streaked straight to the place where her legs were pressed
together. He made a rough sound in his throat and stroked her
again and again, until her nipple was a hard little bud of throbbing
sensation, until she was whimpering, clinging, trying to anchor
herself as her senses threatened to fly apart.

A protest, a plea, parted her lips, but even as she arched in
frantic demand, Marc bent his head and closed his mouth hotly
over the peak he'd tormented and her vision hazed. She fell back
against the sheets, lost in the fierce pleasure of his mouth at her
breast.

He didn't stop until she was quivering and writhing beneath him, and then only so he could deliver the same sweet torment to her other breast.

'I knew you'd be like this,' he rasped. 'Sweet and hot and wanting.'

Amy moaned under the fresh onslaught, barely hearing the husky words. Wanting? She burned. She *craved*. Hot little sparks kept cascading through her. She was aching in places that hadn't even been bruised. She needed him to touch the throbbing place between her legs, needed to part them, to cradle his hard male flesh against her, to have him fill the aching emptiness within, but he kept his own legs clamped about hers.

The thought came to her that he was restraining her so he could hold on to his own control, and with a sound of frustration, she shifted, struggling to get her hands between them, to be rid of the one remaining barrier.

'No, Amy. Wait.' He lifted his mouth from her breast, his breath bathing the wet, rosy tip. 'You really are tiny, darling. I have to be sure you're ready for me.'

'I am ready,' she said with sudden fierceness. 'I want you.'

He gave a short, ragged laugh and kissed her, quick and hard. 'God, you don't even know what I'm talking about, do you? And right now, it doesn't seem to matter.'

He rolled away, shucked his breeches in one swift move, and was back beside her in seconds. It was time enough for Amy to see what he meant.

'Oh, my goodness.'

'Don't worry,' he growled as he gathered her into his arms. 'The seemingly impossible is not only attainable, but, as of this second, as inevitable as the tides.' His mouth came down on hers. He parted her legs with his hand and slid one long finger into her secret, most female flesh.

She gave a muffled cry, startled by the invasion and the intense wave of pleasure that broke over her. The wet, gliding sensation of his thumb on a place she'd never been aware of before was so shockingly, deliciously voluptuous, she forgot about the mind-numbing intimacy of his touch and simply responded; arching, moving in counterpoint to his caresses in a dance as old as time.

The pressure of his mouth turned almost brutally demanding, but his hand remained so gentle the combination made her senses swim. She felt her body melt beneath his fingers, felt her legs widen in wanton invitation, felt the waves building, higher and higher. Then he carefully lifted her bandaged leg over his hip and her eyes flew open at the first seeking touch of his body. Her breath seized. Her heart had raced past frantic long ago. She stared up at him, quivering with a primitive awareness of his size and power, of her vulnerability.

'Marc?'

He framed her face with his hands, holding her still for his gaze as he rocked against her, the gentle movements in stark contrast to the tension shuddering through his body. 'Hush,' he murmured. 'It will be all right, darling. Just be still. I'll try not to hurt you, but if I do…it will only be for a moment.'

His face was hard-edged with passion, his eyes narrowed, fiercely intent, but his voice was so darkly tender she felt it resonate deep inside her, relaxing her, easing his way.

'It doesn't matter,' she gasped, every particle of her being suddenly focused on the place where they joined. He was barely moving, entering her only an inch or two at a time before drawing back. The sensation was driving her wild. She wanted more of him, all of him.

With a small frantic sound she lifted herself, sheer female instinct guiding her to wrap her legs around him—and with an almost audible crack the chains of his control snapped open. A harsh groan tore from his throat. Clamping an arm around her hips to hold her still, he thrust hard, driving himself to the hilt.

A lightning flash of pain streaked through her, gone in seconds. Pleasure followed instantly, flooding her with sensations beyond belief. She trembled uncontrollably, aching for more. There had to be more. She sensed it in the streamers of heat coiling tighter and tighter inside her, but Marc held rigidly still, his breathing harsh against her cheek.

'Are you all right?' he ground out.

'Yes.' Her voice was high and thin, almost soundless. Somewhere in her mind she knew he was waiting for her body to adjust to his, but all she could think of was the urgency building inside her, the incredible sense of joining. One. Inseparable. Hearts beating wildly in tandem, breaths mingling, limbs clinging. And the heavy throbbing of his flesh within hers, the soft secret pulses of her response that made him groan and shudder with the effort at control.

With heart-shattering care he withdrew a short way, then pressed deeper. She moaned and arched, her head falling back over his arm. Steel and heat locked around her. His lips seared her throat. 'Amy...I don't think I can go slow anymore.'

'I don't want you to,' she cried. 'Oh, Marc...Marc..'

'Yes!' he said hoarsely, and pressing his face to her hair, he began to move with a power that had her crying out in mingled shock and excitement. Her senses reeled, recovered, then revelled in his fierce possession. Tension wound, tighter, tighter; heat flooded her until she thought she couldn't take anymore. She would burn, like lightning exploding until there was nothing left.

She sobbed frantically, trying to fight free of the coiling heat, to catch up to her soaring senses, to *breathe*. He muttered something; words of reassurance, of demand, she couldn't tell. Then he slid one hand beneath her hips and lifted her into his thrusts, and the unbearable tension sprang open, flooding her with pleasure so intense she screamed, knowing nothing but the wild pulsing of her body; wanting nothing but the exquisite release washing over her; feeling only him, inside her, all around her, taking her. Blind and helpless with the ecstasy of it, she gave herself up to him.

And with her utter surrender Marc loosed the savage in him. Clamping his mouth over Amy's to swallow her cries, he thrust again and again into the hot silken depths of her body, driving for his own release until the world vanished in a white-hot blaze of completion.

'You *are* going to marry me.'

The gravelly-voiced decree wafted down through the layers of oblivion in which she floated.

Amy stirred and tried to drift upwards. It wasn't the first time she'd surfaced. She vaguely remembered tender kisses following the storm; the comfort of a cool, damp cloth between her legs; the secure haven of strong arms. She'd drifted, feeling utterly replete.

As if something she hadn't even known was missing was now, forever, part of her.

Marc.

She smiled and tried to snuggle closer. And discovered that Marc was lying half-over her. He was heavy. She contemplated a vague protest, then decided it was too much trouble. She couldn't move anyway. Every muscle and bone in her body had melted.

'Amy.'

The soft demand halted another descent into lassitude. Amy opened her eyes and blinked sleepily up at him. 'Hmmm?'

Amusement curved his mouth, but his eyes glittered with a lazy sensuality that caused an echo of pleasure to hum inside her.

She closed her eyes again to savour the sensation.

He put his lips to her ear. 'You know, there's a certain etiquette that must be observed in these situations, Mrs Chantry.'

'There is?'

'One does not go to sleep when one's partner is trying to conduct a conversation.'

'Oh.' Amy prised her eyelids open. Limp though she was, she managed to curl an arm around his neck. 'Not asleep,' she sighed, and stretched languourously beneath him.

Her very limp form was abruptly crushed to the bedding. Marc came over her, thrust her legs apart with his and pressed himself against her in unmistakable demand.

Amy's eyes snapped fully open. She was suddenly feeling a vast deal more wide awake.

'That's better,' he growled, and moved back slightly.

She pouted in disappointment. She'd never pouted before in her entire life.

'Stop trying to distract me,' he ordered. But he bent to stroke his tongue across her lower lip. 'We need to talk.'

'We do?' That was going to be difficult, she mused, because he'd just succeeded in thoroughly distracting her.

'Yes. You're going to marry me.'

'What?' Her brain reeled.

'Amy, see if you can pay attention here. We're getting married.'

'But..' She tried to rally her startled wits. 'How? I mean...oh, Marc, I want to marry you more than anything in the world, but—'

The rest was smothered by a fierce kiss. When he finally let her up for air, her senses were whirling.

'Divorce,' he said succinctly, and smiled.

Amy blinked at the expression. Only a simpleton would have called it nice; the set of his mouth held far too much deadly purpose.

'Divorce? But...the Earl of Hawkridge can't marry a divorced woman. Think of the scandal.'

'Believe me, my little innocent, there'll be a great deal more scandal when people start suspecting you're my mistress. Which they will,' he added when she opened her mouth to argue, 'because, after tonight, I have no intention of staying out of your bed. The only scandal attached to a discreet divorce brought by a woman is when the husband contests the charges, causing some very nasty linen to be aired in public.'

She considered that. 'What makes you think James won't contest? Not because he wants me, but...' She looked up at him, sudden distress shaking her voice. 'I don't want you to give him money. To...to...*buy* me.'

'Amy.' He stroked her tousled curls, then cupped her face in his hands. 'My sweet, beautiful Amy. I'm not going to buy you. I'd never do that to you. Chatsworth won't contest a divorce.' His face went hard. 'If he tries it, he'll end up on the gallows.'

Her swift intake of air had him cloaking the murderous look he knew was in his eyes. 'So might I,' she whispered.

'No.' The answer was immediate, and absolute. 'We can get him on the Bristol robberies, which have nothing to do with you. As for what happened in London, if Chatsworth is stupid enough to mention your name, his rantings will be put down to revenge because you warned Lucinda's family about him.'

'But...Lord Tinsley...'

He lifted a quizzical brow. 'Darling, how often did the Tinsleys see you during the few weeks you spent dusting the furniture? Once? Twice? They'd never recognise you, especially now.'

'No. I suppose...' Her eyes widened when she realised she'd run out of 'buts'. For the first time, hope shimmered on her horizon. She almost believed the tiny golden flame wouldn't wink out if she dared to seize it.

'I'll find out from Lucinda where Chatsworth is staying, and see him in the morning,' Marc was saying, as if that was all it would take. 'He's not at the Green Man, but he must be somewhere within reasonable distance.'

Amy's mind reeled at his unshakable confidence. If nothing else, she believed that James would try to turn the situation to his advantage. Or that he'd turn violent if his plans were thwarted.

She shivered slightly. 'You will be careful, won't you, Marc? James has a temper. I didn't see it until the robbery. One of Lord Tinsley's footmen tried to resist and James beat the man insensible, even though the first blow had subdued him. And the other day...I don't think he meant to hurt me, but if he hadn't shoved past me on that path, I probably wouldn't have fallen.'

'So that's how it happened.' Marc's eyes narrowed. 'Chatsworth can count himself lucky if he lives long enough to make it to the gallows.

She lifted her hand to his cheek. 'Nothing terrible happened,' she said softly. 'I'm still here, thanks to you.'

'Your idea of terrible, and mine, are several hundred degrees apart,' he muttered. Then his voice lowered, went dark. 'But you're right. You're here, in my arms, and—' he gathered her closer until she could feel the throbbing urgency in his body '—if I don't have you again right now, I'll go out of my mind.'

Amy blinked up at him. She'd thought the tension rippling through his muscles for the past several minutes had been caused by anger at Chatsworth. Obviously, she had been grievously mistaken.

'Good heavens, my lord! Have you been in this state the entire time we've been discussing my divorce?'

The smile glinting in his eyes held both wickedness and rueful amusement. 'Thanks to you, Mrs Chantry, I've been in this state since I walked into this house last week. What do you intend to do about such a sorry situation?'

'Hmm,' she murmured, and made a little purring sound in her throat as she savoured the male power beneath her hands. Leashed, his strength enthralled her. Unleashed, it was a ravishment of her senses that she couldn't wait to feel again. 'I shall set my mind to thinking of a solution, sir.'

'Think fast,' he ordered, and pressed his fingers to the soft curls between her legs with an urgency that had a broken cry of pleasure rippling from her throat.

'Shh,' he whispered, easing the pressure to a touch that merely tantalised. His kiss smothered her immediate demand for more. When he lifted his mouth a fraction, the wildfire of excitement had subsided to a simmer. She had the distinct impression that he intended to make her simmer for a very long time.

'What?' she asked hazily.

'It's probably too late, but try to be quiet.'

'I thought you wanted to make me scream.' The mists cleared somewhat. 'You did make me scream.'

'Darling, when we're married you can scream to your heart's content—and mine. No one will hear you from my chambers. But until then we must be discreet.'

'Oh. Well, I'll do my best, sir.'

'Do more than that,' he growled. 'Grandmama's room is right across the hall.'

'Oh, dear.' She laughed up at him with her eyes, and, deciding she wasn't going to be the only one to simmer, slid her hand down his body. 'How very inconvenient for you.'

He clamped his fingers around her wrist and glared at her. 'I haven't made a practice of seducing my grandmother's companions, Mrs Chantry.'

Amy passed her predecessors under rapid review. 'I should hope not, sir.'

For a moment Marc stared in surprise, then his shoulders started shaking in silent laughter. Amy giggled. The little wriggle she gave as she tried to muffle the sound in his throat was too much. Amusement vanished.

'Never mind,' he muttered, loosing her wrist. 'I'll find a way to keep both of us quiet.'

He didn't have to. When simmer turned to incendiary heat, when the leashed power of his body exploded into desperate, driven need, sweeping her away on a tide of exquisite sensation, Amy found a way to keep quiet that proved very effective indeed. For the second time in as many days, she swooned clean out of her senses.

And this time, when she stirred in the warm safety of his arms, she surfaced to the sweetest discovery of all.

'I've been waiting to tell you,' he murmured, and touched his mouth to hers with heart-shaking tenderness. 'I love you, Amy.'

He loved her.

Amy walked along the cliff road towards Ottersmead, trying to suppress the urge to skip every few steps. She'd told everyone she needed a walk in the fresh air, but, of course, she was really hoping to meet Marc on his way back to Hawkridge.

With that goal in sight, she simply couldn't have stayed in the house another minute; she was too restless with anticipation. Happiness bubbled inside her as if she'd drank several glasses of champagne. The whole world looked radiant and fresh and new. The sea was bluer than ever, the sun beamed down with golden radiance, flowers bloomed by the roadside in riotous abandon.

And Marc loved her.

He loved her enough to risk the scandal of divorce so she would be free to marry him.

Her feet executed several skips before she could stop them. The resulting twinges in her thighs reminded her that she'd spent almost an entire night indulging in unaccustomed exercise.

Amy giggled, and skipped again in sheer defiance of twinging muscles. She would never forget such a night. Never. She had followed him, without hesitation, into those dark places where passion held sway, because love had lit the way. Nor had she felt anything less than Marc's true equal. Though the urgency of his desire had seduced her again and again, he'd gifted her with the sense of her own seductive power. He was so very male that, for the first time in her life, she'd gloried in being female.

Amy hugged herself as little thrills winged through her at the memories, tripped around a curve in the road and came face to face with her husband.

'Oh!' She jerked to a stop. The world lost some of its radiant brightness. She blinked and looked around. There was no one else in sight. 'James.'

'Well, well.' His lip curled. 'If it isn't my fortunate little wife, none the worse for her tumble. I was coming to call on you, Amy, but this is better. Saves me the trouble of finding a private place where we can talk.'

She took a step back. 'I don't think we have anything to say to each other.'

'You only need to listen,' he told her, cutting off her retreat by seizing her arm. 'Come on. Over here.'

He began to pull her across to a small grove of trees that stood between the cliff and the road at that point. She expected him to stop as soon as they were out of sight. When he didn't, she began to dig in her heels.

'This is far enough,' she warned as they broke free of the trees. The edge of the cliff lay a mere twenty feet beyond. She kept her gaze away from it. 'I mean it, James. We're out of sight, if that's what you want.'

'What I want?' he repeated, halting and jerking her around to face him. He released her, much to her relief. 'If I ever got what I wanted, Amy, you'd have broken your neck in that fall the other day.'

Her lashes flickered, the only sign that fear slid down her spine at his words. 'Did you push me deliberately?' she demanded.

'Of course not.' He shrugged in dismissal. 'It would've been a convenient accident, nothing more. But since you are still around, and since Lucinda has been packed off to stay with friends for several weeks, and no one will tell me where she is, I need to make some alternate plans.' He came closer, his eyes cold with suspicion. 'I don't suppose you had anything to do with Lucinda's departure, did you, Amy?'

'I know nothing about the Nettlebeds' plans,' she said with perfect honesty.

'Good. Because if I find out you did know something, I'll make sure you suffer another accident, one with more permanent results. I could do it right here and now. There's no one around.'

Amy didn't answer. She was reasonably sure James's threats were empty while she was still of some use to him. Her mind was racing down another track. Marc would have gone first to Nettlebed Place and, since James was annoyed rather than furious, it was clear no confrontation had taken place. With his quarry apparently flown, Marc would be on his way back to Hawkridge.

The thought had barely occurred when she heard hoofbeats, coming fast. Before James could stop her, Amy turned and dashed for the trees.

It was useless, of course—he'd only been a yard or two away—but her intention was to get closer to the road where a cry could be heard over the constant hushing of the sea. When James's fingers closed around her arm, she drew breath and screamed.

'Marc!'

'You bitch!' James jerked her to a halt and wheeled, dragging her back towards the cliff.

Amy didn't bother crying out again; all her strength was needed to slow James down, to give the rider time to catch them. She didn't know if it was Marc—screaming his name had been pure instinct—but she prayed that even a stranger wouldn't ignore a woman's scream coming from the trees.

She went limp with relief when she realised she was right. The hoofbeats stopped abruptly, then came the sounds of a horse being ridden swiftly after them.

Brilliant sunshine struck her eyes a second later.

'Let me go, James,' she said quickly. 'You don't want to arouse any more suspicions.'

It was a desperate bid to gain her freedom, but she knew her scream had already destroyed his plan to use her, indeed had destroyed everything, for what explanation could he give, even to a stranger? She saw the knowledge in his eyes, saw rage explode into violent purpose. As a huge black horse crashed into the open, he dragged her closer to the cliff, shifted his grip to her wrist and flung her out at arm's length.

Amy staggered; she'd been expecting a blow. Then, as she regained her balance, she saw the rider and a sob of thankfulness rose in her throat.

Marc, eyes blazing, mouth set hard; avenging fury astride a wild-eyed, demonic monster. She wouldn't have been surprised to see flames shoot from the horse's flaring nostrils as it reared and pawed the air before Marc brought the animal back under control and turned it to face them head-on.

She glanced quickly at James. He had to release her. What choice did he have?

But his lips drew back in a snarl, and she knew. Revenge. Or distraction to give himself time to escape. He held her at an angle, his body part-way between her and the brink, but one hard swinging pull would be all that was needed to send her staggering. Sheer momentum would do the rest.

She couldn't fight him, couldn't even cling in a bid to take him with her. To do so she'd have to get closer, and his arm was locked, holding her in position.

'Back up!' he yelled. 'Back up or she goes over the cliff.'

Marc didn't hesitate. He didn't argue; he didn't try reason; he didn't ask what James could possibly hope to gain in killing her. In the split second before he moved, Amy saw murderous fury flash in his eyes. He slashed his reins across the horse's neck, drove his heels into the animal's flanks and charged straight at Chatsworth's outstretched arm.

Amy screamed, flinching away instinctively. She was released so abruptly she stumbled. A huge black shape flashed past her. She felt a blast of heat, heard the scream of an angry stallion, then she hit the ground and rolled.

The horse was still screaming. Or maybe it was her. Dazed, she tried to turn, to see...

Then Marc was there, snatching her up in his arms, his hand holding her cheek pressed tightly to his chest so she couldn't see, couldn't hear. When he eased the pressure seconds later, all was quiet again. The screaming had stopped.

'It was James, wasn't it?' she said shakily, clinging to him. 'He went over the edge.'

But Marc wasn't concerned with Chatsworth. 'Amy. Oh, God, sweetheart—' His hands ran over her, searching. 'Are you all right? When I saw you on the ground... Did Demon touch you?'

'No.' His urgency steadied her, strengthened her. She sorted through the blur of the last few minutes and drew back to look up at him. 'You used him...Demon...as a weapon.'

'Yes.' His eyes were still blazing, still violent. 'I would have used anything, anyway I could.'

'I would, too,' she whispered, and burrowed close again. 'Oh, Marc.'

His arms closed about her with fierce protectiveness, pressing her cheek to his heart. The violent pounding beneath her ear gradually slowed to a strong, steady beat. The sun felt warm again, birds resumed their morning chorus; leaves rustled, flowers nodded in the breeze. And she was filled with a passionate sense of gladness that she was alive, that both she and Marc were safe.

James had had choices. And in trying to destroy her, had destroyed himself.

'Do you think we should go down there?' she asked softly. 'Do something?'

'I will in a moment,' he said. 'But there's no possibility that Chatsworth will have survived that fall. There are no convenient ledges at this point; he'll have broken his neck on the rocks.'

Amy shuddered.

His mouth touched the top of her head, then he put her away from him, curving his hands around her arms as though holding her steady. 'Darling, what I have to do could take a couple of hours. You're going to have to be very strong. I want you to go home—Yes,' he emphasised gently when her lips parted on a protest. 'Go home and instruct Mawson to bring the gig to the top of the Inghams' steps. I'll ride back there, retrieve Chatsworth's body and bring it up that way.'

'But...' Amy tried to think. 'Won't you be seen?'

'All the better,' he said somewhat grimly. 'The only thing we wish to hide is your past involvement with Chatsworth and, thanks to his penchant for secluded meeting-places, we'll be able to manage it if I act fast. All you need to say is that while we were walking back to Hawkridge, we heard a cry and discovered that someone had fallen over the cliff. Only Grandmama is to know the truth. Can you do that, sweetheart?' His hands tightened. 'I know it's asking a lot to pretend that you haven't just been terrified for your life, or that Chatsworth was nothing more than a recent acquaintance when in reality—'

She stopped him with a finger against his lips, and a gaze that held all the gentle feminine strength in her nature. 'Marc, it's because of me that *you*'re involved. I can do whatever you ask of me.'

'Why did I even doubt it?' he murmured, and smiled in rueful acknowledgement. 'Go home, darling. I'll be there as soon as I can.'

Chapter Fifteen

'So you sent Mr Chatsworth over the cliff. Well, that will certainly save a lot of trouble.'

Lady Hawkridge nodded thoughtfully while she reviewed the story related to her by her grandson, then smiled benignly at the pair opposite.

From the shelter of Marc's arm, Amy gazed at her employer in astonishment. They were in the library, the dowager ensconced on an armchair, while she and Marc occupied the sofa. No doubt her wits were still somewhat scattered; she was finding it very difficult to reconcile her ladyship's angelic appearance with her ruthless practicality.

Marc apparently had no such trouble. She glanced up to see a look of amusement cross his face.

'I didn't intend to kill him, Grandmama. There was only a second in which to act. Chatsworth might have been armed, he was certainly threatening to send Amy over the cliff, but most people, when charged by a horse, tend to forget everything in the interests of getting out of the way. When Demon's shoulder struck him he must have been closer to the edge than I thought.'

'Of course, dear. However, since you were saving Amy's life, no one will think anything of it.'

'Since no one else was about, they won't know that Amy's life was in danger,' Marc corrected. 'We don't want people wondering why Chatsworth would try to kill someone he'd only just met. Listen carefully. Chatsworth met with an unfortunate accident while out for a walk. In a distracted state of mind owing to the frustration of his ambitions towards Lucinda, he took the wrong path down to the beach, slipped and lost his footing.'

'Quite logical,' agreed the dowager. 'Why, poor little Amy had a fall on the *right* path not two days ago. Very dangerous places, cliffs. We must put up a warning sign.' She nodded decisively. 'Where did you take him, Marc? Not to Mr ffollifoot, I trust.'

'No. I don't want Amy reminded of him every time she goes past the churchyard. I returned him to his last place of abode, fortunately outside our parish boundary.'

'Thank you,' Amy said with real gratitude. 'But, Marc, with Lucinda gone, how did you discover where James was staying?'

'I saw Lucinda before she left, sweetheart. Thanks to Grandmama's note conveying a warning from a supposedly disinterested source, she was shaken enough to let drop that he was putting up at a tavern a few miles down the coast.' His lips curled. 'It isn't one of your more salubrious places. When Mawson and I turned up with Chatsworth's body, the tap-keeper promptly claimed his belongings in lieu of payment. I went through them to make sure there was nothing to incriminate you, and handed them over. There was money in Chatsworth's pockets. If the tap's feeling generous, he might part with enough to pay for a proper burial.'

'Oh, heavens.' Amy bit her lip, guiltily aware that she should be more shocked at this ruthless disinterest in the fate of her husband's remains.

Marc glanced down at her, his eyes hard. 'Don't expect me to feel sympathy for the man, Amy. He would've killed you without compunction.'

'Yes, indeed.' Lady Hawkridge shuddered. 'What a dreadful time you must have had with him, Amy. In London, too. What will you do about his lodgings there, Marc? Search them?'

'Only if Amy thinks there might be anything that could link her to him.'

He sent her a questioning look as he spoke, but Amy was already shaking her head. 'Only our marriage lines, and I have those. I didn't keep James's letters, nor write any myself.' She paused. 'He wouldn't have kept such things. He was very secretive, very careful to keep his plans to himself until he was ready to act.'

Marc's eyes narrowed thoughtfully. 'So his cohorts might not know that he was going by the name of Chatsworth while he was in this vicinity, or that he was in Devonshire at all.'

'Very likely not, judging by what he said yesterday. In any case, I don't think he told anyone he'd married me.' She frowned. 'Do you think his friends might enquire into his death?'

'They'll have to hear about it, first. Frankly, I doubt they'll even enquire into his protracted absence. Given Chatsworth's recent activities, their immediate assumption will be that he's been caught and imprisoned in Bristol to await transportation or hanging. Anyone else involved in the robberies will lie low to save their own skins.'

'The only sensible thing to do,' Lady Hawkridge concurred. She gathered up the stitching she'd been engaged with before Marc had returned to the house and prepared to rise. 'Well, that seems to take care of everything. So comforting to know that we don't have to worry about Amy's former husband popping up again.'

'Oh, ma'am, I'm so sorry to have brought all this trouble upon you. I only hope that poor Lucinda isn't dreadfully hurt after learning that Mr Chatsworth…I mean, James…was a fortune-hunter.'

'Lucinda is young and resilient,' Marc informed her, rising to assist his grandmother. 'When I left her this morning, she was already vowing never to be taken in again. She plans to be an ice-maiden and is going to wear nothing but white, and possibly silver. I give the role three months.'

'Oh dear.'

'And besides, Amy, it wasn't you who caused any trouble,' Lady Hawkridge added. 'It was all Mr Chatsworth's doing. Now, I think you should go upstairs and lie down. The last two days and nights have been so fraught with shocks and surprises you've hardly had any sleep. And we don't want you looking peaky on your wedding day.'

'Uh…'

'Just leave everything to me.' The dowager beamed. 'There's nothing I enjoy more than planning a wedding. And, in this case, we have two nuptials to arrange. However, I think you and Amy should be married first, Marc. We don't want things happening out of their proper order. People can count, you know, and Amy will be very sensitive to such gossip.'

Ignoring the wildly conflicting emotions chasing one another across her companion's suddenly rosy countenance, the dowager tripped towards the door.

Marc crossed the room to open it for her, a wry smile curving his mouth. 'Colborough isn't going to ask me for your hand, is he, Grandmama? Because if he does, I'd feel duty bound to inform him that you're a very dangerous female.'

'I'd rather you didn't, dearest. Acquiring a new wife at Bartholomew's age is quite enough for him. Besides, I'm perfectly capable of bestowing my hand without your permission.' Smiling serenely, her ladyship left the room.

'That puts me in my place,' Marc observed ruefully. 'I can see I'm going to have a great deal of trouble curbing the independent tendencies of the females about the place.'

Amy rose somewhat shakily. Far from wishing to claim her independence, she felt more in need of support than the dowager. No doubt it was the result of all the shocks and surprises, but her legs seemed somewhat reluctant to hold her upright.

'Is it really all over?' she asked.

'It's over.' Marc turned. The glittering triumph in his eyes had her breath seizing. 'And we're just beginning. I stopped by the vicarage on my way home. We'll be married as soon as Mr ffollifoot has the licence ready. Probably in a day or two.'

'A day or two?' Her voice rose to a squeak, then all but vanished. 'Oh, my goodness.'

He started towards her. 'Is that an argument?'

'No, my lord.'

'You realise you won't be independent any more? You'll be mine.'

'Yes, well...'

'I'm over-protective. I'm possessive.'

'Yes, I do believe I've noticed that.'

'My instincts are downright primitive. In fact, when it comes to your safety—' he stopped a pace or two away, his eyes fierce '—it wouldn't be too much to state that I'm a savage.'

Amy took a deep breath. Her legs might be wobbly, but Marc

was clearly the one in need of reassurance. Closing the distance between them, she touched her fingers to his cheek. 'I know,' she said softly. 'That must be why I'm not worried about becoming a nuisance to you when you discover I'm not really as helpless as I look.'

He frowned and captured her hand. 'What?'

'Just something someone once said to me. You know, Marc, when food or clothing was scarce in the poorhouse, I often had to protect Mama's share, and mine, with tooth and claw, so there's really no need to warn me about your instincts.' A dimple peeped at the corner of her mouth. 'Better to worry about what sort of instincts our children will inherit.'

His face went blank. 'Children?'

'Yes.' She tilted her head. 'I presume you do want children, my lord. You'll need an heir for one thing, and a little baby would be—'

'Baby?' he said in such a strange voice that she stopped. His eyes went violently intense. 'A baby?'

He swooped.

Amy found herself lifted, tossed over his shoulder and carried out of the library before she could utter more than a small startled shriek.

She contemplated the marble tiles passing rapidly before her eyes and tried to retrieve her wits. 'For heaven's sake, my lord! What are you doing?'

'Taking you to bed.'

'*To bed?* But it's the middle of the day! What will people think?'

'You're supposed to be resting. No one needs to know what else you'll be doing.'

'But...I didn't mean we had to get started on the project right this minute.'

'Mrs Chantry,' he murmured, in a voice that made her suddenly glad she wasn't ascending the stairs under her own steam. 'We're going to start on the project the minute I get you into my cave. I mean, bed.'

'Oh, my goodness.'

He carried her into his room and deposited her on the bed before she could think of anything else to say.

Head spinning, wits still whirling, Amy struggled up on her elbows, only to sink back down again when Marc strode across to the door, locked it, then turned and paced slowly towards her.

Holding her gaze with his, he removed his coat and tossed it aside. Then, ignoring the havoc his boots were going to wreak on the bedspread, he came down over her and gathered her into his arms.

'That's better,' he growled, and kissed her.

No, she thought hazily, he *sank* into her. And she melted into him. Passion flared, dark and searing, but beyond the meeting of lips, of tongues, of huskily whispered desires, she found a deep well of tenderness, a gentle cherishing, and a need that bade her lay her heart before him, to give him everything, her strength, her vulnerability and all that lay between.

How easy it was. To yield, completely. To take, utterly. His hands framed her face; he took her deeper, until she knew nothing but the total joining of all that they were. Minds touched, hearts merged, souls entwined. When he lifted his head, she was soft and pliant, his. He was hers, until death and beyond; she knew it absolutely.

'I love you,' he murmured against her mouth. 'Love you...love you. My sweet Amy.'

'I didn't believe this was possible,' she whispered back. 'Not really. Until now. Oh, Marc, I love you so. I know I have a lot to learn, that I'm not—'

He silenced her with a gentle finger across her lips. 'Do you want proof that you're a lady?' he asked. 'I know in you I've found the other half of myself. Nothing else matters. I don't care what brought you here, only that I found you. But if you like, if you give me your grandfather's name, I'll write to Ravensdene, have him search his family records to see if there's a link to your mother. Only if *you* wish it, Amy.'

'I think I would like that,' she said after a moment's reflection.

'Then I'll do it, but remember when I said you were a lady waiting for the right setting? Now you have it.'

She thought about that, and a joyous smile spread over her face. 'In your cave?'

He smiled back at her. 'That, too. But most of all—' he bent to emphasise each point with a kiss '—in my home...in my life...in my heart.'

Amy's breath caught at the deep note of sincerity in his voice. She looked into her own heart and saw the tiny flame of hope, so fragile only hours ago, transformed into truth, burning bright and clear and steady.

And as Marc gathered her closer, she saw reflected in his brilliant grey eyes, their future.

The family she'd never had, times of care and laughter, and a love that would grow stronger and deeper through all the years ahead.

* * * * *

In August look for

AN IDEAL MARRIAGE?

by *New York Times* bestselling author

DEBBIE MACOMBER

A special 3-in-1 collector's edition containing three full-length novels from America's favorite storyteller, Debbie Macomber—each ending with a delightful walk down the aisle.

Father's Day
First Comes Marriage
Here Comes Trouble

Evoking all the emotion and warmth
that you've come to expect from
Debbie, AN IDEAL MARRIAGE?
will definitely satisfy!

Visit us at www.eHarlequin.com
PHIDEAL

MONTANA MAVERICKS

Bestselling author

SUSAN MALLERY

WILD WEST WIFE

THE ORIGINAL MONTANA MAVERICKS HISTORICAL NOVEL

Jesse Kincaid had sworn off love forever.
But when the handsome rancher kidnaps
his enemy's mail-order bride to get revenge,
he ends up falling for his innocent captive!

RETURN TO WHITEHORN, MONTANA, WITH

WILD WEST WIFE

Available July 2001

And be sure to pick up
MONTANA MAVERICKS: BIG SKY GROOMS,
three brand-new historical stories about Montana's
most popular family, coming in August 2001.

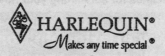

HARLEQUIN®
Makes any time special ®

Visit us at www.eHarlequin.com

PHWWW

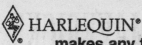

HARLEQUIN®
makes any time special—online...

eHARLEQUIN.com

shop eHarlequin

- ♥ Find all the new Harlequin releases at everyday great discounts.
- ♥ Try before you buy! Read an excerpt from the latest Harlequin novels.
- ♥ Write an online review and share your thoughts with others.

reading room

- ♥ Read our Internet exclusive daily and weekly online serials, or vote in our interactive novel.
- ♥ Talk to other readers about your favorite novels in our Reading Groups.
- ♥ Take our Choose-a-Book quiz to find the series that matches you!

authors' alcove

- ♥ Find out interesting tidbits and details about your favorite authors' lives, interests and writing habits.
- ♥ Ever dreamed of being an author? Enter our Writing Round Robin. The Winning Chapter will be published online! Or review our writing guidelines for submitting your novel.

All this and more available at
www.eHarlequin.com
on Women.com Networks

HINTB1R

New York Times bestselling authors

DEBBIE MACOMBER
JAYNE ANN KRENTZ
HEATHER GRAHAM &
TESS GERRITSEN

lead

TAKE5

Covering everything from tender love to
sizzling passion, there's a TAKE 5 volume for
every type of romance reader.

Plus

With $5.00 worth of coupons inside each volume,
this is one deal you shouldn't miss!

TAKE5

5 Quick Reads. *5* Great Escapes.

Look for it in August 2001.

Visit us at www.eHarlequin.com

HNCPT5R

FREE BOOK OFFER!

In August, an exciting new *Maitland Maternity* single title comes with a FREE BOOK attached to it!

Maitland Maternity **THE INHERITANCE**

by Marie Ferrarella

This brand-new single title revisits all the excitement and characters that you've enjoyed in the *Maitland Maternity* continuity series—but there's more! As part of this extraordinary offer, the first title in Harlequin's new *Trueblood, Texas* continuity will be shrink-wrapped to the *Maitland Maternity* book absolutely FREE! An amazing "2-for-1" value that will introduce you to the wonderful adventure and romance of

TRUEBLOOD, TEXAS

On sale in August 2001 at your favorite retail outlet.

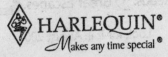

HARLEQUIN®
Makes any time special®

Visit us at www.eHarlequin.com   TBTSPACK